Tea at Kimball Pines

Holly Bebernitz

*For Jenny
Holly Bebernitz
Isaiah 12.5*

PRESS

Tea at Kimball Pines is a work of fiction. Names, characters, places, and incidents are the products of the author's imagination and are used fictitiously. Any resemblance to actual events, locales, or persons, living or dead, is entirely coincidental.

Copyright © 2017
Holly Bebernitz
All rights reserved.

Published in the United States by QuinnRose Press

ISBN: 978-0-9891721-2-7

Cover design: Michael Regina

Printed in the United States of America

www.hollybebernitz.com

Acknowledgments

Anna Harmon: for providing information about the legal matters which affect the characters.

Jacob Leporacci: for sharing his considerable experience with musical auditions.

Michael Regina: cover artist.

Rachael Stringer: proofreading and formatting the final manuscript and preparing it for publication.

Wanda Violet: for taking the author on a tour of the Wardlaw-Smith House in Madison, Florida, which served as model for the Delahunty House.

Aaron & Haley, Aidan and Allison; Paul & Heidi, Ryland and Ella; Ethan & Lindsay: in all ways, in all times, my joy.

Faithful readers: who keep me motivated and encouraged enough to continue writing this series.

Dedicated to Sharon Y. Cobb, the first professional author I met, organizer of the first writers' conference I attended, a constant source of knowledge, encouragement, and inspiration.

Chapter 1

Morning

    Pinetta Fraleigh pedaled her bicycle to the top of the rickety stairs and plunged headlong into a black abyss. Jolting awake, she threw back her great-aunt's quilt and sat up, easing her feet onto the braided rug by her single bed. She was not, she told herself, lost, late, and desperate to get home. She was in her small room off the kitchen and it was time to make breakfast. Something was off kilter—the left shoulder of the flannel shirt she wore over her nightgown had slid down to her elbow.

    Standing, she tugged on the errant sleeve and straightened the garment with as much dignity as if she had been preparing for a job interview.

    Then crossing her arms, she grasped her elbows and prayed God's blessings on Guy Henry Fraleigh.

    Wherever he was.

    The flannel shirt she had made for his 50th birthday was the only thing he had left behind.

    After she dressed in her white blouse and black skirt, she took the letter from her nightstand and re-read it. There was no need. She had checked the details many times. Her youngest sister, Eve Munson, married with two children, was passing through Dennisonville on her way home from Cape Cod. She would be here tomorrow. Pinetta would devote the morning to making her famous cranberry sauce and send ten jars home with Eve. Pinetta's family had always raved about her cranberry sauce—it was the one thing she did better than her sisters.

    After breakfast her four housemates left the kitchen. Pinetta made a second cup of tea and opened the window to let in the November air. Tying her white apron around her thin waist, she took the colander of cranberries from the refrigerator. She placed the fruit in the sink and turned on the faucet. As the water, chilling her hands, splashed over the berries, she gazed out the window and spotted Annie May Goode in her pink coat, skipping and singing on her way to school. Pinetta leaned in to listen, feeling the counter's edge dig into her hip bones.

Annie May spotted Pinetta and paused, mid-skip, to wave. She had once asked her mother why Mrs. Fraleigh always looked sad—even when she smiled.

Her mother had explained, "Some people have had trouble," and it was best not to ask.

Since then Annie May had *always* waved at Mrs. Fraleigh, hoping to cheer her up a little and remind her she had at least one friend in the world, even if the friend was only eight.

Pinetta waved back, recalling she used to sing on *her* way to school when she was Annie May's age, but that was forty-four years ago.

Back when she was Pinetta Jane Pembroke, second daughter of the Alfred Pembrokes, one of the wealthiest families in Sumter.

Now she was Pinetta Fraleigh, castoff wife.

Cook at the Magnolia Arms.

A rambling old house, populated with a dizzying hodgepodge of tenants in a dull little North Carolina town, whose only brush with culture had been when Carl Sandburg dined at the restaurant on the corner of 4th and Main and autographed a menu, now framed and yellowing by the entrance.

While water simmered in the canner, Pinetta stirred water and sugar (less than the recipe called for) in her stainless-steel saucepan—her *personal* saucepan—the one she had brought from home and kept stored in her closet till needed. She added the cranberries, mixing till the berries burst and the beautiful magenta liquid began to sheet from the spoon. Last she added the orange zest. The jars and gingham ribbon for tying around the lids waited on the counter. She reached for her ladle. The doorbell rang. She slammed down the ladle like a gavel on a judge's bench.

Still wearing her cranberry-stained apron, Pinetta opened the front door.

There stood Eve.

"What…what are you doing here?" Pinetta asked. "You're not supposed to be here till tomorrow."

Chapter 1 ~ Morning

Eve laughed, grasped Pinetta's shoulders, and gave her a perfunctory peck on the cheek. Then she leaned back and tilted her head to scrutinize her older sister.

"Mama said you were making your living as a cook, but I didn't believe it. But it suits you. With that apron tied around your waist, you *actually* look like you have hips."

"I'm not making my living as a cook. I'm a caregiver to Mrs. Hubbard. I'm just helping out while we're visiting. It was her decision to come here—not mine."

Eve pushed back a mop of peroxide-blonde curls from her forehead.

"Mrs. Hubbard. Right. I remember." She wagged her finger at the apron stains. "But it *looks to me* like you've been cooking."

Waiting by the curb, engine idling, Eve's husband honked the horn.

"I'm making my cranberry sauce for you to take home," Pinetta said. "Enough for Mama and Miriam and Livie and Nelle…but it's not ready…you're too early."

Looking over her shoulder, Eve waved at her husband. "I know, but Bryan's boss called and said he *had to be* back in the office this morning or the merger would fall through."

"You cut your vacation short?"

Eve nodded. "Isn't it ridiculous? First time in four years we've gotten away and—"

Bryan honked twice and revved the engine.

Pinetta pointed her thumb over her shoulder. "But the cranberry sauce is on the stove. I haven't got it in the jars yet. Couldn't you—?"

"I'm sorry, Net. I can't wait. Bryan is *furious* I made him stop so I could talk to you."

Pinetta's heart softened. "You came out of your way just to say hello?"

Eve hung her head. "No. When Mama found out we were going to Cape Cod, she made me promise to see you on our way home. She didn't want you to hear it through the grapevine."

"Hear what?"

Bryan leaned his head out the window and yelled. "Eve. For cryin' out loud. Come *on*."

Eve backed up. "There's no easy way to say it. Guy Henry got married again."

Pinetta put one hand on the doorframe and stifled a sob with the other.

3

"Don't take it too hard," Eve said. "Mama says you're better off without him."

Bryan stepped from the car. "Eve. Now." Eve edged backward.

"What's her name?" Pinetta asked.

"Who?"

"The woman…he…" Pinetta could not bring herself to say, 'married.'

Eve shrugged her shoulders. "Mama told me, but I forgot. No one we know."

Bryan, glaring over the roof of the car, leaned on the horn. "I'm sorry. I've got to go." She blew Pinetta a kiss and bounded toward the street.

Pinetta hurried to the porch railing and called out as her sister slammed the car door.

She yelled—not her habit. "The cranberry sauce. I have ten jars."

Eve waved as the car screeched away from the curb.

Pinetta closed the front door and returned to the kitchen.

She spooned the cranberry sauce into the jars, screwed on the lids, and lowered them into the simmering water. Then, one by one, she lifted them out and lined them up.

Sealed tight, unadorned, unwanted.

Chapter 2

Barton Carlyle

The day Barton Carlyle turned 50, he draped a tarp over the '63 Ford Fairlane in his garage and boarded a train for Dennisonville, North Carolina. A duffle bag slung over his shoulder, he kept his head down as he walked past his fellow passengers. He sat next to a window, propped his bag in the aisle seat, and leaned back, pulling his faded Panama Jack safari hat over his eyes. He was not a praying man, but his fleeting wish—"Please don't let anyone bother me"—was as heartfelt as any childhood supplication.

Bound for a small town, he could not abide small talk on the way.

He hated both.

After 14 hours, he got off the train and flexed his left knee, never the same since the car wreck in '56. He entered the station and dodged people saying hello and goodbye to each other. He could not remember the last time anyone welcomed him when he arrived at home or anywhere else. Eager to escape the crowd, he headed for the main entrance. Once he got outside, he would stop the first passerby for directions to his son's house.

In a town this size everyone knew everyone else.

He looped his plaid scarf twice around his neck—his well-worn coat offering scant protection against the cold—and leaned his right shoulder into the front door.

A plump woman, seated behind a long table piled with brochures, caught his eye.

He stepped to the center of the table. "Belmont Drive?"

Mary Grace Dodson, secretary of the Dennisonville Historical Society, lifted her eyes to the stranger. Silhouetted by the morning sun pouring through the window behind him, he looked like a mythical messenger lately arrived from Olympus…or an angel. Though she could not make out his features, she had no problem zeroing in on his left hand gripping the strap of the duffle bag on his shoulder.

No wedding ring.

Was *this* the moment she had hoped for?

Was her last grasp at happiness within reach?

Was this the day she could return from her weekly Welcome Table shift and boast to her landlady Ida Willingale she had met the man of her dreams?

She slipped her apple turnover onto her right leg and licked filling from the tip of her index finger. "It's a ways from here, but there are cabs by the curb."

Barton felt the last twenty dollar bill in his pocket. "Walking distance?"

"Goodness, no. Not in this cold. You'd be froze half through by the time you got to the center of town. Maybe if I had a better idea of the place you're looking for?"

"The Magnolia Arms."

Two doors down from her. She hoped her face, suddenly hot, would not give her away.

"306. The nicest young couple manages it and—"

"Not looking to stay. Just trying to locate—" Barton clamped his lips shut. He had been the fodder for gossip most of his life. If he said too much to this garrulous, pushing-40 woman, his errand would be sidetracked before he hailed a cab. "Just trying to locate an old army buddy."

Mary Grace, worried about stray pastry flakes, dabbed a delicate finger at the corner of her mouth. "Everyone in this town knows where the Magnolia Arms is. Grab a cab. He'll take you right to it. You in town for long?"

"Just passin' through…on my way to a job in Florida."

Since lying was second nature—maybe first—to Barton, he spit this out as easily as he had manufactured the army buddy. No need to give this dewy-eyed spinster a chance to run for the nearest phone. If he did not receive the welcome he hoped for…or at least grudging tolerance…he would ask for a lift to the nearest truck stop and bum a ride back north.

Mary Grace called down blessings on Bridey Ludlow for her rigorous training of the Welcome Table volunteers. The 8-hour course, mandated by the Chamber of Commerce, had equipped her for this moment. Forbidding herself to study the color of the stranger's eyes and shape of his mouth, Mary Grace, as rehearsed, leaned over to take a welcome packet from the cardboard

Chapter 2 ~ Barton Carlyle

box on the floor. The turnover shifted; she steadied it. She removed the full-color city map from the manila envelope and unfolded it on the table, smoothing its creases with the same care she would give a linen tablecloth.

Barton set down his duffle bag and leaned over the map.

Their heads almost touching, Mary Grace inhaled. Accustomed to the floral and antiseptic aroma of an all-female household, she found the faint scent of his aftershave intoxicating.

Mary Grace pointed to the train station symbol on the map. "We are here." She slid her finger along the route to Belmont Drive. "And here's the Magnolia Arms."

Barton placed his finger next to hers. Blushing, she pulled back her hand and studied him while he studied the route. He folded the map and tucked it under his right arm.

He bent down for his bag, his head level with hers; her heart nearly beat out of her chest.

Barton turned to go. "Appreciate your help."

Desperate for one more moment, Mary Grace held up a *Dennisonville, North Carolina* souvenir coffee mug. "Would you like one of these?"

Barton nodded at the sign leaning against the front row of cups. "$1.99? Can't spare it."

Cradling the gift like a sacred chalice, Mary Grace offered the mug. "We're running a special today. First five visitors at the Welcome Table get a free mug."

She would slip the five from her coat pocket into the cash box as soon as he was gone.

Barton studied the logo on the cup. "Nice souvenir. Thank you. Hope everyone else in this town is as friendly as you."

When he winked at her, the turnover slid to the floor.

7

Chapter 3

Abbot Cooper

On her 72nd birthday Vesper Kimball awoke before dawn, as she always did. Lying on her back, the edge of the lavender-scented sheet, ironed, folded over once, up to her chin, she forced herself to remember what day of the week it was. It never mattered. Every day was the same, varying only according to temperature or precipitation—sleet, rain—pelting against the central window on the front of her home, Kimball Pines, the largest house in Dennisonville, North Carolina—the house some people called haunted, some abandoned, some (shaking their heads), "a waste of space for just one person."

John Roy Goode, her childhood friend Madge's 14-year-old grandson, who delivered her groceries every other Tuesday, once informed her that taxi drivers offered their passengers a closer view of her house, "even if it ran up the meter." Those who agreed to pay the extra few cents would roll down the window to contemplate the magnificent façade—white, pristine, imposing, Victorian.

When John Roy, thinking Vesper would be honored by her tourist attraction status, added, "Asa Ludlow made *$20 extra* one week doing that," Vesper penned a curt note for John Roy to deliver to his grandmother, instructing her to contact Bridey Ludlow, who was to tell her husband Asa in no uncertain terms was he *ever* to park or even "decrease his speed" when he drove past 17 Second Avenue *ever again*.

After that Asa began his speech when he turned the corner—"See the vine-covered house"—foot off accelerator—"legend has it the lady who lives there"—cab slowing of its own accord—"hasn't seen the light of day"—return foot to accelerator as cab coasted past sidewalk to front porch—"in over twenty years"—accelerate when arriving at crepe myrtle on west edge of property.

Vesper sat up and eased her feet into the pink slippers on the floor. Rising, she put her slender arms into the sleeves of her white satin dressing gown and tied the sash into a symmetrical bow. From the nightstand she lifted the silver-framed portrait of a handsome man—forever young—and kissed it.

"Good morning, Philip. It's my birthday. You understand I have to put your picture away...just for today...in case my son Robert comes to visit."

She placed the photo face down in her nightstand drawer.

On the other 364 days of the year, Philip's photo stayed where it belonged—near her while she slept. On nights when the moon was full, she would leave the curtains open and lose herself in his eyes as she drifted off to sleep. But even on the stormiest night when the sky was black and she could not distinguish the frame in the dark, Philip—*her* Philip—remained a constant presence from the past, permeating, swelling, suffocating her tired heart, worn out from loving.

Vesper walked to the window and drew back the ivory brocade drapes.

She gazed down at Second Avenue and imagined Robert driving up in his long sleek Cadillac. Maybe this would be the year he would surprise her...if he had business nearby and the day's meetings went well. Vesper had never faulted her son for the sterling work ethic he had inherited from his father, Robert, Sr. Neither did she blame her firstborn for his infrequent visits. His absences were his wife's fault. As soon as Pauline had a wedding band on her finger, she had discouraged Robert from spending holidays "at home."

Vesper whispered into the darkness. "If it were up to Robert...things would be different."

Bolstered by this conviction, she stepped into the hallway and walked down the back stairs to the kitchen. Maybe *something* would jar Robert's

Chapter 3 ~ Abbot Cooper

memory today. And even if he was too busy to call this morning, perhaps he would call tonight…or even tomorrow. That would be fine, too. He would apologize. She would say she understood and praise him for working hard. He would send flowers which would arrive the next day or at week's end.

She turned on the kitchen light.

If Robert's brother had lived, they would have reminded each other of her birthday. Maybe Edward would have married a kinder wife, less beautiful and less haughty.

Edward—stricken with pneumonia when he was only two—a sweet, sad memory.

Vesper prepared a poached egg, pumpernickel toast, and cup of oolong tea, and carried her plate and cup to the table. Her maid, Fiona, had arranged the table the night before and left a birthday card on the embroidered placemat. Vesper read the card and leaned it against the jar of raspberry preserves, so she could admire it as she ate. When the grandfather clock in the hall began to chime, she stopped chewing to listen…and to count. One. Two. Three. Four. Five. Six. She swallowed her toast and took another bite as the old fear nibbled at her.

What would become of her clock…Philip's clock…when she was gone?

Shuddering, she closed her eyes and shook her head to erase the thought. If Robert found her in one of her melancholy moods when he arrived, he would glance at his watch after 45 minutes and say he "needed to start home before the traffic got bad."

She simply had to maintain a pleasant frame of mind all day just in case he came.

So, she reminded herself that Robert, unlike his wife, was cultured, with a strong sense of the meaning of legacy. For the sake of the Kimball name alone, he would not allow her possessions to be bartered off in some tawdry estate sale.

Vesper set her plate in the sink and ran water over the remnants of egg yolk on her plate. She made a second cup of tea and walked to the parlor. Edging between the marble-topped lamp table and the front window, she looked out at the leaves blanketing her yard. How she had loved autumn as a child. She and her brother would help Papa rake leaves all morning and then when the pile was almost as tall as Papa, they would leap headlong into the massive mound. Papa would pretend to be angry and then join them.

October had always been her favorite month…until October 29, 1929, Black Tuesday, the day the stock market crashed, crushing all her hopes.

In the faint light of dawn, she remembered.

It was on a day like this Philip March, head down, had shuffled through the leaves on the walk and brought the news his father had lost everything and had taken his own life.

Philip's mother, inconsolable, never recovered from her ruined state or the ignominy of her husband's death. She insisted on moving someplace where no one knew them.

The people of Dennisonville, to prevent the family heirlooms from falling into the hands of strangers, purchased the Marches' belongings at auction.

Vesper's mother bought the grandfather clock and promised Mrs. March she could buy it back "once she got on her feet."

On the day the Marches left, Philip took Vesper in his arms and whispered he would write…come back once his family was settled. Kissing her hand, he vowed to put a ring on her finger within a year.

A year went by. Then two. And then came the news Philip was engaged to a girl whose father had promised him a job in his company.

Vesper married Robert Kimball instead.

Gave him two sons.

Performed the roles of wife and mother.

Was a credit to her husband.

A pillar of the community.

And never stopped loving Philip March.

Holding the saucer under her chin, Vesper tilted back her head to drain the last drop of oolong. As she returned the cup to the saucer, she caught sight of a man on the sidewalk. She blinked and leaned into the window. Robert? Would Robert come so early? He was walking past the gate. Maybe he had wondered if she was awake, and, when he saw no light, decided to come back later. She set down her cup and turned on the lamp. He kept walking. So polite. He did not want to wake her. She knocked on the window.

Chapter 3 ~ Abbot Cooper

When he did not turn his head or slow his pace, Vesper rushed to the front door. She fumbled with the lock and threw open the door as the man reached the corner of the fence.

She stepped onto the porch and cupped her hands around her mouth. "Robert."

He stopped and glanced back.

In the pink slippers, not designed for morning dew and wet leaves, Vesper started down the porch steps, her feet flying from under her. Tilting back, she reached out her hand to break her fall. Down she came, her back scraping against the top step, her hand bending at an odd angle, her wrist wrenching as it bore her weight.

The young man hurried to the gate and struggled with the latch. When it would not yield, he gripped the top of the fence and leaped over in one bound.

He rushed to her and knelt in the wet leaves. "Are you all right? Let me help you."

Vesper whimpered. "My wrist. I think it's broken."

Standing, he took the injured arm in his hands and then eased it onto her lap. "Here. Hold your hurt arm with the other one, and I'll help you stand."

She did as he said. He stepped behind her. When he leaned down to put his hands under her elbows, his cheek rubbed against hers.

Instead of pulling back, she rested her head against his shoulder—a strange, wonderful feeling. Trusting someone.

He guided her up the steps and into the house.

Vesper hardly felt her feet touch the floor.

He paused in the foyer. "Where would you like to sit?"

She nodded her head toward the formal living room. "In there. By the fireplace."

"Is there someone I can call?" he asked.

Vesper studied her rescuer. How had she mistaken him for Robert? This stranger was young and robust, sandy-haired, his blue eyes full of life and good humor.

"My maid will be here at 8:00. She'll call the doctor. He won't be in his office till 9:00."

"Would you like me to wait till she comes? I don't think you should be left alone."

"Yes, thank you, Mr.—"

"Cooper. Abbot Cooper."

"Mr. Cooper. Won't you sit down?"

He brushed his sleeves. "No, ma'am. I have several days' travel on me. I'd get your furniture dirty."

"Well, then, you could bring a chair from the kitchen. Make yourself some breakfast if you like. You'll find eggs in the refrigerator. Bread and jam on the table."

His eyes sparkled. "I'd like that. Can I bring you anything?"

"Tea, if you don't mind. My cup is over there." She pointed to the window.

Holding the cup, Abbot gazed out the window. "It's going to be a beautiful day."

"Yes, it is," Vesper said.

And for the first time in as long as she could remember—she really believed it.

Chapter 4

Truitt Spenlow

Bentley McBain dabbed a spoonful of homemade apple butter on a warm biscuit and admired the silk hydrangeas in the center of the table.

During his final days in prison, he had lain awake at night, dreading what would happen to him when he was released. No one would be waiting to welcome him home; no one would offer him a helping hand. Neighbors would exclude him from their company. He would work in a factory and go home each night to a dingy one-room apartment.

All this he had foreseen.

But he had never imagined homemade apple butter and silk hydrangeas on the table.

Much less a wife and baby boy to kiss him goodbye when he left for work.

Bentley pointed at the flowers with his fork. "Pretty posies. Buy them yesterday?"

His wife Flossie wiped applesauce from the baby's chin. "Uh-huh. Found them at a rummage sale at the Methodist church. I was hoping to find a winter coat for Fletcher."

"Did you?"

"Yes, and three pairs of corduroy pants. I can't believe how this boy is growing."

"You sure you don't want me to come home right after work and help you put things away?" He glanced around the apartment. "We still have so many boxes to unpack."

Flossie lifted the baby from the high chair. "I'm sure. Aren't they rehearsing the Tchaikovsky today?"

"That's the plan." He took the baby in his arms. "Now you be a good boy while Daddy is at work. I'll be home at suppertime."

"Don't forget the checkerboard," Flossie said. She licked her fingertips and smoothed her husband's thinning gray hair. "And go easy on Truitt. He already owes you $8,000."

Bentley handed the baby to Flossie and kissed her goodbye.

Then he tucked the checkerboard under his arm and drove through the brisk November morning, car windows down, singing "La Donna é Mobile" at the top of his lungs.

He had never been happier.

All because of a chance encounter with Agnes Quinn in a hospital waiting room when he had overheard her asking about Jameson Bridger, the friend they had both come to see. Bentley introduced himself. Agnes recognized his name and invited him to lunch.

And that had changed everything.

After Jameson died, Agnes helped Bentley start a new life. He moved to Plainview and got a job on the maintenance staff at Brighton Park Community College. He married Flossie Bingham. Now they were raising her grandson, Fletcher, as their own son.

Bentley spent every day helping people, instead of cheating them, and for the first time in his life had friends…real friends.

The best of them was Truitt Spenlow, the orchestra conductor.

Energized by the prospect of music at day's end, Bentley breezed through his work. Instead of going home at 5:00, he hurried to the auditorium. He took the key ring from the clip on his belt and unlocked the door. Then he tiptoed through the lobby, slipped through the Aisle C door, and stood still until his eyes grew accustomed to the darkness.

Dr. Spenlow was addressing the string section.

As usual, Finn Bigelow, principal cello, was scowling.

As Bentley's eyes adjusted to the shadows, he realized he was not alone in the audience. A few rows ahead, a man and woman whispered to each other. Leaning forward, he squinted his eyes and recognized Dr. Elspeth Sherwood, provost of BPCC, and Dr. Mitchell MacGregor, the new music professor who had joined the faculty in August. Bentley's supervisor, Torbert Hampton, had warned him to steer clear of Dr. Sherwood; he had learned on his own to be wary of Dr. MacGregor. Bentley had seen his type before—young, full of himself.

Dr. Spenlow tapped his baton on the conductor's stand.

Chapter 4 ~ Truitt Spenlow

When the music resumed, Bentley slipped into the middle seat on the next to the last row. Settling back, he pictured himself sitting in the chair behind Finn.

Once a cellist himself, Bentley had tried out for the orchestra after he enrolled as a student at Brighton Park. But Finn Bigelow would not give him the chance to finish his audition.

"This is not a community orchestra for people from all walks of life," Finn had said. "We're training serious musicians. Not people who play for a hobby."

Bentley left. Truitt Spenlow followed him into the hall. "Mr. McBain." Bentley turned back. "You're on the maintenance staff, aren't you?"

"Yes, sir."

"I'll ask Mr. Hampton to assign you to lock the auditorium after rehearsals. You can come a little early. Observe. You'll get an idea of what we expect. Then you can try out again."

Bentley had been coming to rehearsal ever since…arriving earlier each week until at last he was slipping in a few minutes after rehearsal began.

Afterwards, he would talk with Truitt, commenting on the rehearsal, asking questions, discussing the great composers. One night, at Flossie's suggestion, he brought his checkerboard and asked if Truitt would like to play. They had been playing ever since.

The music stopped; Bentley looked up. Dr. Spenlow was gripping his right shoulder. He raised it toward his ear, rotated it, flexed it, bent his head right, left, while the baton, dangling from his hand, cavorted like a marionette on tangled strings.

Silent, the orchestra watched, waited.

"That'll be all till Thursday," Dr. Spenlow said.

Bentley saw Dr. Sherwood jab MacGregor's elbow. They bolted out of their seats and started down the aisle.

"Just a minute," Dr. Sherwood called. "Before you go…"

Truitt spoke louder to the orchestra. "I'll be out of town, so"—he turned to face his replacement—"Dr. MacGregor will take the rehearsal." He turned back to his musicians. "Thank you, ladies and gentlemen. You may go."

Clutching their instruments, the orchestra members took their sheet music and filed out.

Truitt laid the lifeless baton on the open score and stepped down from the podium.

Dr. Sherwood arrived at the stage. "Didn't you hear me say to *wait*?"

Tea at Kimball Pines

"I knew you were here to announce Dr. MacGregor as my replacement," Truitt said, "so I saved you the trouble."

She bristled. "But I wanted to introduce him *properly*. That's why I came to *rehearsal*."

Dr. MacGregor put his hands on his hips. "Look here, Spenlow, you're making this more awkward than it has to be."

Truitt was unruffled. "I did nothing of the kind. You wanted to be introduced. You've been introduced. Now, if you'll excuse me, I'd like to go home."

Elspeth pivoted on her high heels. MacGregor followed her up the aisle.

Bentley remained in the shadows. When the pair exited, he walked to the stage and up the steps. "You okay, Doc? Can I get you anything?"

Truitt sank onto Finn Bigelow's chair. "Water."

Water would not help, but Truitt knew Bentley needed to feel useful.

Bentley slipped backstage to find the cup he had presented to Truitt after last May's all-Beethoven concert—a sturdy white ceramic mug imprinted with *World's Greatest Conductor* in bold black letters. He filled the mug with water and returned to his friend.

Truitt, his bald head glistening under the spotlight, was staring into the dark auditorium.

"Here you go, Doc," Bentley said.

Truitt sipped from the mug. "Sorry we didn't get to the Tchaikovsky tonight."

Bentley sat on the podium. "It's not long till your concert."

"I think it's time I faced the fact there may not be another concert. Not for me." Truitt set the mug on the floor and rested his elbows on his knees. "I can't keep risking performances. It's not fair to my musicians."

Bentley's heart dropped into his work boots. "I thought the doctor was going to try a different pain medication."

Truitt shook his head. "The doctor warned me ten years ago, when I broke my arm, that arthritis would eventually set in. It has. I shouldn't be surprised."

"But you can't give up just like that. You're only 55. Too young to retire."

"I'm not going anywhere. I'll still teach and give lessons." He leaned back. "I can't leave till I win back some of the money I've lost on checkers."

"I brought the board."

Chapter 4 ~ Truitt Spenlow

Bentley brought the folding card table he stored in the wings and set it up under the spotlight. Truitt fetched two chairs.

"You better be careful," Truitt said. "I might win more often now that I'll have time to practice my strategy."

Bentley lined up the black checkers on his side. "Is that a threat?"

Truitt laughed. "More like a promise. I'll tell you one thing. I plan to get back to composing—finish all those pieces I've started and then laid aside."

He had only one unfinished work in mind: "Song of Eventide."

Bentley's voice caught in his throat. "What will happen to the orchestra?"

Truitt made the first move. "I'll stay till the end of the term. Slowly let Dr. MacGregor take over. The Christmas concert will be a good opportunity for him to make his first public appearance, don't you think?"

That night Bentley let Truitt win. They both knew, but neither mentioned it.

Truitt picked up the score and baton and started toward the wings. "Tell Flossie hello."

Bentley walked with him. "I will. We want you to come for dinner once we get settled in the new apartment. That reminds me." He took a notepad from his pocket. "Flossie wanted me to give you our new phone number."

Truitt tucked the paper in his shirt pocket and whistled as he left through the rear door.

Bentley locked the stage door behind him and started toward the lobby. Pausing at the Aisle C door, he turned back and peered at the empty orchestra chairs. Then he locked the auditorium and left for home and the wife and son who loved him.

An hour later his phone rang.

"Mr. McBain?" a voice said.

"Yes."

"This is Officer Ashworth with the Planeview Police. A Mr. Truitt Spenlow has been injured in a car accident. We found your phone number in his pocket. Is he a friend of yours?"

Chapter 5

Prudence O'Neill

Three things infuriated Prudence O'Neill: strangers who joked about her parents' being "Puritans"; acquaintances who nicknamed her "Prude"; and would-be authors, penciled into her calendar because of some flimsy affiliation with her boss Daniel Ogden. So when Mr. Ogden ushered in Agnes Carlyle and introduced her as "an English teacher at his sister-in-law's school," Prudence stepped to the edge of her desk, assumed her half-smile, half-smirk, and pointed the visitor to a chair. She turned, snagging her high heel in the carpet, and glanced at the clock on the wall. Twelve minutes and she would show this girl the door.

Prudence sat behind her desk and sized up the intruder. Young. About 30, she guessed. Appropriate but not stylish dress. Hands gripping chair arms. Eyes darting around office. Ill at ease, but—like all other teachers Prudence had grilled during her tenure as assistant editor—facing the unfamiliar with a reasonable amount of poise. Teachers were notorious for rising to the occasion even when they were unsure. By now Mr. Ogden had laid a fatherly hand on the visitor's shoulder. Prudence studied Agnes' response. If she detected veneration in those eyes, the interview could be whittled down to ten minutes.

"Mrs. O'Neill will take care of you," Mr. Ogden said. "She's the best in the business."

By which he meant "the best" at getting rid of interruptions to the schedule.

The door closed. Prudence donned her reading glasses and feigned interest in the file she held at arm's length.

"So, Miss Quinn…you want to be a writer."

"Carlyle."

Tucking in her chin, Prudence peered over her glasses. "I beg your pardon."

Agnes displayed the wedding rings on her left hand. "Carlyle. I got married in August."

Prudence felt her face go hot. She reached for a red pencil in the pewter mug at the edge of her green desk pad.

"This letter says 'Quinn,' and it was dated"—she scanned the page—"January 31." She laid the paper flat and crossed through 'Quinn' four times.

"No worries," Agnes said. "I still call myself 'Quinn' sometimes."

Prudence fought to regain her advantage. Deflating unwelcome visitors depended on the precise timing of a well-rehearsed line of dismissive questions, and she was already off schedule.

"If you've had this letter since January," she said, glancing at the date, "why did you wait till November to make an appointment? Most people would jump at the chance."

Agnes smiled. Teaching two years at a community college had equipped her to deal with women like Prudence—insecure types who bolstered their fragile egos by glowering at underlings from behind a desk.

The reprimand did not bother Agnes in the least.

She did, however, feel queasy.

"Well, first," Agnes said, "I had to finish the school year, and then there was the wedding to plan, and now my husband and I are still working on our house after last year's ice storm."

Another interviewer with better people skills might have been curious enough to inquire about the storm and the damage, but Prudence, fixated on the time, was not.

She closed Agnes' file and pushed it to the edge of her desk. "I see. Now about your book. Fiction?"

"No. Better."

Prudence leaned back and put her fingertips together. "I'll be the judge of that."

The interview was back on track—the point at which hopeful writers looked dazed and apologized for their presumption.

But Agnes only snickered. She indicated the nameplate which read *Prudence O'Neill. Assistant Editor.* "That *is* your job, isn't it? Says so right there. Interesting name. Do people ask if you—"

Chapter 5 ~ Prudence O'Neill

Prudence held up her hand. "No, my parents were not of Puritan descent and—"

"No, I meant 'O'Neill.' You know…the playwright? Very literary name."

"Oh…him," Prudence said. "Not many people comment on that. Most people can't get past my first name."

"I know what you mean…what it's like to have an old-fashioned name. Do people call you 'Prude'?"

"Not if they want to stay on my good side."

"Me, too. I hate it when people call me 'Aggie.' I don't let anyone get away with it except my dad and my brother." Agnes tugged at her collar. "Whew. I shouldn't have worn this turtleneck. It's hot in here." She swallowed hard.

Prudence seized the moment. "Well, then, let's get down to business, so you can go back outside and enjoy the fall weather. First, you need to be aware how competitive the market is. Beginning writers *think* they know, but they really have no idea."

"Competitive," Agnes repeated, perspiration glistening on her forehead.

For a brief moment Prudence considered offering Agnes a glass of water, but dismissed the idea and pressed on. "We are in the business to make money, so no matter—"

Agnes scooted to the edge of her chair. "I understand."

"—how well-written your particular book may be, if it doesn't meet current—"

Looking terrified, Agnes stood. "I'm sorry. Could you tell me where the bathroom is?"

"Down the hall…that way." Prudence pointed. "Second door on the left."

Agnes bolted for the door and sprinted down the hall.

Smiling, Prudence swiveled side to side in her chair. This was a first. She had rendered people speechless, watched them retreat, dejected, but she had never unnerved anyone in the *middle* of an interview. And what was wrong with that? There weren't enough hours in the day as it was. Why should she spend time on a manuscript she had not solicited from an author she did not know? If they were ever going to make Ogden Publishing truly competitive, they had to be selective, innovative, and above all, ruthless.

Somewhere out there was a truly gifted writer with a unique story. If she could find that person…mentor…mold him, her reputation would be made. She could finally get the recognition she deserved, add achievements to her résumé, and make herself more appealing to a larger publishing house. She was 45. It was high time she rose from "assistant" to a position where she could make decisions and dictate policy.

And maybe…if Daniel were not her boss, he could look at her in a different light.

The clock ticked on well past the twelve-minute slot Prudence had allotted for the interview. Had Agnes Quinn or Carlyle or whatever-her-name-was decided to forget the whole thing and go back to her bucolic life?

While Prudence sat there musing, there was a knock at the door.

She pushed back from her desk, strode to the door, and pulled it open.

But instead of Agnes Carlyle, she found a robust and rumpled man, twisting a faded John Deere cap in his rough hands.

"Who are you?" Prudence asked.

"My name is Ham…uh, Talmadge Hampton. I saw Mrs. Carlyle come from this office."

"Yes?"

He pointed down the hall. "She ran that way."

Prudence folded her arms. "She wanted to know where the bathroom was."

"She's been in there a long time. Could you check on her and see if she's okay? She hasn't been feeling well."

"Are you her husband?"

Ham blushed. "No, ma'am. I'm the caretaker at the Magnolia Arms. Her husband had to teach today, so I drove her here. We told her it was a bad idea, but she wouldn't listen."

"Bad idea?"

"She's been sick for the last week or so. Nestor…that's her husband…told her she should re-schedule, but she said she'd waited long enough for the appointment."

Prudence leaned against the door. "I usually don't check on clients when they're in the bathroom. I can't believe you're asking."

He narrowed his eyes. "Look here, ma'am. If it was me who was sick, I wouldn't bother anybody. But it's Agnes, and if you won't check on her, I'll find someone who will."

Humbled, Prudence shook her head. "That…won't be necessary. I'll be right back."

She found Agnes sitting on the bathroom floor, pale, holding a wet paper towel against her forehead.

Chapter 5 ~ Prudence O'Neill

Prudence stood in front of her. "Are you all right?"

Agnes looked up. "This is my second interview with a publisher, you know. I didn't think anything could be worse than the first one, but it looks like I was wrong."

"Let me help you," Prudence said.

Agnes reached out her hand. Prudence steadied her as she stood.

"I think we're going to have to re-schedule," Agnes said.

"My calendar is pretty full till the end of the year."

Agnes walked to the door and spoke over her shoulder. "January then…or February."

Prudence followed her into the hall where Ham was waiting.

He put one arm around Agnes' shoulder and his other hand under her elbow. She leaned her head against his shoulder as he helped her down the hall.

"I should've listened to you, Ham," Agnes said. "This was a bad idea."

"Don't worry," he said. "You know that truck will give you the smoothest ride possible. You can close your eyes and rest, and I'll have you home in no time."

Truck? They came in a truck? This Prudence had to see. It would make a great story.

She remained in the hall till they left through the front door. Then she walked to the lobby and peeked out the window. Ham was helping Agnes into a white pickup truck. Vintage. Maybe a '30's or '40's model? When he closed the door and walked to the driver's side, Prudence got a closer look. On the door was a logo. A tree—dark green with a sturdy brown trunk. White flowers blooming on the branches. Underneath was printed in bold black letters: *Magnolia Arms*. For reasons she did not understand, she envied the two friends their "smooth ride" home.

Her jaded heart, insulated long ago against dreamy notions, fluttered. She could not imagine why.

Chapter 6

Pinetta Fraleigh

Pinetta Fraleigh wanted to go home—it was that simple.

This thought had become the consuming passion of her narrow, self-enclosed life from the moment she and her employer Millie Hubbard moved into the Magnolia Arms.

Even now—months after being uprooted from her *real* home—Pinetta refused to refer to herself as "residing" at 306 Belmont Drive, Dennisonville, North Carolina.

She nursed her silent protestations every day…every single day…when she slipped away to the kitchen during Millie's afternoon nap.

Sipping from her grandmother's china teacup, Pinetta would allow her mind to wander back to the lovely house on Greenwood Road in Littleton.

As distant and out of reach as a ride in a horse-drawn buggy on a leafy lane.

She returned her cup to the saucer and gazed around the kitchen, clean enough, but in a perpetual state of clutter—an unwashed cup or two in the sink, the newspaper left on the table after breakfast, a clean soup pot left on the stove, instead of stored under the counter. Back in Littleton she had enjoyed her afternoon tea on the sofa in Millie's parlor, but the sofa here was (like the rest of the house) disheveled…worn. Nothing like Millie's firm sofa with a stiff high back and lace-edged linen doilies secured to the arms with straight pins.

Pinetta nibbled at a teacake (her mother's recipe) and wondered again why *everyone* sang the praises of Ivy Leigh Ransom, the previous manager, whose tastes were so alien to her own.

Ivy Leigh *was* a charming woman, but charm had never run a tight ship.

Pinetta noticed a cookie crumb on the table. With delicate wisps of her pinky finger, she edged the crumb into her left hand cupped under the table's edge, stepped to the kitchen sink, and brushed off the crumb into the drain.

She leaned across the sink and pushed up the window. Frosty November air rushed in. Hands on hips, she breathed deeply. Cold air and cold water were good for the body and soul.

She gazed out the window at the yard…rambling and in need of a good raking. The stone walkway…mildewed and not scrubbed nearly often enough. The fountain...cracked and *still* in need of repair.

Why did the Carlyles leave so many chores untended?

Order. That was what was needed. Still sorely lacking in this house even after almost a year of her trying to raise the standard.

Papa would have never tolerated such a cavalier attitude toward running a household.

Pinetta felt her shoulders droop and made a quick adjustment to her posture.

She surveyed the yard a second time and shook her head at the jumble of frost-bitten plants and windblown leaves.

Guy Henry—her former husband—would have felt at home here.

He loved an overgrown yard…reveled in the looping and tumbling of their Confederate jasmine, the teeming azaleas obscuring the view from the windows, even the stubborn wisteria encroaching on the fence every spring, its obstinate vines marring the paint.

The day she took the pruning shears to the honeysuckle, Guy Henry took to the road.

Shuddering, she shook her head to jostle his face from her mind and returned to the table. She was pouring a second cup of rose hips tea when she heard a quick rap at the door.

Without waiting for an invitation, Bridey Ludlow swept into the kitchen. Hugging a clipboard in her sturdy arm, she deposited a *Dennisonville Historical Society* tote bag on the floor and pushed back against the door, closing it with her broad hips.

"Afternoon, Nettie. I just came by to…what in the world is that window doing open?"

Strutting to the sink, Bridey tossed her clipboard onto the dish drainer. Leaning over, she reached for the window. With her ample stomach in the way, however, it took two attempts to get a grip on the sill and nudge it down. Even then, she lacked the leverage to close it completely.

Chapter 6 ~ *Pinetta Fraleigh*

Pinetta's thin lips twitched into an imperceptible smile.

Bridey retrieved her clipboard and joined Pinetta at the table. She grabbed the last teacake off the plate and bit it in half.

Mouth full, she grimaced. "Not very sweet, are they?"

"Sweet enough," Pinetta said.

Bridey pointed to the counter. "Where's the coffee pot? Ivy Leigh always kept a pot of coffee going once the weather turned chancy."

"I serve coffee only at breakfast now."

Bridey clambered up, opened the cabinet door, and grabbed a glass.

"I'll have water then. These cookies are a little dry, if you don't mind my saying so."

Pinetta clenched her jaw. "Was there something you needed, Mrs. Ludlow?"

"I've told you, Nettie, around here we're all on a first name basis."

"And I've told *you*...kindly do *not* refer to me as 'Nettie.'"

Bridey plopped down at the table again. "But 'Pinetta' is so prim and proper."

As usual, Bridey had pronounced "Pinetta" with a short 'i.'

Eyes closed, Pinetta shook her head. "If you must use my given name, at least pronounce it correctly. It's *Pine*...etta. How would you like it if I—?"

Bridey slapped her hefty thigh. "That's right. I remember now. Pine. Etta. Like the tree. Tall and straight with prickly branches."

Pinetta reached for the notepad and pencil on the table. "Mr. and Mrs. Carlyle are not home. Would you like me to leave them a message?"

Bridey flipped through the pages on her clipboard. "Don't be silly. I knew they weren't home. It's Tuesday. Nestor is teaching at Willowbrook, and Ham has taken Agnes to—"

"Then what is it you wanted? Mrs. Hubbard will be awake soon, and I need to prepare—"

Bridey pulled a paper from the stack and slid it toward Pinetta. "Here it is. The schedule for choir tryouts."

Pinetta glanced down. "I beg your pardon."

"We're forming a community choir. For Founder's Day."

"Founder's Day?"

Bridey pushed the paper nearer to Pinetta. "Next summer. We've never had a community choir before, but then we've never had a centennial celebration either, have we?"

The paper lay quarantined between them.

Pinetta straightened her shoulders and leveled her gaze. "I wouldn't know how many or what kind of celebrations you've had. It's no concern of mine. And besides that, I don't sing."

Bridey licked her thumb and continued to rifle through her pages. "I can show you if…I can only…where *is* that *brochure*?" She clamped her hand to her lips and stared at the ceiling.

"Maybe you left it at home?" Pinetta said, hoping Bridey would go there.

Tilting back her head, Bridey giggled. "Silly me. It's in my bag."

She planted her hand on the table, pushed herself up, and bustled across the kitchen. Snatching up her tote bag, she shoved her hand inside and peered into its depths as she walked back. She smacked the brochure on the table.

"There you go. Tri-fold. Full color. Isn't it a beauty?"

The brochure, like the application for choir tryouts, remained untouched.

"I told you," Pinetta said. "I don't sing."

"We don't need you to *sing*," Bridey said. "We need you to *accompany*. And don't bother telling me you 'don't play.' Millie told me you used to be a church pianist."

Pinetta felt her face go hot. "That was a long time ago."

Bridey winked and shook her finger. "Ah-ha. So you admit it."

"I haven't played in years," Pinetta said, voice quivering in spite of herself.

Bridey stashed her clipboard in her tote bag. "I wouldn't ask, but the woman we *thought* would play the piano can't do it this year. Eileen Redmon. Have you met her?"

"No."

"Going through a nasty divorce. Just not up to taking on more responsibility, while her husband…ex-…is selling everything out from underneath her. You think Millie's awake?"

Pinetta stood. "Really, Mrs. Ludlow. You can't just waltz through the door and—"

Speaking over her shoulder, Bridey headed to the hallway. "My Asa wanted me to find out what time she wants him to pick her up for the Garden Club meeting in the morning."

Pinetta followed Bridey into the hall. "The cab driver doesn't call to schedule his customers. The *customer* calls when—"

Chapter 6 ~ *Pinetta Fraleigh*

"Now don't get in a tizzy," Bridey called back. "I'll peek into Millie's room. If she's asleep, I'll let myself out the front door. No harm done. Bye, Nettie, uh…Piney."

On an ordinary day, Pinetta would have outstepped Bridey and blocked Millie's door.

But stung by Millie's betrayal of her secret…and to Bridey Ludlow of all people…Pinetta felt vulnerable and could not summon the will to move.

She heard Bridey tap on Millie's door. The door opened, closed.

Shaken, Pinetta reached for the banister to her right. When she heard nothing further and the front door did not open, she stepped on the first stair and counted the steps as she climbed.

Bridey found Millie sitting in a chair by her window.

"Well," Millie said, eyes sparkling, "how did she take it?"

Bridey dropped her tote bag and sank onto the other chair.

"Just like you said. She's mad as a wet hen."

Millie clapped her hands. "Wonderful. The hard part's done."

Chapter 7

On Belmont Drive

Bridey, like a monarch enthroned, eased back, draping her ample arms over the arms of the chair. "I wouldn't have tangled with that bobcat for nobody but you, Miss Millie. You know that, don't you?"

Millie reached over to pat Bridey's knee. "I do. And I'm grateful."

"For the life of me, I don't see how anyone as cheerful as you manages to put up with someone like her. She is the turned-up-nosiest person I have *ever* met. And believe me, I've met plenty."

Millie shook her head. "Now, Bridey, none of that. If you knew Pinetta's story, you'd feel more kindly toward her."

Bridey raised her eyebrows. This was the chance she had been waiting for.

"You know I've never been one to pry, but…it *would* be helpful to know a few details, especially if I have to spend the next"—she counted on her fingers—"eight months crossing paths with her."

Millie shook her head. "It took me a long time to gain Pinetta's confidence. I can't betray her trust. She's a very private person."

Bridey pressed ahead. "I'm pretty sure bringing up her piano playing hit the rawest nerve there was to hit. Knowing anything else at this point would be small potatoes, don't you think?"

Millie turned toward the window. She had tried so long to draw Pinetta out of her self-imposed isolation. Nothing had worked. It was time for desperate measures.

"All right," Millie said. "I'll tell you as much as I can. What do you want to know?"

Bridey struggled to curb her excitement. She had been chronically curious about Millie and Pinetta ever since they had moved to Dennisonville. The most experienced town gossips had been hard-pressed to acquire even a scrap of information. All anyone knew was that Nestor Carlyle had learned about Millie while he was researching the Bridgers, one of Dennisonville's premier families, and had gone to Littleton to find her.

During the single day he and Millie spent together, they had formed a lasting friendship and had been in contact ever since.

Letters might have remained the extent of their friendship if the winter had not been so brutal, but as the bitter months dragged on, Millie confided to Nestor she was feeling her age.

"Seventy-eight," she wrote, "is too old to be taking care of this big old house, worrying constantly about the pipes freezing."

Nestor had offered to let Millie and Pinetta visit the Magnolia Arms till winter was over.

Winter had come and gone. Spring and summer, too. Now autumn was almost at an end, and Millie was still occupying Ivy Leigh's old room at the front of the house.

Bridey weighed her words. "Well...I've always wondered how you and Pinetta met. You're such unlikely friends."

"I placed an ad in the newspaper."

"For a housekeeper?" Bridey asked.

"I don't remember all it said. Something like '*Wanted: live-in female companion for elderly woman. Light housekeeping, cooking required. Ability to travel,*' as I recall."

"Travel?"

"My husband had been retired for years, but he never wanted to go anywhere. When he left me a wealthy widow, I wanted to see the world, but none of my kids would go with me."

Bridey was intrigued. "So you found someone who would."

"Uh-huh. And Pinetta was the only applicant willing to get a passport. In her 50s, she was near enough my age to be a kindred spirit, but young enough to help me when I needed it."

"And she up and changed her whole life"—Bridey snapped her fingers—"just like that? She doesn't seem the type."

Chapter 7 ~ On Belmont Drive

"Under ordinary circumstances, she wouldn't have. But her husband had left her, and she was devastated by the shame she had brought on her family."

"Why did her husband leave?" *As if I had to ask*, Bridey thought.

"Even after all these years, I still don't know the whole story," Millie said. "But I do know after Guy Henry left—"

"Guy Henry? What a name."

"After he left, Pinetta stayed indoors for weeks. Refused to see anyone. The church choir director called and begged her to come back for the sake of the Sunday morning serv—"

Bridey gasped. "She was the church *pianist*. I still can't picture it."

"I know, but it's true. She wouldn't go back. Couldn't bear the thought of sitting in a pew, much less being on display in front of the entire congregation."

"So your ad gave her the chance to move to a new town. No wonder she jumped at it."

"And my house was exactly what she was used to. Clean, orderly, quiet."

Bridey leaned forward. "So, if you had such an ideal setup…you found a travelling buddy…she had a fresh start…why have you stayed here so long? We've all wonder—"

Wincing, Bridey clamped her lips closed.

Millie lowered her voice. "All right. I'm going to tell you the truth, but only because I need your help. This *has* to stay between us. Promise?"

Pulse racing, Bridey raised her right hand. "Promise."

"I came here under false pretenses."

"You did?"

"Wheedled the invitation out of Nestor…all but invited myself to come. Told him I was tired of taking care of my house, worried about the pipes freezing. But it was all a lie."

"Why on earth…?"

"I needed an excuse to get Pinetta out of Littleton. She can't keep living like a hermit. I want her to find a new life here…with other people…so she can live well after I'm gone."

Tears seeped into Bridey's eyes. "I'm sorry, Miss Millie. And here I thought—"

Millie waved her hand. "No need for an apology. But I can't keep waiting for Pinetta to get out into the community. She needs friends other than Nestor and Agnes and Ham and me."

"Yes, ma'am," Bridey said. "How can I help?"

Upstairs on the third floor Pinetta stared out the arched window on the front of the house.

This was the only secret sin she had ever embraced—waiting till she thought she wouldn't be noticed, tiptoeing up the stairs like a common criminal, sneaking into another person's room without permission.

She had been curious about this room from the moment she had arrived. Stepping from the cab on that frosty winter morning, she had lingered on the sidewalk, gazing up, wondering about the view from the window beneath the towering cupola and widow's walk.

If she had arrived as a tenant rather than Millie's caregiver, she would have asked for a tour of this room and then claimed it as her own on the spot.

But leaving Millie alone on the first floor would have been unthinkable; Pinetta had asked for the small room off the kitchen and taken on the role of cook.

When Nestor's friend, Talmadge Hampton (whom everyone called "Ham"), had arrived to take the job of caretaker, he had moved into the third floor room.

Pinetta had deemed this appropriate.

Though she knew nothing about Ham—and had not asked—she read in his eyes the same deep abiding sadness of her own heart.

So, she did not begrudge him—good and gentle as he was—the solitude and sense of well-being this space provided.

A sudden breeze loosened the few remaining leaves on the walnut tree. Pinetta watched them flutter to the ground. Soon snow would begin to fall, marking the passing of a full year.

And still she and Millie were not home.

She turned from the window and surveyed the room.

The sense of Ham's presence only added to its charm: a quilt (stitched by his mother?) at the foot of the bed; on the dresser a black and white photo of his parents (Ham was the image of his father); carved wooden songbirds (in various stages of completion) on a worktable by the door; a stack of sheet music ("Liebestraum" on top) on an end table by a wooden rocker; on the back of the door, a poster advertising the "Brighton Park Community College Fine Arts Festival," a musician identified as "Lorna Maron" seated at a grand piano.

Sitting in the rocker, she closed her eyes and let her mind drift back to the life she missed.

"Were you looking for me, Miss Pinetta?"

Pinetta bolted up and straightened the collar of her white blouse. Absorbed in her musings, she had not heard Ham coming up the stairs.

"No…no," she said. "I didn't think anyone was home and…it's such a beautiful day…I wanted to look at the leaves. I—"

Ham remained at the door. "It's all right. I don't mind. I think everyone in town has wondered about the view from this window."

"But it's your room, Talmadge, and I'm sorry. It's not like me to be so improper."

"Please, Miss Pinetta, after all this time, don't you think you could call me 'Ham' like everyone else does?"

She ducked her head. "All right…Ham. I'm so embarrassed about my behavior. It's not the way I was brought up. I don't know *what* my papa would say if he knew—"

"Well, I know what *my* dad would say. He'd say, 'Son, you've no right keeping a beautiful view like this to yourself.' So, you're welcome anytime."

Regaining her composure, Pinetta walked to the door. Ham stepped aside to let her pass. "Thank you, Ham," she said. "I'd better check on Millie. She should be awake by now."

"She's in the kitchen. Came out of her room when she heard Agnes and me come in."

Relieved to have a good excuse to leave, Pinetta started toward the stairs. "I should go."

Ham called after her. "Millie's making tea for Agnes. She's still sick—had to walk out of the interview before it was finished."

Pinetta spoke over her shoulder. "I'm sorry to hear that. I'll go down and help."

"Uh, ma'am…"

She stopped and looked back. "Yes?"

"You might want to check on Agnes instead. Lute Monroe is in the kitchen."

Pinetta did not hide her frustration. "What's *he* doing here?"

Ham tried not to grin. "He *said* he had a bag of collard greens for you. But I expect he really wants to talk to you about the chili supper at the church next Saturday."

She leaned against the staircase. "Will he never give up?"

"Probably not," Ham said. "He told me—"

Pinetta held up her hand. "I don't want to know any more. Would you go down and help Millie? Tell Lute I'm with Agnes."

Ham stifled a laugh and walked behind her. When they reached Nestor and Agnes' room, Ham kept walking, headed downstairs. Pinetta paused and knocked on the door.

"Come in," Agnes said.

Closing the door behind her, Pinetta walked to the bed where Agnes was resting.

She produced a polite cough. "Ham said you were still sick. May I get you anything?"

Agnes took the washcloth from her forehead. "Could you wet this and wring it out? I don't want to move. Feels so good to be still."

Holding the washcloth by the corner, Pinetta walked to the bathroom.

She held the washcloth under cold water and perused the counter. Bottles of lotion and aftershave, cans of shaving cream and hairspray, two toothbrushes in a cup—a comfortable muddle of masculine and feminine, poignant evidence of a life shared. She turned off the faucet. As she wrung the cloth, she scrutinized her image in the mirror. High cheekbones, a thin, narrow face, tapering to a square chin; square-lensed, rimless glasses settled on a straight nose. Her hair still auburn without a hint of gray. With wet fingers, she massaged the faint wrinkles at the corner of her right eye.

She wondered if Guy Henry were aging as gracefully as she was.

She returned to Agnes, laid the washcloth on her forehead, and sat in a chair by the window. Never one to initiate conversation, she considered an appropriate comment.

"Ham said the interview didn't go well."

Eyes closed, Agnes whimpered. "It was a train wreck."

Chapter 7 ~ On Belmont Drive

Pinetta, always uncomfortable with honest emotion, would have preferred to mutter some feeble excuse about letting Agnes rest, so she could excuse herself and edge toward the door.

But with Lute Monroe waiting in the kitchen, escape was not an option.

So Pinetta folded her hands in her lap and contemplated what to say next.

Though she found Agnes entirely too immature to be so near 30, she liked her well enough. Still…Pinetta had long been of the opinion *someone* should undeceive Agnes about her "writing career."

Pinetta assessed the situation. Under ordinary circumstances, this would have been the ideal opportunity to address the subject. She and Agnes were alone; the topic had been brought up. But it would have been ill-mannered to wound Agnes when she was in such a pitiable state.

"I'm sure you can re-schedule," Pinetta said.

Agnes, the back of her hand resting on her forehead, went on crying, her words almost unintelligible.

"What's the point? I've had two chances and blown both of them."

"Two? What do you mean? I thought this was your first attempt to…"

Pinetta could not bring herself to dignify Agnes' *hobby* as 'writing.' Jane Austen was a *writer*. Charlotte Brontë was a *writer*. Louisa May Alcott was a *writer*. People were entirely too casual about what words actually meant.

"…at trying to persuade an editor to publish your…story," Pinetta said.

Sick as she was, Agnes recognized Pinetta's dismissive tone. Somewhere, deep within her, a spark of resentment flickered. She fanned it to life.

"*No*. This wasn't my *first* attempt. I wrote *another* book"—her insides, overstimulated, rebelled—"a long time ago. Took it to a publisher…but he wanted to make a comic…a comic—"

Clamping her hand over her mouth, Agnes bolted up and tumbled out of bed. Scrambling to her feet, she made a frantic dash to the bathroom.

Pinetta cringed as Agnes retched. Feeling half-sick herself, she was eyeing the door when Millie stepped in as she knocked.

Calmed, Pinetta pointed to the bathroom.

"Oh, dear," Millie said and rushed to help Agnes.

Pinetta spotted Ham, carrying a tray, waiting outside the open door. She stood and gestured to the round table next to her chair.

Ham glanced toward the bathroom as he made his way across the room and set down the tray. "Is she going to be all right?"

"Millie will look after her," Pinetta said.

Ham backed toward the door. "I'll…I'll…go downstairs. Nestor should be home soon. I'll watch for him and bring him up."

At last Agnes grew quiet. Millie guided her back to the bed and eased her down.

"Bring the tea, Pinetta," Millie said.

Pinetta stepped back. "It wouldn't be wise…for me to catch the flu, since I do all the cooking."

Millie laughed. "Don't be silly. What Agnes has isn't catching." Millie motioned her forward. "Come on. Do as I said."

Pinetta lifted the teacup and approached the bed.

Millie placed the cup in Agnes' hands. "Now be a good girl and drink your tea. It's peppermint. Good for you and the baby, too."

Agnes sipped; then her eyes flew open. "Good for me and *who*?"

"The baby," Millie said. "Surely you've realized…you're pregnant."

"No," Agnes said. "I didn't realize I was…. We've only been married since August. We weren't planning on—what makes you think I'm…?"

"I had four children, dear," Millie said. "I recognize the symptoms."

Agnes grimaced. "Well…I *guess* that makes sense…a baby. A *baby*?"

Pinetta seized the moment. "I have a few things to do before I start dinner."

Millie sat on the edge of the bed. "You might want to wait on that. There's a visitor—"

"I know," Pinetta said. "Lute Monroe is in the kitchen."

The last time she had been forced to hide from Lute Monroe, Pinetta had come up with a plan. If she had to put her life on hold while her would-be suitor hovered in the kitchen, waiting for a word with her, she might as well be useful.

She crept downstairs to the first floor and tiptoed into the dining room. She retrieved her litter pick-up tool, hidden among the fireplace tools, and pulled a black plastic garbage bag from the wicker basket in the corner. Then she stole to the front door and slipped outside, heading for the park. She stepped onto the sidewalk and turned left, heading in the opposite direction of Lute's produce market. With luck, she could reach the end of Belmont

Chapter 7 ~ On Belmont Drive

Drive, turn left onto 8th Street, and be out of sight before Lute gave up his vigil and returned to his store.

Pinetta had taken only a few steps when she spotted Nestor's truck approaching. She calculated. Nestor would go in. Ham would rush him upstairs, leaving Lute in the kitchen. Lute would decide to leave. Be on the sidewalk in seconds. Spot her.

She scurried to Ida Willingale's house and ducked behind a bottlebrush bush. From this vantage point, she could watch unobserved. Once Lute came out of the house and headed in the opposite direction, she could be on her way. Turn the corner.

Holding her breath, Pinetta peered from behind the bush.

Lute Monroe appeared on the sidewalk.

The front door to Ida Willingale's house swung open.

Mary Grace Dodson bounded off the porch.

"Pinetta, was that Nestor that just drove by? Did that man show up yet?"

Pinetta turned and drummed her index finger against her lips to silence Mary Grace.

Mary Grace halted mid-step and lowered her voice. "What's wrong?"

Pulse pounding, Pinetta peeked through the leaves. Lute Monroe had not looked back.

The two women waited: one, desperate for relief; the other, desperate for information.

Lute Monroe turned the corner at the opposite end of the street. Pinetta faced Mary Grace.

"What were you looking at?" Mary Grace asked.

"Nothing. I thought I saw someone—"

Mary Grace grabbed Pinetta's arm. "Was it him?"

"Who?"

"The stranger I met at the train station this morning. He arrived at dawn"—she gazed at the sky—"like he'd ridden in on a sunbeam."

Pinetta eased her arm from Mary Grace's hold. "What *are* you talking about?"

"I was on duty at the Welcome Table this morning. A man…a handsome man…asked where the Magnolia Arms was…well, where 306 Belmont Drive was."

"The only visitor I've had today was Bridey Ludlow," Pinetta said.

Tea at Kimball Pines

Mary Grace took Pinetta's arm again. "All I'm saying is, keep your eye out. This man…may just be the most exciting man to come to Dennisonville in a long time. I hope—"

She hesitated, worried Pinetta would think her foolish.

"You hope what?" Pinetta asked.

Mary Grace blushed. "That he'll stay long enough for us to get to know each other."

Holding her litter pick-up tool like a staff, Pinetta squared her shoulders. "I'm sorry. I have to go. It's my day to volunteer in the park."

"I thought you went yesterday," Mary Grace said, thinking Pinetta looked like Joan of Arc brandishing a lance.

Pinetta eased toward the sidewalk. "The park can't be too clean, now can it?"

"No, I guess not. Will you let me know if the stranger arrives? I gave him directions."

Pinetta nodded, but had no intention of complying with Mary Grace's request. It was none of *her* business *who* stayed at the Magnolia Arms.

As she walked, Pinetta reflected how convenient it would be if Lute Monroe would pursue Mary Grace instead of her. They were perfectly suited for each other. Unkempt, unsophisticated. She glanced at her watch. Almost 4:00. By the time she reached the park, she would have only a few minutes before she needed to start back to prepare supper. She wondered if it was worth the effort, but kept moving. A walk would do her good. After her trying day. First, Bridey Ludlow. Then Ḥam's finding her in his room. And the news of Agnes' pregnancy.

A baby in the house.

Pinetta reached the end of the street and turned left, quickening her pace as her mind raced forward, considering the possibilities. She had already taken on more than her fair share of the housework since the Carlyles had begun teaching at Willowbrook. If they thought she would be happy to take on the role of nanny in addition to all the cooking, answering the phone, *and* checking on the greenhouse, then they—

"Ma'am?"

Pinetta was halfway up the block when she heard a voice behind her. She stopped and turned around. A young man was waving at her from the opposite corner.

42

Chapter 7 ~ On Belmont Drive

She shielded her eyes from the sun. "Were you speaking to me?"

He crossed the street. "I'm looking for the Magnolia Arms. Can you tell me if I'm headed in the right direction?"

Pinetta, habitually suspicious, sized him up. Tall, sandy-haired, mid-20's. Though bedraggled, he had the bearing of a young man well brought up.

He met her stare with benevolent eyes.

She pointed with her pick-up tool. "It's that way. Five houses down. On the right."

He thanked her and walked toward the Magnolia Arms.

She walked back to the corner. Took another look as he walked away. Surely this was not Mary Grace's "stranger." He was young enough to be her *son*. Then, though it was not like her to be impetuous, Pinetta started after him.

"Excuse me," she said.

He looked back. "Yes, ma'am."

"Are you looking for anyone in particular?"

"No," he said. "I'm new in town. I met Mrs. Kimball this morning. She asked if I had a place to stay and recommended the Magnolia Arms. Thought I'd check it out."

Pinetta stepped closer. "You *met* Mrs. Kimball? How?"

"She called to me when I was passing her house this morning. Thought I was her son. She slipped and fell on the steps, so I helped her inside and stayed till her maid came."

"She invited you *in*? That doesn't sound like her."

"I don't think she would have asked me in if she hadn't been hurt."

He continued on his way; Pinetta fell into step.

"Is she all right?" Pinetta asked.

"Just a bad sprain. I didn't mean to stay all day, but it's her birthday. She asked me to celebrate with her. Lovely lady. Are we getting close to the house?"

"It's the next one…there. If you'll tell me your name, I'll introduce you."

"Mrs. Kimball said to ask for Nestor. You know him?"

"I live there," Pinetta said.

His face broke into a broad smile. "You must be Pinetta. (He pronounced it correctly.) Mrs. Kimball told me all about you. I'm Abbot Cooper."

He held out his hand.

Garbage bag in one hand, pick-up tool in the other, Pinetta felt suddenly awkward. Eyes darting from one hand to the other, she stammered.

Abbot laughed. "Here. Let me take that."

His right hand still open, he took her pick-up tool in his left.

When he took Pinetta's hand, she felt as if a locked door had opened and let in the light.

Chapter 8

The Man on the Corner

Teacup in hand, Millie Hubbard sat in the chair by the window, poised in the sublime moment of being needed. Content to remain quiet while Agnes rested, Millie reflected on her blessings. While others her age were becoming museum pieces, exhibited in their own homes, she was forging a new life. The colossal risk she had taken, uprooting herself and Pinetta, moving from Littleton to Dennisonville, was paying off. Though her plan was unfolding more slowly than she had anticipated—Pinetta, remaining predictably intractable—Millie was thriving. She loved…and *was* loved…by a remarkable circle of vibrant young friends.

And now a baby was coming.

How could life possibly be any better?

Eyes closed, Agnes stirred. "Millie?"

Millie placed her cup on the saucer. "I'm here."

"Could I ask you something?"

"Of course," Millie said, sitting next to her.

Agnes peeked through puffy eyes. "When you had children…could you afford them?"

Millie patted her hand. "Dear girl, if couples waited till they could afford children, *no one* would have any. Are you worried about that?"

Agnes squeezed her eyes shut. Tears trickled down her face. "We were going to wait till things settled down. Nestor was going to expand his business. I was going to write. But the repairs to the house, the remodeling after the storm took longer than we thought."

"Now don't get upset. You'll make yourself sick again."

Tea at Kimball Pines

The door opened, and Nestor stepped in. Relieved, Millie welcomed him. He kissed her cheek, and she left the room, closing the door behind her.

Nestor sat on the bed. "Ham said the interview didn't go well."

Agnes reached out; he pulled her close. She buried her face in his shoulder. "It was *awful*. That woman was so snobby…her office was so hot. I had to leave."

"I thought your appointment was with Mr. Ogden."

"So did I. He passed me off to his henchman. And to make things worse…she found me on the bathroom floor after I threw up. I was so embarrassed. She said I could reschedule but—"

He patted her back. "I'll take you back when you feel better. I promise."

She let go of him. Head bowed, she swiped the back of her hand across her wet face. "That's the other thing I have to tell you. Millie thinks I'm…I'm…"

Nestor lifted her chin and gazed into her eyes. "What?"

"Pregnant."

His mouth dropped open, broadening into a smile. "We're going to have a *baby*?"

"That's what Millie said. Are you upset?"

"Why would I be upset?" He hugged her. "Nothing could make me happier."

"But we don't have any money. And I can't teach when I'm so sick."

He eased her onto the pillow. "We'll figure that out. We've figured out everything *else*."

"But where will we put a baby? We'll have to turn one of the rooms into a nursery, and that means one less room to rent and less…"

"You know this house can always take in one more person."

Agnes went back to crying. "If only I could've made it through the interview…Maybe Miss Prissy Pants would have published the book, and we could've made some money that way."

Nestor stood and held out his hands. "Come on. You can take a nice warm bath, put on some comfortable clothes, and we'll sit in the parlor till supper."

She clamped her hand over her mouth. "Don't say *supper*."

He lifted her feet and eased them over the side of the bed.

Agnes, head spinning, eased into an upright position. "I love you."

"I love you, too." He kissed her on the forehead. "Wait here. I'll be right back."

Chapter 8 ~ The Man on the Corner

Nestor went to the bathroom and turned on the water in the tub. He leaned against the sink and peered through the open door at Agnes. Even with her face blotched and eyes swollen from crying, she was still beautiful, the person he most wanted to see at the end of every day…the beginning of every day, and all times in between. He had loved her in silence for so long—kept loving her as she pined for another man. But the moment his rival broke Agnes' heart, Nestor put the finishing touches on the proposal he had been planning for over a year.

Coached by their mutual friend, Ivy Leigh Ransom, he had orchestrated the perfect evening. Roses, candlelight, china, crystal, silver, a gourmet meal with Agnes' favorite dessert. Any other woman would have swooned and fallen into his arms.

But not Agnes.

They had been "friends" for so long, she could think of him in no other way.

He had waited two more months before she said yes.

They were married in this very house, where they had met, in the dining room, the place where Nestor had first professed his love.

Once they became the official managers of the Magnolia Arms, they discovered why newlyweds did not choose a three-story house as their first home. Especially not one in the process of being repaired and remodeled. The basement apartment and two of the second-floor rooms, ordinarily occupied by paying tenants, had been empty except for brief visits by people passing through town. To compensate for their decline in income, Nestor and Agnes had both taken teaching jobs at Willowbrook Community College in Bellport. While she taught British Literature and he taught 18th Century Europe, the writing and gardening were on hold.

Bur Nestor did not mind. Agnes was his wife. Everything else could wait.

He called to Agnes. "Bathtub's ready."

She stood…slowly…steadied herself, and shuffled to the bathroom.

"Will you be okay by yourself?" Nestor asked. "I need to work on the bills."

She nodded. "I'll be down in a few minutes."

When he opened the door into the hallway, he found Ham, grave-faced, leaning against the banister.

"Have you been waiting long?" Nestor asked.

"Not too long. I didn't want to bother you, but there's a guy downstairs. Says he wants a room. Is Agnes going to be okay?"

Smiling, Nestor clapped him on the shoulder. "In a few months."

"What?"

"I'll explain later. This guy. Wants a room?"

"That's what he said."

Nestor started toward the stairs. "Then let's not keep him waiting." When Ham did not follow, Nestor paused and looked back. "What's wrong?"

Ham lowered his voice. "He said Vesper Kimball sent him. Is that possible?"

"We'll find out. If we have a new tenant, it would make Agnes' day."

Waiting in the foyer, Abbot Cooper surveyed the place where he hoped to settle down for a while. Though he did not understand why…the moment Vesper Kimball had said, "Magnolia Arms," he had felt a glint of hope, the first he had entertained since leaving home. For five months, he had ducked into libraries or churches during the day and checked into homeless shelters at night. Through hunger, heat, cold, and drenching rains, he had remained resolute. It would be cold day in July before he crawled back to his father to admit, "You were right."

When Nestor reached the first floor, he held out his hand as he approached Abbot.

"Nestor Carlyle. Manager. Can I help you?"

They shook hands. "Abbot Cooper. Mrs. Kimball sent me. She said you might rent me a room. I'm a little low on cash, but I can pay for a few nights."

"Would you like to stay for supper?" Nestor asked.

"Thanks. Then I wouldn't have to look for a restaurant."

By which he really meant "the Salvation Army."

"I'll show you around." Nestor turned to Ham. "This is our caretaker, Talmadge Hampton. We call him 'Ham.'"

"I'll tell Pinetta there's one more for dinner," Ham said, and left for the kitchen.

Abbot gazed up at the ceiling. "This is a beautiful house. Full of character."

"And full of *characters*," Nestor said, laughing. "Come on. I'll give you the grand tour." He opened the door into the dining room. "We used to run a restaurant here, but it was so successful, we had to relocate. We still eat in here when we have a full house."

Chapter 8 ~ The Man on the Corner

Nestor showed Abbot the parlor, and they stepped across the hall into the kitchen.

"This is Pinetta Fraleigh," Nestor said. "She's our—"

Pinetta, wooden spoon in hand, turned from the stove. "I met Mr. Cooper outside."

"At the corner," Abbot said. "Mrs. Fraleigh gave me directions."

Pinetta stirred her simmering soup. "If I'd known we were having a guest, I would've prepared something a little more elegant."

"Elegance is highly overrated," Abbot said, stomach growling.

"Let me show you the apartment downstairs," Nestor said. "We've had as many as three to share the room, but you can have the room to yourself if you want."

They descended the stairs to the converted basement room. Next to a wooden desk, holding a typewriter and banker's lamp, was a bookshelf lined with tattered paperbacks, leather-bound classics, and catalogs, leaning or lying in haphazard stacks and piles. Twin beds on opposite sides of the room were made up with blue plaid bedspreads and fluffy pillows in starched white pillowcases; a periodic table of elements over one bed, a poster of Einstein over the other. Though Abbot had stayed in some of the finest hotels in Europe, he had never seen a room he liked better.

"What happened to the guys who used to live here?" Abbot asked, as they climbed the stairs to the kitchen.

Nestor crossed the kitchen and opened the back door. "They both got married. So did the guy who lived here before they did."

"Were they all scientists?"

"A physicist and a chemist. The other guy was a pianist."

Abbot followed Nestor onto the screened porch. "Beautiful spot. Do you spend much time here?"

"My wife spends more time here than I do. She's a writer…says it inspires her."

Abbot glanced up at the dried flowers hanging from the rafters. "She put those there?"

Nestor nodded. "Uh-huh. And keeps herbs growing in the flower pots. Something she learned from Ivy Leigh, our friend who used to be the manager here."

Abbot pointed at the greenhouse in the backyard. "What's in there?"

"Roses. Orchids. I hope to grow hybrid day lilies, too. We have two rooms available on the second floor. Want to see them?"

Abbot nodded. He had already decided no matter what the rooms looked like, he was going to stay here as long as possible.

When they reached the second floor, Nestor slipped into the master bedroom to tell Agnes he was giving a new tenant a tour. The news perked her up even more than the warm bath. As she hurried to dress, she asked the visitor's name and if he was staying for dinner.

"You'd better get downstairs and tell Pinetta not to skimp on portions," she said, slipping on her shoes. "You know how she likes to stretch one meal into three."

"Or four," Nestor said. "If Abbot decides he wants a room on this floor, does it matter to you which one he takes?"

"I guess he should move into Posey's room, so we can turn Monty's room into the nursery. Makes more sense, don't you think? It's right next door."

Though former tenants Posey Devoe and Monty St. James had moved out months ago, Agnes could never think of the second-floor rooms as belonging to anyone but them.

Nestor hugged her. "Perfect sense. Feel like walking with Abbot to the third floor?"

"Feeling better by the minute. Maybe we should eat in the dining room tonight."

"I'll go down and set the table. You know how Pinetta hates a change in plans."

Agnes stepped into the hall and waited for Abbot to come out of Posey's room.

"I'm Agnes Carlyle. You must be Abbot."

He took her hand. "I am. And I'd like to take that room. I love the view."

"Would you like to see the view from the next floor?" Agnes asked. "It's even better."

"Is there a room available up there?"

"No, but you still need to see the view. It's a rite of passage before you move in."

When they reached the third floor, she opened the first door on the left.

Chapter 8 ~ *The Man on the Corner*

"This is the study," she said. "You're welcome to use it. When I first came, I was told there was no talking or eating in here, but we've kind of relaxed that rule."

Abbot pointed down the hall. "Whose room is that?"

"Ham. Our caretaker. But it used to be mine."

She walked ahead of him and remained at the door as he entered.

Abbot walked to the window. He gazed out at the quiet street below, the lawn littered with fallen leaves, the roofs of neighboring houses—no two alike. A hint of a smile on his lips, he breathed a long, gentle sigh.

"Don't think I'm crazy," he said, "but I feel like—"

"You've come home?" Agnes asked.

"How did you know?"

"I felt the same way when I first came. I couldn't believe I was actually standing in the house I'd dreamed of for so long. The feeling has never left me."

"You knew about the house before you came? How?"

Agnes laughed. "That is a *long* story. We won't have time before dinner. I'll ask Ham to bring your luggage to Posey's room…uh…your room."

Abbot reached in his pocket. "Do I need to give you a deposit?"

"You can discuss that with Nestor."

Abbot tapped on the window. "Do you know that man on the sidewalk? He's been pacing up and down the whole time we've been talking."

Stepping beside Abbot, Agnes looked out, sizing up the stranger. Hands shoved into his pockets, chin tucked to his chest, he paced, eyes riveted to the ground. He reached the walkway to the porch, hesitated, glanced at the door, pivoted, marched back.

If he would lift his head, Agnes thought, *push back the brim of that Panama Jack hat, maybe I could figure out why he looks familiar.*

"You know him?" Abbot asked.

"Never seen him before. I'll go down and see if I can help him. See you at dinner."

Agnes found herself hurrying, pestered by a nameless fear the stranger would be gone if she did not reach him soon enough. Laying her hand on the banister, she descended the stairs as fast as her queasy stomach allowed.

She reached back into her memory, trying to fit the man into a category—friend from her hometown? College professor? Coworker from

Brighton Park? She chalked up her impressions as the product of her chronically overactive imagination and opened the front door.

By the time she stepped onto the porch, the man had almost reached the end of the street. She hurried to the sidewalk and called out.

"Hello. Were you looking for someone?"

He stopped and turned back. Removing his hat, he ambled toward the house.

"The Magnolia Arms. I looked for a sign, but when I didn't see one, I thought maybe the woman at the train station gave me the wrong directions."

"We did have a sign, but a tree fell on it during the storm last winter. Were you looking for a place to stay?"

"Just for a few days. I'm on my way to Florida." Barton had warmed to his own lie.

"Well, then, you're in luck. We have two rooms available." *And only a few minutes ago, it was three,* Agnes thought. "Have you had dinner?"

"Not yet."

"Then you must join us." They fell into step with each other on their way to the house. "You know they say you should never stay anyplace till you've sampled the food."

He nodded. "I've heard. Have you lived here long?"

"On and off for the last two years. I'm Agnes Carlyle. My husband and I—"

He stopped abruptly. "Carlyle? Nestor's wife? I had no idea he—"

"You're a friend of Nestor's?"

"We…we're from the same…hometown. I haven't seen him in a long time."

She stepped onto the porch and opened the door. "Come in. He's in the kitchen. Won't take but a minute to get him." She paused. "May I ask your name?"

He twisted the brim of his hat. "Barton."

"Mr. Barton."

"No…Barton is my first name."

"Barton is fine," she said, beaming. "We're all on a first name basis around here."

Nestor, a stack of plates in hand, came from the kitchen. He spotted Agnes. "Good news. Abbot said he's going to stay at least a week and Pinetta—"

Chapter 8 ~ The Man on the Corner

"I have good news, too." She pointed over her shoulder. "This man is from—"

Nestor stepped closer and peered around her. His jaw dropped. His face reddened.

"What's wrong?" Agnes asked.

Nestor scowled at the stranger. "What are you doing here?"

"He's from your hometown," Agnes said.

Barton drew in a deep breath. "I haven't been honest with you, Agnes. My name is Barton Carlyle."

She turned from one to the other. "Carlyle?"

"My father," Nestor said. "At least that's the name listed on my birth certificate."

Barton started back toward the door. "This was a bad idea."

Agnes rushed to him and grabbed his arm. "No. We never turn *anyone* away. It's a rule. At least stay for dinner. Do you have luggage?"

"Just a duffle bag. I stashed it behind a bush. I didn't know if I'd be welcome."

"Go get it. I'll tell Pinetta there's one more for dinner."

Agnes returned to the dining room and found Nestor sitting in a chair, his elbows propped on his knees. She knelt beside him.

"I'm sorry," she said. "I know this is painful for you."

His voice was dull, lifeless. "Why did he have to show up today? Today? When I just found out I'm going to be a father? He always ruins everything. How does he do it?" He leaned back in the chair. "He can't stay here. This is my house. Did you tell him to leave?"

"You know I can't do that. He's your father. Besides that, Ivy Leigh would find out, and we'd never hear the end of it."

Her attempt to lighten the moment failed.

Nestor clenched his jaw. "Me and him…under the same roof for the first time in twenty-five years. How does he have the nerve to show up?"

Agnes took both his hands in hers. "Come on. Set the table. I'll get your dad and—"

Nestor stood. "*Don't* call him that. My uncle raised me. He's the only one I call 'Dad.'"

"I'll get Barton," she said. "He can spend the night in the basement. He can sit at the other end of the table during dinner. With Abbot here, we'll have plenty to talk about. You won't have to say a word."

53

Tea at Kimball Pines

Agnes left Nestor and found Barton, duffle bag at his feet, hovering by the front door.

"This way," she said. "We have a basement apartment where you'll be comfortable. I'll introduce you to the rest of—"

There was a knock at the door. Agnes opened it and found Mary Grace Dodson, bearing a freshly-baked pie cradled in an embroidered linen dishtowel.

"Ida sent me over," Mary Grace said, leaning left to see around Agnes. "Vesper's maid called and said you had a new boarder. I knew Pinetta would be busy with supper, so I wanted to welcome him to the neighborhood." She leaned to the right, beaming when she spotted Barton.

Agnes thanked Mary Grace for the pie, but did not invite her in.

Chapter 9

After Midnight

Only when Agnes started toward the kitchen did she remember Mary Grace had been wearing oven mitts. Now the only barrier between her and the pie, minutes from the oven, was a linen dishtowel, not intended for the rigors of extreme heat.

Hands toasting, eyes watering, Agnes hurried. Ordinarily, she would have yelled for Nestor to rescue her. But not this time. He had to regroup if he were going to play 'genial host'—essential if Abbot Cooper were to feel at home…and stay.

She raced past the dining room to the kitchen where Pinetta was slicing warm cornbread into perfect squares. Agnes sprinted in, slid the hot pie onto a crocheted potholder on the counter, snapped on the cold water, and held her hands underneath.

"What in the world?" Pinetta asked.

Eyes closed, Agnes sighed. "What a relief."

Pinetta sneered at the pie. "Where'd *that* come from?"

"Mary Grace brought it over, since we were having company for dinner."

Pinetta cut another cornbread square and lifted it from the Pyrex dish. "How could she possibly know Abbot was here?"

Agnes grabbed a towel. "Not Abbot."

"Me," Barton said.

Cornbread in one hand, knife in the other, Pinetta turned to find Barton standing in the doorway. Broad-shouldered. Worn out leather jacket. Rugged hands holding a hat by the brim. Deep brown eyes. Dark wavy hair. Strong chin. Full lips. Beguiling smile.

From someplace where the air smelled of sea salt, wood smoke, and cypress.

"Sure smells good in here," Barton said, approaching her. "I haven't had a home-cooked meal in a long time." He took the cornbread; his fingers brushed against hers. "Thank you."

Pinetta blushed—a reaction Agnes noticed and mistook as irritation. Pinetta frowned on "grazers," who took food before it was properly served.

Agnes dried her hands. "This is Nestor's father. Barton Carlyle."

Knife still in hand, Pinetta nodded. "Mr. Carlyle."

"Call me Barton," he said, licking crumbs from his fingers.

"As I was saying, we have a basement apartment," Agnes said, pointing him to the door. "Yours while you're here. Dinner's at 6:30."

He followed her to the door. "Thank you. I hope I haven't—"

"Do you play chess?" she asked.

"A little."

"There's usually a game in the evening. But don't let Ham fool you. He seems quiet, but he's ruthless on the opposite side of a board."

Closing the basement door, Agnes rushed to Pinetta. "I have to find Abbot. Tell him Nestor's father has shown up and things might get unpleasant. Can you tell everyone else?"

Agnes left. Pinetta laid down the knife, removed her apron. Then she walked to her room to check her hair in the mirror. She smoothed the back and then cupped her hands under both sides of her page boy cut, fluffing it.

Spotting Abbot in the hall, Agnes divulged the situation. After he assured her he "understood better than she knew," she went to the dining room. No sign of Nestor. Standing behind his chair, she analyzed the seating arrangement to stave off disaster.

She helped Pinetta ferry serving dishes to the dining room and invited the guests to sit down. Introducing those who had not met, she settled next to Nestor, patted his knee under the table, and hoped for the best.

While Nestor remained aloof, the others—even Pinetta—did not disappoint. A seasoned veteran of uncomfortable family dinners, she steered the conversation to general and harmless subjects. Millie, as usual, was charming. When conversation lagged, Ham asked Abbot if he played chess.

"I used to—pass the cornbread, please—but my brother is so competitive I stopped playing and decided to let him and my father beat each other's brains out instead."

Chapter 9 ~ After Midnight

If their situation had not already been so tenuous, Agnes would have questioned Abbot further, but the father/son relationship was the last thing they needed to explore tonight.

Agnes reached for a deviled egg. "How many brothers and sisters do you have?"

"One of each," Abbot said. "An older sister named Priscilla and a twin brother."

"Are you identical?" Millie asked.

Abbot nodded. "He's two minutes older. Got our father's name. And he's heir to—"

"Heir?" Pinetta asked.

Abbot stammered. "What I mean is...he's better suited to the family business than I am. I lack the killer instinct."

"What's his name?" Agnes asked.

"E. Arden Cooper III," Abbot said, his voice tinged with distaste.

"What does the 'E' stand for?" Millie asked.

"Enoch."

"Enoch Arden," Barton said. "So your"—he counted backwards on his fingers—"great-grandmother was a fan of Tennyson? So was my wife—"

Nestor slammed down his spoon. "*Don't* you *dare* mention my mother."

Agnes grabbed Nestor's hand.

Barton lowered his eyes. "My...second wife."

Shoving backward, Nestor sprang up and threw down his napkin. "You got remarried and didn't bother to come back for your son?"

Pinetta dabbed her napkin at the corner of her mouth and eased back her chair. "Would anyone care for dessert? Our neighbor brought an apple pie. She's quite a good cook."

Pinetta did not hold this opinion, but thought it wise to pique interest.

"I'll help you," Agnes said.

"No, I'll go," Nestor said. "I've lost my appetite."

He stormed out; Pinetta followed.

Abbot spread butter on his third piece of cornbread.

Ham spoke up. "I'll wait on dessert. Would you like to see the rest of the house, Mr. Carlyle?"

Barton stood. On his way out, he paused behind Agnes and placed his hands on her shoulders. To her surprise, he leaned down and kissed her cheek.

"Thank you for dinner," he said, and left with Ham.

His tone had an air of finality.

Millie stood and began clearing the dishes. "I hope you won't think our evening meal is always like this, Abbot. Ordinarily, we talk about the most mundane things or at least—"

"Trust me, Mrs. Hubbard, this is the best meal and nicest company I've had in a long time." He looked at Agnes. "If you're worried I'm going to run for the door, don't be."

Relieved, Agnes settled back and wished she had not eaten the deviled egg.

Pinetta returned alone with the dessert. She related Nestor's regrets for not joining them, explaining he had exams to grade. She set a dessert plate in front of Agnes and whispered, "Phone call for you. It's Bentley McBain. There's been an accident."

Agnes leaped up, toppling her chair. "Please excuse me." She hurried to the door.

Pinetta righted the fallen chair and served dessert. Moments like this did not come very often…when she could pretend she was mistress of the house rather than the cook.

Millie swallowed and licked her lips. "The secret to a great apple pie is a perfect balance between tart and sweet. Don't you think so, Abbot?"

Abbot, mouth full, could only nod.

Pinetta examined the delicate bite poised on her fork. "I've never been one to *peel* the apples I use in a pie. The peel adds color and flavor."

Abbot broke off a piece of the flaky crust with his fingers—a breach of etiquette he never would have committed at home.

Millie watched, amused. "Would you like another slice?"

Never had Abbot seen a whole pie set on the dining room table and sliced according to his wishes. During his childhood, dessert had been cut in the kitchen, placed on a china plate, and garnished with a sprig of mint.

Though uncomfortably full, Abbot could not pass up the moment and held out his plate.

Sequestered in the study, Nestor—not grading papers—sat on the worn leather sofa. He left the lights off, letting the gathering darkness engulf him. The nagging memories he had disciplined his mind to resist came fast and unbidden.

Chapter 9 ~ After Midnight

Memories of a five-year-old, dreaming of his father's homecoming. Seeing him, breaking into a run, leaping into his arms. "Did you bring me anything?" Sometime, after he was twelve, the imagined greeting changed to "Where have you been?" Then the dreams stopped.

At no time had Nestor envisioned his father's returning on the very day he would discover *he* was to have a child of his own. The twist of fate was mythological...cruel in its irony. *How* did his father manage to ruin everything?

Nestor heard Ham's voice beyond the closed door.

"And this is the study. You can see it tomorrow, if you're interested. Light's burned out. I haven't changed the bulb. You wouldn't be able to see a thing."

Barton pretended not to know Nestor was inside. He followed Ham to the first floor and stood outside the parlor where Millie and Abbot were playing cards in the corner.

"How about some pie now?" Ham asked.

Barton shook his head. "No. It's been a long day. Think I'll turn in."

On her way from the kitchen, Pinetta, tray in hand, met the men in the hall.

Barton gave a quick nod and winked as he walked past. A meaningless gesture of which he was hardly aware. But Pinetta's heart skipped. She paused to steady herself.

"You okay, Miss Pinetta?" Ham asked. "Could I take that for you?"

She yielded the tray. "I think I might have overdone it today."

"I know what you mean," Ham said. "First, no boarders, and now we have two."

Barton entered the kitchen. Agnes, phone receiver cradled between her right ear and shoulder, was washing dishes.

"Of course, Truitt will be welcome," she said. "Whenever he's well enough to travel…. Don't worry about that. Nestor just said today this house can always hold one more."

Barton halted to imprint the memory of Agnes in his mind. Though he had met her only hours before, he regretted leaving without getting to know her better. There was something about her—a warmth and zest for life—that endeared her to him. His daughter-in-law. He savored the description, the connection, repeating it in his thoughts. What had compelled her to come after him? Invite him to eat? More than he had hoped for. He would write a note, thanking her. Leave it on his pillow. Skip an uncomfortable scene. Avoid explanations and apologies. Catch the train before dawn.

Tea at Kimball Pines

But as rational as the plan was, he couldn't persuade himself to sneak past her. If he didn't say goodbye, he would regret it the rest of his life, and his burdened conscience had no room to file away one more failure.

He tapped her on the shoulder. "Sorry to bother you. Just wanted to say good…night."

She spoke into the phone. "Bentley? Can you hold on a second?" She held the receiver to her shoulder and whispered. "I'll be off in a few minutes. Can you wait?"

He shook his head. "Worn out. Need to get some sleep."

"I teach in the morning, but I'll see you when I get home."

Tears stinging his eyes, he turned away and descended the steps to his room.

Barton opened his duffle bag and took out his toothbrush and pajamas. Then the plastic bag stuffed with photos and newspaper clippings. He had often chided himself for not taking better care his mementoes. But fragments of memories in a tattered plastic bag had no dignity, no identity. Organizing, affixing them into an album, would fuse them into a plot, adhere them into chapters, brand them with the theme of lost opportunity, unmask the main character as a weak man, so crippled by the loss of his wife and infant daughters he could not care for the son he loved.

He rifled through the precious pile, glancing at the only photo of his twin daughters, Vera and Maria (named for their grandmothers), born too soon. Their mother, laboring valiantly to give them life, had lost hers. The girls, too small, had lived only a few hours after their birth. So none of them would be alone, Barton laid mother and babies to rest in the same coffin. Heartsick, he left the son he loved in the care of his brother Owen. Promising to return in a few days, he boarded a train and headed west. Days turned into weeks…then months.

His guilt, insupportable, kept him away.

Still dressed, Barton lay back on the bed.

For the first time in over twenty years, he would sleep under the same roof as his son.

———————∞———————

Agnes hung up the phone and drained the water from the sink. What in the world had she just agreed to? And how would she tell Nestor? Dishtowel in hand, she stepped into the hall and found Ham waiting for her.

She nodded toward the parlor. "How are things?"

Chapter 9 ~ After Midnight

"I think we weathered the storm," Ham said.

"Where's Nestor?"

"I'm pretty sure he's in the study. You look worried. Is anything wrong?"

"Not yet."

"What do you mean?"

Glancing into the parlor, Agnes lowered her voice. "That was Bentley on the phone. Do you remember Dr. Spenlow, the orchestra conductor at Brighton Park?"

"Yeah. He and my dad were good friends."

"He's been in an accident. Several broken ribs, broken arm, torn ligaments in his knee. He needs a place to recover. Bentley and Flossie can't take him in."

"Bentley asked if he could come here?"

"Uh-huh." She shrugged her shoulders. "I told him he was welcome…but I don't know where we'll put him…if Barton and Abbot stay any amount of time, which I hope they will."

"Me, too. Nestor would be a different man if he could come to terms with his past."

Agnes blinked at Ham. He was a simple man. Kind, good, self-sacrificing, but ill at ease in the larger world, nervous and reticent. But no one could cut to the heart of the matter faster than he could. And be exactly right.

Agnes handed him the towel. "I'll say good night to everyone. Will you lock up?"

"Sure." He cleared his throat. "Agnes." She turned to him. "I'm sorry things didn't go well at the publisher's today. I know you were hoping to celebrate tonight."

She resisted the impulse to embrace him—a gesture which would have left him squirming. "Thank you, Ham. But we have new tenants. That's a reason to celebrate."

They stepped into the parlor. Agnes apologized for not joining them and told Abbot she hoped he would be happy at the Magnolia Arms.

Ham watched Agnes climb the stairs and then left through the back door for his nightly inspection of the property.

After three hands of canasta, which Abbot pretended not to know how to play, he said good night. He went upstairs, enjoyed a long bath, put on his pajamas, and sat cross-legged on the floor. Taking his journal from his suitcase, he propped it on his knee and wrote:

November 4, 1978. For the first time since leaving my parents' house at the end of May, I will sleep in a home. Not a cheap motel or a chair in a bus station. A real home. The money my father put in the account for me is still there. He won't have the satisfaction of waving a bank statement under my mother's nose and telling her I've wasted all his money. I think I've finally found the place where I belong. Tomorrow I'll look for a job.

In the study, ten minutes till midnight, Nestor opened his eyes and glanced at his watch. He bolted up, yanking twice on the door, which always stuck. He tiptoed downstairs and into his room. He had not expected Agnes to be awake.

He sat on the edge of the bed. "I'm sorry I ruined the evening."

She reached for his hand. "You did no such thing."

"I've imagined so many times…what it would be like for him to come back. I thought I was prepared. Guess I was wrong."

"There's no way you could prepare yourself for something like that."

"Are you going to try to go to work tomorrow?"

"I think so," she said. "My class isn't till 9:00. I'm going to eat saltines when I wake up. My mom recommended that to my sister-in-law when she was pregnant."

"Okay. Let's get some sleep."

"There's one more thing. I promised a room to another tenant. He'll be here in a week. Maybe two. We'll have to put him in Monty's room and put the nursery plans on hold."

"That won't be a problem. The basement will be free long before then."

"But your father…"

"Leaving tomorrow," Nestor said.

Ham walked the property in darkness, the way as familiar to him as his own room. He checked the greenhouse, screened porch, entered the kitchen, locked the back door, turned out the light in the hall, and then peeked into Millie's room.

Snuggled in bed, she spoke to him. "I heard Soapy on the porch. You might want to check on her before you go up."

"Yes, ma'am. Do you need anything?"

"No. Thank you, Ham." She rolled over and pulled the quilt over her shoulders.

Chapter 9 ~ After Midnight

Ham opened the front door. Soapy, Ida Willingale's white cat, dashed toward him and rubbed against his leg.

"Oh, there you are, Soapy."

Mary Grace Dodson approached from the sidewalk. Ham picked up the cat and met her at the foot of the porch steps.

"What are you doing out so late?" he asked.

"Couldn't sleep," Mary Grace said. "Thought a walk might do me good." She took the cat and peered at the darkened windows. "I guess everyone is asleep. Did they like the pie?"

Ham scraped his finger across the bridge of his nose. "Nestor had schoolwork to do and Agnes got a phone call, so they skipped—"

"No, I meant your guest."

"Abbot?"

"Abbot…" she said with a gentle sigh. "Is that his name?"

"He had a couple of pieces, I think. I was taking Barton on a tour of the house."

Soapy leaped down and ran for home.

"Barton?" Mary Grace asked. "Who's that?"

"The other guest."

Mary Grace tightened the sash of her hot pink quilted housecoat. "Which is which?"

Ham backed toward the steps. "What do you mean?"

"I baked the pie for…I mean, I met a man at the train station this morning. Tall, handsome. Wore a Panama Jack hat."

"Oh, him," Ham said, backing up farther. "That's Barton. Nestor's father."

"Nestor's *father*?"

Stifling a cry, she turned and scurried away in her fuzzy purple bedroom slippers.

Ham wasn't sure what he had said to upset her. He would repeat the conversation to Agnes tomorrow. She would figure out what went wrong. She always did.

———— ⚯ ————

Pinetta Fraleigh, lying awake, heard the front door close. She never had trouble sleeping. Drifted off within minutes of lying down. Not tonight. She put on her bathrobe, tiptoed through the kitchen, peeped into the hall, and watched Ham climb the stairs.

She lingered, eyeing the door to the basement where Barton Carlyle was sleeping. She inched forward. Maybe he was awake. Needed something. Should she tap…gently…on his door? Say, *Barton. Can I get you anything? You didn't eat much for dinner.*

She pursed her thin lips. Soup. Barton's first meal at the Magnolia Arms was vegetable soup. Not a meal for a man like him. Pot roast. Mashed potatoes. That's what was needed. A meal he could sink his teeth into. Homemade bread.

Tomorrow she would ask Ham to drive her to the market. If he asked why they were going in the middle of the week, she would say, "Welcome dinner. For our new tenants." Resolved, she returned to her room and lay down.

Reaching out, she turned the alarm clock to face her.

Past midnight.

A new day.

Chapter 10

You Go Your Way, I'll Go Mine

Alone in her tiny overpriced apartment, Prudence O'Neill was still hunched over a steno pad and coffee-stained manila folders at 1:00 a.m. Plopping back on the sofa, she draped her arm over sleepless eyes, still picturing the ugly scene with Daniel Ogden.

Marching into her office, he had planted both hands on her desk. *"How was the interview with the Carlyle woman?"*

"She got sick. I said we'd re-schedule."

He had rolled his eyes—his most infuriating habit.

"What am I supposed to tell my sister-in-law? You know I have to see her this weekend."

"Not my fault," she had said. *"Or yours either. Don't worry about it. Dinner tonight?"*

Then Daniel brought up the Foley woman again. When Prudence had offended her, Laura Foley had taken her manuscript to another publisher. Her book was now in its third printing. Prudence had apologized, adding "it happens all the time in this business."

She reached for the sweater she had tossed on the floor. How could Daniel be so condescending and so appealing at the same time? Even now, after the scene had looped through her mind for hours, she circled back to the same conclusion.

She adored Daniel—his deep green eyes, the way his dark hair draped over his right eyebrow. Cute smile. Rare, though it was. Vowing to regain his favor, Prudence made a makeshift blanket of the sweater and skidded into a fitful sleep.

When she reached the office the next morning, Prudence called over her shoulder as she breezed past the new receptionist.

"Get that Carlyle woman on the phone."

Pinetta Fraleigh, who took the call at 8:02 a.m., did not like being put on hold, especially when she was on a tight schedule. And Prudence's clipped sentences did nothing to encourage her cooperation.

"This is Prudence O'Neill with Ogden Publishing. May I speak to Mrs. Carlyle?"

Pinetta, occupied with flour, clamped the receiver between her ear and shoulder. "She's not in."

"Do you have a number where I can reach her?"

"No."

Prudence sharpened her tone. "It's important that I speak with her to reschedule her appointment."

"I'll tell her you called."

"When do you expect her?"

"I don't have her schedule memorized," Pinetta said, although she did.

Prudence summoned her executive attitude. "To *whom* am I speaking?"

"*Mrs. Fraleigh.*"

"And who are you...*exactly*?"

"Household manager," Pinetta said. "I'll tell Mrs. Carlyle you called. *Good day.*"

Pinetta hung up and poured the sifted flour back into the canister. The O'Neill woman had driven the cup count completely out of her head.

Timing. *Everything* was about timing.

She had been so fixated on timing, her eyes had popped open after six hours' sleep. Her mind snapped into gear, charting the path which lay ahead. Have breakfast. Make bread dough. Put it to rise. Fix hair. Find make-up Agnes had given her for her birthday. A dab of color on her cheeks wouldn't hurt. Act casual when Barton came into the kitchen. Offer breakfast. Excuse herself to help Millie prepare for the Garden Club meeting, so as not to appear eager to linger over coffee and conversation. Though she was.

Once Millie was on her way, she could leave for the store. Setting her jaw, she poised the measuring cup over the canister. She scooped up a heaping cup of flour, leveled it with a knife, and poured it into the bowl.

Counted one.

Scoop...level...pour.

Two.

Chapter 10 ~ *You Go Your Way, I'll Go Mine*

A firm fist pounded on the back door. Pinetta dropped the cup. It ricocheted off the rim of the bowl and somersaulted onto her navy blue dress, dusting her with flour.

Bridey Ludlow burst in with Lute Monroe in her wake.

"Morning, Piney," Bridey said. "Look who I ran into. Holding this big bag of greens. Said he tried to deliver them yesterday, but you weren't home. That's what I call service."

The door to the basement opened. Barton Carlyle, wearing jeans and a pale blue shirt, stepped into the kitchen.

Pinetta watched the scene unfold in slow motion.

Bridey shifted the bag of collards to her left hand and held out her right as she strode toward Barton. Her booming voice shattered the sanctity of the kitchen.

"You must be Nestor's father." Gripping Barton's hand, she pumped it like a car jack. "We've wondered about you for years." She gestured toward Lute. "This is Lute Monroe. He owns the finest produce store in town. Actually, the only produce store. Do you like greens?"

Barton shook his head. "Can't say I do." He extended his hand toward Lute.

Lute, red-faced, shook Barton's hand. "Welcome to Dennisonville."

Bridey cradled the collards like a bouquet. "Well, now, isn't this nice? You know what I always say, 'Make new friends, but keep the old. One is silver, the other gold.' Right, Piney?"

Lute swiped the back of his beefy hand across his wide forehead, peppered with perspiration. "Mornin', Miss Pinetta. I hope we're not bothering you. I—"

"What in the world, Piney?" Bridey said. "Looks like you had a fight with a flour sack and lost." She lurched toward the sink, dumped in the collards, and snapped on the water. "We'll just put these to soak and all sit down for a nice cup of coffee." She leaned in till she was almost nose to nose with Pinetta. "Goodness me, Piney. Are you wearing *make-up*?"

Lute backed toward the door. "No coffee for me. I have to get back to my store."

Bridey whirled to face him. "Oh, no, you don't. You've got to get acquainted with our new neighbor. May we call you Barton?"

Impassive, Barton walked past Bridey and stooped down to retrieve the cup on the floor. He stood inches from Pinetta's face, placed the cup on the counter, and whispered conspiratorially. "Do you know where Nestor is?"

Though she swallowed hard, Pinetta barely managed a squeak. "He…" She cleared her throat. "He drove Agnes to school this morning. He's going to wait for her till her class is over and then take her to the doctor."

"Nothing's wrong, is there?" Bridey asked, brushing past on her way to the coffee pot.

Pinetta squeezed her eyes shut. How could she have been so careless? "No. Nothing's wrong. Just a routine visit…flu shot."

A plausible explanation.

Bridey filled a coffee mug and handed it to Barton. He thanked her and left the kitchen.

"Not the friendly sort, is he?" Bridey asked. "Is Ham around?"

Pinetta brushed flour from her dress. "Somewhere."

"My Asa is under the weather this morning," Bridey said, thumbing through yesterday's mail. "Won't be able to take Millie to the Garden Club meeting. Sent me to ask Ham to take her."

Pinetta's heart banged against her ribs. "Can't another cab pick her up?"

"I suppose so," Bridey said. "Why?"

"Ham was supposed to take me to the market."

Lute, still hovering by the door, spoke up. "I could take you."

Bridey tossed the mail onto the table and started toward the hall. "Well, there you go. Problem solved. I'll tell Millie." She disappeared through the door.

Like wallflowers at a high school dance, Pinetta and Lute remained rooted to the floor, wilting in the impossible moment.

Pinetta glanced at the clock over the table. Only 8:15. And already her perfect plan lay in rubble at her feet. Eyes cast down, she flinched when she heard Lute open the back door.

In a voice, deep and kind, he said, "I'd have to move some stuff out of the front seat. It won't take but a minute."

Smitten by this noble gesture, Pinetta's conscience stirred and wriggled. She could almost feel her mother's nimble fingers pinching the soft skin on the back of her arm.

Pinetta Jane Pembroke. I'm ashamed of you. You're to be polite to visitors in your home.

She raised her eyes to Lute.

Burly, thickset, with arms extending from his broad shoulders like tree trunks, he looked too much like the cartoon Paul Bunyan to be taken

Chapter 10 ~ *You Go Your Way, I'll Go Mine*

seriously as a suitor. The shadow of a dark beard and his plaid flannel shirt, buttons straining over his ample stomach, only reinforced the comparison.

The scent of Barton's aftershave lingering in her nose, Pinetta was adrift in a sea of unfulfilled dreams, when Millie, gathering her husband's old bathrobe around her, sailed through the door.

"Lute. Thank goodness you're still here," Millie said. "Bridey has just told me Asa can't pick me up for the Garden Club meeting. Could you take me? Ham is nowhere to be seen."

Glancing from Millie to Pinetta, Lute closed the door. "Yes, ma'am, be glad to."

"You're sure I won't keep you from your store too long?" Millie asked.

He shook his head.

"Thank you, Lute. I'm sure Pinetta will be glad to fix you some breakfast while I get ready. Dear me, I hate to be such a bother."

"No bother at all," Lute said, easing toward the table.

Pinetta called to Millie. "Need any help?"

Millie did not look back. "No. Give Lute a good breakfast. It's the least we can do."

Across the hall Barton stood at the parlor window and stared out at the black walnut tree towering above the house. He had envisioned a dozen scenarios about where Nestor lived, but had never imagined a houseful of people and non-stop visitors.

But it's a good thing, he thought. *If there hadn't been so many people here last night, Nestor might have thrown me out the moment I showed up.*

Abbot Cooper bounded in. "Good morning. Sleep well?"

Barton turned around. "Yeah. So well I missed my train."

"Train? You just got here."

"It was a gamble…coming here…but I don't think it's going to pay off."

Abbot stood next to him. "Sorry. I'm going to stay as long as possible. In fact, after breakfast, I'm going to look for a job."

"Mind if I join you?" Barton asked.

"Aren't you leaving?"

"I meant just for breakfast. While I was wandering around town yesterday, I found a restaurant called Mollie's. Great coffee."

"I saw it, too. Ready to go now?"

Tea at Kimball Pines

Barton headed to the door. "Let me get my bag. I'll leave for the station from there."

Pinetta, refilling Lute's coffee mug, glanced up as Barton walked through the kitchen. "Breakfast, Mr. Carlyle...uh...Barton?"

"No, thanks. The kid and I are going to eat breakfast in town." He paused. "Would you tell Nestor and Agnes I said goodbye?"

"You're...leaving?" she asked.

"This was a mistake. I never should've come."

"But...the baby..."

Barton narrowed his eyes. "Baby?"

Lute, scraping his bowl, looked up.

Pinetta fought to breathe. "It's not for sure yet. Agnes is going to the doctor today."

Barton stared at her. For the first time in his life, his timing was right.

Lute wiped his mouth and took his jacket from the back of the chair. "I'd best be getting back. Thanks for the oatmeal, Miss Pinetta."

Pinetta was reeling. "Please don't say anything about Agnes...I never should've—"

"I never repeat what I hear," Lute said. "I couldn't stay in business."

"You going toward town?" Barton asked.

Lute nodded.

"Could Abbot and I ride with you?"

"Sure. Where to?"

"Mollie's."

Pinetta winced. Bad enough Barton was having breakfast in town, but why did it have to be Mollie's? Muriel Porter would cast her spell over him like she did everyone else.

"You could go to Newman's," Pinetta said. "It's closer."

Barton paused at the basement door. "Newman's?"

"It's a place where the men in town go for breakfast. Men like you. They talk about sports. The Tar Heels. Blue Devils. At Mollie's it's more—"

Abbot entered the kitchen. "Ready?"

"Yeah. Let me get my coat." Barton went down to his room.

Desperate, Pinetta turned to Lute. "You can't leave now. You promised to take Mrs. Hubbard to the Garden Club."

Lute settled his Atlanta Braves hat on his head. *You can't leave now?* It was the first time Pinetta had ever asked him to stay. "Mollie's isn't far. I'll be back."

Chapter 10 ~ *You Go Your Way, I'll Go Mine*

Barton came from the basement; the men left.

Watching them through the window, Pinetta breathed a silent prayer of thanks.

Barton had left without his duffle bag. He was coming back.

Headed toward Bellport, Agnes munched on saltines and tried to focus on the road to keep her mind off her weak stomach, which lurched with every curve and slope in the road. Nestor's mood—sullen, withdrawn—did nothing to ease her nerves.

She glanced at him from the corner of her eye. "Did you want to talk about—?"

"I'll drop you off at the library," he said. "You won't have so far to walk."

Road-blocked. She changed course. "What are you going to do?"

"Go to my office. Call to get you an appointment today."

"We could have lunch," she said. "If I get through the morning without, you know—"

"Do the crackers help?"

"A little. Can we talk about—?"

The truck coasted down a steep hill; Agnes' stomach churned.

He shook his head. "I know you mean well, but—"

Panicked, Agnes rolled down her window and stuck out her head. The cold air beat back the rising tide of nausea. Pulling her head in, she leaned back and closed her eyes.

"I'll have to remember that," she said. "Cold air helps. Could you slow down?"

Nestor eased his foot off the accelerator. "Sorry."

Eyes still closed, she wiped perspiration from her forehead. "For your information, I wasn't going to bring up your father. I thought we should talk about Truitt."

"Truitt?"

"The new tenant I told you about last night. You remember. He performed in the Fine Arts Festival last year."

"The skinny guy with the bassoon?"

"No. Truitt played the oboe. He's the orchestra conductor."

"I don't remember. I was kind of distracted that night."

She opened her eyes. "Waiting for curtain call, so you could bring me roses."

For the first time since Barton had arrived, Nestor's face eased into the familiar smile.

"One of my favorite memories." He touched her cheek. "What about Truitt?"

"He was in a bad car wreck. He lives alone and needs someone to help him while he recovers. Bentley called and asked if he could stay with us for a while. Is that okay?"

"Sure." He chuckled. "So strange. This time yesterday we had no tenants, and now there's not an empty room in the house…well, not till Barton leaves."

"Do you think you should call him—?"

The smile evaporated; he shot Agnes a withering look.

She snatched up the paper bag in her lap and threw up.

Clutching her grocery list, Pinetta watched Dennisonville blur past the window as Ham drove her to the store. She had not been this undone since she found Guy Henry's parting note on the mantel of their fireplace. She tried to ignore the voice of reason shouting in her head. This trip to the store was a "fool's errand," her mother would have said. Because Barton might return while she was away, pick up his duffle bag, and be gone by the time she came home. But maybe…maybe he would stay till tomorrow. To find out about the baby.

"So, what do you think, Miss Pinetta? Think I should ask Nestor?"

Pinetta turned from the window. "I'm sorry. What?"

"Do you think it's a good time to ask Nestor about my project? Or should I wait till things settle down?"

"What project?"

"The staircase…up through the cupola…to the widow's walk."

Pinetta rolled down her window. "I'm sorry. I was thinking of…my grocery list. What about the staircase?"

"Should I ask Nestor now or wait till his dad leaves?"

Pinetta blinked at Ham; her voice quivered with helpless rage.

"He *wouldn't leave* without his bag and without saying goodbye. If he finds out Agnes is going to have a baby, he'll want to reconcile with Nestor. It will be his last chance."

Ham could not have been more startled if Pinetta had grabbed the steering wheel and run the truck off the road.

Chapter 10 ~ *You Go Your Way, I'll Go Mine*

"I didn't mean to upset you," Ham said. "Agnes is going to have a baby?"

Pinetta willed herself to calm down.

"I shouldn't have told you. Please…don't say anything till we find out for sure. I'm sorry, Ham. I don't know what's gotten into me today."

Reared in an all-male household, Ham was still baffled by the changeable nature of women and had no idea why Pinetta should be so offended about a total stranger.

On guard, Ham ventured forward. "I know what you mean. Whenever new people move in, I'm always nervous till I get to know them. And Barton is…"

Pinetta put her hand on her hip. "Is *what*?"

The parking lot in sight, he sped up. "He's…restless. Seems like he—"

Pinetta relaxed. "Restless. Yes, that's it. He's restless." *Like me,* she thought. *That's why I understand him.*

Ham eased into a parking place. "Want me to help you or wait here?"

Pinetta reached into her wallet and took out a $20. "Actually, I was hoping you could go to Mollie's for a cake. I won't have time to make dessert."

He laid the money on the seat, opened his door, and walked around to help her down from the truck. "What are we having tonight?"

Pinetta took his hand. "Pot roast and mashed potatoes."

"Roast beef? In the middle of the week? What's the occasion?"

"A…celebration…the baby."

"Agnes will like that," Ham said.

Pinetta hitched her purse over her arm and walked toward the door. To "celebrate the baby"—the perfect story.

—◆—

Muriel Porter showed Abbot and Barton to a table.

"Coffee, gentlemen?" she asked.

Accustomed to truck stop waitresses, Barton eyed her. Tall, slender, confident, about his age, she infused her surroundings with warmth and comfort.

"Yes," Barton said. "And keep it coming."

"New in town? Or just visiting?"

"I moved into the Magnolia Arms last night," Abbot said

"Then you've met Agnes," she said. "One of my regulars."

"Yes," Abbot said. "In fact, Barton is her—"

73

Barton coughed loudly. "You have waffles?"

Muriel pretended not to notice his glaring at Abbot. "Two or three?"

He held up two fingers. Abbot ordered the same and Muriel walked away.

"Why do you care if she knows who you are," Abbot asked, "if you're leaving anyway?"

"I don't like to answer questions."

Abbot unwrapped his silverware. "Hmm. Okay. How about baseball? What do you think of Ron Guidry wining the Cy Young award? Or is that too personal?"

"I mean questions from *women*. They always have an ulterior motive."

"You mean marriage."

"When you get to be my age," Barton said, "women think you're approachable just because you've got a few gray hairs and a paunch. My last wife—"

Abbot propped his elbows on the table. "*Last*? How many have you had?"

"Four."

"Four?"

"The third one doesn't count. With me less than a year."

"*She* probably thought she counted," Abbot said.

"Look, kid. I came with you to kill some time. Not to be lectured. What do you know? Have you ever been married?"

Abbot held up his hands. "Sorry. My mistake. Won't happen again."

Barton withdrew into silence and stirred his coffee, though he had added nothing to it.

Abbot watched, thinking. *Pain hung on the stranger like a mantle, draped on sagging shoulders.* He felt his shirt pocket. No pen. He snatched up his coffee cup and headed to the counter. "Be right back."

Muriel saw him coming and brought the coffee pot from the warmer. She filled his cup.

"Acting like a regular already," she said. "Couldn't wait?"

Abbot whispered. "Gotta pen?"

She reached into her apron pocket and slid a pen toward him. He grabbed a napkin from the holder, scribbled out his idea, and shoved the napkin and the pen in his pocket.

Muriel shook her head. "Oh, no. Not another writer..."

Abbot picked up his cup. "What do you mean?"

Chapter 10 ~ You Go Your Way, I'll Go Mine

"I've watched Agnes make notes on napkins for years."

"Agnes is a writer?"

"Get back to your friend. He'll get suspicious if we stand here talking."

Walking back, Abbot studied Barton. Strong jaw, weathered hands, inscrutable face. A son he had not seen in over twenty years? Four wives? If Barton stuck around long enough to let his guard down, his story could be a chapter in itself.

Abbot was writing a book.

He had not traveled far before he realized the quaint towns, eccentric people, and kind souls who offered him help, would make a first-rate story. He had a spiral notebook full of entries. Now settled, he could compile them into a manuscript.

He set his cup on the table and slid into his chair. "I should've asked if you wanted a refill."

"Look who's here," Barton said, nodding at the door and waving.

Muriel greeted Ham and pointed to Abbot and Barton.

He approached their table. "Mind if I join you?"

Barton pulled out a chair. "You eat here often?"

"No," Ham said. "Mrs. Fraleigh sent me to buy a cake."

"She doesn't drive?" Abbot asked.

"I don't know," Ham said. "Maybe. But we only have trucks, and she says it's not lady-like for a woman to drive them."

A server approached the table with waffles. Ham ordered coffee.

They ate in silence. Barton was desperate to interrogate Ham. Questioning women—even the sweet old lady—was not at option. Women could not be trusted to keep secrets. But if anyone would give him honest answers about Nestor, it was Ham.

Muriel returned with coffee. "So, Ham…I hear there's going to be a community choir for Founder's Day. You going to try out? Agnes says you're very musical."

Ham blushed. "I'm not a singer. I'm a whistler, and there's not much call for those in a choir. How about you?"

"Haven't sung in years," Muriel said. "But even if I did, I wouldn't sing for Donovan Strode. They say he's a shoo-in for the director job."

Abbot perked up. "Who's he?"

"Choir director at the high school," Muriel said. "But I shouldn't say more than that. Wouldn't want to prejudice you, in case you want to try out."

She winked at Abbot and strolled away.

Barton skewered a bite of waffle. "Ham. What kind of name is that?"

"Nickname. My name is Talmadge, but no one's called me that since third grade."

"You've known Nestor a long time?" Barton asked.

"No. I only met him last year when he came to visit Agnes."

"How did you know her?" Abbot asked.

"She was a teacher at my school."

"You were a teacher?"

Ham laughed. "No. The janitor. Well, assistant janitor."

"Teachers didn't hang out with janitors at my school," Abbot said, chilled at the memory of uniforms and assemblies.

"You don't know Agnes," Ham said. "With her everybody is a potential friend, till they prove otherwise. That's how she won over Dr. Grinstead."

"Who?" Barton asked.

"Jonas Grinstead. The man who built the Magnolia Arms."

"Wait a minute," Abbot said. "The guy who built the house where we're staying was a teacher at your school?"

Ham nodded. "Uh-huh. Agnes met him on her first day. She called it *destiny*."

Abbot took out Muriel's pen. "Could you start at the beginning? You lost me."

"Jonas came here thirty years ago," Ham said. "He'd always wanted to build a house and finally had some property here. He rented a room in a boarding house where Margaret lived."

"Margaret?" Abbot asked.

"His wife. Well, she is now. It was love at first sight. But Jonas was being chased by a girl back home—Olympia, the daughter of the man who gave Jonas the property."

"Hold on a minute," Abbot said, reaching for another napkin. "I wish I'd brought my notebook. Okay. Olympia. Got it."

"Olympia showed up and told Margaret she and Jonas were engaged."

"Out of sight, out of mind?" Barton asked.

"No. It was a lie. But Margaret was so hurt she sent Jonas packing without giving him a chance to explain. So, once he was finished with the house, he moved away to Plainview."

Abbot scribbled. "And got a job at your school. What's the name of it?"

"Brighton Park."

"And this was thirty years ago, you said?"

Chapter 10 ~ You Go Your Way, I'll Go Mine

Ham nodded. "Jonas became a math teacher. Never married. Lived alone. He got to be friends with my dad. Used to come to our house for supper. I grew up knowing him."

Muriel approached with the coffee pot and a spiral notebook, which she placed in front of Abbot. "Here. Stop using my napkins." She refilled their cups.

Abbot looked up. "You just happened to have a notebook in the kitchen?"

"I keep them on hand for Agnes. She's always asking for paper. Need anything else?"

"No, thanks," Barton said.

"I need a cake for dessert," Ham said. "What do you recommend. For company?"

"Carrot cake. I'll box it up. Let me know when you're ready to leave."

She laid the check on the table and walked away.

"Can you finish?" Barton asked. "Where does Nestor come in?"

Ill at ease about sharing confidences, Ham stuck to the facts.

The more Agnes found out about Jonas, the more she wanted to know. Quizzing Jonas' friends, she gradually pieced his story together and won Jonas over. Once she learned about the Magnolia Arms, she was convinced it was where she belonged.

When Jonas had a heart attack and faced his mortality, he decided to reconcile with his past. He sent Agnes to the Magnolia Arms. He had no idea Margaret was still there and unmarried. Agnes saved the house and reunited Margaret and Jonas.

"Nestor was the gardener at the time," Ham said. "That's how he met Agnes. He was in love with her within a week, but it took her longer to come around."

Abbot flipped to a new page. "What a story. Is she going to publish it?"

"No," Ham said. "But she has written the history of the Bridger family."

"Bridger?"

"The original owners of the property. Miss Millie is Julia Bridger's sister."

Abbot scraped his hand through his hair. "How did they find *her*?"

Muriel approached. "Your cake's at the cash register, Ham. Ready?"

Grateful to be rescued, Ham stood. "Yes, ma'am. Thank you."

"Wait," Abbot said. "Can't you stay?"

"Not my story to tell," Ham said. "Ask Agnes. I don't know much about writing, but I know you shouldn't write someone else's story unless you ask."

When Ham arrived at the store, he found Pinetta waiting outside. He placed the bags in the back of the truck and helped her into her seat. Pinetta tapped on the cake box between them.

"What did you buy?" she asked.

"Carrot cake. Muriel recommended it."

Pinetta stared out the window. "Did you run into anyone we know?"

"Just Abbot and Barton."

"Did you talk to them?" She clutched her purse. "Do…they like it here?"

"I don't know. They asked me more questions than I asked them."

"About what?"

"Agnes, mostly."

After Ham brought the groceries into the house, he left to pick up Millie. On his way to the Delahunty House, a historically preserved ante-bellum home where the Garden Club met, he reviewed his plan to build a spiral staircase.

At last he could repay Nestor and Agnes for the kindness they had shown him. If it hadn't been for them, he would have never survived the last year, when he lost the only woman he had ever dared to love.

With everyone gone, Pinetta's day unwrinkled. She changed into a housedress and apron, washed and peeled potatoes and carrots. She seasoned the pot roast with the Pembroke family secret recipe and slid it into the oven as Millie and Ham arrived home.

After lunch, when Millie went to her room for her nap, Pinetta tiptoed into the dining room and opened the china cabinet. Chiding herself for using Ivy Leigh's dishes without asking, she lifted out the meat platter, serving bowls, and gravy boat.

This dinner would be one Barton would always remember.

When Agnes and Nestor arrived at home, they were delighted to smell supper as they opened the kitchen door.

Agnes pointed to the box on the counter. "A cake? From Mollie's? What's the occasion?"

Pinetta wiped her hands on her apron. "I thought I'd be prepared…just in case you came home with good news. So…are you?"

Chapter 10 ~ You Go Your Way, I'll Go Mine

Agnes nodded. "I am. Due in July."

Pinetta extended her hand. "Congratulations. I'm happy for you."

At 6 p.m. the residents, all glad to be home, made their way to the dining room.

Millie, first to arrive, was so stunned at the beautiful table she covered her face with both hands and then slowly swung them open to enjoy the full effect. In all the years Pinetta had prepared meals, she had never served dinner on china…except at Christmas. What had softened Pinetta's heart Millie could only guess, but it didn't matter. This elegant table was the first sign Pinetta's façade might be cracking.

Abbot, delighted to be having dinner in the same home for the second night in a row, bounded down the stairs, eager to tell his good news. Hoping for a shot at being an office boy, he had gone to the office of the *Dennisonville Chronicle*. When the assistant editor found out Abbot had graduated from Florida State with a degree in English, he hired him on the spot. He would start work on Monday—as a reporter.

Pinetta was the last to be seated. She had changed back into her navy blue dress, washed and ironed and free of flour, and reapplied a dab of blush to each cheek.

At the head of the table, Nestor sat as grave and quiet as he if he were about to announce bankruptcy.

Millie spoke up. "Is there anything we should know before you say grace, Nestor?"

"Yes. Agnes and I are going to have a baby."

Abbot applauded. "That's great."

Barton looked at Agnes. "Congratulations."

She smiled, but said nothing.

Pinetta whispered a sigh of relief. Instead of this being Barton's farewell meal, it would be the first of many. Well…the second. She still regretted the soup last night, but that couldn't be helped. She had to start from where she was.

After Nestor prayed over the meal, Pinetta reached for the meat platter and handed it across to Barton. He laid a slice of meat on his plate.

"Smells delicious," he said.

The words "secret family recipe" were on the tip of her tongue when the doorbell rang.

"I'll get it," Ham said.

Pinetta stiffened. *What now?*

Nestor passed the meat to Agnes. "Feel like eating?"

"Gonna try," Agnes said, glancing at Pinetta. "Can't pass up my own celebration dinner."

Ham reappeared. "Uh, Agnes. It's for you. That woman…from yesterday."

Prudence O'Neill stepped in and set her suitcase on the floor.

Chapter 11

A Change of Heart

"Mrs. O'Neill," Agnes said, peering over the bowl of mashed potatoes in her hands, "what…what are you doing here?"

Rumpled and away from her office, Prudence felt more like a child summoned to the principal's office than an executive. Her plan to apologize, ask for directions to a hotel, and make a quick exit would not work in this setting.

One on one, she was brilliant, but facing an audience, even a small one, was another matter, ever since she had drawn a blank during a college production of *Our Town*. Scanning the faces, Prudence aimed her comments at nobody in particular.

"I…wanted to say…I was sorry we…didn't get to finish our…"

Ever maternal, Millie patted Barton's arm. "Get the lady a chair. She looks done in."

Pinetta clenched her narrow jaw. That voice—the very woman who had interrupted her bread making this morning. Standing in *their* house. Sitting down to dinner.

Hours yet till midnight, Pinetta's carriage was turning into a pumpkin. But the "stepsister" who had spoiled the ball was far from ugly. She was a beauty—stylish, sophisticated, and years younger than Pinetta.

Abbot stood. "I'm Abbot Cooper."

"Prudence O'Neill," she said. "I didn't mean to interrupt."

Millie noticed Pinetta's jaw jutted forward—never a good sign.

Still holding the potatoes, Agnes waited till Ham returned to his chair and then passed the bowl to him. No need to defer to Prudence in her own home. She could wait her turn.

"O'Neill," Nestor said, without a hint of a smile. "You're from Ogden Publishing."

"You're a publisher?" Abbot asked.

Prudence ignored Abbot and turned to Nestor, sizing him up as the kind of man you would regret picking a fight with.

"Yes," she said, studying the bowl of beans Barton had handed her. "Mrs. Carlyle left…so abruptly…Mr. Ogden was…upset…uh, disappointed…and…"

Laughing, Agnes held up her hand. "No need to explain. He didn't want to face his sister-in-law. Who can blame him? I used to work for Elspeth Sherwood. I know how she is."

Pinetta, crestfallen, said nothing for the rest of the meal. The succulent roast, creamy mashed potatoes, even the picture perfect homemade bread, all took a back seat to Prudence O'Neill. Only the carrot cake from Mollie's veered the conversation back to food.

When Prudence asked for advice about the nearest hotel, Millie spoke up.

"Motel? Nonsense. There's an empty room upstairs."

Agnes gaped at Millie.

"Right next to me," Abbot said.

"For now," Nestor said. "We're expecting a tenant in a few days. My wife's friend."

Pinetta laid her fork on her plate. *Another* tenant. What was next?

Too tired to argue, Prudence yielded. "If it wouldn't be too much trouble. I can be out of here first thing in the morning."

"New tenant?" Millie asked.

"Truitt Spenlow," Agnes said. "The orchestra conductor at my old school. He's been in an accident and has no one to look after him while he recuperates."

"Then it's all settled," Millie said. "Do you need to call your husband, Mrs. O'Neill, to tell him you're staying here tonight?"

"I'm not married," Prudence said, displaying her left hand. "Divorced."

Pinetta marveled Prudence could admit this disgrace so freely.

Agnes leaned forward and peered around Ham. "Supper was delicious, Pinetta."

"Yes, it was," Barton said. "Haven't had a meal like that in a long time."

Pinetta lifted her eyes to Barton's. "Thank you. I'm glad you…all…enjoyed it."

Ham pushed back from the table. "I'll help with the dishes."

Chapter 11 ~ *A Change of Heart*

Thankful he had provided her a graceful exit, Pinetta took Millie's plate and then reached for Barton's. When he added his plate to the stack, his fingers touched hers.

"Delicious meal," he said.

She floated down the castle steps and returned to the kitchen.

Nestor left his place. "I'll take your bag upstairs, Mrs. O'Neill, if you'll follow me."

"I'd like to talk your wife first…in private. If I could."

"Sure," Nestor said, picking up her suitcase on his way out.

Tilting his chair back on two legs, Barton called over his shoulder. "Need help, son?"

Shaking his head, Nestor disappeared into the hall.

Abbot turned to Prudence. "I'd love to talk to you later. I'm a writer, too. Just got a job with the *Dennisonville Chronicle*. Start Monday."

Prudence wagged her hand at him. "Never do interviews outside my office."

"I don't want an interview…exactly. Just to run an idea past you. See if—"

"Maybe tomorrow," Prudence said. *In your dreams*, she thought.

Barton slapped Abbot on the shoulder. "Come on, kid. Let the ladies talk." As he had the night before, Barton stepped behind Agnes and kissed her cheek. "Congratulations," he said. "I'm happy…for both of you."

Millie claimed to have letters to write and closed the French doors on her way out.

Prudence leaned her elbows on the table. "Congratulations?"

"I'm going to have a baby," Agnes said, sipping water to settle her stomach. "We just found out today. That's why I bailed out of your office in such a hurry."

"That's a relief. My boss thought…I…thought I upset you so much I made you sick."

Agnes laughed. "Don't be silly. I've dealt with women *way* more…well, let's just say it wasn't you that made me sick."

"Still…Daniel insisted I…I mean, Mr. Ogden…I've come to apologize."

Prudence rattled off her prepared and insincere speech; Agnes, amused, studied her guest.

A veteran of scuffles with imperious women, Agnes was positive she was not the first potential client Prudence had offended. Why should she care in this case? What had motivated her to come all this way to apologize to a fledgling author?

Only one explanation fit the facts. Prudence O'Neill was smitten with Daniel Ogden. For his sake only had she transformed to this pitiable state. Only love could turn her prickly veneer into this disheveled figure leaning over a plate of half-eaten food.

"Why are you smiling?" Prudence asked.

Jolted from her musings, Agnes shrugged. "I was just thinking how upset I was last night and now…here you sit in my own house."

"So, could we get back to your book?"

"Not tonight. Too tired. Would you like to see where you'll be staying?"

By the time Agnes led Prudence to her room, Nestor was long gone. Ordinarily, he would have delivered the luggage and rejoined his guests to play host. Instead, he retreated to the third floor, entered Ham's room, and walked to the window.

When he had first arrived at the Magnolia Arms—a disillusioned Ph.D. candidate, worn out from too much study—this was the only room available. Ivy Leigh Ransom had apologized, explaining the room was seldom used and not ready for a guest.

"If you can live with a little dust tonight," she had said, "I'll clean up in here tomorrow."

"No need," he had said. "I'll only be here a night or two."

That was five years ago.

Since then Nestor had established himself as a master gardener, opened his own business, married the woman he loved, and now he was to be a father. And yet here he was, alone, in the dark, as exhausted and confused as the night he arrived. The raucous ghosts he had spent years trying to silence had been roused. Their sleep disrupted, they hounded him, reminding him no matter what façade he wore now, inside he was still the little boy on the front porch of his uncle's house, waiting for the father who had left without a word of goodbye.

"I thought I might find you here."

Startled, Nestor turned to find Ham standing in the hall. "Sorry. I brought up that woman's suitcase and…thought I'd—"

Ham turned on the light and sat on the bed. "Have a little time to yourself?"

Sighing, Nestor leaned against the desk. "Try to get my head together. I should be downstairs, celebrating with Agnes…and instead I'm up here, acting like a spoiled kid."

"I wouldn't say that."

Chapter 11 ~ A Change of Heart

"You never say anything bad about *anybody*."

Ham laughed. "I wouldn't say that *either*. Actually, I was hoping I'd find you here. I've been wanting to talk to you about something and haven't had a chance."

"What is it?"

Ham pointed his thumb at the window. "That."

"What do you mean?"

"You're not the first person I've found standing there. When anyone wants to be alone and think, they come up here for the view."

"Agnes will never love another room as much as this one," Nestor said. "Tomorrow I'll remind everyone to respect your privacy. You deserve it as much as—?"

"No, that's not it. I want to move into the study. No one uses it much since Monty moved away…well, except for last night—"

"The study? Don't you think it's a little cramped? I mean, it's a great place to spend the afternoon reading, but—"

Ham took a notebook from the nightstand. "I want to build a staircase."

Nestor took it and flipped through pages of penciled diagrams and measurements. "Staircase. You mean, from—?"

Ham pointed up. "To the windows in the cupola. Starting where you're standing. Ending at a platform. A view from every direction. Have you been up there?"

"Not in a long time. "Ivy Leigh wouldn't allow it. Not since she had to call the fire department to rescue Edna Flite from the widow's walk." He laughed at the memory.

"My point exactly," Ham said.

"This will take a lot of materials. I don't know if we can afford it. Not right now."

"I have money…to get started, at least."

"On the salary I pay you? I don't think so," Nestor said.

"When I was a baby, my dad opened a college fund for me. He never stopped believing I might go. I've never had the heart to ask him for the money. But I would for this."

"I can't let you spend your own money on this house," Nestor said.

Ham ducked his head. "It's my home, too."

"I'm sorry. I didn't mean—"

Ham got up. "I have to go down now. You look those over and let me know."

Tea at Kimball Pines

On his way down Ham spotted Prudence O'Neill gazing up from the foot of the stairs.

"You need something, ma'am?" he asked.

Giggling, she backed away. "No. You caught me snooping. I just wondered—"

"What's up there?"

She nodded.

He met her at the foot of the stairs. "I'll show you tomorrow, if you want. But right now Nestor is up there working. We shouldn't bother him."

Prudence returned to her room, closed the door, and plopped on the bed. She had never done anything so reckless. All to please Daniel—prove what sacrifices she was willing to make. She could hardly wait to call him tomorrow. *You'll never guess where I am*, she would say. *With the Carlyle woman.* He would be amazed at her resourcefulness. He would stammer, apologize for being at a loss for words. *No need to thank me*, she would say. *I'd do anything for you. I hope you know that now.* Before he could profess his love, she fell asleep.

Still in her clothes, she awoke disoriented and squinted at the light coming through the window. Morning? She *never* slept all night. Sitting up, she stretched her arms overhead and sighed contentedly. Time to call Daniel. Then hurry to the train station.

She took clothes from her suitcase, grabbed a towel from the dresser, and peeked into the hall. Finding it empty, she slipped into the bathroom to shower. Then she dressed and took her suitcase and purse downstairs, leaving them in the hall.

Agnes rushed past her on her way to the bathroom. "Can't talk," she said. "Breakfast."

Was this an invitation to eat, or had breakfast made Agnes sick? Either way, Prudence had to call Daniel. She stepped into the kitchen. The elderly lady and two men she had met the night before were eating oatmeal and cinnamon toast. Agnes' husband was not there. Neither was the handyman. The lady who had cleared the dishes after supper was leaning against the sink, her arms crossed like a sentinel.

Abbot Cooper hopped up and pulled out a chair.

"Thank you," Prudence said, "but I need to call my boss and let him know I won't be in."

He pointed to the phone. "Over there."

Chapter 11 ~ A Change of Heart

Prudence dialed Daniel's private number. If only he could see her rubbing shoulders with these simple people, he would appreciate the lengths she had gone to.

"Long distance?" Pinetta asked.

Prudence nodded. "Put it on my bill."

Ham bumped into her on his way through the back door. "Sorry, miss." He blew on his stiff fingers. "Cold this morning. Any coffee left?"

Prudence turned her back to the room. Receiver held tight against one ear, she pressed her finger into the other. "Hi, Daniel? It's me. Did you find the note I left on your desk?"

Standing, Abbot sidled to the sink. He gazed out the window, straining to hear what Prudence was saying. If she were leaving, he would offer her a ride to the station. Might be the closest he would ever get to an honest-to-goodness publisher.

If there was one thing his father had taught him, it was you never got anywhere in business simply by working hard. You had to "know someone." If he could pitch his book to Prudence, he was certain he could sell it.

Annoyed by Abbot, Prudence turned further into the corner and cupped her hand over the receiver. "But Daniel, you told me you wanted me to…I thought you'd be pleased."

"Ham," Millie said. "Will you take me to the bank later this morning?"

Ham sat next to her. "Sure. Do you mind going to the hardware store first?"

"Starting another project?" she asked.

Ham nodded. "I didn't want to tell anyone till I ran it past Nestor."

"What is it?" Barton asked.

"A staircase," Ham said, beaming. "To the top of the house."

Barton propped his elbow on the back of his chair. "You have experience with that kind of work?"

"Ham is a jack of all trades," Millie said. "He can do anything."

"Could you use an assistant?" Barton asked.

"You a builder?" Ham asked.

"Had a lot of jobs in the last few years, but…yeah…you could say I'm a carpenter."

Prudence's hoarse whispers were growing louder. She held her hand over the receiver and turned to Pinetta. "Excuse me. Ma'am?"

Pinetta stiffened. "Yes?"

"Is there somewhere I can finish this conversation in private?"

"Millie's room, but you'll have to ask her."

Prudence laid down the phone and stepped toward Millie. "Could I finish my call in your room? I'm talking to my boss."

"Of course," Millie said. She led Prudence out.

Ham asked Barton if he would like to take a look at the plans he had drawn up, and the men followed the ladies into the hall.

When everyone was gone, Pinetta hung up the phone, prepared her tea, and sat in her usual chair. Was there no end to this chaos? Her nerves were in tatters. At least the O'Neill woman would leave today. The sooner the better.

Agnes, gray-faced, came back to the kitchen. "Where'd everybody go?"

"Ham is showing Barton his plans for the staircase. Did you know about it?"

"Uh-huh. Nestor told me last night."

Pinetta attempted a casual tone. "Did you know Barton is a carpenter?"

"Really? That's good news." Agnes walked to the towel drawer, took out a dishcloth, and wet it with cold water. "That would be a good excuse for Barton to stay."

She wrung out the cloth and wiped her face; Pinetta cringed.

"You want him to stay?"

"Of course. He and Nestor need to establish some kind of relationship… even if all they do is part as friends."

"You think that's possible?"

Washcloth on her forehead, Agnes sat down. "Nestor has a good heart. He'll come around." She laid her head on the table. "Oh, I am so sick. At least now I know why."

"Can I get you something to drink?"

"No," Agnes said, raising her head. "But could you go upstairs and get the box of saltines on my nightstand?"

"Of course."

Pinetta, eager to finish the conversation about Barton, strode from the kitchen. Before she could reach the stairs, Prudence brushed past her, snatching up her purse from the floor. She rifled through it, pulled out her wallet, and bustled into the kitchen.

Pinetta tiptoed to the door and stood out of sight, listening.

Prudence was asking if she could pay a month's rent in advance.

"A month? What about your job?" Agnes asked.

"I don't *have* a job. He fired me. After all I've done for him. He *fired* me."

Chapter 11 ~ A Change of Heart

Pinetta leaned against the wall. A month? *That* woman in the house for a month?

The doorbell rang.

Pinetta straightened her shoulders and marched toward the foyer. She was in no mood for another disruption.

So help me, if that's Mary Grace Dodson again...

Ready to let fly, Pinetta smoothed her apron and opened the door. Her pinched mouth eased into a pleasant expression when she found a distinguished man instead.

"May I help you?"

"Is this the Magnolia Arms?" he asked.

"Yes."

"My name is Grant Hubbard. Millie is my mother. I've come to take her home."

Chapter 12

A Delicate Balance

Like a car stuck in second gear, November lurched and thudded by.

The day before Thanksgiving, Agnes awoke at ten minutes till six. Reaching for the box of saltines on her nightstand, she sat up and waited for the inevitable wave of nausea to sink her.

Nothing happened. White box unopened in her lap, she remained suspended in the sublime moment, blinking her eyes at the dark window.

Thanksgiving. Tomorrow. Her third at the Magnolia Arms.

Last year she had packed a bag, taken a train, and looked forward to Nestor scooping her up in his arms when he met her at the station. Now she lived here. She was Nestor's wife. And he had not scooped her up in his arms in days.

She returned the crackers to her nightstand and glanced at Nestor's side of the bed. Empty. Three weeks ago she would have found it strange if he left for his class before dawn. But not now. Since his father had arrived, Nestor stayed up late and got up early. He barely spoke to anyone…even her…and looked for any excuse, however flimsy, to leave the house. Agnes had tried to reach him, but failed; Barton cast a dark, impenetrable shadow between them. So far reasoning with Nestor had done nothing to bring about a truce with Barton, even a tenuous one.

A lump in her throat seized her. She had everything she had ever wanted, but had never felt more helpless and alone. The friends she depended on, Ivy Leigh and Margaret, were far away, living their dreams in homes of their own.

She reveled in their happiness—happiness with which they credited her. But she would have given anything to walk downstairs and find them in the

Tea at Kimball Pines

kitchen, lingering over coffee, swapping stories, laughing, waiting for *her*. Ready to advise about this impossible situation.

But they were not here. The burden rested on Agnes' shoulders alone. Nestor was no help. In fact, *he* was part of the problem. One thing was certain: she would not allow the feuding Carlyle men to hold the entire household prisoner.

Not on Thanksgiving of all days. Millie's last day at the Magnolia Arms. Truitt's first.

Ham was counting down the days till his father Torbert arrived, bringing Truitt in the '59 Cadillac, chosen from their collection of classic cars to guarantee the smoothest ride.

Pinetta was bustling about her work, busy, withdrawn, weeping when no one was looking, ever since Millie's son Grant had announced her "services were no longer needed."

Barton waited in vain for a kind word from Nestor—grief etched on his face.

With so much at stake, Agnes turned to the one person who could help her. Muriel Porter.

Agnes had stipulated no one could know she was coming.

She eased up off the bed, held her breath. It was true—she was not sick. Not yet anyway. Maybe it was a sign. She stepped to the bathroom, turned on the light, and squinted at the mirror, hoping to find the "glow" expectant mothers are reputed to have. Not there. She smoothed her naturally curly hair, slipped on her jeans and favorite sweater, and crept downstairs. Relieved the house was still quiet, she was tiptoeing toward the foyer when she spotted a light under Millie's door. Worried Millie might be ill, Agnes stepped closer and called through the door.

"Millie? Are you all right?"

Millie opened the door and whispered. "What are you doing up at this hour? You don't have school today."

"Going on a little errand. Do you need anything?"

"Actually, yes. Could you close this suitcase and hide it in the closet?"

Agnes stepped in. "Sure. But why? Everyone knows you're leaving Friday."

"I don't want to ask Pinetta to help me…she's so sad."

Agnes stowed the suitcase. "You look nice. Going somewhere this morning?"

"A little farewell breakfast of the Garden Club. At Newman's."

Chapter 12 ~ A Delicate Balance

"Ham taking you?"

"No," Millie said. "Gretchen Tate is picking me up."

"I don't know what those ladies will do without you, now that you're going home."

"I'll miss them, too, but it will be wonderful to be with my children again. Since Grant has been overseas with the Department of Defense, we haven't been together…all of us…in a long time."

"They're all coming for a reunion?"

Millie nodded. "Apparently, they've been arranging it for a while and wanted to surprise me. One or the other has been hinting for me to come home. Finally, they had to ask outright."

"I'm glad you're waiting till after Thanksgiving to leave. It will mean a lot to Pinetta…to all of us."

Millie sank down on the edge of the bed. "Please don't say any more. I can't stand it."

Agnes sat next to her. "I didn't mean to upset you. I just wanted you to know—"

Millie's voice broke. "Oh, Agnes, if I don't tell someone the truth, I think I'll bust."

"What's wrong?"

"I *asked* Grant to come here and put on that show, because I didn't have the courage to leave on my own…and leave Pinetta behind."

"I thought you two were best friends."

"We are. And that's why I *have* to leave her here." She took Agnes' hand in both of hers. "You'll help her, won't you, Agnes?"

"I don't understand."

Voice trembling, Millie revealed her plot to involve Pinetta in the Community Choir and Founder's Day celebration—to force her out of isolation and into the real world.

"So your son *doesn't* want you to come home?" Agnes asked.

"He does. They all do, but he would've never *insisted*. It was an act I asked him to put on. For Pinetta's sake. You know how she is about family loyalty."

"Actually, I don't. I hardly know her. Not because I haven't tried."

"My point exactly. If she doesn't have me to focus on, she'll *have* to turn to someone else. Be her friend, Agnes. Don't give up on her."

Agnes glanced at her watch. "I'm sorry. I have to go. But we'll talk later. I promise."

She grabbed her coat and Nestor's plaid scarf from the coat rack by the front door and drove to Mollie's. She tapped on the door and then tucked her hands in her pockets, shivering while Muriel snapped on the lights and hurried over, keys in hand.

When she opened the door, Agnes smelled coffee.

Muriel pulled her in, locked the door, and straightened the "Closed" sign. As she helped Agnes with her coat, she lifted the edge of the scarf.

"What is the meaning of this?" Muriel asked.

"It's Nestor's."

"And where, may I ask, is the holiday scarf Flossie knitted for you?"

The red-and-yellow scarf with pumpkins embroidered at the edges was an inside joke.

Agnes laughed and embraced her, comforted by the familiar lavender scent of Muriel's hair, perfectly coiffed...even at six in the morning.

"Flossie is staying at home this year. In their new apartment."

Muriel motioned her to a table near the kitchen. "Sit over there, and I'll turn out the lights. If I don't, Asa Ludlow will stop and ask if I'm open."

As Agnes walked to her chair, Muriel stepped behind the counter. "I made decaf. You're supposed to cut down on caffeine when you're expecting. Want something to eat?"

"Plain bagel," Agnes said. "I feel better today, but still don't want to risk anything."

"Toasted?"

"Yes."

Muriel snickered. "You or the bagel?"

"Both. Thanks for coming in early."

"Early? Don't be silly. The day is half gone." She set the mug in front of Agnes.

"The restaurant's really taking shape," Agnes said, glancing at the portrait of Muriel's great-grandmother on the wall. "It looks more like the Drifters' Rest every time I come in."

Hovering near the toaster, Muriel glanced around the room. "Old habits die hard."

"You miss the Drifters' Rest?" Agnes asked.

"I do. But this place keeps me on my toes. I never know what's coming next."

"Me neither," Agnes said. "At least not for the last couple of weeks."

"How's Nestor? Speaking to his father yet?"

Chapter 12 ~ A Delicate Balance

Agnes shook her head. "No. He would've made Barton leave by now if we hadn't found out he was a carpenter. He's helping Ham build his staircase."

"I heard about that. How many staircases does one house need?"

"One more, according to Ham."

Muriel served the bagel. "Does Ivy Leigh know? She still talks about—"

"Edna Flite getting stuck on the widow's walk," Agnes said, laughing.

"Tell me when it's finished. I'll come over for the unveiling."

"Won't be finished for a long time. You know what a perfectionist Ham is. I wouldn't be surprised if Barton is stalling as long as possible. Hoping Nestor will come around."

"It must have been hard for him to come back after all this time."

Agnes sighed. "It's so hard on Nestor, and it doesn't help that I'm encouraging Barton to stay."

She patted Agnes' hand. "You're doing the right thing. Don't doubt that."

"I'm glad to hear you say that. It makes it easier to ask"—inhaling, tears flowing—"I know it's last minute, but could you invite Barton for Thanksgiving? It would make things—"

Muriel held up her hand. "I've already invited him. And the other two."

Agnes dabbed a napkin under her eyes. "The other two?"

"Abbot and Prudence."

"When?"

"Yesterday."

"I...I don't understand. Why would you—"

"They all come in a couple of times a week. Barton sits by the window. Usually alone. The other two like that corner table. Sit there hunched over a pile of paper."

"I had no idea you knew all of them."

Muriel shrugged her shoulders. "I wouldn't say I *know* them. Barton is more like a shadow than a man. And the other two only talk to each other. Very hush-hush."

"That's what they do at the house," Agnes said. "I think Abbot is trying to talk Prudence into publishing his book. But it makes no sense. She was fired, not even an editor anymore."

Muriel waved her hand. "I don't know anything about that. But when Mary Grace told me you were expecting a new tenant *and* Ham's father, I thought you could use a little help."

"Mary Grace. That makes sense. And you came up with a plan all by yourself." Agnes began crying again. "You don't know what this means to me. I have no one to turn to."

"You have Nestor."

Agnes wailed. "No. I don't. He's furious with me for trying to force him to forgive his father. I'm losing him."

Muriel took a tissue from her pocket and held it out. "No, you're not. He's not mad at you. He's in pain. Don't forget that."

"It's hard to remember when I feel…so…bad."

"I've never had a baby," Muriel said, patting her hand, "but I know plenty of women who have. This is all normal. Now finish your bagel and go home and help Pinetta. I'm sure she's worse off than you are. Her whole little world will crumble when Millie leaves."

Agnes wiped her nose. "You knew Millie was leaving?"

Muriel bit her lip. She had weighed every word during this awkward interview, and now…so near to sending Agnes home…she had gotten careless. Rookie mistake.

"The Garden Club ladies wanted to hold the farewell breakfast here. But I told them I was booked. Party of one." She stood. "I'll get some more coffee. You relax."

Agnes sniffled, wondering if the bagel would stay down.

Walking away, Muriel rolled her eyes at her own stupidity.

You nearly blew that one, old girl. How would you have explained that to Nestor?

Twenty-four hours earlier, he had sat in the same chair where Agnes was now and asked Muriel for the same favor. Take Barton off his hands for one day. Thanksgiving had so many memories for him and Agnes. Two years ago—they had met. Last year—he had proposed. This year—the baby. He was planning a surprise and had not counted on the house being full of guests. Especially not one as unwelcome as his father. They needed room at the table. And Agnes needed "one day when things could be like they used to be." Could Muriel help?

She had agreed, offering to invite Abbot and Prudence, too, so Barton would feel less awkward about being singled out.

Agnes managed to eat half the bagel. Muriel refused to let her pay.

On the way home Agnes pulled over to the curb, hopped out, and threw up in the trash can at the entrance to Robert Kimball Memorial Park. Then got back in her car and fell asleep.

———∞———

Pinetta, a jumble of nerves and muddled emotions, was making cranberry sauce again. Though the ten jars she had made for her family were still lined up in her closet, *fresh* cranberry sauce, "a little on the sweet side," was Barton's preference.

Chapter 12 ~ A Delicate Balance

She knew this because she had drafted Ham to quiz Barton about his favorite holiday dishes. Today she would check "Make Cranberry Sauce" off her list of sacred tasks.

Even though the instructions were Barton's, she winced slightly as she poured in the required portion of sugar and a dab extra.

The mixture began to simmer. Alone in the kitchen, she opened the window a few inches, welcoming the frosty air to fill her lungs and jar her senses.

She had been jittery for the last two weeks. Fidgety. Hardly knowing what to do with herself. Her stomach quivered unexpectedly throughout the day. Her sleep, usually sound, was disturbed by dreams of Guy Henry, college days, childhood. She would wake in a cold sweat and glance at the clock, counting down the minutes till she could rise and make her way into the dark kitchen to prepare coffee for Barton. Just drawing nearer to the door of his room, thinking of him a few steps away, sleeping, thrilled her.

And now as she bustled about in the kitchen, the noise of tools, the clean smell of cut wood drifted downstairs. Barton was upstairs building. If he had been anything but a carpenter, Nestor would have shown him the door by now.

But he would stay…at least till the staircase was finished.

So, on this sublime morning she measured, mixed, mused in the fragrant kitchen.

She was preparing the meal for her first holiday with Barton.

Risking her heart. After being without love for so long.

Steam rose. Sauce bubbled.

Painful. Exhilarating. Loving someone.

Berries popped.

She raised the wooden spoon. Watched the ruby-colored liquid cascade down.

Sweeter than usual.

Laying the spoon aside, she adjusted the flame under the canner on the back burner.

Add the orange zest. Fill the jars. Tighten the lids. Lower them into the hot water.

She had been mistaken about the coldness of her heart.

Embers still glowed there. Barton had ignited them.

A gust of wind swirled leaves past the window. Under ordinary circumstances, her first thought would have been *wet leaves on a driveway become wet leaves on the floor.*

Today—she sang.

"And the autumn weather turns the leaves to flame, and I haven't got time for the waiting game. And the days dwindle down to a precious few…September…November…"

She closed her eyes and pictured herself setting a perfectly browned turkey in the center of the table. Barton would lean in to inhale. Then, as a joke, tuck his napkin under his chin.

"Hand me that drumstick—"

Pounding on the back door, Bridey Ludlow, cornucopia earrings dangling from her fleshy ears and a pumpkin brooch fixed to the shoulder of her burnt orange sweater, barreled in.

"Morning, Piney. If it wasn't colder than a well digger's butt, I could've stood by your window all day, listening to you sing. You have a nice voice. You should join the choir."

An armed robber would have been more welcome.

The intruder deposited a dingy picnic basket on the counter. "I heard you were expecting a crowd for dinner, so I brought my award-winning strawberry-rhubarb pie." She pulled out the pie plate. Pink juice had seeped out and baked to the sides of the dish. "I overfilled it again. Don't know when I'll learn. Made a terrible mess in my oven." She pushed the jars aside to make space. "Didn't have time for a *pea*-can pie, so I brought the nuts." She plopped a plastic bag of pecan halves next to the pie. "You make good pie crust? Not everyone can."

Pinetta kept her head down. "Puh-*cahn* pie is too sweet."

Bridey skirted Pinetta and opened the freezer. "Then I'll just put them in here. There's always fudge to be made for Christmas. Or fruitcake. How are you holding up?"

"Holding up?"

Bridey helped herself to a coffee mug from the cabinet. "What with Millie leaving. I must say I find it disgraceful…her kin putting you to the curb without so much as a fare thee well."

"They're not putting me to the curb. Millie won't need me now that her son is home from Germany. Besides, it wouldn't be appropriate for me to intrude on their reunion."

Chapter 12 ~ A Delicate Balance

Bridey tilted the percolator precipitously. The lid fell off, showering coffee grounds over the counter. She tossed the lid into the sink and ignored the mess. "Say what you will. I know you're heartbroken." She emptied the pot into her cup. "Coffee pot's empty." The chair creaked as she sat at the table.

Pinetta eyed the pie. Once Bridey left, she would scrape the whole mess into the trash and put the dish to soak in the sink.

"Millie gave me a job when I needed one," Pinetta said. "I gave an honest day's work for an honest day's wage. Now it's time for me to move on."

"Move on, my hind foot," Bridey said, spooning sugar into her cup. "You have no choice. But it's a good thing. Once you don't have Millie to use as an excuse, you can get out more."

Pinetta turned off the burner and moved the saucepan onto a trivet next to the stove. She wet a dishcloth and swiped the coffee grounds off the counter and into her hand.

"Is there something you need?" Pinetta asked. "I have a lot to—"

Barton, dappled with sawdust, entered from the hall. "Any coffee left?"

Pinetta whirled around, hiding her hand behind her back as if he had caught her stealing. "I can make a fresh pot. Won't take a minute."

"My fault," Bridey chirped. "I'm such a greedy Gertie." The doorbell rang. "I'll get that."

Bridey planted her hands on the table and pushed herself up, her thighs grazing the table's edge. The sugar bowl teetered; coffee sloshed.

When Barton stepped aside to let her pass, Pinetta turned and brushed the coffee grounds into the sink. She rinsed her hands, holding them under the water longer than needed, so she could regain her composure. Then took a clean towel from the drawer and turned around.

Barton righted the sugar bowl. "Doesn't know her own strength, does she?"

"I guess not."

"Hand me that towel. I'll clean this up." She did as he said. He carried Bridey's cup to the sink and poured the rest down the drain. "So that was the last of the coffee?"

"I always make a second pot about the middle of the morning. Won't take a minute."

She filled the percolator with water; Barton nodded at the saucepan. "What're you making?"

"Cranberry sauce. I…make it for my family every year. I thought—"

Tea at Kimball Pines

He stepped closer and peered into the saucepan. "Smells delicious. My mom used to make cranberry sauce. Is this for Thanksgiving?"

Pinetta nodded. "I wanted to make it today to leave time tomorrow for everything else." Her hand wobbled as she measured the coffee. She hoped Barton did not notice.

He picked up the spoon and stirred the sauce. "You'll have to save me some."

"Save you some?" Pinetta asked.

"I'm taking Prudy to Thanksgiving dinner at Muriel's place," Barton said.

Pinetta plugged in the percolator. "Prudy?"

"She hates it when I call her that," Barton said, laughing. "You already made a pie? What kind is it?"

Pinetta's voice trembled. "I didn't make *that*. Mrs. Ludlow brought it."

"Didn't think so, but had to ask. Totally out of character for Mrs. Fraleigh to let a pie boil over in the oven. Woman of your standards? Never. Yell when the coffee's ready?"

"I'll...bring it to you."

"No need to—" Barton slapped his forehead. "What was I thinking? You've probably never *yelled* in your whole life. Too genteel. Have your friend call. I'm sure we'd hear *her*."

"She's not my—"

He winked as he left.

Helpless, Pinetta watched him go.

Mrs. Fraleigh? He thinks of me as 'Mrs. Fraleigh'? Woman of standards? Genteel? Were those compliments or—

Bridey returned. "Someone here to see you. Told him to wait by the door." Pinetta did not answer. Bridey waved her hand in Pinetta's face. "Yoo-hoo. *Door*."

"Who is it?"

"If I told you *that*, you might not go. You'll just have to see for yourself." She walked behind Pinetta and nudged her with her shoulder. "Go on now. I'll let myself out the back door."

Still dazed, Pinetta started moving. *Save me some? Was that what Barton said? Dinner with Prudy? He calls her Prudy?*

Hardly feeling the floor beneath her feet, she glanced at the dining room as she passed by. China and crystal stacked on the table. A folded tablecloth

Chapter 12 ~ A Delicate Balance

lay at one end. Everything was ready, but the one she was doing it all for would not be there.

Mired in misery, she was within a yard of the visitor before she noticed his shocking similarity to Guy Henry. Tall and gaunt, he was outfitted in black pants, black turtleneck sweater, and an ill-fitting tweed jacket with brown suede patches at the elbows. His short, brittle hair, dyed auburn, was gray at the temples. Unaware of her approach, he mumbled to himself as he rifled through a stack of paper cradled in his right arm. Pinetta coughed politely. He looked up, squinted at her, disapproving, his thin lips a straight, blank line under a narrow moustache.

"You're not at all what I pictured," he said.

"I *beg* your pardon."

Index finger tapping his chin, he scrutinized her like a parent exasperated with a child's bad behavior.

"Mrs. Ludlow wasn't entirely honest," he said. "She *said* you were practically a professional musician. Nothing about being a cook."

Pinetta glanced down at her bib apron. Temper rising, she reached behind her back, fumbled with the square knot, undid it, and ripped the apron over her head, skewing her glasses.

"I'm *not* a cook. Every woman in this town, if she's worth her salt, is in the kitchen this morning. You *can't* leave all the preparations till Thursday. The meal would be a disaster."

Donovan Strode, choirmaster at Dennisonville High School, wisely removed his hand from his chin and lowered both hands to his sides, standing at attention.

A single sheet of music fluttered to the floor.

"No need to be offended," he said. "Mrs. Ludlow said you'd had classical training, and so I naturally assumed you would be a person of—"

"Mrs. Ludlow wouldn't know a *real* musician if she trampled one on her way to the buffet table. Now. *Who* are you and *what* do you want?"

Clearing his throat, he took a business card from his coat pocket. "Dr. Strode. Head of the music department at Dennisonville High School. I'll be your conductor."

Pinetta refused the proffered card. "*My* conductor?"

He returned the card to his pocket. "For the…community chorale. Founder's Day?"

"Oh…that. I'd forgotten all about it."

Donovan, sensing a lapse in her defenses, rallied. "The first meeting of the planning committee is next Monday. I want to announce tryouts and introduce you."

"There's no point in my attending a 'planning' meeting."

"Attendance isn't optional for staff," he said.

"I'm not on anyone's staff."

Donovan's patience had depleted. His cheeks reddened. "I was told you had agreed to serve as accompanist. That makes you part of my staff, since I'm in charge."

Pinetta squared her shoulders. "Let me make one thing perfectly clear. I agreed to help *only* as a favor to Mrs. Hubbard. And I have never been, nor ever will be, on anyone's 'staff.'"

"That's two things."

If Agnes, hand clamped over her mouth, had not rushed headlong through the front door and dashed to the hall bathroom, Donovan and Pinetta might have stood there, like warriors from rival tribes, half the morning.

"If you'll excuse me," Pinetta said, "I need to help Mrs. Carlyle."

Right eyebrow raised, Donovan held out the scores.

Draping her apron over her arm, Pinetta remained where she was.

Donovan glanced at the stray sheet of music on the floor.

Pinetta raised both eyebrows.

Donovan stooped to pick up the page, placed it on top of the stack, and approached.

Pinetta accepted the music and nodded at the door.

Donovan, uncertain who had won, retreated. He had hoped to inveigle her into an impromptu audition. Now he would have to wait to find out what she was capable of. At least she was temperamental. Always a good sign in a musician.

He got into his Audi and pulled away from the curb. When he spotted Mary Grace Dodson in the rearview mirror, hurrying toward him, waving, he pressed on the accelerator.

Pinetta stared at the door. Only yesterday she had been giddy with anticipation. She turned toward the kitchen. Moments ago she had been singing…like a schoolgirl. Now she walked with leaden steps into the parlor, approached the piano, lifted the music high with both hands, and let it fall with a thud on the bench. She returned to the kitchen, took the trash can from beneath the sink, and lowered the strawberry-rhubarb pie, plate and all,

Chapter 12 ~ A Delicate Balance

onto a bed of sweet potato peels, poured the cranberry sauce on top, and garnished the whole mess with the bag of pecan halves.

Mist formed inside the frosty plastic bag as it nestled into the warm mixture.

Agnes, looking gray, stole into the kitchen and sank onto a chair.

Pinetta calmly returned the trashcan to its place under the sink and closed the cabinet door. Slipping her apron over her head, she pulled the ties into a square knot.

"Can I get you anything?" Pinetta asked.

"Water. I'm sorry, Pinetta. I meant to come home and help you with dinner, but I fell asleep in the car. And now I'm going to have to lie down till I feel better."

Pinetta filled a glass. "Ice?"

"Hmm," Agnes said. "I have good news at least. We'll have three less for dinner."

Placing the glass on the table, Pinetta sat down. "It would have been nice to have had a little warning."

Agnes propped both arms on the table. "Fewer guests is good, isn't it?"

"All I'm saying is—"

Pinetta drew in a lungful of air. Head tilted back, eyes fixed on the ceiling, she whimpered, her chest heaving.

Astounded, Agnes looked up. In the year she had known Pinetta, she had witnessed only two emotions in her: forced acquiescence or suppressed disdain. She had *never* seen her cry.

Agnes slid onto the chair next to Pinetta and slipped her arm around her shoulders.

To her surprise, Pinetta did not resist.

"I'm sorry," Agnes said. "I didn't stop to think how much you're dreading saying goodbye to Millie. I shouldn't have said—"

Pinetta shoved back from the table and bent over double, resting her head on her knees. "Bag. Bag."

Agnes leaned in. "What?"

Head still down, Pinetta stabbed the air, pointing to the pantry. "Paper bag. I'm...I'm..."

Agnes scurried to the pantry and returned with a paper lunch sack. Pinetta sat up and pressed the bag to her face, blowing in and out, till her breathing slowed.

Ham entered from the hall. "What's wrong?"

"Pinetta," was all Agnes could say.

Kneeling by Pinetta's chair, Ham spoke in a low voice. "I came to check on you, Miss Pinetta. Barton just told you he won't be here for Thanksgiving, didn't he?"

Pale and perspiring, Pinetta nodded once.

Ham stood. "Let me help you up."

She slipped her hand into his. He put his other hand under her elbow as she got up from her chair. "Come on. You need to rest. There's nothing that can't wait till later."

Agnes, dumbfounded, was still at the table when Ham closed the door to Pinetta's room.

"You should check on her in a few minutes," he said.

"What was *that* all about?"

Holding his finger to his lips, he moved closer. "You don't know?"

"She can't be that upset about having fewer guests," Agnes said.

"It's not that. Haven't you noticed?"

"Noticed what?"

He spoke barely above a whisper. "She's in love."

Agnes grabbed his arm. "You don't mean…with Barton?"

He nodded.

"But…her? No way in the world. Barton would *never*—"

"You don't choose who you love," he said. "It just happens."

"But how do *you* know? Did she tell you?"

"She didn't need to tell me. Haven't you noticed our meals have gotten better since Barton got here? Dessert every night. Roast beef for no reason."

"I haven't exactly been…on good terms with food lately."

Ham took a mug from the cabinet and filled it with coffee. "Good point. I've got to get back to work. Check on Pinetta later?"

"Sure."

After Ham left, Agnes laid her head on folded arms on the table. Too tired to go upstairs to bed and too sick to move, she tried to make sense of the scene she had just witnessed. *Pinetta Fraleigh? This brittle woman, starched, sour, terse, weeping in unbridled anguish? Capable of that kind of passion?* Agnes' stomach rumbled. She gulped. Recalling Millie's advice about peppermint tea, she crept to the cabinet, hoping to find one lone teabag. Finding two, she filled the kettle with water and placed it on the stove. Steam rose; she grew hot.

Chapter 12 ~ A Delicate Balance

Desperate, she undid her top button. No effect. Too late to make it to the bathroom. She yanked open the door under the sink, pulled out the trashcan and threw up on top of the pecans on top of the cranberry sauce on top of the strawberry-rhubarb pie.

The sight of which made her heave again.

She mustered the strength to move the trashcan to the back porch, washed her face at the sink, and somehow managed to make tea. She shuffled to the table and sank down, panting, propped helplessly over her cup. She inhaled, hoping the smell would soothe her nerves.

Check on Pinetta? Who's going to check on me? she thought.

When Agnes had left Muriel, she was certain her life was back on track. She had planned to hurry home, help with dinner preparations, tidy up the house, clean the bathrooms. It had all seemed so possible. Yet here she was—summoning the courage to drink the tea she was sure to throw up only minutes later. And why was there a pie in the trashcan? Pinetta—of all people—was lying in bed after hyperventilating. Nestor, true to form, would be gone most of the day, concocting some feeble excuse about his absence when he came home after dark.

Why had she ever believed she could fill Ivy Leigh's shoes as manager of this house? In the four months she had lived here, her life had been one continuous string of failures. First, there were no guests, and now there were too many. She hardly knew Nestor any more. She had no one to talk to...except Ham. She breathed in the peppermint again. *If only someone would bring the saltines from the nightstand.* Through puffy eyes she spotted Pinetta's teacakes on a pumpkin-shaped plate. *Maybe those would help. They were so bland. Dry.*

She took a cookie and nibbled. Sweet. Moist. Buttery. Pinetta had rolled them out in powdered sugar instead of flour.

Ham was right, Agnes thought. *Pinetta has fallen for Barton. She's sacrificed her principles for the man she loves.* The thought of this almost made her laugh.

The doorbell rang. She groaned. There was no one to answer but her.

She grabbed a handful of napkins in case she couldn't make it to the door and began the long journey down the hall to the foyer. When she reached the foot of the stairs, she paused to call to Ham. But her feeble voice did not carry over the racket reverberating from the third floor. Whoever was at the door would just have to come back later.

The doorbell rang again. Then a knock. And a hello as the door swung open.

"Anybody home?" said a familiar voice.

Agnes screamed, ran, and fell into Ivy Leigh Ransom's arms.

"What are you doing here?" Agnes asked.

Ivy Leigh patted her on the back. "Couldn't miss Thanksgiving at the Magnolia Arms."

Agnes peered over Ivy Leigh's shoulder at Mr. Hampton, suitcases in hand, and behind him, Truitt Spenlow, leaning on a cane with his right hand, his left arm in a sling.

Standing back, Agnes swiped the napkins across her face. "Mr. Hampton. And Dr. Spenlow. Come in. Come in."

"Hello, Agnes," Truitt said.

Mr. Hampton wrapped her in his strong arms. "How's Mrs. Carlyle?"

"Better now," she said, letting go and wiping her eyes. "But nothing's ready. We weren't expecting you till tomorrow. And I had no idea Ivy Leigh was—"

Ivy Leigh put her arm around Truitt. "I'll explain all that later. Truitt needs to rest. Can I put him in my old room for now?"

"Sure," Agnes said. "Millie won't be home till later. She won't mind."

"Where's Ham?" Mr. Hampton asked.

Agnes pointed up. "Follow the racket all the way up."

Mr. Hampton kissed her on the cheek and climbed the stairs.

Agnes, rooted in place, marveled at her unpredictable life. Hopeless only seconds ago, her world had righted itself. The heartbeat of the house, Ivy Leigh Ransom, had returned.

Closing the bedroom door behind her, Ivy Leigh rejoined Agnes, took her by the shoulders, and, standing at arm's length, looked into Agnes' eyes, appraising her.

"Nestor said you needed me," Ivy Leigh said. "But he didn't say how much."

Agnes clung to her friend. "I've tried to be like you, but...I can't do it. Every day, I...wait...*Nestor* said I needed you? He asked you to come?"

"A week ago."

Agnes stood back. "He's not mad at me?"

Arm around Agnes, Ivy Leigh guided her down the hall. "Of course, he's not mad. Now, what can I do first?"

"Get the saltines off my nightstand?"

Chapter 12 ~ A Delicate Balance

"And then?"

"I hate to ask."

Ivy Leigh led her into the parlor and eased her onto the sofa. "Don't be silly. What is it?"

"The kitchen trash. I threw up in it. It's on the back porch. Could you tie it up and put it in the garbage can outside? The thought of it still makes me…"

Agnes held both hands over her face.

Ivy Leigh slipped off Agnes' shoes and lifted her feet onto the sofa. Then she waited while Agnes lay back on the throw pillows.

"Be still," Ivy Leigh said, pulling an afghan over Agnes' legs. "Lie here and look out at our old walnut tree. I'll get your crackers and be right back."

Behind her closed door, Pinetta was curled up, shivering. What would her mother say if she could see her *in bed* in the *middle* of the day? She had made a fool of herself. How could she ever face Agnes again?

Maybe, she thought, *I could say I'm sick and stay in my room till Thanksgiving is over.* Sitting up, she waved her hand as if shooing a fly. Pembroke women *never* behaved this way. The meal she had planned was for Millie, too.

Chastened, Pinetta stood, straightened her skirt, and peeked out her bedroom door. Finding the kitchen vacant, she hurried to take out the garbage before anyone spotted the mess. The cabinet door squeaked as she pulled it open.

"Hello, Pinetta."

Pinetta whirled around. When she saw Ivy Leigh entering from the hall, she backed up and pushed the cabinet door closed with her foot. "Mrs. Ransom, what are you doing here?"

"At the moment, taking care of something for Agnes. She threw up in the trash can and set it on the porch. I'm going to take it to the garbage can on the driveway. Be right back."

When Ivy Leigh stepped outside, Pinetta rubbed her temples. Think. Think. How can I explain all the food in the trash? I broke the pie plate? Burned the cranberry sauce?

But when Ivy Leigh came back, she didn't mention it. "Whew. I wouldn't do that for anyone but Agnes. Bless her heart. She is *literally* a mess."

Pinetta stiffened her backbone. "It's nice to see you. I didn't know you were coming."

Ivy Leigh grabbed the dish soap and washed her hands. "A little surprise. Nestor invited me to come along with Ham's father to bring Truitt. He said Agnes needed cheering up."

"The last few days have been hard for her. May I get you anything?"

"Tea would be nice. I'm parched."

Adopting her company manners, Pinetta busied herself with cups and spoons. "Where *is* Dr. Spenlow? I'd like to meet him."

"He's in Millie's room. Actually, I'm glad to have a chance to talk to you alone. Truitt is far from well. Some of his care will fall to you. Are you all right with that?"

"Of course." Pinetta set a cup in front of Ivy Leigh. "Is Mr. Hampton upstairs with Ham?"

"Yes. Rushed up there the moment we arrived. How have you been?"

Pinetta's attention was arrested by Ivy Leigh's graceful fingers tapping on the "To-Do List," lying useless by the sugar bowl.

"Busier than usual," Pinetta said. "We have three new tenants. Plus I've been helping Mrs. Hubbard get ready to go home."

Ivy Leigh smiled benevolently. "And Agnes has been sick. You've had your hands full. Nestor said everything's been off kilter since Barton arrived."

Heat rose in Pinetta's face. Averting her eyes, she jiggled the lid on the sugar bowl. Telltale behaviors not lost on Ivy Leigh, who knew unrequited love when she saw it.

"Old wounds are the hardest to heal," Pinetta said.

Ivy Leigh picked up the list. "Shall we get to work? It's been a while since I fixed dinner for eight. It's a good thing three of your boarders won't be here. Otherwise, it would be eleven."

"How did you—?"

Ivy Leigh read the list. "You *made* the cranberry sauce? That's ambitious."

"I…had to throw it out…burned it. Someone came to the door. I lost track of time. How did you know Barton…and the others…wouldn't be here?"

"Nestor told me." She squinted at the list. "I left my glasses in the car." She stood to go.

"How did Nestor know?" Pinetta asked. "He and Barton never talk."

Ivy Leigh laid the list on the table. "Nestor asked Muriel to invite them."

Chapter 12 ~ A Delicate Balance

"He *asked* Muriel to invite them? Why?"

"To take pressure off Agnes," Ivy Leigh said, pausing at the door. "Let her have one day with nothing to worry about. Nestor's thoughtful like that."

"It was Nestor's idea?"

"Uh-huh. After I find my glasses, I'll check on Agnes and then we'll get started. Do you have an extra apron I could borrow?"

"In my room. I'll get it."

Hand on her heart, Pinetta returned to her room. Barton hadn't chosen Prudence over her. Dinner at Muriel's wasn't his idea. It was Nestor's. Barton had agreed, because he was a man of principle with a noble heart.

She loved him all the more.

Pinetta took an apron from the closet and returned to the kitchen as Ivy Leigh, glasses on, walked through the back door and Mr. Hampton entered from the hall. Hand extended, he walked to Pinetta.

"Hello, Pinetta. Haven't seen you since the wedding. How are you?"

"Fine. I was just telling Ivy Leigh how busy we've been."

"That's what Ham told me." He approached Ivy Leigh, took her hand, and kissed it. "I'm going to get my tool belt out of the car. Anything else I need to bring in?"

Pinetta envied this simple display of affection.

Why had love never been like that for her?

Why was it always so painful?

After muffins, fruit, and polite conversation, Millie thanked the Garden Club ladies for breakfast and said goodbye. She wanted to get back to the Magnolia Arms and spend as much time as possible with her friends, her family for the last year.

Like Goldilocks, she found a stranger asleep in her bed. Kind-hearted, she did not wake him, but sat quietly by the window, watching. He resembled her husband—pleasant face, bald on top, white wavy hair on the sides and in back.

Truitt stirred and opened his eyes.

"You must be Dr. Spenlow," Millie said. "You're a musician, aren't you?"

"Used to be," Truitt said. "Now I'm a cripple."

Abbot and Prudence remained at Vesper's house long past breakfast. So long that she invited them for lunch and then dozed quietly in the wooden rocker in the parlor while they pored over her family photos spread out on the coffee table.

Prudence called to her. "Vesper. Vesper." When she did not stir, Prudence whispered to Abbot. "This is a good start, but we need more. Did you find a diary yet? Journal? Anything?"

"No, I've looked everywhere, except her room. I don't feel right going in there."

Prudence laid her hand on his arm. "She'd never know." She glanced at Vesper. "Go look. I'll keep an eye on her. If she wakes up, I'll say you're in the bathroom."

"I don't know…"

Prudence pressed closer. "You don't have to steal it. Just thumb through and see if you can find out more about this Philip guy she talks about. *That's the real story.*"

"It's not right to pry into something that personal," Abbot said.

"What do you think we've been doing for the last two weeks? She knows we're interviewing her for your book. You made that clear."

"Yeah, but she thinks we're researching the Kimball family."

"That story is too bland," Prudence said. "If you want to write a book that will sell, it's about this poor old woman pining away in this big old house after Philip…what was his name?"

"March."

"Yeah, Philip March." She lowered her voice. "Now get upstairs and find that diary."

On the way home from his class, Nestor felt almost cheerful. By the time he arrived, Ivy Leigh would be there. Agnes would be happy. Thanks to Muriel, he and Agnes could enjoy the day tomorrow. He hated the distance between them.

Agnes was not to blame—he knew that—caught in the middle between him and his father. But she had a chronic compulsion to rescue strays. Animals, people. It didn't matter. If someone was in pain, she felt responsible to fix it.

It was one of the things he loved best about her.

He pulled into the driveway a little before noon and found Ivy Leigh washing dishes. When she saw him, she dropped the dishcloth in the sink, swiped her hands against her apron, and wrapped her arms around him.

Chapter 12 ~ A Delicate Balance

"How are you?" she asked.

"Fine now," he said.

She gestured toward the table where Millie and Truitt were having lunch. "Have you met Dr. Spenlow?"

Nestor held out his hand. "Yes. At Brighton Park last year. How are you, Dr. Spenlow?"

"Now, Nestor," Millie said. "I was just telling Truitt we don't stand on ceremony here."

"Truitt," Nestor said. "We're glad to have you."

Truitt thanked him.

Nestor turned to Ivy Leigh. "Where's Agnes?"

"Napping on the sofa."

Nestor stepped into the parlor and knelt next to Agnes. When he kissed her, she opened her eyes and hugged him.

No words were necessary.

Ivy Leigh settled into the kitchen as if she had never been away. Pinetta was relieved dinner no longer rested on her shoulders. She had lost all interest in the final result. She fell into step, following Ivy Leigh's directions without questioning.

After lunch, Millie led Truitt into the parlor.

"I always take an afternoon nap," she said, "but I'll be back to check on you. In the meantime, make yourself at home."

Truitt, leaning on his cane, gazed around the room, cluttered, comfortable. His eye fell on the stack of music on the piano bench. He walked over, pushed the music to one side, and sat down. He took the selection from the top of the stack. A choral medley from *Oklahoma*. He laid his cane on the floor and played "People Will Say We're in Love" with his right hand. Piano had never been his instrument, but it could be played with one hand—unlike his oboe, which he had left at home. No point in bringing something he couldn't use.

Pinetta, carrying coffee upstairs to Barton and Ham, paused, unseen, at the door. The sight of Truitt, hunched over the keyboard, touched her.

Ivy Leigh made vegetable soup and cornbread for supper. Only Prudence and Abbot were absent—still at Vesper Kimball's house. Muriel, eager to see Ivy Leigh, had invited everyone for dessert at Mollie's. Torbert and Barton, worn out from working, declined. Pinetta also remained behind, claiming Truitt needed company. She lingered in the kitchen, pretending to clean. When Barton passed by on his way to bed, she would offer him a cup of coffee…and join him. But he breezed through, muttering, "G-night" and closed the basement door behind him. Pinetta folded the dishtowel and draped it over the oven door handle.

For one more night they were sleeping under the same roof.

Pinetta found Truitt, in pajamas and robe, in the parlor. An open book in his lap, he was seated in a chair next to the piano.

"May I get you anything?" she asked.

"Do you play?"

"Excuse me."

He pointed at the piano. "Do you play?"

"I was our church pianist for many years."

"Does that music belong to you?"

"No. Millie volunteered me to accompany a community choir for Founder's Day next summer. I'm going to try to get out of it after she leaves."

"Would you play something for me?"

"I haven't played much since I've been here. Actually, in years. I'm rusty." She held up her hands as if this were proof.

"Anything at all. This is a beautiful piano."

Pinetta lifted the odious choral selections from the bench and deposited them on the floor. Then she played *Claire de Lune* by memory, the notes spilling from her fingers as if she had played them yesterday rather than two years ago. The stillness of the house, the knowledge Barton was nearby, the end of a day well spent—especially after it had begun badly—enveloped her. She felt as if her heart, long-welded, was creaking open. She took the inexplicable feeling of well-being as some kind of sign. A turning point. A *coda* in the song of her life.

"You have a lovely touch," Truitt said, when she finished.

She rubbed her hands together. "I guess it's like riding a bicycle. You never forget."

"Could you help me to my room? I'm sleeping upstairs for tonight. That young man…what's his name?

"Abbot?"

"Yes. Abbot. Volunteered to sleep in the basement so I could have his room. I'm not sure I can make it by myself."

"Of course." Standing, she put her hand under his elbow and steadied him as he pushed up from the chair.

Chapter 12 ~ A Delicate Balance

"May I call you Pinetta?" he asked.

"Yes…Truitt," she said, walking beside him up the stairs.

"I was dreading coming here," he said. "I live alone. The thought of being surrounded…in a houseful of people…"

"We respect each other's privacy." She opened the door to Abbot's room. "You'll only need to make the climb one more night. After Millie leaves, you'll move into her room."

"You'll miss her."

"I will. But it's time for me to have a life of my own. Do you need help with anything?"

"Yes. Could you come in for a moment?"

Pinetta followed him. He pointed with his cane at the open suitcase on the floor. "Underneath those clothes on the right. There's a folder. Could you get it for me?"

She obliged, pulling out a tattered manila folder, the tab labeled "Song of Eventide."

"Is this what you wanted?" she asked.

"Yes. Will you play it for me sometime? After you've practiced?"

She thumbed through the staff paper. "You wrote this?"

"It isn't finished. Not sure it ever will be."

Pinetta carried the music to her room.

On Thanksgiving Day Nestor offered his place at the head of the table to Ivy Leigh. She declined, adding, "You're the manager now. I'm visiting," and took her place next to Torbert.

Nestor knew better than to argue.

He addressed the group. "It's our tradition, before we say grace, to say what we're thankful for."

Holding Torbert's hand, Ivy Leigh said, "This man," and announced they were engaged. Torbert added he was thankful for his son and that "Ham has found the place where he belongs."

Ham expressed thanks for his father, the prospect of a new mother, whom he already loved, and the progress made on the staircase the last two days.

Nestor said he was thankful for his wife and baby.

Agnes, never a woman of few words, clung to Nestor's hand and turned to their guests. "I'm thankful I don't have to leave tomorrow like I did last year. I'm thankful for my husband, who kept loving me, even when I was foolish, thankful for all of you, especially Ivy Leigh, who I want to be like when I grow up."

Truitt, seated between Agnes and Pinetta, said, "I'm thankful for a place to stay till I'm better. I hope I won't be too much bother."

Pinetta wanted to say she was thankful for a second chance at love, but only said, "I'm thankful for Millie, who gave me a chance at a new life," not knowing how true this was.

Millie, forcing a smile, said she was thankful for her adopted family, especially Pinetta, and promised to call once a week. Then added, "You'll have to build another room, Nestor, if I'm going to have a place to stay when I come to visit. And I *will* come to visit."

After dinner, everyone, except Truitt, helped clear the table and clean the kitchen. Ivy Leigh left with Torbert and Ham to visit the friends she had not seen yet. Millie asked Nestor to take her on a farewell drive around the city and invited Truitt and Pinetta to ride with them.

Agnes, hoping dinner would stay down, returned to the sofa in the parlor. She had almost dozed off when she heard the back door open and footsteps in the kitchen.

Then Barton stepped into the parlor. "What are you doing here by yourself?"

"Everyone has gone for a drive. I didn't want to risk it. Did you have a nice time?"

He pulled up a chair and sat next to her. "Yeah. This is great. I didn't know how I was going to catch you alone."

Agnes sat up. "Is something the matter?"

"Not yet. But you'd better keep an eye on Abbot and Prudence. They're up to something."

Chapter 13

Partings

Pinetta Fraleigh was the only one to brave the bitter early morning air to wave goodbye from the porch. To Millie, snuggled between Nestor and Ham on her way to the train station, and to Ivy Leigh and Torbert, driving to Highway 501.

Both vehicles out of sight, Pinetta stepped inside the warm house. Pausing in the doorway of Millie's room, she imprinted the scene on her mind. Then stripped the bed, remaking it with white sheets and a striped bedspread, transforming the room to Truitt's.

Gathering up the pink-flowered sheets, she headed to the washing machine.

Barton, going upstairs to work, surprised her in the hall.

"They're gone then?" he asked.

"Yes."

He touched her arm. "You okay?"

She clutched the laundry tighter. "Yes. Thank you for asking."

"Good. Send Abbot up to tell me when breakfast is ready. He and Prudence are heading to Raleigh today, so they'll be awake soon."

He gave her arm a quick squeeze—his hand, warm and strong, nothing like Guy Henry's bony fingers, perpetually cold.

She called after him "Be careful not to—"

He peered over the banister. "What?"

She stopped herself. *Don't nag about everyone being asleep.*

"Be careful…not to…bump into Agnes if she's running to the bathroom."

Tea at Kimball Pines

This made no sense. Agnes had her own bathroom. But it was better than nothing.

"I'll tiptoe past," he said.

Humming, Pinetta entered the kitchen and opened the cabinet to get her teacup.

On top of the dinner plates—out of place—was a pie plate, holding an envelope.

She lifted out the dish and set it on the counter. The envelope was addressed to her. She opened it and read:

Dear Pinetta,

During the many years I've known her, Bridey Ludlow brought more than one pie over here. I never had the nerve to throw away the whole pie plate like you did, but not because I didn't want to. Here's a replacement, so you won't have to explain. I'm glad you decided to stay when Millie went home. Agnes is going to need you, and so is Truitt.

~Ivy Leigh

Pinetta read the letter again on her way to her room, placed it in her dresser drawer, and marched back to the stove and into the future.

Nestor and Ham drove home in silence, bearing the same grief. Millie had become a mother to them—though none of the three had ever stated the obvious—drawn them to her heart, nurtured, loved them, called them "her boys." She had never smothered, interfered, nor clamored for their attention. Only nurtured them gently, filling the shoes of the remarkable mothers they could barely remember, but whose memory they revered. They had found joy in tending to Millie, lavishing their unspent love on her.

"I sure am going to miss her," Ham said.

"Me, too. House won't be the same without her."

"Let's send her a box for Christmas. Get Muriel to make some of those almond cookies."

Nestor smiled. "Good idea."

Ham fixed his eyes on the road. "She's right, you know. If she's going to visit, we'll have to build another room." He glanced at Nestor. "Probably a good idea anyway...considering."

"Considering what?"

Ham recalled the speech he had rehearsed. "What with Founder's Day coming. Old friends coming back. We don't want to farm people out like—"

Chapter 13 ~ Partings

"If you mean like we did this week, that's not likely to happen again. My father won't be here much longer. That'll free up the basement. Truitt is only temporary. Things will be fine."

Coached the day before by Ivy Leigh, Ham did his best to "be subtle."

"For now. But don't you think we should plan for the future?" Pausing: "If the house could support itself, you could spend more time in your greenhouse. Agnes could write."

Nestor knew a conspiracy when he heard one. "Sounds like you've been thinking about this for a while."

"Dad and I talked about it…while we were working."

Nestor's hands tightened on the steering wheel. "About—?"

"For one thing, we need another room. The dining room is big. We could take part of it and make another room on the front of the house with a nice view of the street."

"And—?"

"You're going to need a room for the baby. And you and Agnes need privacy. A place of your own, separate from the rest of the tenants instead of on the second floor."

"And where *exactly* would we build this room?"

"Close in the screened porch."

Nestor shook his head. "Agnes would never agree to that. It was Ivy Leigh's place. Her herbs, the dried flowers. Agnes would never let us tear out those cedar rafters."

Ham took a deep breath. "You wouldn't have to. Besides that, it was Ivy Leigh's idea."

"What?"

"We talked about it yesterday…me and my dad and her…when we were out driving. Ivy Leigh said we need to plan for the future…not just 'hang on for dear life' to what we've got."

"What about money?"

"I told you when I started the staircase. My college fund. Dad said I could use the money for whatever I wanted. And this is it."

Nestor was not convinced. "Permits."

"I'll take care of it."

"Building plans."

"Dad and I did some sketches last night. When he gets home, he's going to talk to Jonas Grinstead. If anyone would know how to add onto the house, it's him. In the meantime—"

Scowling, Nestor turned to him. "In the meantime, *Barton* can help you get started. Is that what this is all about?"

Warned Nestor would object, Ham remained stalwart. "If you'd come upstairs and see what your father's done…you'd have to admit he—"

"Who put you up to this?"

"Nobody," Ham said.

They lapsed into silence the rest of the way home.

When they arrived at the house, they found Pinetta, leaning against the sink, and thumbing through a tattered Betty Crocker Cookbook.

"Is Millie all right?" Pinetta asked.

"Yes," Ham said. "She's excited about seeing her family."

"Is Agnes awake?" Nestor asked, breezing by.

"She hasn't come down yet," Pinetta said. "Do you want breakfast?"

Nestor shook his head. "No, but could you make a couple of lunches for me and Agnes? We're going on a little trip today."

"Of course. Plenty of leftovers. Turkey or turkey?"

Too distracted to respond, Nestor kept moving, but Ham stopped and turned around.

"Miss Pinetta. You made a joke. Miss Millie would be proud."

Pretending to take inventory of the pantry, Pinetta glanced over her shoulder at Abbot and Prudence as they gobbled oatmeal and guzzled coffee. *Eating like truck drivers*, she thought. *Why does a woman as cultured as Vesper Kimball allow them in her home?*

Prudence wiped her mouth and dropped the napkin in her bowl. She stepped to the phone.

When she hung up, she snickered. "I'll never get used to life in a small town. Five minutes for a cab to show up? Amazing."

"Where are you going today?" Pinetta asked, hoping she sounded nonchalant.

"Vesper's house. Pick up a car and then drive to Raleigh."

Pinetta watered the fern in the window. "Pick up a car?"

"Yeah. She has three," Prudence said. "Mint condition and they just *sit* in her garage. I asked her if we could borrow one today."

Pinetta managed an offhand tone. "Don't you work today, Abbot?"

"Special assignment," he said. "Researching an article I pitched to the editor."

Chapter 13 ~ Partings

Pinetta was not convinced. "Since you're going to Raleigh, would you do me a favor? Go to the health food store for more tea. Rose hips for me, peppermint for Agnes."

"Good idea," Prudence said. "We'll buy oolong for Vesper."

Pinetta started toward her room. "I'll get my purse." She stopped and turned around. "You two are spending a lot of time with Mrs. Kimball."

Before Abbot could respond, Prudence spoke up. "She's filling us in on some of the older houses in town. Historic preservation is a hot topic right now. You know…the article?"

"That's why we're going to Raleigh," Abbot said, reddening. "Archives."

If Pinetta had not been anxious to get them out of the house, she would have questioned Prudence further. But eager to plan the day's meals for Barton, she handed them a $20 bill from her wallet and said goodbye. Gladly.

An hour later Agnes and Nestor climbed in their truck. Supplied with lunch, saltines, and empty paper bags, just in case, she assured him she "felt fine." Any risk was worth taking, if she could have time with the husband she loved.

"Where are we going?" she asked.

He turned right at the corner. "Someplace I should've taken you a long time ago."

She scrutinized her clothes. "Am I going to meet someone? I would've dressed better."

"You look fine. Now no more questions. Just relax and enjoy the ride."

Agnes fiddled with the lunch sacks. Something was wrong. Nestor was trying too hard to sound pleasant, his voice hollow and strained.

Dense mist blanketed the windshield. Nestor turned on the wipers.

"Thank you for inviting Ivy Leigh," Agnes said. "I feel better now that I've seen her."

"Sometimes I wish she would move back. Nothing's been the same since she left."

Stung, Agnes turned away, reminding herself what Ivy Leigh had said. *Nestor is not mad at you.* But he sure sounded like he was.

Afraid she would cry if she tried to talk, Agnes propped on the armrest and studied the rolling hills, fences, and old farmhouses rushing past the window. After an hour of steady speed and meaningless conversation, Nestor pulled into a gas station.

"You might want to go to the bathroom," he said. "We're heading off the main road."

When she returned from the restroom, she found him at the cash register.

A lanky, gray-haired man was handing change to Nestor. "I *thought* that was you at the gas pump. Good to see you again. How have you been? Heard you got married."

Nestor pocketed the money. "I did. Four months ago."

Agnes stepped beside him.

"This your wife?" the man asked, extending his hand.

Nestor put his arm around her. "This is Agnes."

"Pacer Mullins. Used to be this guy's boss."

"Really?" Agnes asked, happy to see a smiling face. "Was he a good worker?"

"Was going to make him assistant manager before he went running off to that Yankee school. You still in Dennisonville? Heard that ice storm last year hit y'all pretty hard."

"Yeah," Nestor said. "We're doing great. I had a friend help with the repairs. Things were slow for a while, but house is full now and we're still building."

Agnes blinked at Nestor. Who was this cheerful, personable guy chatting with an old friend about how good things were on Belmont Drive?

Pacer's voice softened. "Are you on your way to visit your mama's grave?"

Agnes' heart sank. *Cemetery?*

Nestor nodded. "I've never taken Agnes there."

Pacer spoke to Agnes. "You take care of this guy. And if he ever needs straightening out, you know where to find me." Turning to Nestor: "Don't be a stranger, hear?"

Clouds gathering, Nestor drove down a rutted dirt road. The day turned grayer, mist heavier. Reaching the corner of a low stone wall, he drove alongside to the arched entrance of Evergreen Cemetery. He turned, curved right, and pulled off the path.

Parking under a gnarled tree, he got out and walked around to the passenger side. Warning Agnes not to slip on the wet leaves, he helped her out and took her hand. Silent, he led her past two headstones to a third.

He pointed to the inscription. "You need to see this."

Chapter 13 ~ *Partings*

Clinging to his hand, Agnes read:

Katherine Quentin Carlyle
1927-1953
Maria Enid Carlyle
Vera Evangeline Carlyle
September 10, 1953
Earth has no sorrow that Heaven cannot heal

"I know you and Ivy Leigh are concocting a little plan to get my father to stay," Nestor said, his voice edgy, "but I thought if you saw this for yourself, you'd understand why I can *never* forgive him and why it would be better for all of us if he would just—"

But a very different scene played out than the one he had intended.

The wife he had hoped to reason with sank to her knees on the wet ground. "So sad. They're buried together? Why didn't you tell me?"

Nestor went down on one knee beside her. "I wanted you to see what my father walked away from and how he—"

She pulled free of him and scraped frantically, sweeping away the pile of dead leaves on the grave. Her voice shattered the stillness of the cemetery. "Look at this mess. Someone should be taking care of this. Why didn't we bring flowers? You *knew* we were coming."

She sprang up and sprinted, slipping, toward the stone wall, leaned over it, and vomited. Then she plopped down, cross-legged on the wet ground, and cried.

Nestor, heartsick, hurried over and tried to pull her up, but she wouldn't budge.

"Please get up," he said. "The ground is wet. You'll catch cold."

Head bowed, she sucked in a lungful of air and lifted her eyes, brimming with tears, to meet his. Exhausted, sick, and grieving over a woman she had never met, Agnes was powerless to stop the flow of words, and spilled them out, only half aware of what she was saying.

"I *know* what you're doing. You thought if you brought me here and showed me that"—she pointed to Katherine's headstone—"I'd feel sorry for you and understand why you hate your father."

Bending over, he put his hand under her elbow. "Please get up. I didn't mean to—"

She scrambled up, facing him. "But when I look at that grave, do you know what I see? A young father, crushed by the loss of his wife and daughters, weeping over *that grave*."

"Please, Agnes, get in the truck. It's cold. I'm sorry. I'm sorry."

She stood her ground, gesturing wildly at the grave, her voice growing hoarse. "I'm sorry he was too *weak*. He should've stayed…tried to be a father to you, but when he knew he couldn't, he did what was best for *you*." She poked his chest. "He left you with a family who loved you. And you turned out all right, didn't you? Never lacked for anything, did you?"

"I know," Nestor said. "I know." He stepped beside her and edged her toward the truck.

"He didn't have to come back," she said, jerking free, striding ahead. "He could've stayed away. But *something* made him want to find you. Did you ever one time stop to think what courage that took? I'm sick and tired of watching you ignore him. If an old stray dog came up to the house, you'd at least give him some scraps."

When they reached the truck, Nestor took off Agnes' wet coat and gave her his. Then he settled her in the front seat. All cried out, heart emptied, weeks of unspoken words unlocked and let loose, she sniffled one final time as he closed the door.

As Nestor started the truck and drove slowly away, Agnes looked back.

"Next time we come we're bringing flowers," she said, her voice as gray as the day.

She moved the sack lunches to the floor, laid her head on Nestor's leg, and pretended to sleep as they drove home.

When they came into the kitchen, they heard music coming across the hall.

"Come on," Nestor said. "You need to go to bed and get warmed up."

Resisting, Agnes stopped at the parlor door and peeked in.

Pinetta was seated at the piano. Truitt in a chair next to her.

Agnes opened the door.

"Don't you want to go upstairs?" Nestor asked.

"No." Agnes walked past the piano on her way to the sofa.

Pinetta looked up. "You're back early. I thought you'd be gone most of the day. Your picnic get rained out?"

Chapter 13 ~ *Partings*

Nestor followed Agnes to the sofa and helped her take off her coat. "Things didn't work out like we planned."

"Like *you* planned," Agnes mumbled. She sank down and reached for the afghan at the foot of the sofa. Pulling it over her shoulders, she curled up, facing away from the others.

Confused, Pinetta left the piano. "Can I do anything?"

"Not now," Nestor said. "Let her rest. She was sick again." He motioned for Pinetta to follow him into the hall and closed the door behind them.

Truitt stood and gathered up the music.

"Beautiful song," Agnes said, her voice muffled by the sofa.

"I'm sorry. What?"

Eyes still closed, Agnes turned her head. "Beautiful song. Schumann?"

"No. Spenlow."

"I didn't know you were a composer. What's it called?"

"'Song of Eventide.'"

Pinetta returned and spoke to Truitt. "Nestor has phone calls to make and asked us to keep an eye on Agnes. I need to take coffee to Barton and Ham. Could you sit here a while?"

"Sure." He lowered his voice. "What's wrong with Agnes? Flu?"

"No. Morning sickness. With some women it lasts all day."

She left the room. Truitt started playing. His left arm, still unhealed, in his lap. His right hand playing the melody. He began to sing.

When the day begins to fade, evening comes, and all is night, I think of you...I think of you...

Rain, slow, ceaseless, sleeting, slipped from the seamless gray sky.

Lulled by his soothing voice, Agnes drifted off. *I think of you. I think of you.*

The cemetery reappeared. Leaves blanketing a grave, three names etched on the headstone. The woman who might have been a second mother. Girls who might have been like sisters. Agnes mourned, as if she had known them, loved them, buried them this morning.

On the third floor Barton stopped hammering to peer outside. How many gloomy days like this had he been stranded in a dingy bus station when his wife at the time had had enough and said goodbye? He shuddered at the memory.

For now, at least, he had a roof over his head, a place to hang his hat for a few days more. Companionship—though not with his son. The work was ahead of schedule. Once done, Nestor would ask him to leave.

Ham stepped up the unfinished staircase and stared out the round window facing north. "Looks like snow. I hope Millie will be okay. It's a long way home for her."

"It's always a long way home," Barton said. "Wherever you're going."

Descending the stairs, Ham sat on the second step. "I'm sorry things haven't worked out liked you hoped."

Slipping the hammer into his tool belt, Barton leaned against the window ledge. "Can't complain. Got more than I hoped for. If it hadn't been for Agnes…and you…Nestor would've kicked me out long before now. But he's not going to put up with me much longer. Now that we're almost done."

"Maybe. Maybe not. I don't want you to get your hopes up, but if you can be patient a little longer, things may work out."

"I have to face facts. I came to my senses too late."

Pinetta, tray in hand, appeared in the hall. "I wondered why it got so quiet up here. I brought coffee. Are you going to stop for lunch?"

Barton looked at his watch. "You're always on schedule, aren't you?"

Pinetta's forehead wrinkled. Was this a compliment?

"I try to be," she said. "Good nutrition is important."

Good nutrition is important? Stop talking. Saying nothing would be better.

"We'll be down in a while," Ham said.

Pinetta started down. On the second floor she met Nestor coming from his room.

He was carrying a suitcase.

"Nestor?" she said. "What are you doing?"

Holding up his hand to silence her, he whispered. "Is Agnes still asleep?"

"She was a minute ago. I came up to check on—"

He stepped closer. "I don't want anyone to know I'm leaving."

"Leaving?"

"Sh-hh. Meet me in the greenhouse. After I put this in the truck."

She followed him downstairs. He went through the front door. She walked past the parlor to be sure Agnes was still asleep and slipped out the back.

Nestor unlocked the greenhouse, and they stepped inside. "Where's your coat?"

Chapter 13 ~ Partings

"A little cold never hurt anybody," she said. "Now, what's wrong?"

"I just got off the phone with Margaret. I asked her if I could come visit for a few days. I'll drive the truck to the station and leave it there. Ham can pick it up later."

"But why?"

"I have to get away from here for a while." He ducked his head. "I hurt Agnes this morning. I've never done that before."

"What happened?"

He described Agnes' breakdown at the cemetery; crimson flooded Pinetta's face.

"You took a pregnant woman to the grave of a woman who died in childbirth? Don't you know the *moment* a woman knows she's pregnant, she starts worrying about her baby?"

"I…didn't think—"

"Well, you *should have*," Pinetta said, trembling with rage. "I had two miscarriages."

The cold rain dripped off the roof.

"I'm sorry," he said. "I didn't know."

"I never talk about it. But take it from me. You *must not* take Agnes back there again. Do you understand?"

"Yes. That's why I have to leave. My feelings for my father are clouding my judgment. I thought I could keep quiet till he was gone, but now…who knows when he'll leave?"

Pinetta folded her hands to stop them from shaking. "I don't know what happened between you two, but I've always believed a father deserves—"

Nestor's face darkened. "*Not now*. I only wanted to tell you what I was doing, so you can tell Agnes where I'll be. If I tell her myself, I won't be able to leave. And I *have* to go."

At the same time Nestor was driving to the train station, Abbot and Prudence were touring Raleigh, looking at office space in affordable neighborhoods.

"Irony, that's what it is," Prudence said, a city map unfolded in her lap. "Turn here."

Abbot obeyed. "What do you mean?"

"When I came to find Agnes, I was trying to save my career. I thought if I could apologize, my boss would welcome me back. But instead he fired me."

"That's the irony?"

"Left at the next corner. There." She pointed. "No. Because I was chasing after one author and found another." She patted his knee. "And your story is *way* better than hers."

"You mean the one you want me to write about Vesper?"

"There's 3402," she said. "Park here. We'll walk. Yes, of course, about her. That house is a museum. Frozen in time. People will buy the book for the photos alone."

He grabbed the umbrella and joined her on the sidewalk. "Don't we need some kind of permission?"

She strode toward the empty building with a "For Rent" sign in the window. "I've already figured that out. Better to market it as an 'unauthorized' biography anyway. Readers like those best."

"I hate to take advantage of her like that. She's been so nice to me."

Prudence waved her hand dismissively. "She never goes out. How will she know? Unless someone tells her, and no one will. Now where's that realtor?" She pressed her face to the window. "Think. This may be the home of O'Neill Publishing. And *you* will be my first client. How does that sound?" She motioned him forward. "Come on. Look inside."

Agnes opened her eyes and uncurled her right arm, cramped from being tucked under her chin so long. She rolled onto her back and blinked at the ceiling. Then peered out at the tree branches swaying in the wind. *What time is it?* She rolled over and sat up, surveying the empty parlor, door closed. *Why is it so quiet? No one would be out in this weather.* Light-headed, she steadied herself on the coffee table and stood up. *Hungry. Is that possible?* She walked to the door and opened it, scanning the hall as if expecting a ghost.

"Nestor?" she called.

Pinetta, hearing her voice, appeared in the kitchen door. "He's not here."

"Upstairs?"

"No."

"I need to find him. I said some things I shouldn't have."

"He won't be back for a while. I made soup. Want to try some?"

Agnes paused. "I probably should. Smells delicious. That's a good sign, isn't it?"

"It is." She beckoned her toward the kitchen. "Come. Sit down, dear."

Chapter 13 ~ *Partings*

Groggy as she was, Agnes couldn't believe what she was hearing. *Dear?* Pinetta never used pet names. Much less for her.

Agnes sat in the chair nearest the door. "It's so quiet. Where is everyone?"

Pinetta ladled turkey noodle soup into a bowl and set it on the table. "Barton and Ham are running errands. Took Truitt with them. Abbot and Prudence are in Raleigh."

"This smells so good," Agnes said, leaning over the bowl.

"Try the broth first. If it settles all right, you can try a mouthful of noodles. If you can keep this down, you'll feel better. You need some nutrition after—"

"After what?" Agnes asked, blowing on her spoon.

"After…you slept through lunch. It's half past three."

Pinetta, while chopping carrots and celery, had rehearsed her inevitable conversation with Agnes and vowed to keep away from the subject of Nestor as long as possible.

"My mom always made soup the day after Thanksgiving," Agnes said. "What time was Millie supposed to get home?"

"In time for dinner."

"Are you all right? I hate saying goodbye to my friends."

Pinetta sat across from her. "Better than I thought I'd be."

"How do you think Truitt is doing? I haven't been able to spend much time with—"

The doorbell rang. Pinetta answered and escorted Fiona Wilton into the kitchen.

Fiona, a shy girl of twenty, was Vesper's maid, a position she had inherited from her mother. Though often quizzed by the people of Dennisonville about "how Vesper Kimball lived," Fiona guarded Vesper's privacy like a knight, armored, bearing a shield.

Slim, green-eyed, with mousy brown hair, Fiona arrived for work every morning by six, served Vesper's breakfast, and prepared lunch, which she left in the refrigerator. Then she drove to Bellport for classes at Willowbrook. Fiona hoped to become a nurse.

"Hello, Fiona," Agnes said. "Have a nice Thanksgiving?"

Fiona pulled out a chair. "I did."

"Are you sure?" Agnes asked. "Doesn't sound like it."

"I always dread the holidays for Mrs. Kimball. We invite her to our house every year, but she stays home in case her son shows up. He never does. I went over after dinner and took her a plate and sat with her while she ate. It was all I could do."

Agnes frowned. "Has anyone ever tried to talk to him?"

"He doesn't come around enough for anyone to do that."

"It's nice Mrs. Kimball has you, Fiona," Pinetta said.

"No one can take the place of your own children, no matter how much you love them. But Robert Kimball is not why I'm here. I've come about your tenants."

"Abbot and Prudence?" Pinetta asked.

Fiona nodded. "At first I was thrilled Mrs. Kimball was finally inviting people in. She adores Abbot. I think in some ways he replaces Robert. Or maybe Edward."

"Edward?" Pinetta asked.

"The son she lost when he was two," Fiona said.

"So what about Abbot and Prudence?" Agnes asked.

"Abbot won Mrs. Kimball's heart the moment she met him, when he helped her after she fell. When I came to work that morning and found a man in the house, I couldn't believe it."

"He's charming," Agnes said. "No doubt about it."

"But then that woman started coming with him," Fiona said. "I didn't like her from the very start. She's always snooping, picking things up, walking around the house."

"Have you missed anything?" Pinetta asked.

"Not that I've noticed," Fiona said. "But I'm not sure about the upstairs. I don't go through Mrs. Kimball's things. And there are four other bedrooms besides hers."

"So what made you decide to talk to us?" Agnes asked.

"Day before yesterday, I was putting away some laundry in Mrs. Kimball's room, and I found Abbot going through her dresser. He *told* me she had sent him to find her glasses."

"You didn't believe him?" Pinetta asked.

"She'd never allow a man in her bedroom. Besides that, I was in the house. She would have called for me."

"I asked them just this morning about why they're spending so much time with her," Pinetta said. "They *said* they're writing an article on historic homes."

Fiona shook her head. "He's writing a book about Mrs. Kimball. I've seen it."

Chapter 13 ~ Partings

"Does she know that?" Agnes asked.

"Yes, and she's thrilled. She's always been worried about preserving her family history. But why she trusts *them* to write the story, I don't know."

"What can we do?" Agnes asked.

"Can you find out what they're up to? It's not my place to tell Mrs. Kimball who she can invite into her own home. But if I had my way, neither of them would be allowed in again."

"I'll talk to Nestor," Agnes said, "and call you later. Try not to worry."

Fiona wrote down her phone number and stood to go. "Thank you. I feel better."

"I'll walk you out," Pinetta said and led Fiona into the hall.

Agnes tapped her fingers on the table. *We cannot have this,* she thought. *I'll call Ivy Leigh. She always knows what to do.* Before she could reach the phone, it rang.

"Magnolia Arms."

"Agnes? This is Josh McGarry. I'm returning Nestor's call."

"I'm not sure where he is right now. Can you hold on till I find him?"

"No. That's all right. He left me a message, asking if I could teach his class this week. Tell him I'll be glad to."

"Teach his class?"

"While he's out of town."

Agnes did not want to appear uninformed. "Okay...I'll tell him."

She hung up the phone, opened the back door, and stepped onto the driveway. Both trucks were gone—Nestor's and Ham's.

Pinetta returned to the kitchen the same time Agnes did.

"That was Dr. McGarry on the phone," Agnes said. "He said Nestor's out of town."

Till this moment Pinetta had distanced herself from the day-to-day concerns of the household, thinking of herself as a guest, temporary. But now, Agnes had no one but her.

"Nestor told me what happened at the cemetery this morning," Pinetta said.

"Oh. So...he went for a drive? He does that when he needs to think."

"He asked me to tell you again how sorry he is."

"Did he say when he'd be back?"

Pinetta pulled out a chair. "Could you sit down a minute?"

Agnes complied. "You're scaring me. Where's Nestor?"

Pinetta sat next to her. "He thought he should get away for a few days. To get some perspective. So…he called Margaret."

Relief washed over Agnes' face. "He went to see Jonas and Margaret?"

"Took the train. The men have gone to pick up the truck."

Agnes sprang up and threw her arms around Pinetta. "Thank you. I'm glad Nestor had you to talk to. You're a good friend."

In Pinetta's walled heart, a tiny fissure opened.

Chapter 14

Tables for Four

The day after Thanksgiving Jonas Grinstead drove his sister Iris to the Plainview train station. Recently widowed, she had chosen to spend the holiday with her "little brother Jonesie" rather than endure her first holiday alone without her husband. They waited on the platform till the last possible minute. Then Jonas hugged her and watched as her train departed for Texas, where their other sisters would be waiting to meet her.

When Jonas came home, he found his wife Margaret testing Christmas tree lights.

"Is Iris all right?" she asked, a tangle of green cords dangling from her hand.

"Yes. She mentioned Christmas again. I didn't have the heart to tell her we're going to the Magnolia Arms. Still want to shop for a tree this afternoon?"

Head down, she pretended to focus on her task. "Yes...but we'll have to come home early for dinner, so we can get back to the station."

Jonas plugged in the strand of lights, all working. "What for?"

"Nestor's coming for a few days."

"Really? Why?"

Margaret relayed her conversation with Nestor, ending with his anguish over the trip to the cemetery. She braced herself for Jonas' reaction. Where Agnes was concerned—the nearest he had come to having a daughter—he was a bear defending a cub.

Margaret had expected a puzzled look, maybe a wrinkled lip, but not a frown so fierce his lips turned white.

"No. No. This is not acceptable," he said, shaking his head and starting up the stairs.

She called after him. "Where are you going?"

"To pack a bag. Nestor can spend the night, but first thing in the morning, I'm taking him home. He can't leave Agnes at a time like this. Doesn't he know her *at all*?"

"He wouldn't leave her, if he didn't feel it was best. You don't know Nestor like I do."

He met her at the foot of the stairs. "And *you* don't know Agnes like *I* do. She puts up a good front, but she's very sensitive. Who's taking care of *her* while he's gone?"

Tugging on his hand, she guided him to the living room. "Pinetta…and Nestor's father."

"Pinetta? She doesn't have a compassionate bone in her body. And how long has Agnes known Nestor's father? A few days? He's a *stranger*."

"—and Ham." Only this silenced Jonas. Margaret drew him to the sofa and sat next to him. "For your information, Agnes likes Barton. You know how she is about underdogs."

"She's trying to force them to reconcile, isn't she?"

"Being a peacemaker is her life's calling. She got us back together, didn't she? And there couldn't have been two people more stubborn than us."

Ham found Nestor's truck at the Dennisonville train station; he stopped and held out the keys to Barton.

"Nestor wouldn't want me driving his truck," Barton said. "I'll drive this one."

"He's not here now, is he? Besides, that truck belongs to Agnes. Jonas gave it to *her*."

Barton took the keys. Truitt, seated in the middle, slid over to the passenger side when Barton got out.

"There's always someone coming or going around here, isn't there?" Truitt asked.

Ham pulled forward and waited for Barton. "What do you mean?"

"First I came. Then Millie left. Now Nestor. It's like there's a revolving door."

"It's just how life is around here. Some people stay a few days. Some longer. Depends on why they came in the first place…and what they need."

Chapter 14 ~ Tables for Four

"I've always wondered why *you* moved here. Everyone at Brighton Park thought you'd take over for your dad when he retired."

Ham had only one reason. Lorna Maron. She had arrived at Brighton Park, broken-hearted, fleeing her past. A gifted pianist, she had stopped playing when her boyfriend, threatened by her success, had cast her aside. Courage gone, she fell victim to stage fright.

Agnes had persuaded her to return to the piano and asked Ham for his help. Every day for months he escorted Lorna to the rehearsal hall and waited backstage as she practiced. While he watched her from the wings, he fell in love.

He mistook her kindness for mutual interest and resolved to declare his intentions, not knowing Lorna was already in love with someone else. The night of her comeback performance, Ham waited backstage with a dozen roses to present after her encore.

And then watched, doomed, as Oliver Martin Farrell presented Lorna with his own bouquet. Bereft, Ham could not bear the pain of seeing Lorna every day. He quit his assistant janitor job at Brighton Park and moved to the Magnolia Arms.

But never revealed the real reason to anyone.

"It was supposed to be temporary," Ham said, "but after I'd been here a while, I felt like I belonged. Dad understood. He always wanted me to have my own life."

"I *get* that. The feeling you belong. There's something about that house. Makes you feel like…it's the place you should've lived your whole life."

"Agnes thought that after she'd only seen a *photo* of the house."

"I never thought of staying here. But I could pay rent here as easily as anywhere else. Make a fresh start. Maybe teach music like I planned."

"You'd be welcome to stay, Doc. And you'd be doing Agnes a favor. She's at her best when she has someone to take care of. And to be honest, we could use the money."

Truitt stroked his chin. "I'll talk to Agnes when we get back. I've never done anything so reckless—just up and move for no good reason."

Barton pulled into the driveway behind Ham. He grabbed the umbrella off the seat and helped Truitt up the steps into the kitchen. "Easy there, Doc. You don't want to fall and undo all your progress."

Truitt thanked him and went to find Agnes.

Tea at Kimball Pines

When Ham came in, Barton met him and held out his hand. "Thanks for letting me help with the staircase. At least I did *something* for Nestor. I'm going to pack now. I hate to ask—"

"Pack? Why?"

"I can't stay here…now that I've run my son out of his own home."

"You can't leave. You'll break Agnes' heart. Besides that, the work's not done."

"Agnes won't want me to stay." Barton said. "Now that Nestor—"

"Wait here. I'll prove it to you."

Ham stepped across the hall, bumping into Truitt, hurrying to his room.

"Agnes says I can stay," Truitt said.

"We're going out for dinner," Ham said. "Want to join us?"

"Not this time," Truitt said. "Gotta call my landlord and get the ball rolling."

Agnes and Pinetta, books in their laps—neither reading—looked up when Ham entered.

"You two get your coats," Ham said. "Barton and I are taking you out for dinner."

"I'm too much of a mess," Agnes said. "And I can't eat anyway."

All Pinetta had to hear was 'Barton.' She hopped up. "He's right. A change of scenery will do us all good. I'll get my coat."

Ham watched her go and sat next to Agnes. "I'll drive Pinetta. You ride with Barton. He's trying to leave. You have to talk him out of it."

"He said that?"

"Just now. If he goes before Nestor comes home, all this trouble will have been for nothing."

While Agnes was upstairs getting ready, Ham called Muriel. He explained they were on their way—and why. "No questions about Nestor. And be prepared. Agnes looks terrible."

Muriel reserved Agnes' favorite table and greeted them at the door when they arrived. Grateful for Ham's warning—she had seen Agnes at her worst, but nothing like this—she escorted the party of four to their table and sent a server.

They placed their orders and sank into an awkward silence. Though each felt obligated to comfort the others, none of them felt like talking.

Pinetta, thanks to Ham's subtle maneuvering, was seated next to Barton, so close his arm brushed hers as he reached for the sugar. She could hardly breathe.

Chapter 14 ~ Tables for Four

Ham, whose talk with Truitt had drawn Lorna from the shadows of his mind, needed time to coax her back out of sight.

Barton added the pain on Agnes' face to his catalogue of sins.

And Agnes wished in vain she could take back what she said to Nestor.

So, they sat together, each alone, stirring cream into coffee and squeezing lemon into tea, till Agnes breached the silence.

"Fiona Wilton came by today."

A brilliant stroke. With five words, Agnes converted the tattered company into a casual gathering of friends who had met to share the news of the day.

Their talk turned to Vesper Kimball and her need for protection.

Though not one of them had ever met her.

Sneaking out without saying goodbye was the hardest thing Nestor had ever done. But once he drove away, he felt strangely relieved. He had not been himself since his father had arrived. Resentment had risen from the tomb he thought was sealed.

Nestor boarded the train for Plainview. He stared at the ceaseless rain pelting the window and thought of how often he had put Agnes on this train and vowed, if she ever agreed to marry him, they would never be parted again.

Yet here he was, hurtling away from her as fast as the wheels clacked over the tracks. She would be better off without him…for now.

The train pulled into the station. Jonas took his suitcase; Margaret wrapped her arms around him. Nestor relaxed and breathed in her warmth.

They caught up on the mundane news on the way home. After a sandwich, Nestor went upstairs for a bath and then fell asleep in the room Jonas had designed as a study for Agnes.

Downstairs Margaret dialed Ivy Leigh every hour. At last she answered.

"This is Margaret. Have a good—?"

"What's wrong?"

"What do you mean 'what's wrong.' I just wanted to see if you got home safely."

"In the first place," Ivy Leigh said, "you never call this late for *any* reason, and in the second place, I hear it in your voice. Is Jonas all right?"

"Yes. We're fine. I wanted to invite you for lunch tomorrow…with Nestor."

"Nestor? He's *here*?"

Margaret told the story. "Can you come at 9:00? I'm sending the boys to the Drifters' Rest in the morning to 'discuss building plans,' so you and I can figure out what to do."

Both half-sick—for entirely different reasons—neither Pinetta nor Agnes ate much. While the men discussed Stanley tools and the next day's chores, Pinetta gazed out the window. The rain had stopped. The stars were out. A sublime end to the day.

"Hello."

Marooned in her thoughts, she had missed Agnes' trying to signal her. Lute Monroe, red knitted cap in hand, had lumbered up and wedged the toe of his boot against Barton's chair.

"Fancy finding you folks here," Lute said. "You been Christmas shopping today?"

"Hello, Lute," Agnes said, glancing at Pinetta. "No. We just wanted to relax a while. But"—she glanced at her watch—"we were just saying how we ought to go home."

Taking Agnes' cue, Ham pushed back his chair. "I'll get the check."

Lute twisted his cap. "I was wondering if you folks were coming to the meeting Monday night."

"What meeting?" Barton asked.

"The planning meeting. For Founder's Day. I know Pinetta is coming. She's playing the piano for the choir."

Leaning one elbow on the table, Barton peered at Pinetta. "You play the piano, too? Is there anything you can't do?"

Agnes stood and took her coat from the back of the chair. "The only thing Pinetta can't do is be disorganized."

Pinetta managed a smile, thin and straight as a tear in a sheet of paper.

Ham paid the bill and hurried back to the table. "Would you ride home with me, Agnes? We need to talk about Truitt. Barton can take Pinetta home."

"Glad to." Barton said, placing his hand on Pinetta's chair.

Lute stepped back. Pinetta rose, said good night, and, light as a feather, walked ahead of Barton to the door. Lute watched her go.

Agnes touched his arm. "I'll see you at the meeting, if I'm up to it."

Chapter 14 ~ Tables for Four

"Sure," Lute said. He pulled his cap over his ears and trudged away, head down.

"Poor Lute," Agnes said, buttoning her coat. "We don't need to talk about Truitt, by the way. I already told him he could stay."

Ham lowered his voice. "I know. I made that up so Pinetta could ride with Barton."

Prim and composed, Pinetta sat motionless as Barton drove. She imprinted each detail of the beautiful night on her mind. She wished Barton would talk, so she could respond. But he was silent, distant. Thinking about Nestor? She thought of reassuring him.

"I'm sure Nestor is there by now," she said. "I could call the Grinsteads when we get back. I don't know them well, but I'm sure they wouldn't mind."

"No. It's all right. I'm used to going to sleep wondering what my son is doing."

"Awful, isn't it? Wondering where people are?"

He glanced over. "Who do you wonder about?"

She bit her lip. The first personal question he had asked, and the answer was *my ex-husband*. "Millie. It's going to be hard…getting used to being without her."

"But she didn't leave because she can't stand the sight of you."

She wanted so much to touch his arm. "Nestor will be back after he's had time to think. You'll see."

"You sound like Ham," Barton said. "He told me not to give up." He stretched out his arm on the back of the seat. "What do you think? Should I stay?"

"Yes," Pinetta said. "If you leave, you'll never know what might have happened. If you stay…things might work out."

The next morning Jonas pounded on Nestor's door at 8:00. "Rise and shine."

"I'm awake." Nestor rolled out of bed and hurried to dress. When he came downstairs, he found Margaret holding his coat at the front door. He slipped his arms into the sleeves.

"Better hurry," she said. "Jonas is already in the car."

He kissed her cheek. "I've missed you."

"I've missed you, too. Now get going."

Ivy Leigh arrived at 9:00. They went to work. By the time the men returned, lunch was ready, and the Christmas tree, angel-topped, dazzled in the corner.

Nothing like a cozy atmosphere to encourage open, honest communication.

At least that was the plan.

Margaret, watching from the kitchen window, studied the men as they got out of the car. Nestor, looking sullen, swiped his hair from his forehead as he stalked to the house. Jonas, lagging behind, rolled his eyes once Nestor's back was turned.

Margaret called to Ivy Leigh. "I don't think things went well."

Sprinting to the door, Ivy Leigh swung it open as Nestor reached the porch.

"You haven't changed much in 24 hours," she said, too pertly.

"I wish that were true," Nestor said, giving her hand a quick squeeze as he brushed past her on his way upstairs.

"Uh…lunch is ready," she said to the back of his head.

"Down in a minute."

Jonas went to the kitchen where Margaret was taking oatmeal cookies from the oven.

"Hi," she said. How'd it go?"

He took a glass from the cabinet. "I did what you said—talked about nothing but the house. Didn't bring up Agnes. But it wasn't easy. I wanted to take him by the scruff of—"

She silenced him with a peck on the cheek. "Thank you."

The four of them gathered at the table: men, exasperated, at opposite ends; women, still hopeful, across from each other. Complete strangers, thrown together, would have been more at ease. When they joined hands to say grace, Nestor gripped the women's fingers; their touch consoled him. Margaret opened her eyes to peek at Ivy Leigh, who shook her head, forbidding her to cry. Blessing concluded, they passed dishes without being asked, served their plates without comment. Like latecomers crammed onto the last remaining seat on the bus, they wondered who would wriggle first, so they could all get comfortable.

Ivy Leigh zeroed in on Margaret, who read her meaning. *You first.*

A veteran school teacher, Margaret was an expert at forced pleasantness. Eyes wide, voice lilting: "Did you make any progress on the remodeling plans?"

Chapter 14 ~ Tables for Four

Jonas spooned potato salad onto his plate. "It's going to take a lot of work."

Blank-faced, Nestor sipped from his glass.

Ivy Leigh jumped in. "Think, not long ago, you were worried about keeping the rooms full, and now you're adding on to the house. By the way, how's Truitt?"

Nestor blinked. "Truitt? I don't know."

Margaret giggled. "What do you mean, 'you don't know'? You only saw him yester—"

Nestor slammed down his glass. Water shot up, spraying Ivy Leigh. "I *didn't* see him *yesterday*, because I sneaked out of my house like a burglar with the silverware in my suitcase."

Without a word, Ivy Leigh dabbed water off her chin and her placemat.

Jonas threw down his napkin. "All right, that's enough. This is ridiculous." Elbow on the table, he pointed at Nestor. "Tell us *why* you're here."

The women froze. Nestor rubbed the space between his eyes. Moments passed. Then he patted Ivy Leigh's arm—"Sorry…for the mess"—and faced Jonas. "Where do I start?"

Jonas pointed his thumbs outward. "You know the Bobbsey Twins. What one didn't tell me, the other one did. So, I know all about your dad. There's no need—"

"Barton," Nestor said.

"Excuse me."

"I refuse to call him *dad*."

"Okay. I know about 'Barton.' What we need to do is figure out where you go from here. Because, if you think I'm going to stand by while you make Agnes miserable—"

Under the table Margaret gripped her husband's knee. "What Jonas is *trying* to say is we want to help…if we can. Isn't that why you came? To ask for help?"

Nestor slouched in his chair. "Yeah. That, plus I thought Agnes could use a break from me. She's been so sick…and I'm making her worse. I know that."

"You got that right," Jonas said. "I can't believe you actually had the nerve to take her—"

Ivy Leigh threw up her hands. "Are we back to that?" She glared at Jonas. "Nestor's *here* now. Being mad at him will get us nowhere."

Jonas pulled on his left ear. "You're right. Pass the pickles."

"Sweet?" Ivy Leigh asked, eyebrows raised.

"Kosher," Jonas said, retreating so the women could brood over their young.

Nestor smirked. "I just spread joy and sunshine wherever I go, don't I?"

"Actually, you do," Ivy Leigh said. "That's why I hate to see you like this. You hardly said two words to me while I was there for Thanksgiving. I felt like a stranger."

Nestor shrugged. "It's a big house. I've gotten good at hiding out."

"Well, you can't hide out any longer," Margaret said. "Your father…uh, Barton…is back in your life, whether you like it or not."

"And whether he leaves or stays," Ivy Leigh said, "he'll be a factor in your life from now on. You know that, right? Agnes is not going to let go of this."

"She can never let well enough alone," Nestor said.

Jonas reached for the pepper. "I'm glad she didn't let me alone. If she had, I'd still be moping over Margaret instead of sitting here next to her."

"Agnes said I treat stray dogs better," Nestor said, ducking his head. "Maybe if I'd *known* Barton was coming…but he showed up out of nowhere. I wasn't ready."

"It's understandable," Margaret said. "All those years without a word? No one would've known what to say."

"Agnes had no problem," he said.

"Of course not. She has no history with him," Ivy Leigh said. "But remember last year when her brother Toby 'showed up out of nowhere'? She wasn't going to let *him* stay either."

"Till I talked her into it," Jonas said.

"I forgot about that," Nestor said. "I'll have to remind her when I get home."

Margaret shook her head. "Not a good idea."

"Did Agnes tell you the advice I gave *her*?" Jonas asked.

Nestor piled ham on a slice of bread and folded it. "Yeah. You said to think of herself as Toby's friend. But this isn't the same thing. We're not talking about childish fights over the last cookie or whose turn it was in the front seat of the car."

"All right, then," Ivy Leigh said. "If you can't think of Barton like *that*, can you consider him a tenant? Someone who wandered in, needing help?"

Chapter 14 ~ Tables for Four

"Remember that Mr. Colville?" Margaret asked. "Meanest man who ever walked through the door, and within 48 hours Nestor had him planting petunias, happy as a lark."

"That was different," Nestor said. "He'd had a hard life. Once I got him by himself and let him talk, I understood..."

Backed into a corner, he clammed up.

"You sent him home to his family," Ivy Leigh said. "Remember?"

"Yeah," Nestor said. "I told him he had nothing to lose."

"Maybe someone said that to Barton," Margaret said. "And that's why he came looking for you."

"Think about what you're asking me to do," Nestor said. "You want me to forget he took off while I was crying myself to sleep every night because I missed my mother?" Red-faced, he slammed both hands on the table. "He wasn't there when I *needed* him."

Margaret sat back. "We're not asking you to forget. That's impossible. And you have every right to be angry. All we're saying is now that Barton's back, you can't make him leave without...at least listening"—her voice faltered—"to his side of..."

Fingertips pressed to her lips, she fell silent.

Jonas reached for her hand. "What's wrong, Meggie?"

"Listen to me. Telling Nestor *not* to do the very thing I did to you." She turned to Nestor. "I sent Jonas away without...and look what it cost me. Years..."

Clearing her throat, Ivy Leigh lifted the pitcher and refilled half-full glasses.

"Don't say any more, Meg," Jonas said. "We agreed never to do this."

Nestor tapped his knife on the edge of his plate. "I'm sorry, Margaret. I'm sorry I came in here, dragging all my problems—"

"We *all* 'dragged our problems' in here," Jonas said. "You think there are only four of us at this table?" He shook his head. "Your father came with you. So did Agnes. Marshall Ransom came with Ivy Leigh, even though she's in love again and—"

Margaret interrupted. "Jonas. Don't."

"It's okay," Ivy Leigh said. "He's right. Nestor knows. He was with me when Marshall died. So were you, Megs."

"My father goes *everywhere* with me," Jonas said. "I'll go a while without thinking of him, and then sometimes, out of nowhere, something reminds me…I sneaked away from home without telling him, and he died before I could get back. I never got to tell him how sorry I was."

"Agnes told me," Nestor said.

"My mother said he forgave me," Jonas said. "Even repeated what he said. But I'd have given anything to hear the words myself. Your dad would, too. You owe him that much."

"You think he wants me to *forgive* him?"

"Why else would he have come?" Margaret asked. "He took a terrible risk facing you."

"You won't know till you ask," Ivy Leigh said.

Nestor shook his head. "I can't see myself doing that."

Ivy Leigh folded her arms. "Well, you'll have to figure something out. I've decided to have my wedding at the Magnolia Arms. And you'll need Barton's help to be ready in time."

Margaret's mouth dropped open.

Nestor's brow furrowed. "And when did you decide *this*?"

Ivy Leigh ran her finger around the rim of her glass. "I was going to tell you while I was there, but you didn't give me much of a chance, did you?"

"When's the wedding?" he asked.

That's what I'd like to know, Margaret thought.

"April…or May. March…maybe. In the spring."

Eager to move on, Jonas seized the moment. "You can stay here a few days longer. We'll need time to draw up the plans. Now, can we please change the subject so we can eat?"

Talk turned to the holidays and President Carter's brother Billy. When the meal was concluded, the men left the table; Jonas to his workshop, Nestor to call Agnes.

Humming, Ivy Leigh gathered the dishes and headed to the sink.

When Margaret was certain the men were out of earshot, she stepped next to her friend, presiding over a mound of suds, and whispered.

"You know perfectly well you're getting married at Charlotte Wrayburn's house next *month*."

"That was before," Ivy Leigh said.

"Before *what*?"

"Before Barton Carlyle showed up. Hand me that silverware and start drying."

Chapter 14 ~ Tables for Four

Margaret obeyed. "But Agnes will be"—she counted on her fingers—"five or six months pregnant by the spring. She can't host a wedding. What are you *thinking*?"

"She won't have to lift a finger. You and I will do everything. Pinetta can't cook worth beans, but she's great at organizing. Muriel will cater."

"Who'll run the Drifters' Rest while you're pulling off this out-of-town wedding?"

"Annabelle. She did it while I was gone for Thanksgiving, didn't she?"

Margaret wiped off the counter. "Have you forgotten I have job? I can't just leave in the middle of a semester. I'm head of the department."

"When's your spring break?" Ivy Leigh asked.

Agnes wasted no time. She was confident Nestor would return in a better frame of mind, but he might still insist Barton leave. These few days might be her only chance to learn where Barton had been, why he had stayed away.

She let him talk, crying while he described Nestor's mother, scowling when he listed the wives he had married and left. She did not reproach him, but often imagined grabbing him by the collar and shouting, *Did you never think about Nestor?*

Pinetta lavished her attention on him, understated though it was. She tried new recipes, made dessert every day, and kept Barton and Ham supplied with coffee while they worked. She scheduled an appointment at Mimi's Beauty Salon "for a trim" and asked to ride to Bellport with Agnes so she could get started on her Christmas shopping. She dropped Agnes off at the college and then headed downtown for a new dress, something bright for the holidays. Then to a gift shop for a journal. She had not kept one for years. But there was so much to write…now.

The night before Nestor came home, Agnes was working on the bills at the kitchen table when Prudence came in.

"You're up late," Prudence said.

Agnes kept her eyes on her checkbook. "You're *out* late."

"Just got in from Raleigh. Been painting my new office."

"So you'll be leaving soon?"

Prudence took off her coat. "No. I'd like to stay a while longer, if that's all right."

143

Tea at Kimball Pines

Agnes sealed and stamped the electric bill. "Long commute to Raleigh. I wouldn't think it would be worth your time."

"The office won't be ready for a few weeks...or months. It depends."

"Will Abbot go with you?"

Prudence reddened. "What do you mean?"

"You're working on a book together, aren't you? The one on Mrs. Kimball?"

Coat over her arm, Prudence backed toward the hall. "No. Not about *her*. Abbot is writing a...travel journal about his experiences in small towns. This is just one chapter."

Agnes laid down her pen. "Interesting. Who else has he interviewed?"

Hand behind her, Prudence steadied herself against the doorframe. "I'm not sure. People at local businesses...restaurants. Church activities, maybe?"

"Here's an idea," Agnes said. "Why don't I set up some interviews for Abbot? That way, he can get the whole story."

Prudence produced a fake grin. "Good idea. I'm sure he'd appreciate the help." She stepped into the hall and then turned back. "What about your book?"

"Right now, it's the least of my worries."

Nestor was coming home. As Agnes waited at the station, she remembered how often he had stood here, waiting for her. The train came into view, slowed, stopped. Nestor appeared. She rushed into his arms. He swept her up, twirling her around.

"I'm glad you're back," she said, "but you'd better put me down. I'm still a little queasy."

"Sorry," he said. "Wasn't thinking. I'm just happy to see you."

"I missed you," Agnes said. "I have so much to tell you—"

Someone tapped on her shoulder.

"Excuse me. Can you tell me the way to the Magnolia Arms?"

Agnes turned around...and stepped into the arms of Jonas Grinstead.

Chapter 15

Under Construction

Nestled between Nestor and Jonas, Agnes turned from one to the other.

"I can't believe it," she said. "A week ago I thought my life was ruined. And now here I am, riding along with my two favorite people in the world."

Nestor patted her leg. "You're not going to get rid of me that easily."

Jonas, satisfied Agnes was happy, let the couple talk as he gazed at the familiar sights of Dennisonville and fought back the nagging melancholy they evoked.

Until today, he had returned only twice in thirty years—Christmas, after his reunion with Margaret, and last August for Agnes' wedding. *All's well that ends well?* True or not, memories still stung—like an amputee convinced his missing leg was aching.

As Nestor drove, Jonas' thoughts journeyed back to living here, building the Magnolia Arms. The house had never been out of his thoughts—from the first sketch to viewing the building site to locking the door on the finished house, abandoning it.

The house was to pay homage—atonement for refusing to run the family farm, disappointing his father, leaving without a goodbye. But once Jonas met Margaret, his purpose changed. The house would be theirs. They would build a future. Raise a family.

He would name his first son for his father. Denver.

But after Jonas lost Margaret, the house became a symbol of his failure. Taking a last look at the finished house, he had backed out of the driveway, driven down Belmont Drive, and out of Dennisonville. In this very truck.

The rainy day he had met Agnes in the parking lot at Brighton Park, she had noticed the Magnolia Arms logo on the truck door. The memory of their first meeting—his irritation, her indomitable spirit—never failed to warm Jonas' heart.

Agnes, slipping her arm through his, brought him back to the present.

"What are you smiling about?" Agnes asked.

"Just glad to be here."

When they arrived, Jonas opened the front door for Agnes and then followed her in. He paused, bracing himself against the flood of memories. But met an old friend instead.

Truitt shook his hand. "I didn't know you were coming. Where's Margaret?"

"You know how she is about missing work. She said to tell you hello. You sure look better than when we visited you in the hospital after your accident."

"Almost well. Cast should come off in a few days. And my knee is better. Still sore."

Nestor came in with Jonas' bags and headed to the basement, where Jonas would stay. In the kitchen, he found Pinetta, paging through her *Good Housekeeping* cookbook.

"Welcome back," she said. "Whose are those?"

"Jonas is here. He's going to help with the remodeling…and keep an eye on me."

"So…you've decided to patch things up with your—?"

He paused at the basement door. "Try."

After Nestor started down the stairs, Pinetta clasped the cookbook to her heart. Just what she wanted to hear. Barton was staying. Things could only get better.

When Nestor came up from the basement, he found Jonas waiting in the hall.

"Let's go upstairs and take a look," Jonas said.

"Now?" Nestor asked.

He followed Jonas upstairs. When they reached the third floor, Jonas called to Ham.

Barton stopped working. "He's up top working on the platform. Who are you?"

"Jonas Grinstead. I came back with your son."

"You're the builder," Barton said. "I've heard a lot about you. I'm—"

"Barton Carlyle," Jonas said, shaking his hand.

Ham came down. "Jonas. Didn't think we'd see you till Christmas."

Chapter 15 ~ Under Construction

"Margaret thinks now that I'm retired, I can just pick up and leave whenever I want to."

"Come to help?"

"Brought the plans," Jonas said.

Ham turned to Barton. "Okay if I take a break, boss?"

Nestor cringed. *Boss? Not in this house.*

Jonas and Ham started downstairs. Nestor followed. Jonas turned to him. "Not you. Stay here and talk to your father."

"Now?" Nestor asked.

Jonas did not respond and left.

Alone, the Carlyle men faced each other.

"Glad you're back," Barton said.

"Prodigal son returns." He pointed to the study. "Want to sit down?"

Heart pounding, Barton walked in and sat on the sofa. Nestor pulled out the desk chair.

The room seemed airless.

Barton cleared his throat. "Have a good trip?"

"Did you?"

Barton propped his elbows on his knees. "What?"

"The trip you were on for twenty years. It took you long a time to get back."

"I got lost."

The first volleys fired.

"How did you find me?" Nestor asked. "I've wanted to ask."

"Found a magazine someone left on a bus. *Our State.* Thumbing through it. There was your name big as life. Picture of this house. Article about your garden. The Julia Bridger Rose."

"That makes sense."

Barton relaxed. "I still have it. I've about worn it out, re-reading it—"

"All those years did you *ever* one time think about me…or my mother?"

Barton narrowed his eyes. "Did I ever…?" He bolted up. "Come with me."

Nestor followed Barton to the first floor.

"Wait for me in the dining room?" Barton asked. "I'll be right back."

He went to his room, took the plastic bag of photos from the drawer, and rejoined his son. He opened the bag and poured out black-and-white pictures, faded color photos, tattered newspaper articles onto the table like sacred offerings on an altar.

The precious pile bore silent, irrefutable proof.

Nestor, speechless, stroked the pictures with a tender hand, spreading them out, sorting through them, pausing over an Easter photo of himself, basket in hand.

"How old was I?" he asked.

"Little over a year. Your mom made that outfit, but you wouldn't wear the hat." Venturing a hand on Nestor's shoulder, Barton leaned in and pointed. "See it in her lap."

When Nestor did not pull away, Barton slid out a chair and sat next to him.

The chasm between them narrowed to common ground…Katherine Carlyle…the woman they both loved.

An hour passed—brief questions, quiet answers. Stories told.

They reached the bottom of the stack. A wedding photo.

"You look happy," Nestor said.

"We were."

Nestor caressed his mother's image with his fingertips. "You loved her."

"More than life itself."

Nestor rested his head on his hand. "I understand…better than I used to. Now that I have Agnes." He looked up. "But I hope I'd be man enough to stay with my son, no matter what."

"You're a better man than I was…am," Barton said. "I know that."

"Actually," Nestor said, gathering the photos, "you made me who I am."

"Why do you say that?"

Nestor slipped the photos into the bag. "Because somewhere along the line I decided never to be the kind of father you are." Standing, he cradled the tattered bag in his arm. "Mind if I keep these a while…to show Agnes?"

"Take all the time you need."

When Pinetta entered the kitchen the next morning, she found a lipstick-stained cup in the sink. The coffee pot, half full, was hot. Prudence. Here and gone. Pinetta tasted the coffee. Too strong. She poured it out, rinsed the pot, started over.

Jonas came to the table first. She could not help thinking how handsome he was. In a different way from Barton. Every bit as masculine, but with refined features. He had the air of an artist. Even in jeans and a flannel shirt.

She served his coffee. "Did you sleep well?"

Chapter 15 ~ Under Construction

"Not really. I haven't been married that long, but I'm used to waking up next to my wife. I don't feel"—he chuckled—"it sounds silly…"

"What?" Pinetta asked.

"I don't feel 'whole' without her. Romantic notion, I know. But it's true. I don't know how I lived so long without her."

She sighed. "I know what you mean."

"Miss your husband?"

Ham bounded in before she could respond.

But her answer—she realized in that moment—would have been 'no.'

No. She did not miss Guy Henry Fraleigh.

Barton had replaced him. Moved him aside. Taken up residence. He was her every waking thought. This silent admission was so jarring she blushed when Barton entered moments later. She cracked the tenth egg into a bowl before Ham caught her attention.

"That's enough, Miss Pinetta. Unless you're going to have breakfast, too."

She managed a nervous laugh. "No."

While they ate, she hovered like a hummingbird, a gentle presence. Darting to the table to refill cups, retreating to the sink to dry dishes. All the while admiring them. The men of her family wore suits and ties and fretted about monogrammed shirt cuffs. Their hair was cut short, slicked down, tamed. Jonas wore flannel. Barton, faded plaid, collar frayed, sleeves rolled up. Ham, a janitor's uniform shirt, dark green, starched, with a blank space above the pocket where his name tag had once been. Their hair was smoothed, but untrimmed. Barton's hair brushed the top of his ears.

Her mother and sisters would have looked down their noses at these men. Called them "scruffy." Pinetta found them rugged. Charming. And Barton…appealing.

The men talked shop, thanked Pinetta, and left the table at 9:00.

Half an hour later Bridey Ludlow rapped on the door as she shoved it open. Dropping her bulging tote bag, she made a beeline for the coffee pot.

"Morning, Piney." She lifted the coffee pot to see if it was full. "Is it true?"

"Is what true?"

"Jonas Grinstead is here." She plunked down the coffee pot and stepped around Pinetta. "Did he leave Margaret?"

Pinetta nudged the coffee pot aside to see if the countertop was scratched. "No. He didn't *leave* Margaret. Whatever gave you that idea?"

Bridey swung open the cabinet door and rifled through the dishes. "Did I leave my Minnie Mouse mug here? I can't find it anywhere."

"No." The cabinet door barely missed Bridey's ear as Pinetta closed it. "You didn't leave your mug here."

"Are you sure?"

Eyeing the sink full of suds, Bridey plunged in her hands, searched, pulled out her hands and tapped them on the sink edge. Snatched up a towel, dried her hands, slung the towel over her shoulder. Grabbed a mug from the dish drainer, filled it to the brim, and sloshed coffee on the floor as she sashayed to a chair, her hips moving independently of her body.

"You all practiced up?" Bridey asked, reaching for the sugar bowl.

Pinetta took the towel from Bridey's shoulder and knelt to mop up the coffee. "Practiced up for what?"

"For choir tryouts." She nabbed the last biscuit from the serving plate and bit it in half.

"Got any apple butter?"

"No." There were two jars in the pantry.

"Ivy Leigh always kept apple butter," she said, mouth full, crumbs spraying. "Well, no matter. I came by to give—what's his name? Albert? The boy who lives here?"

"Abbot?"

"Abbot, that's it." Swallowing, she looked down at the floor. "I came by to give him…mercy me…where's my bag? I thought I brought it in."

"By the door," Pinetta said.

"Hand it to me, love. My poor old bones are wore out. I've been up since 6:00."

Pinetta lifted the bag and held it at arm's length as she approached.

Bridey licked her fingers and sorted through the bag. "Albert…Abbot…whatever his name is…asked me to bring an application. He wanted one for that woman, too."

"Prudence?"

"Yeah. The snooty one?"

For the first time since Bridey invaded, Pinetta focused on what she was saying. "They're *both* trying out for the choir?"

Chapter 15 ~ Under Construction

"Uh-huh." Bridey pulled out two crinkled sheets and laid them on the table. "Maybe they're going to settle down here, you think? She seems too old for him, but there's no—"

Abbot, who always ran late, burst into the kitchen. "Any coffee left?"

Pinetta nodded in the direction of the pot; Abbot filled a mug. "My alarm clock didn't go off. I've got to buy a new one."

"Your boss must be lenient," Pinetta said. "You run late an awful lot."

"I'm the last one to leave every night." He filled a mug. "Have to lock up."

"They fired Jess?" Bridey asked.

"Who's that?" Pinetta asked.

"Janitor at the paper."

"He...has the flu," Abbot said.

"No, he doesn't. I saw him just yesterday." Bridey picked up the application and held it out to Abbot. "Brought this for you."

"What's this?"

"Application you asked for. Choir tryouts?"

Abbot folded the paper and put it in his coat pocket. "Oh, yeah. When is it?"

"10th of December. Blue Room in the Delahunty House. Come with Pinetta."

Abbot buttoned his coat. "I hate to ask, Mrs. Ludlow, but could you drop me off at the newspaper office? I usually ride with Prudence, but she already left."

Standing, Bridey shouldered her tote bag. "No problem. We should get to know each other better if you're going to stay here and get involved in the community, like people say."

When Abbot opened the door, Truitt, face chapped by cold, stepped in.

"Truitt," Pinetta said, "I didn't know you'd gone out."

"Felt like a walk. Time I got my strength back."

Bridey pinched his cheek. "Good for you. Nothing like fresh air to get the blood pumping." She reached in her bag. "Here. Why don't you try out for the choir? Do you good."

After Bridey and Abbot left, Truitt propped his cane against the wall and sat down. Pinetta offered tea; he accepted.

"Should you be out alone?" she asked. "Maybe someone should walk with you."

"Didn't go far. I'm healing faster than I thought. Can't wait to get this cast off my arm." He removed the sling and draped it over the other chair. "I want to get back to the piano…with both hands…work on my piece. I'm feeling inspired. Music in my head."

She set his cup in front of him. "I guess we'll have to work out a practice schedule. I have to start learning the choir music."

Truitt stirred his tea. "I didn't want to come here, you know. I thought I liked living alone, having things a certain way. But it's strange…none of that matters now."

Pinetta sat next to him. "I heard the men talking at breakfast. After they finish upstairs, they're going to start working in the dining room. Will you be able to work with all the racket?"

"I was a teacher for over thirty years. I'm used to racket." He stood. "All right if I take my tea into the parlor? I'd like to get to work now."

He left his cane by his chair, stepped across the hall, and sat at the piano.

Up till now the most purely happy moment of Truitt Spenlow's life had been attending his high school senior prom with the stunning Brenda McDonnell. She could have had her pick of any athlete or the student body president, but she turned them all down in favor of Truitt, president of the chess club and first chair oboist in the band. Everyone, including Truitt, was baffled. He never found out why she went with him. Had her parents bribed her? Was her own heart naturally tender? Was it a dare? No matter. She restored Truitt's faith in the human race.

In her honor he had begun composing "Song of Eventide," homage to the perfect, full-mooned spring evening when he had driven her home and kissed her cheek when they said good night. They had graduated together, gone to different colleges, lost touch.

But his resolve to immortalize the sublime moment—in song—never left him. The business of teaching, rehearsing, had waylaid his composing, stalled his progress. When he had time, he was not inspired. When he was inspired, there was no time.

Who would have believed a car wreck would turn all that around? Give him a fresh start? With these people…in this house…where for the first time he felt like he belonged. Where again his faith in the human race had been restored.

Agnes awoke and rolled over to make sure she was not dreaming. Nestor…still asleep…was next to her. Home. For the first time since Barton

Chapter 15 ~ Under Construction

arrived, he had not crept out of bed before dawn. They had the whole delicious day—Saturday—ahead.

She eased up onto her elbow, propped her head on her hand, and gazed at the man she loved—father of her child. The man she had dreamed of her whole life without knowing. Nothing like her foolish romantic fantasies. Thank goodness.

Breakfast in bed. Why hadn't she thought of it last night?

Lifting the covers, she sat up and eased her feet onto the floor.

"Where do you think you're going?" Nestor asked, eyes still closed.

"To get breakfast. How long have you been awake?"

"A while. I was thinking about what we could do today."

Agnes put on her robe and tied the sash. "Me, too. What do you have in mind?"

He opened his eyes. "Feel like a short trip out of town?"

"Uh-huh. And when we get back, we have another stop to make, if that's okay."

After breakfast Nestor brought pots of yellow strawflowers, purple pansies, and garnet mums from the greenhouse and placed them on the floorboard of the truck. Agnes sat next to him as Nestor drove to the cemetery. She brushed debris from Katherine's grave; Nestor arranged the flowers. Content, they drove to Mollie's Restaurant for lunch, leaving with two pink cake boxes. They delivered the German chocolate to the Magnolia Arms and changed clothes. Agnes held the coconut cake in her lap on the way to Kimball Pines. Fiona, expecting their visit, admitted them.

Hands folded in her lap, Agnes sat next to Nestor on the antique brocade sofa in Vesper Kimball's living room. Late afternoon sunlight shone through sheer curtains on the bay window looking out onto the street. Another world away.

"I'm still not sure we should be here," Nestor said. "Are you positive this is what you want to do? Waltz in here and tell Mrs. Kimball you don't trust Abbot Cooper?"

"You don't think I'd come here without a plan, do you?" Agnes asked. "I've been thinking about it for days…ever since Fiona told me what was going on."

They were whispering like schoolchildren whose teacher had left the room.

Nestor propped his elbow on the embroidered linen doily pinned to the sofa arm. "This whole thing could backfire in our faces."

Agnes poked him in the ribs. "I don't think you should do that."

"What?"

"Lean on that."

He slid his arm onto his lap. "Probably right. Think anyone *ever* sits in here?"

Agnes surveyed the room: wide gold oval-framed photos, faded fleur-de-lis wallpaper, tasseled lamp shades, Oriental ginger jars, weathered volumes on tall mahogany bookcases.

"I can't believe you've lived in Dennisonville all these years, and you've never been here. Weren't you curious?" she asked.

"Everyone in town is curious. It's like having our own Miss Havisham." He shuddered. "This is too much like my piano teacher's house, except she kept plastic on her furniture."

Leaning forward, Agnes gazed at the face of a pensive porcelain shepherd, blue-robed, staff in hand, tending a flock of unseen sheep on the glass-topped coffee table.

"*Legend has it the lady who lives there hasn't seen the light of day in over twenty years.*"

"What?" Nestor asked.

"The day I got here. Asa Ludlow was driving me to the Magnolia Arms in his cab. We drove by this house. He pointed out the window, and that's what he said. I'll never forget it."

"She's legendary, all right. Once I asked Ivy Leigh if I could deliver flowers here…just to get a look inside, but she put her foot down. 'If Mrs. Kimball wanted visitors,' she said—"

"'I'd invite them.'"

Vesper Kimball, diminutive, beautiful, was standing in the arched entry.

Nestor jumped to his feet. Agnes, dumbfounded, stared at the fragile figure in burgundy chiffon, a cameo brooch pinned at her lace collar.

Vesper walked to the Queen Anne chair opposite the sofa. "Ivy Leigh brought soup once, when I had the flu. Came to the back door. Didn't ask to come in. Peerless cook. Is she well?"

"Yes," Agnes said, pulling Nestor onto the sofa. "She's getting married again…to a friend of ours. We're having the wedding at the Magnolia Arms. You'd be welcome—"

Nestor gave her a quick nudge.

Vesper rested her hands on the chair arms. "Mrs. Ransom remarrying after so long. I still remember Major Ransom's funeral. Whole town turned

Chapter 15 ~ Under Construction

out…the paper said." She turned to the family portrait suspended by a long gold cord over the fireplace. "Can one love twice?"

"Ma'am?" Agnes asked.

Vesper closed her eyes. "A line from Tennyson."

"*Enoch Arden,*" Nestor said.

Opening her eyes, Vesper peered at him. "A gardener who reads poetry."

"I've always liked Tennyson. Re-read that poem not long ago. Someone reminded me."

"Lovely story—*Enoch Arden*. I've always thought Philip Ray was the hero. Loving Annie so long. Fiona tells me you're the manager at the Magnolia Arms now. Is that right?"

"Yes," Nestor said, taking Agnes' hand. "We both are."

"Abbot says the house is full," Vesper said. "A tenant in every room?"

"It's true," Agnes said. "And we're expanding. Ham is building another staircase"—she pointed up—"to the cupola, and we're taking part of the dining—"

"Ham?" Vesper asked. "Like in *David Copperfield*?"

"I guess so…I never thought about it before."

This was a lie, but somehow it seemed wise to bolster Vesper's sense of superiority.

"So, you're here about my book?"

Caught off guard, Agnes stammered. After days of contriving the perfect way to bring up the subject, Vesper had beat her to the draw.

"We…uh…were just concerned about what Abbot might include in the story. Apparently, he's going into quite a bit of…detail you might—"

Vesper's cheeks glowed pink. "I'm not so old and dotty that I don't know what's going on under my own roof. I've read a few chapters."

Nestor intervened. "Have you told your son about the book? If someone were writing about my mother, I'd want a say in what—"

"*My son,*" Vesper said, "is an important man, much too busy running his company…his father's company…to be bothered about proofreading a book. Even one about his own family."

"That may be true," Nestor said, "but he—"

Vesper turned to Agnes. "Isn't that why *you're* here?"

"What do you mean?" Agnes asked.

"Mrs. O'Neill said she wants to hire you as the final proofreader. She told me you're an author *and* an English teacher. But she still wanted me to meet you and give my approval."

Nestor blinked; Agnes' jaw dropped.

Fiona, eavesdropping in the hallway, stepped in. "Should I serve tea now?"

"Yes, thank you," Vesper said. "And the cake."

When Vesper turned away, Fiona mouthed 'Sorry' to Agnes and disappeared.

Agnes stood. "Do you mind if we eat at the table? I tend to spill things when I'm balancing them in my lap."

Vesper grimaced. "You can't manage a cup and saucer at your age?"

"Knock stuff over all the time. If Ivy Leigh were here, she'd tell you. Right, Nestor?"

"Very well," Vesper said. "Go and tell Fiona. The kitchen is down the hall on the left."

Leaving Nestor to his own devices, Agnes hurried to the kitchen. Fiona, hands trembling, was cutting the cake with a sterling silver knife.

Agnes rushed in. "Fiona, what in the world? No one was supposed to know I was—"

Fiona kept slicing. "Keep your voice down, *please*."

Agnes whispered. "We agreed not to tell anyone I was coming. How did—?"

"It's my fault. The other day I caught that O'Neill woman in the nursery."

"Nursery?"

"Edward's room. The son who died when he was two. When I saw Prudence going through his cedar chest, handling his little clothes, I stormed in and slammed the lid."

Agnes frowned. "The nerve of that woman."

Fiona carried the plates to the table. "Then I said, 'You may think you're going to get away with this, but you're not. I told Agnes what you're up to. She's going to put a stop to it.'"

"That makes sense now. Prudence came up with a Plan B. Got to Vesper before I did."

"I'm sorry, Agnes. All this time I've kept my mouth shut, and now when we're just about to get rid of these two, I ruin everything."

Agnes squeezed her arm. "Maybe not. Vesper let us in the house. That's a good first step. It'll be easier to get in next time. And now…I can find out what's in that book."

Chapter 15 ~ Under Construction

"Tell her tea is ready. I don't want her to think we're in here talking about her."

Agnes backed toward the door. "I need to rescue Nestor anyway. He will *not* be happy I left him alone with her so long. I barely talked him into coming here in the first place."

Backing toward the door, she was preparing to sprint on tiptoe to the parlor when she spotted Nestor and Mrs. Kimball in the hall.

Standing at the grandfather clock. Vesper had slipped her arm through Nestor's.

"I've never actually seen a Howard Miller clock," Nestor said. "Is this cherry veneer?"

"Windsor cherry. And a swan's...neck...pediment," she said, lingering over every word...as if each left a pleasant aftertaste.

Nestor looked closer at the pendulum. "The brass is pristine. A gift from your husband?"

"No. It was my mother's. She bought it from a family who moved away...suddenly. They couldn't take it with them."

"You've taken good care of it. It looks brand new."

Squinting her eyes, she peeked up at Nestor. "It's my most valuable possession."

In this light, if she tilted her head just so...he was the image of Philip March.

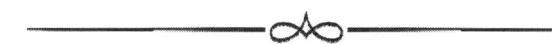

At day's end Ham secured the house, climbed the stairs, and lay on his back in bed. Hands under his head, he stared at the ceiling. He used to go to sleep, worn out from emptying trash, oiling hinges, repairing wobbly desks.

This was bliss—to be exhausted from *building*, forging a legacy, creating something beautiful to leave behind. He might never find a wife, have a family of his own, but if he could build...someday...someone would know he had lived.

Beyond the closed door he heard steps in the hall. Rising, he opened his door and looked down the hall. Truitt Spenlow, in bathrobe and slippers, was standing at the arched window at the foot of the spiral stairs.

Ham stepped into the hall. "Doc? You okay?"

Truitt turned around. "Sorry. Didn't mean to wake you."

"I wasn't asleep yet." Ham joined him at the window. "Beautiful night."

"Yes, it is. Look at those stars."

Ham touched the unfinished banister. "You won't believe the view from up there."

"I'd like to see it. Would it be a nice place to—"

"What?"

"I was just wondering if it would be…you know…a romantic spot. I mean, if there was some lady you had your eye on…you could invite her up there and…talk."

"Yeah, I guess so."

"Ham. You've been here a while, and you know Pinetta pretty well, don't you?"

"As well as anyone can know her, I guess."

"And you know me." He raked his hand over his bald head. "I know I'm not much to look at. But do you think someone like her could ever be interested in someone like me?"

Ham focused on the view. "I don't see why not. You have a lot in common. She's a cultured woman—knows a lot about music. She's hard to get to know, but once you do—"

"Could you help me? I haven't dated much…at all…since college."

"I'll do what I can, but I don't think I'm the one to coach you through—"

Truitt was not listening. "She's so beautiful. I've never met anyone like her."

Chapter 16

At the Delahunty House

The Delahunty House was the only historic Dennisonville home open to the public. Though tourists were allowed to glimpse Hyacinth Hall from a respectful distance, linger on the sidewalk to admire the ancient trees of Buckeye Lodge, or crane their necks as they rode slowly past Kimball Pines, at the Delahunty House, for a donation of $3 ($1 for children and seniors), they could actually pass through the wrought iron gate onto the circular stone driveway, climb the steps to the porch circling around all four sides, and walk through the north door into the foyer, 10:00 a.m.-5:00 p.m., Tuesday-Sunday, year-round.

There on the wall of the library was the printed, framed story of the original owner.

Mrs. Gloria Delahunty, one of three heirs to the shrinking Delahunty fortune, had refused to sell her share of the house to her greedy cousins and encamped in a downstairs room with four of her six children, sleeping on the floor and burning the wooden furniture in the fireplace to keep warm during the winter, until an anonymous patron (speculation ran rampant it was Ian Penderleith, Mrs. Delahunty's childhood sweetheart) bought the house and bequeathed it to the city with the stipulation the house be entered into the national registry of historic homes and always bear the name of Delahunty.

Now the house served as the sanctuary of the Dennisonville Historical Society. And since all the officers of the society were also members of the Dennisonville Garden Club, they voted themselves the privilege of holding their monthly meetings in the Blue Room, strictly roped off from the public; the tour of the foyer, library, and dining room being judged sufficient to justify the $3 fee.

Until Bridey Ludlow circulated a petition that auditions for the Founder's Day Community Chorale should be held in the Blue Room.

Thirty feet square, with a high ceiling, rows of tall, arched windows looking out onto the oak-lined street, and a glistening wood floor, the Blue Room was the perfect venue for musical evenings.

What better way to encourage timid people to audition? Bridey surmised. Let them into the house for free. Then allow them to linger in the Blue Room and admire the chandelier and the crown molding until they were called on to sing.

Sign-ups for auditions would triple, once word got out. No telling what hidden talent they might discover. And besides that, photos of large crowds, invested in the success of the festival, would play well in *The News & Observer* in Raleigh.

Maybe the governor would see the article, be intrigued, find the devotion of his fellow Tar Heels charming, and attend the festival to see what all the excitement was about and snag a free publicity photo with voters.

This was Bridey Ludlow's dream. To put Dennisonville on the map. So, she pushed the idea through, ramrodding and cajoling, till the community *bought* in and the Dennisonville Historical Society *gave* in.

Therefore, on December 10th Mrs. Harriet Oxley-Friend, President of that auspicious body, supervised—under protest—the moving of the large round table with Macassar ebony veneer and maple inlay from the Blue Room to the library. She then stationed herself by the door, as metal folding chairs, on loan from three church fellowship halls, were ferried in. Why choir tryouts had to take place at the Delahunty House she could not fathom, but outvoted by the planning committee, she had been forced to comply. If one scratch appeared on the original wood floor installed by Harry Winterson eighty years ago….

Well, she dared not even think of such a thing.

But if it happened…*if* it happened…Bridey Ludlow, the odious woman who had master-minded this foolhardy scheme, would get the business end of a chewing out the likes of which she had never heard.

Leaving nothing to chance, Mrs. Oxley-Friend arrived at 6:00 p.m. to take up her post by the front door. A lined plastic garbage can at her side, she was poised to stare down anyone who tried to sneak past with chewing gum, soda can, or Styrofoam coffee cup—lidded or not.

Even Esmé Inch, the first judge to arrive, was not spared.

Chapter 16 ~ At the Delahunty House

"Excuse me," Mrs. Oxley-Friend said, eyeing Mrs. Inch's Thermos. "Would you like to leave that with me? Accidents happen."

Esmé, barely 5' tall, peered up. "No, I would *not* like to leave it with you. I taught elementary school for 40 years. I think I can manage to drink from a cup without spilling."

She strutted into the Blue Room and claimed her place at a long table at the back of the room. Legal pads, pencils, pre-printed forms, and three pocket calculators were available for the judges' use.

Mary Grace Dodson, grateful for the distraction Mrs. Inch had provided, arrived next (sneaking in three packs of Lance peanut butter crackers in the bottom of her tote bag) to post herself at the registration table in the hall.

Donovan Strode parked his red Audi at the rear of the building and entered through the kitchen. Pausing in the door of the Blue Room, he studied the seating arrangement to make sure his instructions had been followed. Six rows of eight chairs, divided by a middle aisle, which led the way to a Yamaha baby grand piano at the front of the room. The long judges' table at the rear of the room. Satisfied, he took the center judge's chair and pulled back his shirt cuff to check his Rolex watch.

He cut his eyes at Mrs. Inch. "Eileen's not here yet?"

"No. I was the first. Had my husband drop me off, since parking is—"

"Yes, yes," Donovan said, rubbing his forehead.

He had always found Esmé tiresome. She was not supposed to be here. The committee had been forced to draft her at the last minute when Grover Crisp, high school band director, had opted out of auditions, due to his "mother being ill."

A revelation made only after Donovan and Grover had almost come to blows earlier that morning in the teacher's lounge. Yet another disagreement over the upcoming Christmas concert. Grover had phoned Eileen Redmon, the third judge.

"Sorry, Red," he said. "I know I said I'd help you out, but I cannot put up with Donovan *one more minute*. It's bad enough I have to work with him, but I'm being *paid* to do that. I'm not going to *volunteer* to spend another *minute* with him…not even for you."

"But the two of us could outvote him," Eileen had said, trying not to sound as desperate as she felt.

Tea at Kimball Pines

"My mind's made up. As mad as I am, if I showed up tonight, there would be an ugly scene and that wouldn't do anybody any good. You can do this. You're up to it. I'm not."

The planning committee was notified, and Esmé, retired elementary school music teacher, who had never awarded an Honorable Mention or Certificate of Participation—even to a first grader—was summoned as a replacement.

And so Esmé and Donovan waited, while Eileen walked the two blocks from her apartment, hoping a good chill from the frosty night air would steel her for the task ahead. Hands in pockets, she watched her breath form silvery clouds as she reviewed her strategy. *Keep quiet, write positive comments to the singers, submit the forms without explaining, and hurry out the minute the last note is sung. Tomorrow, call everyone Donovan insulted and tell them they did well.* No…. That would mean answering more questions about why she had refused to serve as accompanist.

Longtime organist for First Baptist Church, Eileen had been the logical choice to accompany the Founder's Day chorale. She was, after all, a daughter of Dennisonville. Even after twenty years, people still marveled she had come home after college, rather than "writing her own ticket to Carnegie Hall." With her dark wavy hair, brilliant green eyes, and beautiful smile, she seemed destined for life under the spotlight. On high school graduation day, people had resigned themselves to losing Eileen to the waiting world. Who were they to hold her back? But she had come home to the community she loved.

And they loved her all the more. Were so devoted to her that her ex-husband moved his second wife—a prissy blonde secretary half his age—to California to avoid being bombarded with questions about "why he had let Eileen go."

She kicked at a pine cone on the sidewalk. No one could blame *her* for what was about to happen. She *tried* to persuade the committee to ask Dr. Ellingham, the choir director at the Presbyterian Church, to lead the chorale. But *no*, they said. *People from all over the state know Donovan. No telling who might show up to watch him conduct. We might make the news in Raleigh.*

"Let Raleigh have him," she muttered as she stepped onto the porch.

"What was that?" Mrs. Oxley-Friend asked.

"Nothing."

"Not like you to be late, Mrs. Redmon."

Eileen removed her scarf. "Is it 7:00?"

"6:45."

Chapter 16 ~ At the Delahunty House

"Then I'm not late, am I?"

"Judges were to arrive at 6:30. That's what I was told."

Eileen opened her mouth, caught her breath, and forced a weak smile. If she unleashed her temper now, there would be no hope of making it through the evening.

"I guess I didn't get the memo."

She brushed past Mrs. Oxley-Friend and entered the Blue Room, pausing for a moment to look over the crowd. There was her mother's best friend, Verbena…and Mrs. Tate…both so pure of heart, and both sure to have their spirits crushed.

"Joining us?" Esmé asked. "Or did you want to audition? *Since you're not playing.*"

"No. I'm not trying out," Eileen said, and took the remaining chair, nudging it toward the end of the table…away from Donovan.

Serving her community was one thing; enduring Donovan's snide comments was something else.

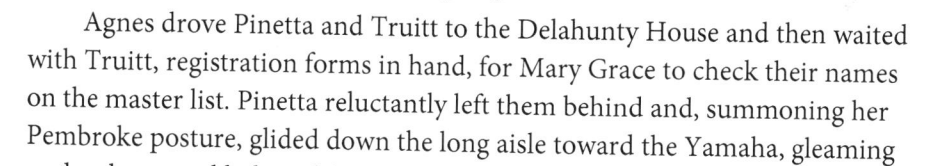

───────── ⚭ ─────────

Agnes drove Pinetta and Truitt to the Delahunty House and then waited with Truitt, registration forms in hand, for Mary Grace to check their names on the master list. Pinetta reluctantly left them behind and, summoning her Pembroke posture, glided down the long aisle toward the Yamaha, gleaming under the crystal lights of the chandelier.

She had hoped Barton might join the choir, but no such luck. Trying to appear at ease, Pinetta slid onto the piano bench. Laying her fingers gingerly on the keyboard, she played a song she knew by heart while people milled about the room.

"The Song is Ended" by Irving Berlin.

When Agnes and Truitt reached the front of the line, Mary Grace glanced up and then leaned left to peer at the line of people behind them. "Is Mr. Carlyle coming later?"

"Nestor likes acting, but not singing," Agnes said, though she knew Mary Grace had not meant *that* 'Mr. Carlyle.'

"The other men are working on the house," Truitt said, touched by the sad look in Mary Grace's eyes. "They'd work 24/7 if it wouldn't bother the neighbors, right, Agnes?"

She took his hint. "Yes. All the other men are working on the house."

"Not all of them. Abbot's here," Mary Grace said, tilting her head in his direction.

Tea at Kimball Pines

"Abbot?" Agnes scanned the crowd. "Prudence, too?"

Mary Grace handed them their numbers. "She's not trying out. I think she just came along to supervise him."

"What's with the numbers?" Agnes asked.

Mary Grace shrugged. "Dr. Strode's idea."

Numbers in hand, Agnes and Truitt started down the aisle.

"Mind sitting near the front?" he asked.

"Anywhere is fine. Look at Pinetta. The picture of poise."

"Star quality," Truitt said. "She's a natural, but doesn't know it."

When they reached the row where Abbot and Prudence were sitting, Agnes paused.

"Hello," she said. "Didn't expect to see you two here."

"Hello," Prudence said. "These small town community affairs always make great stories. Drama just waiting to happen."

"Do you both sing?" Truitt asked. "I would've helped you, if I'd known."

"Just me," Abbot said.

"Do well," Agnes said. "We'll see you later. Truitt wants to sit up front."

They left; Abbot whispered to Prudence. "Can we leave...now that they've seen us?"

"No," Prudence said. "If you're going to finish your book, we have to make it look like we're 'involved' in the community—not just trying to take advantage of Vesper."

He slumped in his chair. "But we *are* taking advantage of her, and I don't like it."

"You want to get published, don't you?"

"Yeah."

"All right then. I'm telling you—no one wants to read some stupid book about you running away from home. But an old lady like Vesper stuck in a time warp? That's different."

Lute Monroe had been parked outside the Delahunty House since 6:15. When he saw Pinetta arrive and go into the house, he waited five minutes before he left his truck and climbed the porch steps. Mrs. Oxley-Friend scrutinized him and nodded curtly at the door mat. He leaned his hand against the door frame as he wiped his shoes. When he removed his hand, she examined the paint for smudges.

"I've never been here," he said. "Inside, I mean. Which way do I go?"

Chapter 16 ~ At the Delahunty House

When she pointed left, Lute gaped at the enormous diamond on her manicured hand. "Pretty ring. Where would a fellow buy one of those?"

She laid her hand, red fingernails glistening, on her pearl necklace, in case he had not noticed it.

"Tiffany's," she said.

"Who's she?"

"Not *who*. *Where*. My husband bought this from the flagship store…in New York."

"I couldn't go all the way to New York for a ring. I have a business to run."

She dropped her hand. "Try Charlotte. Shoes clean? You're holding up the line."

Lute followed the sound of the piano to the Blue Room. He stopped in the doorway to gaze at Pinetta, picture himself standing near her, singing, pausing at the end of his song to lean in and say in a low voice, "That was for you." He still wasn't sure he could go through with it…the whispering part…but even if he made a fool of himself, he had to seize this moment. He had nothing to lose.

"Lute," Mary Grace said. "You have to check in first. *Lute*."

Tom Gibbons, owner of the hardware store, tapped Lute's shoulder. "Over there, big guy."

Lute stepped to the table.

"You nervous or something?" Mary Grace asked.

"A little," Lute said.

"Wouldn't catch me trying out," she said. "Sing by myself for Donovan Strode?"

"If that's what it takes," Lute said.

Cap—and heart—in hand, he started toward the piano, each step bringing him nearer to Pinetta and the fulfillment of his dream.

"Can I sit with you, Agnes?" Lute asked.

Agnes slid over. "Sure. Truitt was helping me with my stage fright."

"Stage fright?" Lute asked. "You?"

The thought of Agnes' being nervous was strangely reassuring.

At 7:00 on the dot, Donovan, glasses perched on top of his head, clipboard in hand, sauntered to the front. Pinetta stopped playing, but refused to acknowledge him.

"Good evening," Dr. Strode said.

A few daring souls dutifully replied.

Tea at Kimball Pines

"Welcome to tryouts for the community chorale. I'm Dr. Donovan Strode, and I'll be your conductor." He ran his pencil down the list. "As usual, we have a *plethora* of altos. So, don't take it personally when we weed you out."

"Hmmm," Esmé Inch said.

Eileen shot her a withering look. "Aren't *you* an alto?"

She bristled. "*Mezzo soprano*. There's a difference."

"We won't announce results tonight," Donovan said. "So, after your audition, you're free to leave. In fact, we prefer that. Mrs. Ludlow will notify you if you made it. Questions?"

No one had the nerve to appear ill-informed.

"No?" Donovan said. "Good. Who's Number 1?"

Verbena Vernell, short, plump, hair cut pixie-style, rose slowly. Beloved in the community, she had calmed many an angry customer in her 25 years at the tax collector's office. Hesitant, she addressed Donovan as he strolled past on his way to the back.

"We were all wondering…we have to try out in *front* of everyone else? We thought we would wait outside and be called in one at a time."

Murmurs of assent followed.

Waving dismissively, Donovan did not slow. "If you can't sing to an audience, now's the time to find out."

Still at her chair, she adjusted her wire-rimmed glasses. "But singing a solo is different from singing with a group. Most of us are average singers. We find strength in numbers."

"That's right," one said.

"I get too nervous," said another.

Donovan rejoined the judges and scooted his chair to the table.

Eileen clenched her jaw. "This is not the way to inspire confidence."

"I'm not interested in building confidence," he said. "I'm interested in bravado."

Without a word Truitt got to his feet and started toward Verbena. The room fell silent. When he reached her, he extended his hand. She took it and walked beside him to the piano.

"Honestly," Esmé said, shaking her head. "Silliest thing I ever saw."

Lovely, Eileen thought.

"Start the exercises, Mrs. Fraleigh," Donovan said. "Sing on, 'ah.'"

Verbena warbled up and down a few scales before Donovan ordered Pinetta to hand over the sight-reading exercise.

Chapter 16 ~ At the Delahunty House

"What's this?" Verbena asked.

"Something I wrote myself," Donovan said. "Do you know how to sight read?"

"If you hum a few bars," Verbena said.

Esmé snickered; Eileen fumed.

The exercise concluded, Verbena performed a tenuous version of "Blue Skies," omitting the finger snapping she had practiced.

"You may go," Donovan said. He raised his voice. "Everyone…sing loud enough we can hear you in the back. You're not singing in the shower. This is a performance."

Verbena made a beeline for the front row. "Could I sit here?" she whispered to Truitt. "My poor old knees are shaking so bad I can't make it back to my chair."

"You did a great job," Truitt said. "Put Sinatra to shame."

Prudence O'Neill got up to leave. Abbot tried to follow.

"What are you doing?" she asked. "Stay here and get in that choir."

"But why are you leaving?"

She nodded at Donovan. "I had enough power-hungry men in my life. I'm not listening to this another minute. But you *have* to stay. I explained that."

Abbot sank down and determined to do what he had always done when his mother insisted he "sing for company." Give a lackluster performance and make a quick exit.

The grisly process repeated four times before Donovan called, "Number 6," and Truitt Spenlow stood. Though wearing khakis, a plaid shirt, and white cable-knit sweater, he approached the piano with as much dignity as if he were mounting a conductor's platform in black tie and tails.

"Brace yourself," Agnes said to Lute. "This is going to be good."

Truitt sailed through the vocal exercises, nailed the sight reading (opting to hit an impromptu high note at the end) and then dazzled the assembly with a few bars of "O sole mio," before Donovan interrupted.

"Thank you. I've heard enough."

Eileen slammed down her pencil. "Well, I haven't. Go ahead, *Dr.* Spenlow."

A smattering of applause rippled across the audience.

Pinetta played an arpeggio, and Truitt continued.

When he finished, everyone, except Donovan, sprang up for a standing ovation.

Truitt bowed and gestured toward Pinetta, who declined to stand.

Before Donovan could call "Number 7," Eileen raised her voice.

"Serafina Rummage."

Donovan glared at her.

A lithe young woman with long blonde hair sashayed forward. Placing her delicate hand on the piano, she lifted her chin slightly and said, "Roo-MAZH."

Agnes swallowed a laugh.

"What's that?" Eileen asked.

"Roo-MAZH. The accent is on the second syllable," she announced in a breathy tone.

"Syl-LAB-ble," Agnes whispered to Truitt.

"Sorry," Eileen said. "What will you be singing tonight?"

Serafina shaded her eyes from the chandelier overhead. "'Cock-eyed Optimist' from *South Pacific*."

Serafina, eccentric, but proficient, was the first soprano added to the choir.

Dinah Latimer, red-haired junior high school secretary (codenamed "Bulldog" by the faculty and staff) and Corby Dudman, bow-tied high school economics teacher, followed. After their many years of daily encounters with adolescents and administrators, it would take more than Donovan Strode to throw them off balance.

Neither was gifted, but both sang on pitch, unwavering.

The audience clapped again, cementing their unspoken pact to stand together.

After each audition, one or two more would opt out, leaving their numbers in their chairs or depositing them with Esmé on their way to the door.

Those stalwart enough to continue followed Verbena's example and remained behind, stationing themselves at the front to mount a battlement between singer and Strode.

Agnes was next. A veteran of piano recitals and college theatre, she fixed her eyes on a spot just above the heads of the judges and imagined herself in the Magnolia Arms talent show two years before. She gave a creditable performance. Even for an average alto.

Eileen smiled at Agnes. "Thank you, Mrs.—"

"Number 10," Donovan interrupted.

"Carlyle," Eileen continued, glaring at Donovan.

Chapter 16 ~ At the Delahunty House

Gretchen Tate, eased into the aisle. Manager of the Whispering Pines Motor Lodge, she was famous for dispensing homespun advice and home remedies. Ever since Agnes had stayed at the Whispering Pines her first night in Dennisonville, the Tates had held a special place in her heart. Though Moe Tate was becoming senile, sometimes alarming guests with his nocturnal wanderings, his wife refused to send him to a nursing home and cared for him herself, never complaining. There was no one in Dennisonville who did not love Gretchen Tate. Agnes reached out and squeezed her hand as she passed.

Though Gretchen had witnessed the previous auditions, she still had to be coached through the vocal exercises. The sight reading completely eluded her.

Donovan did not attempt to hide his distaste. "That's enough. Your selection?"

Pinetta waited for Gretchen to hand over her music.

"Didn't bring any music. I've been listening to Patti Page sing for years. Won't need the piano."

Pinetta folded her hands in her lap.

In a pure, sweet…quavering…tone Gretchen began to sing:

I was dancin' with my darlin' to the Tennessee Waltz, when an old friend I happened to see. Introduced her to my loved one and while they were dancin'…

Her confidence shaken by her failures, she could not go on.

Agnes' heart ached. She was on the verge of a rescue, when Truitt began to sing.

My friend stole my sweetheart from me.

Locking her eyes on Truitt, Gretchen sang with him.

I remember the night and the Tennessee Waltz and I know just how much I have lost.

Voices scattered throughout the room—tender soprano, gravelly bass—joined.

Yes, I lost my little darlin' the night they were playing the beautiful Tennessee Waltz.

Eileen Redmon, along with the entire crowd, joined in.

Esmé Inch wrote "No" on Gretchen's form.

Donovan rolled his eyes. "Thank you," before the song was finished. "Number 11."

Tea at Kimball Pines

The song died out. Truitt walked back to the piano and offered Gretchen his hand.

"Thank you," she said. "I don't know what happened. If you'll come to the motel Monday, I'll treat you to coffee and pastry. I don't expect I'll be seeing you in choir practice."

Gretchen sat next to Verbena.

Tom Gibbons was a reputable baritone, followed by Hal Mayberry, bass, one of the few men who had not stormed out in a huff. His folding chair creaked as he raised his 6'4" frame. Turning slowly, he glared at Dr. Strode like a mongoose at a cobra. Reading his meaning, Donovan allowed him to finish an entire verse and chorus of "I'm Getting Married in the Morning," before he asked him to sit down.

When Donovan called 23, Abbot Cooper was still weighing his options.

As a child, Abbot had been considered a gifted singer. And because the private schools he attended had choirs and because his parents were always benefactors, he was awarded any solo part a performance featured. Once his voice changed, he was relegated to the tenor section and eventually quit altogether, claiming he needed the time to study. He had not been alone on a stage since he was 13. He was still waffling on what to do when Agnes turned around to see who was next. Spotting him, she raised her eyebrows, as if to say, "Well?" He walked forward.

Before Pinetta could begin, he sang a middle C and proceeded up the scale.

Abbot had perfect pitch.

He sailed into the sight-reading piece he had memorized after hearing it once and before Pinetta could transfer *West Side Story* to the music stand, he began, "There's a place for us…somewhere a place for us…"

She waited, found a place to catch up, and played as she never had.

"Somehow…someday…somewhere…"

At the end, there was no applause. Only silence.

The young stranger people had seen around town, but did not know, became theirs; every man's friend, every mother's son, every girl's dream.

He bowed low—old habits die hard—and left the stage and the building.

Stunned, Agnes turned to Truitt. "Did you coach him?"

He shook his head. "First time I've heard him."

By the end of the long evening, the first two rows on both sides of the aisle were lined with survivors and only two men remained unsummoned.

Chapter 16 ~ At the Delahunty House

Wyatt Blackwell, a retired history professor from UNC Chapel Hill, had relocated to Dennisonville to care for his 90-year-old mother. An imposing figure, thinning hair on top, with soft, wavy white hair combed back over his ears and brushing his collar, he was handsome and debonair even at 68. When Donovan called his number, 42, (most of the 30's had escaped by then), Wyatt drew himself up to his full height and turned to face the conductor.

"*Dr. Blackwell*," he said. "Haven't been a number since I was in the army."

Donovan's glasses slipped from the top of his head and crashed onto his nose.

Eileen stifled a laugh.

Pinetta straightened her already straight posture as Wyatt took the stage. "Old Man River" never sounded so good.

When Wyatt found a seat behind Agnes, she turned and mouthed 'thank you.'

He patted her shoulder. "Hang together or hang separately."

Lute Monroe, a bundle of nerves by then, did not wait for Donovan to call him. Still holding his cap, he pushed himself up and flexed his knees. When he passed Agnes, she nabbed his cap.

"I'll hold onto this," she said.

He let go and faced the music.

The weary assembly was about to find out what only Lute's family and John Roy Goode, hired to stack produce after school and on weekends, knew.

Lute Monroe could sing.

Pinetta sounded a chord. He soared up and down the scales. Like Abbot, he had memorized the sight-reading pieces and sang with such verve even Esmé Inch looked up from her judging sheets.

Pinetta lifted the final number from the piano bench and played the introduction, her mind elsewhere. *Finish this and we can go home,* she thought, while Lute, wiping sweat from his forehead, breathed a silent prayer his meaning would be understood.

He opened his mouth and sang:

I'm glad I met you. You, wonderful you. I can't forget you. You, wonderful you. You're like a breath of spring. A whole new thing has happened...

One by one, ladies closed their eyes or bowed their heads to dream of the men they loved...or would have loved...or had once loved. If they did not *look* at Lute, his stomach straining against his shirt buttons; hair uncombed, plastered to his head; work boots scuffed at the toes, they could imagine anyone…singing *those* words…with that voice…to them.

Even Esmé Inch let her eyes droop closed as she dreamed of her Frank.

On the verge of tears, Eileen turned away, so no one would see.

Mary Grace Dodson was transfixed, as if seeing Lute for the first time.

Eyes glued to her music, Pinetta played, oblivious to the noble man laying bare his soul a few feet away. Pesky visions of the long months ahead swarmed around her. Week after week of leaving Barton behind to spend hours rehearsing in some stale chorus room. Bad enough. But to trade time with the man she loved for watching Donovan Strode badger these well-meaning people—his hapless chorale—who hummed quietly while they worked, or sang lustily, hymnbook in hand, on the back row of some church choir on Sundays.

It was not to be born.

Lute's intended message drifted unopened into the dead letter office of Pinetta's heart.

When he finished, he wiped his face with a dingy handkerchief, turned away from the breathless audience, and steadied himself against the piano.

"That was for—" Lute began, when the sound of pounding feet shattered the moment.

Mary Grace Dodson, waving a tryout form like a battle flag, was hurtling to the front. "Wait. Wait. I've been counting. There aren't enough sopranos…and…I…sing…soprano."

If Pinetta had not been a Pembroke, she would have launched herself off the piano bench and shaken Mary Grace till her teeth rattled.

Panting, Mary Grace addressed the dazed audience. "I wasn't going to try out, but I've been keeping track and…Dr. Strode is right…there are too many altos…."

Serafina unscrewed the lid on her water bottle and handed it to Mary Grace, who sipped and went on. "I filled out a form"—she held it up—"and I want to…"

Jaw jutted forward, Pinetta hit middle C.

A little too hard.

Mary Grace fanned herself with her paper before laying it on the piano. "Give me a minute. I haven't caught my—"

Pinetta ripped through the vocal exercises, forcing Mary Grace to catch up and keep pace, which she accomplished with surprising success.

Chapter 16 ~ At the Delahunty House

Dumbfounded, Lute was still rooted in place. So close…to speaking four simple words to Pinetta. How had everything gone wrong? He stepped away from the piano, took his cap from Agnes, and walked quietly up the aisle, past the judges, and into the hall.

Eileen Redmon jumped to her feet, toppling her chair as she hurried after Lute.

"Redmon. Where are you going? Sit down," Donovan said.

She ignored him.

On stage, Mary Grace, whose mother had driven her to voice lessons in Charlotte every week for six years, was flying through the sight reading.

Lute had one foot out the front door by the time Eileen caught up with him.

"Mr. Monroe," she said, reaching out her hand. "Lute."

Pulling on his cap, he turned back. "Ma'am?"

"I…I wanted to thank you for the song. Your voice. I've never heard one so—?"

He shrugged. "Nothing I did. Born with it. My mother called it a gift."

"She was right about that. Why have I never heard you sing? In a town this size, all the musicians know each other. All I've ever known about you is—"

"I sell produce?"

"Yes."

"I used to be sing…till I was 16 and—" He ducked his head. "Long story. But when I heard about this choir, I thought it might be a good time to try again."

"I'm glad you did."

"*Climb…every…mountain,*" wafted into the foyer.

Without the piano.

"I need to get going," Lute said. "Have to get up early in the morning."

"Of course, you know you made the choir," Eileen said. "Dr. Strode was impressed, and it's not easy to impress him."

"I don't care nothing about impressing *him*."

"No," she said. "Neither do I. See you at rehearsals?"

"I suppose. Good night."

"*Follow every rainbow…*"

Eileen tiptoed back into the Blue Room and returned to her place. Not bothering to sit down, she wrote "10" in every box on Mary Grace's judging sheet while she was still singing. Then Eileen walked around Donovan, handed the paper to Esmé, and stationed herself in the aisle.

"*Till...you...find...*"

"What are you doing, woman? We're not finished," Donovan said.

"I am," Eileen said.

"*Your...dream.*"

Esmé held up a stack of paper. "The scores need to be tallied."

"Tomorrow," Eileen said, marching forward.

The fifteen survivors, huddled together in groups of two or three, congratulated Mary Grace and then praised each other, excusing any missed notes or forgotten words, remarking how Mrs. Inch "hadn't changed one bit since we were in elementary school."

Agnes hugged Mary Grace. "I didn't know you could sing."

"Oh, yes," Dinah said. "Mary Grace and I used to be in the Dreamettes."

"Dreamettes?" Agnes asked.

"Our girls' ensemble in junior high," Dinah said. "We wore royal blue dresses. Sang at the high school prom." She demonstrated. *Bewitched...*"

Mary Grace slipped her arm around her friend. "*...bothered and bewildered am I.*"

They giggled like school girls.

Eileen was making her way through the crowd, when Verbena grabbed her arm.

"Thank you for helping me with my song," Verbena said. "When I looked up and saw you smiling, just like your mother, it gave me courage. I hope I was good enough."

Eileen embraced her. "If it were up to me, you'd have a solo."

Pinetta left the piano, marched across the room, and positioned herself near Agnes, who was busy answering everyone's questions about the mysterious Abbot Cooper.

If Agnes read Pinetta's body language—pursed lips, tapping foot—she gave no indication.

Pinetta decided to appeal to Truitt. Maybe together they could convince Agnes it was time to go. She spotted Truitt talking to Wyatt Blackwell and walked over.

"I only sing for fun," Truitt was saying. "My first love is conducting. Followed by—"

Wyatt narrowed his eyes. "You're a conductor?"

"Yes, at the college where Agnes and I used to teach. I'm retired now."

Chapter 16 ~ At the Delahunty House

"You taught voice?"

"No, I was an orchestra conductor. I'm hoping to give woodwind lessons once my arm is completely healed. If there's any demand in this town."

"You're a professional musician...with a degree?" Wyatt asked.

Pinetta's patience was exhausted. "Yes. He has a Ph.D. Sorry to interrupt..."

Wyatt smiled at her. "I'm glad you came over. It gives me a chance to thank you for your very fine playing. Strode should have introduced you."

"He would've gotten around to it sooner or later," she said. "Truitt, don't you think—"

A piercing voice resounded from the back of the room.

"Attention, everyone," announced Mrs. Oxley-Friend. "The clean-up crew is here. I'm going to have to ask you to leave and finish your conversations elsewhere."

"Well," Wyatt said. "The *grand dame* has spoken. Could we meet for coffee in the morning, Truitt? At Mollie's? 8:30? I'd like to talk about the choir."

"I'll be there," Truitt said.

When Wyatt left, Pinetta squeezed Truitt's elbow. "Let's go. I'm exhausted."

"Me, too. Where do you suppose Agnes is?"

"Maybe she's at the truck."

They stepped into the hall and found Agnes talking to Eileen by the front door.

Agnes called to them. "Truitt. Pinetta. Come here. Eileen wants to meet you."

Pinetta complied, only because this would bring her nearer to escaping.

"This is Truitt," Agnes said.

Eileen held out her hand. "Dr. Spenlow, it's nice to meet you."

"And this is Pinetta."

"I enjoyed hearing you play," Eileen said. "You did a great job."

"Thank you," Pinetta said curtly.

"I'll see you in the morning, then," Eileen said. "Good night." She started out and then turned back. "Because of you three, I'm going to sleep better tonight than I have in months."

"Wonder what she meant by that," Truitt said.

"Guess we'll find out in the morning," Agnes said. "She invited herself over."

175

Tea at Kimball Pines

Nerves frayed, Pinetta remained silent all the way home, while Agnes and Truitt reviewed the performances. At least the night she had long dreaded was over—her fears faced. Tomorrow, after she had rested and could manage to sound positive, she would call Millie and tell her how well auditions had gone. Millie would be pleased. There was some satisfaction in that. Rehearsals were not scheduled to begin till January. She could devote all her efforts to preparing for Christmas. Her first Christmas with Barton. Surely he would stay through the holidays. He and Nestor were getting along so well.

They drove onto Belmont Drive. Pinetta's heart raced when she saw the kitchen light still on. Maybe, as she had hoped, the men were sitting at the table, having coffee, talking over the day's work.

Barton would stand and help her with her coat. Pull out a chair. Offer her a cup of tea. It would be the most natural thing in the world for her and Agnes and Truitt to join them, talk for a while.

"Guess everyone is still awake," Agnes said. "I could use a snack, and I can't wait to tell Nestor what happened."

When they stepped inside, only Ham was waiting.

He pulled out a chair. "Miss Pinetta, could you sit down a minute?"

"Is something wrong?" Agnes asked.

"I'm afraid there is," Ham said.

Pinetta feared the worst—Barton was hurt. Nestor had driven him to the hospital.

"Where are the others?" Pinetta asked.

"They've gone to bed. I told them I'd tell you the news."

"Tell me what?"

Truitt sat next to her.

"Your sister called," Ham said. "It's your father. He had a heart attack."

Pinetta gasped. "Papa? Is he in the hospital?"

Ham hung his head. "They tried to save him, but they couldn't. He's gone. I'm sorry."

Pinetta could not make sense of what she was hearing. Her father. That formidable presence who had hovered over all their lives. Gone? Couldn't be.

She bolted up. "I should go home. Do they want me to come tonight?"

"No," Ham said. "Your sister said your mother doesn't want you to travel at night. They'll pick up you at the train station tomorrow afternoon."

"I'll have to face them again."

"Face them?" Truitt asked.

Chapter 16 ~ At the Delahunty House

"I haven't seen any of them...well, except Eve, since I left home...after my divorce."

Helpless, Truitt looked over at Agnes.

She put her arm around Pinetta. "Come to your room. I'll make you a cup of tea."

"I have to pack," Pinetta said.

Agnes guided her to her door. "I'll help you."

"Who'll do the cooking while I'm gone?"

"We'll manage," Agnes said.

"I'll take you to the station," Ham said.

"Good night, Pinetta," Truitt said, as she left the room. He turned to Ham. "What time will you leave for the station, Ham?"

"There's a train at 6:30."

"I'm going with you. Can you drop me at Mollie's on the way home?"

The next morning Pinetta rose before dawn as usual and made the last pot of coffee she would serve Barton for...who knew how long? She finished packing and made her bed, surprised at how melancholy she felt about leaving her room. She brought her suitcase to the kitchen and sat quietly, waiting for Ham to come downstairs.

The basement door opened. Jonas came into the kitchen. Barton followed.

Jonas sat next to her and took her hands in his. "I'm sorry about your father."

"Thank you," she said. "He lived a long, full life."

"There's something to be said for that," Barton said. "Living a good life. Not everyone does. Hope you have a good trip. We'll be thinking about you."

She lifted her face to gaze into his eyes. "Thank you. I'll miss you...all."

Ham and Truitt drove Pinetta to the train station and waited with her on the platform.

"Will you call us when you get there?" Ham asked. "So we don't worry?"

"Yes. I hate to leave." Then she added: "Agnes isn't that great of a cook."

"We'll miss you," Truitt said. "And not just because of the cooking."

Pinetta boarded the train for Sumter, South Carolina. Suitcase in hand, she kept her head down as she walked past her fellow passengers. She sat next to a window, settled her bag in the aisle seat, and propped her elbow on the arm rest. Leaning her head on her hand, she stared out the window as the train pulled out of the station.

One week. That would be respectful enough. She would be home in time for Christmas. With Barton. How she wished he were going with her to meet her family.

Three hours later Eileen Redmon arrived at the Magnolia Arms. Agnes, washing the breakfast dishes, dried her hands and answered the door.

"Hello, Eileen. Pardon the mess. We're remodeling."

Eileen looked puzzled. "Remodeling? I've always thought this house was perfect."

"Ham talked Nestor into it," Agnes said. "Adding another room on this floor and turning the porch into a master bedroom and a nursery. Have you been here before?"

"Yes, to visit Margaret when she lived here. We taught together at the high school."

"Of course. I should've known that. Come in the kitchen. We'll try to talk, but if there's too much racket from the porch, we'll move to the parlor."

Eileen sat at the table. "How many men are out there? Sounds like an army."

Agnes took cups from the cabinet. "Just three. My father-in-law and Ham and Jonas, Margaret's husband."

"I'd heard he was here."

"Would you like to meet him?"

"Love to. He's a legend in this town."

Agnes opened the back door and waved to Jonas. He shut down the table saw.

"Someone here wants to meet you," she said. "A friend of Margaret's."

"Be right there," he said. "Need coffee anyway." He removed his safety glasses as he came into the kitchen. "I guess our days of being served are over now that Pinetta is gone."

"You guessed right," Agnes said, laughing. "This is Eileen."

Eileen extended her hand. "So you're the lucky man who married Margaret."

"I am."

Ham was right behind him. "Hello, Miss Eileen. Haven't seen you in a while."

Chapter 16 ~ At the Delahunty House

"I've been keeping to myself, except for going to school. Tired of so many questions."

"Sorry to hear about your husband," Ham said. "And your house."

She added cream to her coffee. "At least he left me the piano."

"You're...divorced?" Agnes asked.

Eileen nodded. "Yeah. That's why I bailed out of playing for the choir. I can't concentrate on anything at the moment."

Brushing sawdust from his clothes, Barton entered. When he saw Eileen, he stopped where he was, fixed his eyes on her, and brushed his hair from his forehead.

"Didn't know we had company," he said, straightening his collar.

That smooth voice. The wistful look.

Agnes noticed and for Pinetta's sake, introduced Barton as her "father-in-law, Mr. Carlyle."

"So you're Nestor's father," Eileen said.

He sat across from her. "I am. And it's 'Barton.'"

For the first time, Agnes understood how Barton had wooed and won four wives.

And was grateful Pinetta had been spared from watching his latest conquest turn a rosy shade of pink.

Chapter 17

Pinetta Phones Home

"Telephone for Mrs. Fraleigh," the maid said. "A Mr. Hampton."

Eleven pairs of eyes turned to the open French doors of Alfred Pembroke's study.

Trying not to smile, Pinetta set her cup and saucer on the end table as she stood.

"Not now," Miriam, her oldest sister said. "We haven't finished discussing the music for the service."

Of all Pinetta's sisters, Miriam was most like their mother. Elegant, imposing, bossy.

"Hampton? Do we know a Hampton?" Mrs. Pembroke asked. "Is he coming for the funeral?"

"No, Mother," Pinetta said, edging toward the door. "He's an acquaintance of mine."

"Can't he call back later?" Eve asked. "We've been at this for hours. I'd like to finish before dinner."

Pinetta hesitated, but only for a moment. "Ham…Mr. Hampton… wouldn't call unless it was important. It would be rude not to answer." She gladly closed the doors behind her.

"Would you like to use the phone upstairs?" the maid asked.

"No, the kitchen phone will be fine."

The kitchen staff was surprised to see Mrs. Fraleigh hurry in, and even more surprised when she stooped to pick up an apple peel and drop it in the sink.

She snatched the phone. "Hello?"

"Hello, Miss Pinetta," Ham said. "How are you?"

She leaned against the counter, comforted and content for the first time in days.

The cook, stirring lemon custard, glanced over her shoulder, puzzled at the presence of a Pembroke daughter in the kitchen.

"I'm all right," Pinetta said. "We've been so busy. I haven't had a chance to call."

"I understand," he said, Agnes at his elbow. "We were just wondering when…you might be coming back. Margaret's on her way, too, and we wanted to…plan our trips…to the station."

Agnes frowned and rolled her eyes.

"I won't be back as soon as I thought," Pinetta said. "So many people have so far to travel. My father's business associates, old fraternity brothers. Relatives I've never even heard of." She cupped her hand over the receiver. "All curious about the will."

"Oh. Well. Uh…when's the funeral? We thought four days—"

"Not till Tuesday."

"So…will you be coming back on Wednesday?" he asked.

Agnes nodded approval.

"I don't know," Pinetta said. "There's so much to tend to. Two of my sisters think Mother should move to a retirement community. The grandkids have been hinting about what they'll take with them. I think it's going to get risky after the funeral. How's everyone there?"

"We're fine. Fine. I wanted to call and tell you—"

"Are the new rooms finished yet?"

"Almost," Ham said.

"I can't wait to see them." She paused. "Is Barton still there? Since you're still working?"

Ham looked at Agnes. "Yes. Barton's still here. We plan to start painting tomorrow."

Agnes waved her hand, urging him to continue.

"So," Pinetta asked, "he'll still be there when I get back?"

The maid approached Pinetta. "Ma'am? Your mother sent me for you."

"I have to go, Ham. Thank you for calling. Tell everyone I said hello. *Everyone*, okay?"

The phone went silent. Ham hung up.

"What happened?" Agnes asked.

"I don't know. She said she had to go."

"So she's coming back on Wednesday??"

Chapter 17 ~ *Pinetta Phones Home*

"No. The funeral is Tuesday. She thinks the family will start arguing after that."

"That buys us a few more days," Agnes said. "I wish you could've told her."

"Why do I have to be the one to tell her?"

"Because of all the people in this house, she likes you best."

He sighed. "I wish I could get this over with. I'm tired of dreading it."

The following week Pinetta stood at the grave of her father, Alfred Arthur Pembroke, as freezing rain dripped off black umbrellas, soaked black coat sleeves, chilled black-gloved hands.

The day could not have been more gray and dismal—a point the funeral director made when he suggested burial be delayed till Thursday.

But the Pembroke sense of propriety held firm.

After the service, Pinetta guided her mother to the limousine and climbed in beside her.

While her sisters, their husbands, children, and grandchildren followed behind in a long procession of family cars.

Alone, at her mother's elbow, Pinetta felt like a child, too young to ride with the others.

Her mother squeezed her hand. "You're a good daughter, Pinetta. I knew you'd come to your senses sooner or later and come home where you belong."

They returned to the Lutheran church for lunch hosted in the fellowship hall.

Sick to death of fielding questions from her mother's well-meaning friends—"Where are you living?"—"Coming home now that your father's gone?"—"Still playing the piano?"—Pinetta stationed herself squarely among her great-nieces and great-nephews and pretended to be occupied with their care. When one too many people encouraged her to eat, she relented, serving herself token portions of mushroom-souped-casseroles and fruit-cocktail-in-Jello-salads, leaving it all uneaten, the hot food melting the cold, soup and Jello puddling in the center of a paper plate. She wondered what was on the menu at the Magnolia Arms and wished she were there.

When the meal was finally over, the family caravanned home. The children burst through the door and raced for the Christmas cookies in the kitchen and then to the television in the den. Pinetta, desperate to be alone, offered to carry the youngest child upstairs. She put him down for a nap and

Tea at Kimball Pines

retreated to her old room. Closing the door, she sat in the window seat and stared at the glowering clouds.

Her "respectful week" of mourning was stretching into two. And she was still impossibly far from home. Home. When had she begun to think of the Magnolia Arms as "home"?

Flickering images, fragments of memory fluttered through her mind. Cool air from the open kitchen window. Lifting her hand from warm, soapy water to wave at Annie May Goode on the sidewalk. The scent of Ham's Old Spice aftershave as they rode together to the store. The creak of the stairs as she climbed to the third floor. The arched window opening out onto the world of stars, clouds, rain, falling leaves, drifting snow. Carrot cake from Mollie's. Tea with Agnes. Coffee with Barton. Snuggling into bed in her cozy room off the kitchen. Busy mornings. Quiet evenings. Pleasant conversation.

She jumped up, took her suitcase from the closet, and opened it on the bed.

There was a knock at the door. "Pinetta. It's Miriam."

"Come in," Pinetta said, slipping off her black shoes.

Miriam, doused with Chanel No. 5, swept in. "Mother sent me to get you. Bryan insists they start home today and"—she pointed at the suitcase—"what are you doing?"

"Packing."

"What on earth for?"

"So I don't have to do it in the morning."

"You're leaving Mother to spend Christmas *alone*?"

Pinetta squinted at her eldest sister, chin tucked, hands folded. In that posture, with that white streak in her dyed-black hair, she looked too much like Cinderella's stepmother.

"Isn't she going home with one of you?" Pinetta asked, opening the closet.

"No. Giles and I have reservations at a B & B in Charleston. Livie's flying to New York. Nelle will be in Boston with her in-laws. And Eve…well, you know how Bryan is. You'd *know* all this if you hadn't spent most of the week moping in your room."

"I haven't been moping."

"Please, Pinetta, I don't have time to argue. The fact of it is the rest of us need to get home. You're the only one with no plans."

Hangered clothes draped over her arm, Pinetta whirled to face her sister. "What makes you think I have no plans?"

Chapter 17 ~ Pinetta Phones Home

"Livie said the woman you worked for went home to her children."

"What does that have to do with anything?"

"It means you have no obligations...and no one to get back to," she said, lecturing. "We just naturally assumed you'd stay with Mother through Christmas. Maybe till New Year's."

Tears stinging her eyes, Pinetta threw the clothes into the suitcase, hangers and all. "I have a *home*. A beautiful home. In Dennisonville. I've lived there a year and—"

"It's not your *home*. You're the cook. Not, by the way, what we were raised to be, now that you mention it."

"I didn't mention it, and what business is it of yours what I do? At least I'm doing something honorable...helping people...not just going to stuffy club meetings and benefits."

Temples throbbing, Pinetta went on, barely conscious of what she was saying.

"And they don't think of me as a cook. They think of me as a friend. We do things together. Talk about something other than how much money we have."

"I *beg* your pardon." Miriam would have been less startled if Pinetta had slapped her.

Pinetta stormed to the dresser, pulled open a drawer, yanked out her underwear, slip, and nightgown, threw them in the suitcase, and slammed it shut, stray sleeves hanging out.

"What in the world has gotten into you?" Miriam asked. "You're talking like a lunatic."

Pinetta sank onto the bed. "No, I'm not. In fact, since I've been here, I'm seeing things more clearly than I have in a long time. For the first time in my life I know what I want."

Miriam stepped to the door. "Isn't that what you said when you *begged* Papa to let you marry Guy Henry? Look how that turned out. And *now* he's married *again*."

Cut to the heart, Pinetta sprang up. "I'm getting married, too, you know."

The words were out of her mouth before she knew what had happened. "*What?*"

It was too late to turn back. And Pinetta relished the stunned look on Miriam's face. They would part in the morning. What could it hurt to savor this moment?

"He was going to come home with me for Christmas, but when Papa died so suddenly, there was no chance to arrange things. It wasn't the right time."

Miriam opened the door. "Does Mother know about this?"

"No, Mother doesn't know."

"We'll discuss this *later*. Come say goodbye to our sister."

Pinetta opened her suitcase and stuffed in the dangling sleeves. "I'll come say goodbye, but I'm not discussing anything. Not with you or anyone else."

She followed Miriam downstairs to the front door where the family had gathered.

When Eve hugged Pinetta, she whispered in her ear. "Keep your eye on Miriam's kids. They'll walk away with half the house, if you let them."

Advice Pinetta remembered when the next morning Pembroke claws were bared.

Miriam's son laid claim to his grandfather's golf clubs. When Livie's son complained, Miriam reminded him of the money he had received for college tuition and demanded fairness.

Nelle wanted to take the piano. Pinetta objected, since she was the only one to inherit their father's musical talent, to which Nelle replied, "You have no place to put it."

Pinetta yielded, reminding herself she was going home to the beautiful grand piano in the parlor. And if she ever got back to the Magnolia Arms, she was never leaving again.

Miriam put an index card bearing her name on the John Gould prints in the study. When Livie protested, Miriam argued she and Pinetta, as the elder daughters, had "grown up poor" before their father achieved success. They deserved more now. Again demanding fairness.

"Don't you agree, Pinetta?" Miriam asked.

"I might have a year ago," Pinetta said. "But not now. I've met too many people who are satisfied with what they have...and they're much happier than any of you."

And easier to get along with, she thought.

The longer the sisters put off leaving, the crankier they became. Livie and Nelle, who had flight reservations, were furious Miriam, who was driving to Charleston, would be left behind to "pillage the house." They appealed to their mother, pleading their cases, and resorting to tears. Mrs. Pembroke, who hated to deny her daughters anything, was at a loss to keep them at

Chapter 17 ~ *Pinetta Phones Home*

peace. When she began to weep, regretting she "had not gone first and left Alfred behind, who always knew what to do," Pinetta had had enough and decided to call the person she trusted most.

Millie Hubbard.

"I was only going to stay a week," Pinetta said. "Once the funeral was over, I thought I could leave, but my sisters are fighting over who's going to take what. My mother is in tears."

"You can't leave her alone to referee them," Millie said. "She's not up to it. Situations like this can alienate families for years. You don't want that, do you?"

"But why does it have to be up to me to keep peace?"

"Because you've learned more than your sisters in the last year and because you have a good heart. You always took good care of me. You can't do less than that for your own mother."

"I don't know what to do."

"We had a lawyer friend. Had the same problem with a client. He bought colored stickers, assigned a color to each sibling, made them draw numbers to see who would choose first, and then marched them through the house, taking turns marking what they wanted. Sounds childish, but it worked."

Pinetta followed her advice. Once the process was complete, she volunteered to make an inventory and mail them each a copy.

"*After* I get home," she added.

Leaving their loot and their mother in her care, the sisters went in pursuit of a perfect holiday.

Pinetta scheduled a mover to pick up the piano, hired a local gallery owner to pack and ship the Gould prints, and boxed up her father's first editions and all his golf sweaters.

She kept his golf hat and desk lamp for herself.

Two days later, her duties fulfilled, Pinetta followed her mother down the aisle of the Lutheran church and sat next to her during the Christmas Eve service.

Mrs. Pembroke sang lustily, dabbing at her eyes only once during "O, Holy Night," reminding Pinetta it was "Papa's favorite."

Staring at the flickering candles, Pinetta mouthed the familiar words without thinking, while she rehearsed the phone call she intended to make when they got home. She would ask about the weather. The house. Everyone else…*then* tell whoever answered, she needed to speak to Barton about a

Tea at Kimball Pines

building project. When he came to the phone, she would say her mother was going to convert their old carriage house to an apartment for her grandson. What was his advice? None of this was true. Only a ploy to hear the sound of Barton's voice—all she wanted for Christmas.

On the way home Mrs. Pembroke rambled aimlessly about the service, the days long gone when "all five of my girls were lined up on the pew beside me. Remember?"—sighing—"Every year I had Mrs. Robertson make matching Christmas dresses. Till Miriam turned 13 and refused to wear what the rest of you were wearing. *It's a Wonderful Life* will be on tonight. I had cook save some of the fruitcake. When we get home, you slice it while I get ready for bed. Then we'll watch George Bailey. Just like we used to."

Pinetta followed her mother into the house and watched as she climbed the stairs.

Halfway up, her mother paused. "Aren't you coming?"

"In a minute. The fruitcake. Remember?"

When she heard her mother's bedroom door close, she tiptoed into her father's study and closed the French doors behind her. Sitting at his desk, she dialed the Magnolia Arms.

Agnes answered. "Hello?"

"Hello, Agnes. This is Pinetta."

"We were just talking about you. Can you hold on a minute?" Agnes laid down the phone and stepped into the hall, calling to Ham in the parlor. "Pinetta's on the phone."

Pinetta propped her arm on her father's desk. "How's the weather there?"

"Freezing," Agnes said. "We're hoping for a white Christmas."

"Is everyone all right? I heard the flu was going around." Not true.

"Yes. Everyone's fine. Margaret's here. And Ham invited Fiona over tonight. She's been helping us out since you've been gone."

Ham had entered the kitchen; Agnes motioned him forward.

Pinetta moved on to Question 3. "Did you take the turkey out of the freezer?"

Agnes laughed. "Yes, Margaret reminded me."

Question 4. "Are the new rooms finished?"

"Yes. But we haven't moved anything in. Waiting till after Christmas."

"How's…Truitt?" Pinetta asked.

Ham stood next to Agnes.

"We hardly see him anymore," Agnes said. "Once the choir list came out, he started going to rehearsals."

Chapter 17 ~ Pinetta Phones Home

"I thought they didn't start till January."

"They don't. These are practice sessions. Organized by Wyatt Blackwell. Truitt works with the men one night, women the next. We're trying to get ready to face Donovan."

Pinetta peered into hall to watch for her mother. "Who's playing the piano? Eileen?"

"No," Agnes said. "I am. Just till you get back. Want to talk to Ham?"

"Ham? No. Actually…I was wondering if I could talk to Barton for a minute."

Agnes winced. "Barton?"

"Yes…my mother has an idea to convert our old carriage house into—"

"If it's building advice you want, I'll get Jonas. Talk to Ham while I'm gone." Holding her hand over the receiver, Agnes whispered. "She's asking for Barton. This is it."

Biting his lip, Ham took the phone. "Hello, Miss Pinetta. Merry Christmas."

"Merry Christmas," Pinetta said, irritated her script was off track. "I didn't want to bother Jonas…since Margaret's there. I thought Barton would be the best—"

Pinetta's mother opened the door. "Who are you talking to?"

"My friends…in Dennisonville. I wanted to tell them Merry Christmas."

"Did you take the fruitcake to the den?"

"No. I thought I'd do this first."

She rolled her eyes. "Never mind. I'll do it myself. Don't be long."

Her mother walked away, leaving the door ajar.

Agnes tugged on Ham's sleeve. "What happened?"

"Her mother came to the door. I think she's in trouble."

"Her mother?"

"No," Ham said. "Pinetta."

"Try to get back on the subject."

Pinetta lowered her voice. "Ham?"

"Yes. I'm still here."

"I can't talk much longer. Is there any way I can talk to Barton for just a minute? He's still there, isn't he? I mean everything's okay between him and—?"

Mrs. Pembroke, holding two dessert plates, reappeared at the study door, and nodded in the direction of the den.

Tea at Kimball Pines

"Be right there," Pinetta said and returned her attention to Ham. "I can't talk much longer. She'll badger me with questions. Please, could you get Barton?"

Ham squeezed his eyes shut. "I can't. He's not here."

"You said he was."

"He's still *staying* here, but he's not here right now." He let out a sigh. "There's no easy way to say this." Agnes laid her hand on his arm. "Barton and Eileen have been spending a lot of time together. She invited him to go home with her for the holidays. To meet her family."

Pinetta hung up the phone and clamped her hand over her mouth to stifle a cry.

Her mother called. "Are you off the phone yet? The movie's started."

Pinetta walked across the thick hunter green carpet and stepped into the hall.

"Just a minute." She steadied her voice. "I'm going to get ready for bed."

"Bring napkins with you. The Christmas ones."

Grasping the banister, Pinetta climbed the stairs and made a dash for her room. She yanked the brocade pillow off the bed and buried her face in it, sobbing like a lovesick teenager.

Here. In this spot she had wept over her first schoolgirl crush. Grieved when she had no date to the prom. Mourned Guy Henry. And now here she was again, crying over the man who was supposed to change everything, but hadn't.

She pulled off her clothes, left them in a pile on the floor, and pulled her nightgown over her head. Stumbling into the bathroom, she ducked her head to avoid her reflection in mirror, and splashed cold water on her face.

Still in a daze, she returned to her room and slipped on her robe, tying the sash as she started down the stairs.

If Mother asks if I've been crying, she thought, *I'll say I miss Papa.*

But Mrs. Pembroke, engrossed in her holiday ritual, did not look up when Pinetta came into the room and sat in the tall wingback chair next to hers.

Just in time to watch George Bailey select a suitcase for the trip around the world he would never take.

Chapter 18

Moving Day

Mrs. Pembroke fanned out her cards on the table. "Gin."

Pinetta tallied the score and put down the pencil. "I'm going upstairs now."

"Not now," her mother said. "You might win the next one."

All the Pembroke girls knew better than to win at gin rummy when facing their mother as an opponent. Better to lose than endure her pouting.

Pinetta scraped the cards together into a neat stack and left them in the center of the table. "I need to finish packing."

"Pack?" Mrs. Pembroke asked, shuffling the cards. "What's your rush?"

"I've been here two weeks. I'm not exactly rushing."

Tears puddled in Mrs. Pembroke's eyes. "But…it's Christmas. We haven't had a second piece of pie, and tomorrow we need to return gifts…and have turkey noodle soup."

Pinetta stood and pushed her chair under the table. "I've already called Mrs. Pratt. She'll be here in the morning to take you shopping and out to lunch."

"You're leaving *tomorrow*?"

"No. Tonight."

"Tonight? *Why?*"

The scene was unfolding exactly as Pinetta had predicted; she delivered her next line.

"I need to go home."

"You are home," Mrs. Pembroke said, as if scolding a four-year-old.

"No, Mother. I'm not. This is your home. Not mine. Not any longer."

And there it was—the slight tilt of the head, the look of disdain Pinetta knew so well.

"But it *could* be," Mrs. Pembroke said. "You could move back into your room or any other room in the house. You always liked Miriam's room better than yours. Take it."

Pinetta edged toward the door and the hall. "I don't want to live in Miriam's old room. I'm not a child whose older sister has left for college."

Not that Miriam could've graduated, she thought.

Her mother smacked her lips. "I know you're not a child, but you're acting like one."

Pinetta whirled around. "You watched my sisters squabbling over Papa's things like junkyard dogs over a trashcan, and you're calling *me* a child? How can you say that?"

Mrs. Pembroke regrouped. "I'm only trying to reason with you. I understand why you had to get away after your divorce. You were embarrassed. I understand that."

"Do you *really*?"

"Of course. But that was long time ago. You don't need to wear that hangdog expression anymore. As mistress of *this* house, you would—"

"I don't *want* to be mistress of this house."

Coached by Miriam, Mrs. Pembroke had rehearsed her own script.

"You don't have to live *here*. You could buy your own house now that you have your inheritance. Finally put Guy Henry behind you. Now that his new wife is expecting—"

Pinetta felt the room spin. "*What?*"

Mrs. Pembroke clasped her hands to her cheeks. "I wasn't supposed to tell you." Then she rallied, taking aim. "But why shouldn't you know, if it will make you face reality?"

Pinetta could barely manage a whisper. "She can't be pregnant. She's…in her forties."

"Barely 40," her mother said, pressing her advantage. "Mid-life pregnancies happen all the time. They're leaving town to be near her family. There's no *reason* you can't move back."

"How long have you known?" Pinetta asked, her voice sticking in her throat.

"A couple of weeks."

"Why didn't you tell me?"

"Miriam said not to. She said if you knew, you'd never move back."

"She was right," Pinetta said, walking away.

"Where are you going?"

"I told you. To finish packing."

Chapter 18 ~ Moving Day

"I don't know what's gotten into you, Pinetta. You used to be so sensible. But you've changed. You're not the same person you were when you left here."

Pinetta faced her mother. "You mean that?"

Mrs. Pembroke straightened the cameo brooch pinned at her collar. "Yes, I do."

"Thank you. That's the nicest thing you ever said to me."

Agnes was waiting for Pinetta when her train arrived the morning after Christmas.

Having too much…and nothing…to say, they smiled as politely as strangers.

Agnes offered a hug. Steeled not to cry, Pinetta remained aloof.

In a feeble attempt to help, Agnes reached for the suitcase.

"No, thank you, I'll carry it," Pinetta said, and followed Agnes to the truck.

They rode in silence. Pinetta, nestled in the seat, quieted her soul with the familiar sights of the town she had once despised.

"You missed the turn," Pinetta said.

"We're going to Mollie's," Agnes said. "I thought you could use a little time before we went back to the house, so we could talk…about Barton."

"Ham told you?"

"Yes. That day in the kitchen when…you know…the paper bag?"

Pinetta felt her face go hot. "I'll have to move out. I thought about it all night. I can't stand by and watch Eileen…I mean if she's going to come over all the time…"

"We already talked about that and made arrangements…for you."

Pinetta felt like she had been kicked in the stomach. *Just like that? After a year of cooking for them? Was Miriam right? Is that all I am to them? An employee?* She fought to preserve her dignity. "So Fiona…helping out. That worked well for all of you?"

"Yes. We would've been lost without her. The holidays. Company. The rooms to finish. Margaret and I were always out shopping. That left Fiona in charge."

"Who took care of Vesper while Fiona was at—?"

"She did everything. She'd fix breakfast for Vesper, get her lunch ready, leave it in the fridge, then come to our house. Went back and forth every day. She's amazing."

"Of course, she could manage both jobs. She's young…"

"And she's been saving money to go to college full-time. Did you know she wants to be a nurse? So, the extra money we paid her was a big help. It was a win for everybody."

Wounded, Pinetta had nothing left to say.

Muriel met them at the door and guided them to an out-of-the-way table near the kitchen.

"Anything you want," Muriel said, laying her hand on Pinetta's shoulder. "On the house. I was sorry to hear about your father."

Pinetta nodded her thanks. "I'll have whatever Agnes is having. With tea."

"All right. But you should know Agnes has no imagination when it comes to breakfast." She wrote on a ticket. "Two bagels."

"Wait," Agnes said. "We'll have scrambled eggs and toast with apple butter."

"Excellent choice," Muriel said. "Add bacon…hash browns." She walked away.

"How was your trip?" Agnes asked.

"Long."

"Is your mother all right?"

"About like you'd expect. Her friend's coming today to take her to lunch."

"Was it nice to see—?"

"We don't have to make small talk," Pinetta said. "Just tell me what happened."

Agnes launched out. "Remember after the auditions when you and Truitt saw me talking to Eileen? And I told you she'd invited herself over? She wanted to talk about Donovan."

Muriel returned with coffee and tea. Setting down the cups, she reached across the table and slid the sugar bowl in front of Pinetta.

"I never take sugar," Pinetta said.

"Just this once," Muriel said. "It'll do you good. Be right back."

Pinetta added a spoonful of sugar. "Never mind about Donovan. Go on about Barton."

Agnes could hear Ham's voice in her head. *Just give her the facts. Don't mention how happy Barton is.*

Agnes began with Eileen's visit the morning Pinetta left. How she met Barton. He took her on a tour of the house. She stayed through lunch. He

Chapter 18 ~ *Moving Day*

called her that night. The next day he took the day off. Then things snowballed.

"Sometimes Eileen ate with us," Agnes said. "Sometimes he went over there."

Pinetta covered her face with her hands. "That's enough."

Muriel brought breakfast; Pinetta straightened up and placed her napkin in her lap.

"Eat up. Before it gets cold," Muriel said, and left them to talk.

"She's being awfully solicitous," Pinetta said. "What have you told her?"

"Nothing. She's being nice because you just got back from your father's—"

Pinetta stabbed a bite of egg. "I guess the whole town is laughing at me behind my back."

Agnes lowered her voice. "No. No one knows how you feel about Barton, except me and Ham. I had to tell Nestor, because—"

Pinetta cut the bacon with her fork. "You *had* to tell Nestor? Why?"

"He's my husband. And besides that, we had to include him in the plans."

"Oh, of course. The *plans*." Pinetta gaped at the door. "When did *that* happen?"

Lute Monroe and Mary Grace Dodson, arm in arm, had walked in.

Agnes glanced over her shoulder. "Oh, that. You left too soon to see the aftermath of Lute's performance. Half the women in town were star-struck."

Pinetta laughed bitterly. "Only me."

"What do you mean?"

"Only I could lose two men at the same time. One I loved, and one I didn't."

They drove home. Agnes parked in the driveway. "Ham wants us to come in the front door. You go ahead. I'll get your bag."

Pinetta climbed out and studied the Magnolia Arms, as if seeing it for the first time. The tall windows, the wide porch, the cupola. She could hardly wait to get inside and close the door on the bleak world, leaving it behind.

She climbed the porch steps, opened the door and entered, breathing in the fresh smells of wood, paint, varnish; the staircase rising before her, the hallway beckoning, the kitchen door and her own dear room only a few steps away. So different from the imposing Pembroke house she had left last night—its heavy drapes, antique furniture, dark walls, thick carpet, massive, mahogany staircase with wrought iron railing, leading up to long dark halls,

Tea at Kimball Pines

hung with austere family portraits, and more formal rooms, draped, antiqued, carpeted, moth-balled.

And here, best of all, gentle Ham waited. He took both her hands in his. "'Morning, Miss Pinetta. We missed you."

A lump in her throat, she clung to him. "Oh, Ham. You're my best friend."

Hesitating, he placed his arms gently around her.

Suspended in the sublime moment, Pinetta heard Truitt's "Song of Eventide" drifting from the parlor. She let go of Ham and swiped her hand across her face. "Did Truitt finish his song?"

"Not yet," Agnes said. "But he's close."

Nestor came from the kitchen. "You're back. Ready for the grand tour?"

"Let me take this to my room first," Pinetta said, picking up her suitcase, "and—"

Agnes grabbed the bag. "I'll take it. You go with Ham."

"Is this room finished?" Pinetta asked. She pointed to the closed door on her left.

Ham moved between her and the door. "Yes. But...you can't go in there."

Puzzled, Pinetta drew back her hand from the doorknob.

"What he means is," Nestor said, "someone's already moved in."

"And Ham wanted you to see the third floor first," Agnes said. "Work your way down."

Heartsick, Pinetta followed Ham up the stairs. Fiona had already taken her place.

They passed by Abbot's room on the second floor.

"Is Abbot at Vesper's again today?" Pinetta asked.

"No. He's in Raleigh. Moving Prudence into her new office."

They climbed the stairs to the third floor.

"Does Prudence ever mention *Agnes'* book?" Pinetta asked. "That's why she came here in the first place."

"Agnes said she'd rather not publish her book as let Prudence do it."

Ham reached the top step and stood back, letting her go ahead.

Pinetta stepped onto the third floor, turned, and saw.

The door at the end of the hall was gone, a wide arched opening in its place, the beautiful window visible from where she stood. Sunlight poured in, spilling onto the floor. In that instant—how?—her pain eased. She moved closer to the window, gazed out, then up the spiral stairs. Placing her hand on the banister, she glanced down at the floor, pictured the unfinished pieces scattered in sawdust. How had those measured-and-cut parts, curved,

Chapter 18 ~ *Moving Day*

straight, short, long, been brushed off, fitted together, painted white, or stained, varnished, to create this stairway leading away from the world below?

"Wait till you see the view from up top," Ham said.

Pinetta began to climb, expecting him to follow, but he stayed in place.

"Aren't you coming with me?" she asked.

"No. You need to be by yourself."

She reached the landing in the cupola. Stood at the round window on the front of the house, and then, one by one, at the other three, each offering its own perspective. Roofs, treetops, courthouse, park. The town once despised. Now home.

After a few moments, Ham called up. "Well. What do you think?"

"I could stay forever."

"There's more to see, when you're ready."

Hand caressing the banister...Barton had built...she descended.

They walked down the hall. Pinetta pointed to the former study. "Have you finished moving in?"

"Yes. Day before yesterday."

She hesitated outside his room. "Can I ask you something? Personal?"

"Sure."

"Is the poster of Lorna still on the back of your door?"

"No."

Pinetta ducked her head. "How did you get over...losing her?"

"I didn't lose *her*. She was never mine. But I let go of the dream. That's the hard part. When you've imagined a future you always knew...deep down...was impossible."

They both knew he wasn't talking about Lorna.

"You're right. I always knew I'm not the kind of woman Barton would ever—"

"You can't help who you love," Ham said. "Barton showed up at the wrong time. You were lonely. You thought he might be the one for you. There's no shame in that."

"But I'm a rational woman. I never should have allowed myself to—"

"Sometimes your heart runs away with you before your mind can catch up. But love doesn't have to be that way. Sometimes it slips in before you even know it."

"Not for me," Pinetta said. "The sooner I face that, the better."

"I used to think that, too, about myself. I'm not very smart. I don't have any talent—"

"Don't say that. You're—"

He turned the doorknob. "I've spent a whole year grieving over Lorna. But because of you, I found the perfect girl for me, right under my nose."

"Because of me?"

Opening the door, he pointed to the roll top desk—at a framed photo of Fiona Wilton.

"If you hadn't left for your father's funeral," Ham said, "Fiona wouldn't have come here to work. No telling when we would've talked to each other. She's as shy as I am."

"She's a lovely girl." *Even if she did take my place.*

He closed the door. "She doesn't make my heart race the way Lorna did. But she loves me for who I am. Come on. They're waiting for us."

They walked down. Truitt was standing at the foot of the stairs. "Welcome home, Pinetta. We missed you."

"It's good to be back," she said. "Where's your cane?"

He grinned. "Can't run around the block, but I'm getting there."

They entered the kitchen. Spotless. Fiona had left everything in perfect order.

Pinetta felt a pang of jealousy. She glanced toward her room, longing to open the door and retreat inside, claim exhaustion, and promise to see the rest of the house later.

Ham stopped and pointed to the new door at the rear of the kitchen. "Nestor and Agnes will show you their new room. We'll wait here."

Pinetta opened the door. Margaret's blue chairs, moved from upstairs, were in front of a bay window which offered a view of the backyard. Then Agnes opened the door to the baby's room, crib against one wall, wooden rocker in the corner.

They went back through the kitchen, Pinetta's heart folding in on itself with each step. As they passed by the parlor, she glanced at the unlit Christmas tree.

Time to toss that out, Pinetta thought. *Just like me.*

They walked toward the new room at the front of the house. *Fiona's room.* Ham and Truitt were waiting.

Smiling broadly, Ham opened the door. "Miss Pinetta. Welcome home."

Pinetta caught her breath. Fiona had not moved in.

The room was hers—her bed, quilt, rug, furniture, all transported from her old room by the kitchen and arranged exactly as before.

Walls a pale shade of rosy pink. Sheer, white curtains hung at the large window. Her suitcase, waiting to be unpacked, beside the bed.

"We fixed it like your old room," Ham said.

Pinetta squeezed Agnes' arm. "It's mine?"

Chapter 18 ~ *Moving Day*

Agnes was buoyant. "We called Millie about the paint color and curtains."

"I don't know what to say," Pinetta said. "I thought—"

"I wanted to tell you when you got off the train," Agnes said. "But these guys insisted on surprising you. I told them it was a bad idea. I've been *dying* since the moment I picked you up."

Nestor slipped his arm around Pinetta. "I never meant for you to stay in the room by the kitchen for so long. I always thought you deserved better."

"Is everything okay?" Ham asked. "We can change anything you don't like."

"It's perfect," Pinetta said.

"We'll let you girls talk," Nestor said. "Ham and I have a few errands to run."

"And I have voice students coming," Truitt said.

"Voice students?" Pinetta asked.

"Lute's not the only one who made a name for himself," Agnes said. "Truitt's the most popular guy in town at the moment. Every time the doorbell rings, it's for him."

Truitt explained. "We decided to have lessons here, so Donovan wouldn't find out. He thinks of himself as a one-man show. So they say."

"Donovan should be grateful," Agnes said. "Everyone has improved. Even Gretchen and Verbena."

"They made the choir?" Pinetta asked.

"Only because there 'weren't enough sopranos,'" Truitt said. "That's how he put it."

"He would've had enough," Agnes said, "if half the crowd hadn't run for the door before they even got to sing."

"Water under the bridge now," Truitt said. "But we'll be ready when rehearsals start."

After the men trooped out, Pinetta sat on the bed and ran her hand across the quilt. "I stayed awake all night worrying about what I'd do when I got back. Where I'd live."

"This is your home," Agnes said. "We wouldn't *let* you move out."

"I thought you were adding this room for a new tenant."

"We were. But one night we started talking about how much we missed you and how the house wasn't the same. One thing led to another and we decided to surprise you."

Pinetta blinked away tears. "This is the nicest thing anyone ever did for me. And it will make everything so much easier."

"What do you mean?"

"I won't have to see Barton every morning…in the kitchen. I'll be in *here*."

"Well, not exactly," Agnes said. "Not if you take the job I found for you."

"What job?"

"With Vesper."

"What?"

"It's kind of complicated. Want to rest a while first?"

"No," Pinetta said. "I'm wide awake."

"Good. The kettle's simmering on the stove. Come on."

They went to the kitchen table where all serious business was discussed. Pinetta took her usual chair. "I haven't asked how *you're* feeling."

"Fine. Morning sickness stopped, just like everyone said. In fact, I've been busy while you were gone. Fiona's not the only one who's been back and forth to both houses every day."

"You've been going to Vesper's?"

The doorbell rang. Agnes served Pinetta's tea. "I'll get that. Truitt's first lesson."

She disappeared down the hall and returned with Verbena Vernell and Gretchen Tate.

Verbena brushed past Agnes and hurried around the table. Bending down, she wrapped her arms around Pinetta. "We're so glad you're back. People said you might stay in Sumter."

"We didn't want to lose you," Gretchen said, giving way to tears. "If it hadn't been for you, I'd have never made it through that audition."

"Truitt says you're the best accompanist he's ever had," Verbena added. "There'll be no stopping us now. Best Founder's Day choir ever."

"We've never had a Founder's Day choir before, dear," Gretchen said.

Truitt opened the parlor door. "I thought I heard you two out here. Come in."

Verbena giggled. "First things first. Excuse us."

Beaming, they joined their teacher, closing the door behind them.

"Has this been going on the whole time I've been gone?" Pinetta asked.

"Uh-huh. Except for Christmas Day. All this time we thought Truitt needed peace and quiet, when the best therapy for him has been work. It'll be the same for you. You'll see."

"Think so?"

"I do. Vesper has a lot to lose if we don't help her."

"You mean, 'interfere'?"

Agnes took a single page from a file folder on the table. "Call it that if you want to. If it means Vesper's being spared from having this published." She read aloud:

Chapter 18 ~ Moving Day

Pale, frail, and tragic, Vesper Kimball moves about her house like a restless spirit, seeking quiet from the incessant lament of her wounded heart. Visitors are unwelcome. They might upset her delicate balancing act, the tightrope she walks every day, back and forth, between the gray present and the rosy past, those she loves forever out of reach. Philip March, who broke his promise to marry her; Robert Kimball, Sr., she married by default, but never loved; Edward Kimball, lost to pneumonia at a tender age; Robert Kimball II, alive and well, but, intolerant of his mother's melancholy, perpetually absent.

Pinetta frowned. "That's despicable. How could he write that?"

"And *this*," Agnes said, tossing the paper to Pinetta, "is *not* the manuscript he's showing her. This chapter was in a makeshift office upstairs."

"You went snooping?"

"That's what Nestor said. But I don't call it that. Vesper invited me. I told her I'd always admired the house. She said Fiona could show me around. So, we went upstairs."

Pinetta tapped on the page. "How did you know where to find this?"

"Fiona. Don't let her fool you. She's mild-mannered, but she's a bulldog where Vesper is concerned. And she doesn't trust Prudence as far as she could throw her. When—"

The phone rang. Agnes answered. "Hello. Oh, hello again. Who? No. No one's come by. Okay. We'll keep an eye out." She hung up and came back to the table. "That was Muriel. Someone was at Mollie's. Asking about Abbot."

Pinetta walked to the stove to refill her cup. "Anyone we know?"

"No. Some businessman. Said he found one of our newspapers at a train station on his way to Charlotte. Saw Abbot's name in an article about the choir."

Pinetta stirred sugar into her tea. "He knows Abbot?"

"Family friend. Said they haven't heard from him in months, and they're worried."

"Did Muriel tell him anything?"

"Nope. She's as tight-lipped about her customers as a lawyer about his clients. But she wanted us to know in case he showed up. Everyone in town knows Abbot lives here."

The doorbell rang. They stared at each other.

"He couldn't be here *that* soon," Agnes said.

Pinetta pushed back from the table. "I'll get it."

On her way she heard a knock and then another. She opened the door to Donovan Strode.

Tea at Kimball Pines

"That answers one question," he said, frowning. "I came to see if you were back."

She folded her hands. "I got in this morning."

"Good. Talk was that you'd stay in…I forgot. Columbia or something?"

"Sumter. Is that all you needed? To see if I'm back? Because Agnes and I are busy."

"I came to give you a rehearsal schedule. I finalized it while you were gone." He fumbled with his briefcase. "Could I come in and set this down so I can open it?"

Pinetta allowed him in. Donovan waited for an invitation to a chair. When none came, he knelt and opened his briefcase on the floor.

The dulcet tones of Verbena and Gretchen's vocalizing, edging up the scale—"Ma-me-may-mo-moo. Ma-me-may-mo-moo. Ma-me-may-mo-moo"—floated into the foyer.

Donovan looked up. "What's that?"

"Practicing."

"Who is it?"

Pinetta had no intention of allowing Donovan to interfere. "Agnes maybe?"

"But who's she singing *with*?" His lips curled.

"I couldn't say." She snagged the schedule and glanced at the first date. "I'll see you on the…6th."

He snapped his briefcase closed and stood up.

Agnes stepped into the hall. "Hello, Donovan."

He glanced at Pinetta. "I thought you said Agnes was singing."

"Guess I was wrong. Like I said, I just got in. I haven't—"

Donovan clenched his jaw. "I *heard* rehearsals were being held without me, but I didn't believe it." He pointed down the hall. "It's Spenlow, isn't it?"

"Is that why you're here?" Agnes asked. "To spy?"

"*I'm* the conductor," he said, tapping his chest. "I set the standards for performance, and I'd rather not have some *amateur* teaching technique to *my* choir. He'll undo everything."

"Truitt's not an amateur," Agnes said, face reddening. "He's as qualified as—"

"He plays the *oboe*," Donovan said. "Vocal training is another matter entirely."

At that moment the sisters-in-song, inspired by their teacher, sounded a dizzying high note somewhere in the vicinity of the correct pitch. Joyous laughter and applause erupted.

Chapter 18 ~ Moving Day

Eyes closed, Donovan shook his head. "We can't have that." He looked at his watch. "I have some time now. I could—"

Pinetta edged closer to Agnes, their shoulders touching.

"We were just getting ready to leave," Pinetta said. "Thank you for stopping by."

Donovan yanked up his briefcase and stomped to the door.

Pinetta darted around him to open it.

Serafina Rummage, her finger poised on the doorbell, jumped back, gasping. "Dr. Strode. I didn't expect to see you here."

"Apparently not," he said, with frightening calm. He marched down the porch steps, speaking over his shoulder as he made his exit. "We'll discuss this at the first rehearsal."

Serafina watched him go and turned to Agnes. "Discuss what?"

"The rehearsal schedule," Pinetta said. "Would you like to see it?"

They escorted Serafina to the parlor and then returned to the kitchen table.

"That was awkward," Pinetta said.

Agnes laughed. "You told him it was *me* singing?"

"I said it *might* be you. And it might've been." A smile broke across Pinetta's face. "You *might've* walked across the hall while I had my back turned." She began to laugh.

"Did you see the look on his face when you said, 'Thank you for stopping by'? Classic." Still giggling, Agnes held her sides. "I haven't laughed like this in a long time."

"I'm usually not that quick on my feet," Pinetta said. "I guess you're rubbing off on me, after I've watched you wriggle out of sticky situations for months. Twisting the truth."

"Me?" Agnes asked, feigning offense. "I never lie."

"There you go again."

Agnes tilted her head back, cackling to the ceiling. Pinetta folded her arms on the table, laid her head down, and gave way to hilarity.

Agnes took a deep breath and sighed. "I always knew we were kindred spirits."

"Me?" Pinetta asked. "No. You're so cheerful. Always looking on the bright side. Seeing the best in people. Glass half full. I've always admired that about you."

"You *have*?" Agnes asked.

They laughed again. Nervous, explosive, lopsided laughter like longtime friends with an inside joke. The kind of laughter Agnes and Pinetta had never shared till today.

"Why are you laughing?" Pinetta asked, half-snickering, half-sighing. "Can't a person give an honest opinion around here?"

"I believe you. I just never saw it coming."

And the whole process started again.

Pinetta grabbed a holly-print napkin and held it over her face, wiping the tears streaming down. "Mercy. I'm such a mess." She crumpled the napkin in her hands. "I'm so sorry."

"Sorry? For what?"

"For being so hard to get along with. We could've been friends all this time, if—"

"It wasn't your idea to move here. I know that. You only came because of Millie. And I know it's been hard on you. Especially…lately. But look how far you've come."

"How far I've come?" She held her thumb and finger together, suggesting an inch. "I came *this* close to making a fool of myself."

"How?"

"I bought Barton a shirt for Christmas. I'm glad now I didn't give it to…. Wait. It was in my closet." She held her hands over her face. "You moved everything. Did anyone see it?"

Agnes shook her head. "Just me. I didn't let the guys touch your personal things. The box is in your new closet. Along with the jars of cranberry sauce. What's up with that?"

"It's a long story. And would take way too much time to tell."

"Then let's get back Vesper. We don't have much time. You have an appointment with her tomorrow morning."

"Tomorrow?"

"I had to make an executive decision," Agnes said. "I hope you don't mind."

"I don't mind. I'm just glad to have a place to live. And a job. Excuse me just a minute." She stood and walked to the phone. "I need to call my mother and tell her I'm home."

Chapter 19

The Next Chapter

The following morning Agnes and Pinetta arrived at Kimball Pines at 9:30. Fiona ushered them into the living room where Vesper, dressed in a black skirt, white ruffled blouse, and blue cashmere sweater, waited, looking regal in her Queen Anne chair. Fiona went to the kitchen for tea. Agnes walked ahead of Pinetta to the sofa, sat on one end, and patted the cushion next to her. Pinetta needed no such coaching. Accustomed to formal settings and fastidious women presiding over their estates, she was fully at ease, and glided into place as if she were a frequent visitor.

"Nice to see you again, Agnes," Vesper said and turned to Pinetta. "You must be Mrs. Fraleigh. Agnes tells me you've been to your father's funeral. I'm deeply sorry."

"Thank you," Pinetta said. "You have a lovely home."

Fiona returned with tea and, with a quick wink at Agnes, left the room.

"Did you have a nice Christmas?" Agnes asked Vesper.

"Too quiet. I had hoped Robert would come, but his wife got sick at the last minute. Fiona's mother brought dinner and this lovely fruitcake. Care for some?"

"No, thank you," Pinetta said, who would forever associate fruitcake with her mother, plates in hand, on that dreadful Christmas Eve.

Vesper sipped her tea. "Agnes says you're from Sumter."

"Yes," Pinetta said. "But after I lost my husband…after he left…I moved to Littleton, where I worked for Mrs. Hubbard."

"Did you enjoy being a companion?"

"I did. I was a homebody before I went to work for Millie. But she wouldn't let me sit and grieve. So, we did a lot of travelling."

Tea at Kimball Pines

Vesper straightened the ruffles of her blouse. "Your world will be a little narrower working here. Will you be comfortable with a simpler life? A little cooking and cleaning?"

"Yes," Pinetta said. "I won't be going anywhere anytime soon."

"Pinetta's the accompanist for our choir," Agnes said. "Rehearsals start soon."

"I used to sing," Vesper said. "So…Pinetta. May I call you Pinetta?"

"Please do."

"Would you like to work for me?"

"I would. But isn't there anything else you'd like to ask?"

Vesper shook her head. "Agnes told me all I needed to know. She thinks very highly of you. But I wanted to meet you before I offered you the job. You understand."

"Of course. When would you like to me to start?"

"Tomorrow morning. I want Fiona to have a little time off before she starts her classes. It's time she spread her wings. This really isn't a job for a young woman."

Agnes grinned. "It's all settled then."

"One more question, Pinetta," Vesper said. "Do you have office experience?"

"I worked in my father's office from time to time. Why do you ask?"

"Prudence says once my story is published, I'll be getting a lot of mail. I told her I can't do interviews, but I can autograph books and send them. Are you willing to help with that?"

"Yes," Pinetta said. "Your book is one of the reasons I'm here."

Halfway to North Carolina Eileen finished her crossword puzzle. She studied the road ahead for a moment and then turned to Barton. "Are you sure you want to go through with this?"

He adjusted the rearview mirror. "I've never been more certain."

"But you just settled down, and you and Nestor are getting along. Do you want to risk damaging your relationship with him again?"

"I've proven to him I've changed. I think he's forgiven me. He's trying anyway. Besides that, I'm taking up a room they could rent. I don't want to wear out my welcome."

"But you hardly know my brother. Are you sure you want to go to work for him?"

Chapter 19 ~ The Next Chapter

He took her hand. "You don't want to stay in Dennisonville forever, do you?"

"No. It'd be nice to live in a town where the only thing people know about me is that I'm Jim's little sister. And I *don't* want to be around when word gets out that you proposed."

"We don't have to tell anyone. I'll say your brother offered me a job in his construction company, which is true. And you want a fresh start, which is also true."

Eileen shuddered. "I dread telling my students I'm leaving."

"They're young. They'll bounce back. And there's some music teacher somewhere who's been waiting for a job to open up. You can say goodbye to Donovan Strode forever."

"I like the sound of that."

He glanced at his watch. "We'll be at my house in couple of hours. We'll pick up my car and be in Dennisonville by late afternoon. Tomorrow we'll break the news."

"That we're *leaving*...not that we're getting married. Right?"

"Right. That can wait till later. Much later."

She smoothed his graying hair over his ear. "I love you."

He grabbed her hand and kissed it. "I love you, too."

At the piano Truitt was scribbling notes on the final bars of his score, when he heard the back door open. Thinking Pinetta and Agnes were home from Vesper's, he left the parlor and peeked in the kitchen. Abbot Cooper was rifling through the cabinet.

"Where have you been?" Truitt asked.

Cup in hand, Abbot turned around. Disheveled, dark circles under his eyes, he looked like he had not slept in days. "Helping Prudence move. Sometimes I wish I'd never..."

"Sit down," Truitt said. "Let me help."

Abbot did not argue. "I *have* to go to work. My editor is expecting the story on historic homes at the end of the day, and"—he sighed—"I'm nowhere near finished."

Truitt poured a cup of coffee and placed it in front of Abbot. "Too bad you missed the holidays here. We had a good time. When did you get in?"

"Last night. This morning. After midnight. I don't know. I spent Christmas in a restaurant talking business with Prudence. Well, talking about *her* business."

"She's a very driven woman," Truitt said, sitting across the table. "Not that I've been around her much. But I know the type. As many years as I taught school."

Abbot took a cold biscuit from the plate on the table. "I used to think it was destiny...meeting Prudence here. I mean what are the odds I'd meet a *publisher*?"

"You don't think it's 'destiny' now?"

"More like some kind of weird Greek tragic twist. Me wanting to prove something to my father. Her wanting to prove something to her old boyfriend. It's a bad combination."

"What's wrong with proving yourself to your father?" Truitt asked, only to keep him talking.

Abbot rubbed his forehead. "Because I've let Prudence talk me into doing whatever it takes to market my book." *Even if it means betraying Vesper,* he thought.

"What's your book about?" Truitt asked, though he knew.

Abbot washed down the biscuit with a swig of coffee. "Originally, a travel journal. 'Rich kid leaves home with nothing. Depends on strangers for help.' Thing is: I had good notes. Interesting people. Places I stayed. But that's all out the window now."

"Why?"

"Prudence says it won't sell. No one wants to read about a 'spoiled kid running away from home.' Says once I make a name for myself, I can write anything I want."

"That's a pretty broad statement."

Drifting in his own thoughts, Abbot did not hear. "She says I should keep working and focus on how I'll feel when I sell the movie rights."

"And when is all this supposed to happen?" Truitt asked.

"She wants a first draft by the end of January."

"Can you manage that?"

Glancing at his watch, Abbot stepped to the sink and poured out his coffee. "I'm hoping once she leaves I can get more done...without her standing over my shoulder all the time."

"She's leaving?"

"Yeah. We moved her stuff into an apartment not far from her new office."

Truitt weighed his words. "It's none of my business, but you could ask Pinetta for help. Now that she'll be at Mrs. Kimball's house every day, you two could collaborate—"

Chapter 19 ~ The Next Chapter

Abbot whirled around. "What do you mean?"

"Fiona's going to college full-time, so Pinetta's going to work for Mrs. Kimball. She's a well-educated woman—could probably advise you, if you let her read what you're writing."

Abbot went white. "I can't do that."

"Why not?"

"She doesn't know the story...she can't just start in the middle..."

Truitt shrugged. "She can start from the beginning."

Turning on the faucet, Abbot splashed cold water on his face, then grabbed a dishtowel. Leaning against the sink, he held the towel to his eyes and groaned.

"Are you all right?" Truitt asked.

Abbot tossed the towel on the dish drainer. "I have to go to work." He paused at the back door. "Where's Pinetta now?"

"With Agnes at Mrs. Kimball's. For an interview. But I think it's only a formality."

"They're there *now*?" Abbot asked.

"Yes. They left a while ago."

"I *told* Prudence I should've taken that manuscript with me."

Truitt lifted the folder from the table and held it out. "You mean this?"

Abbot dashed back and nabbed the folder. "They've *read it*?"

"Some of it."

Abbot shook his head. "They know. I'll never be able to stay here now."

"You have to stay," Truitt said. "You made the choir."

———∞———

Upstairs, Prudence was packing. Intending to stay here only long enough to apologize to Agnes, she had brought few clothes and gradually accumulated a second wardrobe, one item at a time, from Elsie's Dress Shoppe on Main Street. Smirking, she examined a pink blouse, suitable for life in Dennisonville, but *never* anywhere else. She added it to the clothes piled on the floor with note attached: *Donate to church bazaar.* Church bazaar? The fact she was in a town where this was considered a cultural highlight was sign enough it was time to move on.

Opening the nightstand drawer, she removed Daniel Ogden's photo and gripped it between taut fingers, ready—once again—to tear it to bits. But, as usual, she stopped herself, caressing his image with her fingertips. Tucking the photo in a pocket of her suitcase, she considered the terrible risk she was taking, starting her own publishing company, courting Daniel's clients, mending fences with the ones she had alienated. But what else could she do? There were two things she loved in the world: Daniel Ogden and her work. If she couldn't have one, she'd have to settle for the other.

Abbot Cooper—exactly the kind of young, eager, talented writer she had been hoping to discover—was a windfall. What were the odds she would find him just sitting here, waiting, when she arrived to smooth things over with Agnes? It was destiny—Abbot, willing to do anything to prove himself to his father; and her, determined to prove something to Daniel. The perfect combination. Once Abbot finished the book, she would market it as an "unauthorized biography," and the reading public would gobble it up. People reveled in stories about eccentric, lonely people trapped in their tortured pasts.

She opened the dresser drawer, took out three sweaters, and retrieved the large manila envelope hidden underneath. Precious loot cradled in her arm, she made sure her door was locked and plopped on the bed. She opened the clasp and peeked inside at the dozens of photos she had accumulated after persuading Vesper the "family history" needed illustrations. Vesper brought out her photos; Prudence selected several and courteously provided a consent form for her to sign. Then while Vesper and Abbot consulted on the story, Prudence scoured the rooms upstairs for any secret mementos which might be hidden.

Her snooping paid off. In a poetry book in Vesper's room, Prudence found a photo of a beautiful young woman in a long, lacy dress. Head bowed, a bouquet of daffodils in her hands, she was gazing at a tall, handsome man in a tuxedo. A stately home with roses blooming by the porch steps provided the perfect backdrop. On the back was written "Philip and Vesper, Spring '24." This was not Vesper's husband. It was the man Vesper had secretly grieved over for fifty years. Slipping the photo in back of her steno pad, Prudence had sneaked out.

This photo would go on the cover.

A knock at the door startled her. She slid the photo into the envelope, tossed it in her open suitcase, and slammed it shut.

Breathing slowly to calm herself, she opened the door to Ham.

"Truitt told me you're leaving today," he said. "Will you need a ride to the station?"

"No. I'm going to call a cab."

Chapter 19 ~ The Next Chapter

"I'll do that for you," Ham said. "Hope you enjoyed your stay." (He usually said, 'We enjoyed having you,' but did not think it warranted in this case.)

"Yes...thanks. I stayed longer than I meant to."

Ham took a step, paused, and turned back. "So...when will you publish Agnes' book?"

"What?"

"Agnes' book," Ham said. "Isn't that why you came? To talk to her about it?"

"Uh...yes. Once I set up my office, I'll get back in touch with her."

Twenty minutes later Prudence was in the back seat of Asa Ludlow's cab on her way to the train station.

He studied her in the rearview mirror. "You're that publisher lady, ain't you?"

She was in no mood to talk. "Yes."

"People say you and that Cooper fella are going to put this town on the map. That right?"

Prudence squinted. "How are we supposed to do that?"

"With that book on the Kimballs."

"The family history. How do you know that?"

"Everybody knows *that*. You've been the talk of the town ever since you showed up."

"Me?" She thought she had kept a low profile. "What are people saying?"

"Just wondering how in the Sam Hill you got into that house, when people who've lived here all their lives wouldn't dare knock on the door."

"It wasn't me. It was Abbot. Vesper's sappy about...uh...very fond of him."

"Is that right? Don't that beat all? So...what's it like? The house, I mean?"

Though Vesper had long ago sent word Asa was forbidden to conduct impromptu tours past her house, he had ignored her instructions. In fact, his narration had taken on new dimensions since Abbot and Prudence had arrived. Now he added:

For the first time in years Mrs. Kimball has allowed visitors in her home. An up and coming young author by the name of Cooper is writing her family history. *He and his publisher are in there at this very moment, working on a book to be released soon.*

So, when Prudence O'Neill climbed into his cab, Asa considered it the best luck he'd had in a long time. If he could get her to talk, he could provide an insider's look about the most mysterious house in town.

Prudence, though she considered Asa intrusive, could not resist the opportunity to create interest in the book. "Like stepping into another century. Heavy drapes. Family portraits in gilt-edged frames. Doilies on the furniture. Persian rugs. A grandfather clock that chimes the hours."

Gaping into his rearview mirror, Asa ran up over the curb. He jerked the steering wheel; the tire thudded back onto the road, but he did not miss a beat. "People say the nursery where her little boy died is exactly the same as when—"

"True," Prudence said. "The crib is still there. Rocking horse. Toy chest."

Asa wagged his head slowly. "Hmm. Cobwebs?"

"No. The house is clean as whistle, top to bottom. The little maid keeps it that way."

Asa pulled up to the curb at the train station. "Wonder if it will stay that way now that she's leaving."

Prudence opened her door. "Leaving?"

Asa got out, took the suitcase from the trunk, and set it on the sidewalk. "Yeah. She's going to college. My missus heard Pinetta's going to take her place."

"Pinetta?" Prudence took two fives from her purse. "That's not good."

"Why not?"

"Never mind. Keep the change."

―――――∞―――――

Nestor was puttering in his greenhouse when he heard the door open.

"Hello?" a voice called.

Nestor waved. "Back here. By the potting bench. Keep walking."

Truitt maneuvered between the rows of wooden tables. "What are you planting?"

"Haven't decided," Nestor said, garden spade in hand. "I just wanted to get started. I haven't felt like working in here lately. My dad knocked me for a loop, but I'm pulling out of it."

Truitt buttoned his sweater. "I know what you mean. I'm feeling better by the day."

Chapter 19 ~ The Next Chapter

Nestor pointed at Truitt's arm. "You mean physically?"

"Yes. But it's more than that. I used to think music was my life. Even when I came home to my empty apartment, I knew I'd be back with my orchestra the next day. And it was enough."

Nestor laid down the garden spade. "But now?"

Truitt rubbed the back of his neck. "Now I have…something else."

"Pinetta?"

Truitt gaped at Nestor. "How did you *know*?"

"I used to be in love with a woman who only thought of me as a friend." He removed his gloves. "I recognize the look. And I sympathize. Believe me."

"Ham told me about you and Agnes and said I should ask you for advice. I've only dated one woman, but that was a long time ago. And Pinetta is not exactly the easiest person—"

"To get to know?"

Truitt nodded. "She's very private. Polite. But private."

Nestor spooned dirt into a clay pot. "She seems different since she came back. "I'm not sure what happened while she was gone, but she's…I don't know…not quite so…brittle."

"Ham said the same thing. He thinks I should ask her out for New Year's Eve. But not to spring it on her. Work up to it…gradually. What do you think?"

Nestor nodded. "He's right. Start with something thoughtful…but not intimate."

"What do you mean?"

"Romantic lunch for five."

When Agnes and Pinetta came home, they found Ham taking down the Christmas tree.

Agnes sank onto the sofa in the parlor. "Where is everybody?"

"Abbot's gone to work," Ham said. "Prudence is just plain gone."

"When did this happen?" Agnes asked.

"Not long after you left."

Pinetta picked up an empty ornament box and began to fill it. "Did Prudence say anything when she left?"

"Just that she'd stayed longer than she meant to and she'd be in touch with Agnes about her book."

Agnes sneered. "I'd like to 'get in touch with her' about *her* book."

"You mean Abbot's book?" Pinetta asked.

"No. It's *her* book. Abbot just doesn't know it. Where's Nestor?"

Ham reached up for the angel on top of the tree. "He *was* in the greenhouse."

"That's good news," Agnes said.

"But"—Ham peeked at Pinetta from the corner of his eye—"Truitt asked him to go with him to Mollie's."

Pinetta closed the ornament box and picked up another. "They went out for lunch? Don't you have leftovers?"

"Yes." Ham kept his eyes on the tree. "But he told Nestor he wanted to do something nice for you. Since you were gone all morning. So, you wouldn't have to fix lunch."

"Me?" Pinetta asked.

Ham hesitated. "You…and Agnes."

By the time the tree was bare, Truitt and Nestor had returned. The five friends gathered in the kitchen, utterly content, over tomato bisque and chicken salad sandwiches.

Muriel had suggested almond cookies for dessert.

Agnes took one sip of soup and leaned back in her chair. "This is so good."

"Truitt's idea," Nestor said, kicking him under the table.

Truitt snapped to attention. "Uh…a 'welcome home' for Pinetta. And…to congratulate you on the new job. You got the job, didn't you?"

"I did," Pinetta said. "Start tomorrow."

"You should've seen her," Agnes said, waving her spoon. "Had Vesper in the palm of her hand the minute she started talking."

Pinetta grinned. "I wouldn't say that."

"It's true," Agnes said, warming to her subject. "Pinetta is a perfect fit for that house. People like me don't belong there, but Pinetta—"

"Is as antiquated as the drapes in the parlor?" Pinetta asked.

"No," Agnes said. "You belong in that kind of grandeur. You give the house…meaning. Like you were born to oversee it. Confess. You already have plans."

"Well," Pinetta said, "that depends on Vesper's budget. The drapes need attention. The rugs."

"So does the grandfather clock in the hall," Nestor said. "But I didn't mention it."

Chapter 19 ~ The Next Chapter

"My point exactly," Agnes said. "But Pinetta will get away with it. Mark my word."

"I wish I shared your opinion of my abilities," Pinetta said.

"I share them," Truitt said.

Silence fell.

"Me, too," Ham said.

Truitt cleared his throat. "So...what do you do around here on New Year's Eve?"

"It's different every year," Nestor said, "depending on who's living here at the time." He turned to Agnes. "This will be our first New Year's together. We should go out."

Truitt spoke up. "Why don't we all go out?"

"Not me," Ham said. "Going to Fiona's."

"What do you think, Pinetta?" Nestor asked. "Feel like celebrating?"

"Why not?' she said. "I haven't been out for New Year's in—"

The back door swung open, and Barton, duffle bag over his shoulder, sauntered in.

"What's this?" he asked, grinning. "Little post-holiday celebration?"

The color drained from Pinetta's face. Truitt noticed.

Barton set down his bag, walked to the table, kissed Agnes on the cheek, and patted Nestor's shoulder. "How was Christmas?"

"Fine," Agnes said. "How was yours?"

"Good. Eileen's family welcomed me with open arms. Lovely people."

Pinetta, eyes riveted to her plate, said nothing.

"Have you eaten?" Agnes asked. "We're just about finished, but I could make you a sandwich and we have cookies." She held out the white box.

"Already ate," Barton said. "But I'll take some coffee."

Pinetta did not hop up to serve Barton; Ham wanted to applaud.

Barton took a cup from the cabinet and filled it.

Truitt fidgeted. The perfect lunch and easy transition to New Year's Eve had been sidetracked by Barton's arrival. Pinetta was wilted.

"We were just talking about New Year's Eve," Nestor said. "Do you have plans?"

His back to the room, Barton stiffened. He picked up his cup, sipped slowly, and decided now was as good a time as any. He turned around. "I'll be in Louisville."

"You're going back?" Agnes asked. "Why didn't you just stay there and come home in another week?"

Barton leaned against the sink. "I came home to pack. Eileen's brother offered me a job. He has his own construction company. It's a great opportunity."

Agnes left the table and hugged Barton. "I'm happy for you."

"Thank you." He kept one arm around her. "It's time I moved on. I'm taking up a room you could rent. And you'll need the money now that the baby is coming."

"When are you leaving?" Nestor asked.

"Tomorrow. Jim—Eileen's brother—is starting a remodeling job and wants me to help him. They have a spare room I can stay in till I find my own place."

"You're going to move there permanently?" Ham asked.

Barton nodded. "Louisville is a good fit for me. Just the right size."

"Do you have to leave so soon?" Agnes asked.

"I do," Barton said.

"Then we should have a going away dinner," Agnes said. "Something special."

Barton picked up his bag. "No. I'll be out the rest of the day. I promised Eileen I'd help her this afternoon. I don't want to go off and leave her with so much to do by herself."

"What does she need help with?" Ham asked. "I could go over so you could spend—"

Barton walked to the basement door. "No. Thanks. We've made plans. Nestor, I went by my old house and picked up the Ford. Want to go for a quick ride?"

"I do," Agnes said.

"I've got room for all of you," Barton said.

"Not me," Pinetta said, standing. "I need to get ready for work in the morning."

"I have voice students coming," Truitt said.

"How about you, Ham?" Barton asked.

"What year is the car?" Ham asked.

"'63."

"I'll get my coat," Ham said.

The men left the room. Pinetta brought the glasses to the sink.

"Are you all right?" Agnes asked.

Chapter 19 ~ The Next Chapter

Pinetta walked to the sink and turned on the faucet. "You know why he's going to 'help' Eileen, don't you? She's moving, too. They're going to get married."

Agnes took a towel from the drawer. "He looked happy, didn't he?"

"Why would *anyone* marry a man who'd been married four times before?"

"Would you?" Agnes asked.

"In a heartbeat."

The following morning Pinetta rose before dawn, slipped into the kitchen, and made tea. Taking her place, she stared into the familiar room. So much had changed since she had first sat here, drinking tea, nursing her unspoken resentment at Millie's decision to bring her here. Now Millie was gone. And within an hour, Pinetta would leave for Vesper's house. She gazed at the new door on the opposite wall. Beyond, Nestor and Agnes slept. The baby's room waited. And from the basement apartment, Barton Carlyle, packed, ready to go, would walk up the stairs for the last time.

Pinetta would not be waiting. Best to preserve what little dignity she had left.

She poured her tea in the sink and returned to her room for the keys to Vesper's 1947 burgundy Buick Roadmaster. Ham had taken her to pick up the car yesterday. She buttoned her coat, straightened her quilt, and left her room.

In his bathrobe, Truitt waited in the hall. "Good morning."

"I didn't expect anyone to be up."

He spoke quietly. "I thought someone should see you off on your first day."

"Sorry I woke you."

He moved closer. Standing in shadows, he found the courage to speak. "I'm not. I like seeing you first thing every morning."

"I have to go now."

Pinetta left through the front door and hurried to the driveway. *I like seeing you first thing every morning*? Why in the world did he say—? She gasped when she saw Barton's Ford parked behind Vesper's car. Blocked in. She stood there. Staring. Refusing to believe her perfectly-timed plan would have to be changed. Keys in hand, she went back into the house and down the hall to the dark kitchen. She tiptoed to Barton's door and knocked. No response. Knocked again. Quietly called his name. Turned the doorknob.

She started down. Barton had fallen asleep watching the small TV on the dresser, leaving her just enough light to see by. At the bottom step, she paused and tapped on the wall.

"Barton."

Her eyes adjusted to the dim light; she gazed at him sleeping.

"Barton."

He rolled over. She could see his face in the dim glow. Her heart fluttered. *Stop this. Stop this right now. He's leaving. You'll be late for work. Wake him up.*

Calling his name, she stood next to the bed. Reached out. Touched his hair. Then his shoulder.

"Barton."

He opened his eyes, squinting. "Mrs. Fraleigh? Is something wrong?"

"Sorry to wake you. Your car's parked behind mine. I'll be late for work."

He sat up, ran his hand through his hair. "No problem. I wanted to get an early start anyway. What time is it?"

"6:15"

He rubbed his eyes. "Coffee ready?"

"No."

"That's okay. I'll stop by Newman's on my out of town." He stood and stretched. "Let me grab my coat and put on some shoes."

Pinetta could not turn her eyes away. Unlike Guy Henry, who wore sensible plaid pajamas in the winter, Barton had on a white t-shirt and sweatpants. How could he look so appealing at this time of day? At his age?

She started up the stairs. "Go through the front door. We don't want to wake Agnes."

She waited by the front door till she heard Barton coming, then walked ahead to the driveway. Chiding herself for the lump in her throat, she hurried to the Buick and fumbled with the cover Vesper had insisted she keep on the car "at all times."

Barton caught up to her. "Here. Let me help you with that," he said, his breath visible in the frosty air. She stood back. When Barton pulled the cover off the hood, he whistled. "Is this the old lady's car?"

Arms clasped around herself, Pinetta shivered. "One of them."

Chapter 19 ~ *The Next Chapter*

"It's a beauty. Suits you. Classy lady driving a classy car." He faced her. "I never really saw you as chief cook and bottle washer."

"No?"

He shook his head. "You don't belong in a kitchen."

In an instant she pictured herself asking what he meant, heard him say, *You belong with me*, pulling her close, kissing her.

But all she could do was repeat, "No?"

He folded the tarp. "Open the trunk. I'll put this in for you."

They walked behind the car. She unlocked the trunk. He put in the tarp and closed it.

"I picture you as"—he tilted his head to study her—"headmistress of an exclusive girls' school or executive secretary to a lawyer or a bank president. How *did* you end up here?"

Pinetta brushed past him and unlocked the car door. "Long story. I'm glad you made peace with Nestor. Long overdue."

He followed her and opened her door. She climbed in and fixed her eyes on the steering wheel. "I hope you'll be happy in your new home."

She reached out for the door handle. He held the door to keep her from closing it and knelt down. "I appreciate all you've done for me. And for my family." He leaned in and kissed her cheek. "You're a remarkable woman, Pinetta Fraleigh. Take care of Nestor and Agnes. I'll be back this summer when the baby's born."

She closed the door, started the engine, and backed out into the dark street. Still standing in the driveway, Barton blew her a kiss.

She drove. Turned the corner. Pulled over to the curb. Laid her head on the steering wheel. Refused to weep. Willed herself to fight off the rising tide of panic. Then straightened up. Leaned back. Breathed in and out. In and out.

Above the trees the sky glowed pink.

A new day.

Chapter 20

Resolutions

On New Year's Eve Truitt Spenlow studied his reflection in the mirror. Outfitted in the gray suit he had purchased in Raleigh, he judged the effect *not bad*. He was dressed for a "date," his first intimation of romantic interest in Pinetta.

In her room across the hall, Pinetta removed the plastic bag from her mauve floral print dress. She put it on—for the first time in over a year. Dabbing on blush, she gazed in the mirror and entertained only one thought.

What is Eileen Redmon wearing tonight to spend New Year's Eve with Barton?

Everyone in town had been shocked to learn Eileen was moving to Louisville to "be near her brother." Newsworthy enough. But when word got out Barton was *also* leaving for Louisville, everyone put two and two together and got four.

The news surged through the streets of Dennisonville like the Great Flood of 1916.

Pinetta, however, was blissfully insulated from the chaos. Long before the townspeople arrived at Mollie's or Newman's to sip their coffee and chatter about Eileen's "running off with Nestor's father," Pinetta was breakfasting at Vesper's kitchen table, reading the morning paper under the high white ceiling…alone. Safe inside Kimball Pines all day, she was spared from the commotion at the Magnolia Arms where Truitt's students and curious neighbors repeated the same questions over and over. *Were there any clues Barton and Eileen were serious? Hadn't Barton been married before? Several times? What did Nestor think? Would the wedding be here?*

Pinetta picked up her coat and purse and stepped into the hall to wait at the front door. Eyes closed, she pictured Barton walking toward her, dressed for an evening out, ready to whisk her away to a romantic dinner for two.

Instead—Truitt's door opened. The scent of Aqua Velva wafted into the hall.

Startled to see her, he stepped back. "I should have known you'd be ready before I was. I was going to…. Wait here. I'll be right back."

He hurried to the kitchen. Pinetta heard voices, then Agnes appeared in the hall and walked toward her.

"They bought corsages for us," Agnes said. "It's a surprise."

Nestor and Truitt, boxes in hand, joined the ladies in the foyer and presented the flowers. Agnes and Pinetta took turns pinning on each other's white carnations and daisies.

Forcing a smile, Pinetta straightened the ribbon. "Thank you. It's beautiful."

Truitt helped her with her coat, careful not to crush the blossoms. *First step*, he thought. *Now she knows this is a date.*

He thinks this is a date, Pinetta thought, vowing never again to agree to a "party of four."

Nestor opened the door. "I'll warm up the—"

A woman outside, preparing to knock, gasped, and held her hand to her chest.

"You startled me," she said, catching her breath. "I'm sorry to bother you. I can see you're on your way out, but this won't take long. Is this the Magnolia Arms?"

"Yes," Nestor said. "Come in. Out of the cold."

She stepped inside and stood still, looking around at the walls, the ceiling, and then tilted her head to peer around them into the hall.

Truitt glanced at his watch. Their reservations were in 90 minutes.

Eyeing the stranger, Agnes concluded she had never seen a more beautiful, refined woman. Petite, with shoulder-length brown hair and deep brown eyes, the lady wore a dark purple turtleneck sweater, black slacks, black boots, and a long beige camel hair coat. On her left hand was the largest diamond Agnes had ever seen.

Pinetta fervently hoped their visitor was looking for a place to stay. Then she could offer to remain behind. A new tenant could not be ignored.

"Is there something we can help you with?" Nestor asked.

The woman repeated her question. "This *is* the Magnolia Arms?"

Chapter 20 ~ Resolutions

"Yes," Nestor said. "If you need a place to stay, we have a room available upstairs."

She grabbed his arm. "Don't tell me Abbot left. Am I too late?"

"No," Nestor said. "He lives here, but he's not here right now."

Bowing her head, she sighed. "Thank goodness."

Agnes thought the woman might faint. "You know Abbot?" she asked.

"I'm his mother. Joan Cooper." Her eyes brimmed with tears. "He's not here?"

Nestor raised his eyebrows at Agnes. She nodded.

"Let me take your coat, Mrs. Cooper," he said. "Have you had dinner?"

"I'm not hungry," she said. "But I would like to sit down. I'm exhausted."

"This way," Agnes said and walked beside Joan Cooper to the parlor.

Slipping off her coat, Pinetta started toward the kitchen.

Nestor whispered to Truitt. "I'm sorry. We can't just go off and leave her like this."

"I know," Truitt said. "I'll call the restaurant and cancel the reservation."

Nestor patted him on the shoulder. "We'll re-schedule."

Alone in the kitchen, Pinetta put on the kettle to boil and removed her corsage. Nestor entered, holding the two empty florist boxes.

"Guess you won't be wearing flowers tonight," he said sheepishly.

She returned the corsage to the box and stored it in the refrigerator. "Was tonight meant to be a date?"

He ducked his head. "Yes."

"I'm not ready for that."

"Would you have been 'ready' if my father had been going out with us instead?"

"How can you say that to me?" Pinetta asked.

Nestor lowered his voice. "Because I was once in Truitt's shoes. And believe me, it's not easy being the nice guy women want for a friend. That's why I—"

Truitt entered the kitchen. "I cancelled the reservation. Just as well. Now we don't have to worry about coming home in all that traffic." He rubbed his arm. "Still a sore subject."

Nestor walked to the phone. "I'll call the newspaper office to see if I can find Abbot."

"Anything I can do to help?" Truitt asked.

Tea at Kimball Pines

"No," Pinetta said, still smarting from Nestor's comment. "Thank you for the flowers."

Truitt blushed. "You're welcome. I'm sorry you didn't get to wear them."

She placed cups and saucers on the counter. "I'll wear them to Vesper's tomorrow."

Agnes had guided Joan into the parlor, invited her to sit on the sofa, and then sat in the wingback chair across from the coffee table.

Joan examined her surroundings. "This is a lovely room. I see why Abbot likes it here."

"We've enjoyed having him," Agnes said, not quite true, but the polite thing to say.

"How long has he been here?"

"Since the first week of November."

Joan sank back into the sofa. "I'm so relieved. All during Thanksgiving dinner, all I could think about was Abbot in some sleazy motel…or worse. He was *here* in this lovely house."

"Well, not here exactly. We had…um…an overflow problem, you might say, and a friend of mine invited him to her restaurant, along with a couple of our other tenants."

Joan leaned forward. "So…he's made friends? He's kind of a loner at home."

Truitt and Pinetta entered. He sat on the other end of the sofa. Pinetta served tea and took the vacant chair next to Agnes.

Joan held her cup with both hands and sipped slowly.

Nestor came in and pulled up a chair from the corner. "Sorry. I couldn't reach Abbot. His editor must have him doing some kind of New Year's Eve story. On location."

"Editor?" Joan asked. "He's working for a newspaper?"

"Yes," Agnes said. "And…he's writing a book."

Joan set down her cup. "A book? That's good news. He's always had an artistic side, but his father never encouraged it."

"He's in our choir," Truitt said.

Joan turned to him. "The community choir."

"How did you know?" Truitt asked.

"That's how I found you," Joan said. "A friend of ours was on a business trip and saw your local paper in a train station. He read the article about—"

Chapter 20 ~ Resolutions

"The choir tryouts," Agnes said. "Yes. Muriel—my friend who owns the restaurant—called us and said a man had been asking about Abbot."

"He called us the moment he got home," Joan said. "I can't tell you how relieved I was. I wanted to come right then, but…Abbot's father…wouldn't let me leave."

"How long has it been since you've seen Abbot?" Pinetta asked.

"The end of May. This isn't the first time he's left after an argument with his father, but he always came back after a few days. But this time…"

"We've taken good care of him," Agnes said. "He hasn't gone without a meal, thanks to Pinetta."

Joan scanned their faces. "I'm sorry. I haven't even asked your names."

Nestor took care of the introductions and repeated his offer to let Joan stay the night.

"I'd like that," she said. "But I should call my husband and let him know where I am."

Pinetta took her to the kitchen.

"Well, I never saw this coming," Agnes said. "She sure doesn't look old enough to be Abbot's mother. I'm dying to know the whole story."

"Not tonight," Nestor said. "Not unless *she* brings it up."

"Where do you suppose Abbot is?" Agnes asked.

———∞———

Abbot, a plate of hors d'oeuvres in hand, was mingling with the crowd at Harriet Oxley-Friend's annual New Year's Eve party. Outfitted in a rented tux, he nibbled on stuffed shrimp as he studied the stuffy guests. He knew he was not there as a reporter. He was the entertainment. Harriet had heard him sing at tryouts and chased him down as he left the Delahunty House. *You must give a recital at my home*, she had gushed. He had politely declined. She had visited the newspaper office. His editor had assigned him to cover the story.

In this town no one resisted the edicts of Harriet Oxley-Friend.

So, there he stood. Pressed and dressed and doing as directed. Months and miles away from home, he felt like he was right back where he had started—captive to the well-to-do. Suddenly he was eight years old again, shuddering at the memory of his nanny's cold fingers' straightening his collar as she bustled him downstairs to "sing for company."

"You can run, but you can't hide," he muttered, as Esmé Inch sidled up next to him.

"What did you say?" she asked.

"Nothing," he said, popping another shrimp into his mouth.

"I'm looking forward to hearing you sing again," she said. "Without being a judge."

Abbot, chewing, squinted at her dangly silver earrings, too long for her pudgy face and short neck. He swallowed. "You've got me confused with someone else. I've been a lot of places in this town, but not the courthouse."

Gazing up, she giggled. "Not *that* kind of judge." She touched his arm. "At the choir tryouts. I'm sure you read my comments on the judges' sheets, which were returned to you."

"I never got them," Abbot said.

She bristled. "I'll have to speak to Donovan. I can't imagine why you haven't gotten them by now. Maybe you overlooked them. Being so busy with your book."

Crabmeat stuck in Abbot's throat. "How did *you* know about that?"

Glad she finally had his attention, Esmé licked a bit of macaroon from her fingertip. "Everyone knows about *that*. You know, I used to date Robert Kimball, back when—"

Abbot set his plate on an end table. "People know the book is about—?"

Esmé, unaccustomed to being interrupted, went on. "—we were in high school. If we hadn't gone to separate colleges, things might have been different, but I'm still friends with—"

Abbot noticed Harriet, decked out in an emerald green sequined dress, prancing toward him. He whispered to Esmé. "You know Vesper's son?"

Delighted she had struck a nerve, she smirked. "We went all through school together. I'm friends with his wife. So, when I heard about the book, I wrote to her. You can imagine how—"

Harriet arrived. "We're ready for you, Abbot."

He grasped at something to say. "Could I get a glass of water?"

"Of course," Harriet said. "Your husband's looking for you, Esmé."

Pleased to have Harriet take notice of her for any reason, Esmé turned to go.

"Wait," Abbot said so loudly even the servers turned to look. "I wanted to ask Mrs."—he pointed to Esmé.

"Inch," Esmé said.

"Mrs. Inch…about rehearsals…" he said.

She turned back. "Yes?"

"You wrote to Robert's wife about the book?"

Chapter 20 ~ *Resolutions*

She smoothed the tasseled sash around her ample middle. "Yes. I was surprised they knew nothing about it. She said Robert would look into it as soon as he could get away."

Esmé joined her husband in the formal living room.

Abbot gulped down the water the server handed him on a silver tray.

As he walked toward the piano, grim prospects flitted through his mind: Prudence, furious about the wrench in their plans; Robert, fuming over strangers' taking advantage of his mother. *We can't be sued,* Prudence had said, *for relating facts everyone knows anyway.*

Abbot resolved this evening would be his final public appearance in Dennisonville. Tomorrow he would go to Kimball Pines, gather up his manuscript, and leave town. He had seen photos of the imperious Robert Kimball. He had no intention of facing him. Too much like his father.

He walked to the piano, thinking of Vesper. He dreaded the moment she would discover what he had been doing. But Prudence was right. The story could make him famous. And if he weren't here to watch the aftermath, it would be easier.

Abbot reached the piano, bowed to the guests, announced his first number, and sang, "Gray skies are gonna clear up. Put on a happy face. Brush off the clouds and cheer up. Put on a happy face…"

When Abbot was not home by 10:30, Joan, too tired to wait any longer, asked to be shown to her room. Agnes and Pinetta walked up with her, showed her the bathroom, and gave her some towels. Agnes loaned her a nightgown.

Joan asked to see Abbot's room. Agnes let her in. Joan rested her hand on the shirt Abbot had thrown over a chair. "He didn't bring any pictures of our family."

"Men never think of things like that," Agnes said. "And he really hasn't spent much time here. He's been focused on work."

Agnes said what she thought her own mother would want to hear, and it was enough. Nodding, Joan clutched the nightgown and towels, slipped into her room, and closed the door.

Agnes and Pinetta walked downstairs together.

"Wait till Abbot finds out his mother is here," Agnes said.

"Think he'll go home with her?" Pinetta asked.

"Not likely. Not till he's finished that book."

Truitt and Nestor were waiting at the foot of the stairs.

"Shall we stay up and see in the New Year?" Nestor asked.

"Not me," Agnes said, taking Nestor's hand. They said good night and went to their room.

Truitt turned out the parlor light. "At least let me walk you home," he said to Pinetta and offered his arm.

She hesitated, but then put her arm through his. He deserved that much.

When they reached their rooms, Truitt faced her and took both her hands in his.

"Tonight didn't work out like I'd planned," he said.

She tried to pull away, but he held on. "I appreciate the thought."

"Will you go to Vesper's tomorrow?" he asked.

"Yes. She'll need someone, holiday or not."

"Will you stay all day?"

Pinetta straightened her shoulders. "That depends on—"

"Because I thought we might at least take a drive…or something."

Pinetta cleared her throat. "Truitt, I don't want you to get the wrong idea about me. I'm happy to be your friend, and I'm looking forward to working with you on the—"

Still gripping her hands, Truitt leaned in and kissed Pinetta tenderly. Then he took her face in his hands and kissed her again.

"I was saving that for midnight," he said. "I love you, Pinetta Fraleigh. There. I said it. Good night."

Dazed, Pinetta leaned against her door. She had not been kissed in…she could not remember. Long before Guy Henry left, they barely spoke. Though she had dreamed of being in Barton's arms, the warm reality of a man's lips on hers was…wonderful.

Truitt?—short, bald, puppy dog eyes, square jaw—appealing? Opening the front door, she stepped onto the porch. The moon hung low, white, lustrous, behind the bare tree branches. She blew out her breath, watched it cloud and drift away. She felt…alive.

Compelled to lead "Auld Lang Syne" at midnight, Abbot could not file his story till almost 2:00 a.m. He came home late and crept into his room. He turned on the lamp, tossed his wallet on the desk, and flopped down on the bed.

A new year. And what did he have to show for it?

Chapter 20 ~ Resolutions

Finally got away from home, he thought. *Proved I can make it on my own. Still haven't touched my bank account. Earning my own money. Pretty soon...I'll need a business account.*

He sat up, unbuttoned his shirt, and dropped it on the floor. A pang of guilt pricked him.

At Vesper's expense.

"I'll dedicate the book to her," he whispered to the dark. "Write something nice."

And who knew? Maybe the Philip Marches of the world would read the book and realize the damage they do to the women who love them. It was a public service—exposing them.

Embracing this soothing deception, he rolled over and went to sleep.

———⚭———

After lying awake most of the night, Pinetta rose before dawn and headed to the kitchen. She made tea and took her corsage from the refrigerator. By 6:15, flowers on the seat beside her, she was steering Vesper's car up the driveway of Kimball Pines. She entered through the kitchen and tiptoed upstairs. Finding Vesper still asleep, Pinetta brought Abbot's manuscript from his makeshift office and, over breakfast, continued reading where she had left off the day before. Turning pages, she tried in vain to quiet her noisy conscience. She should *not* be poring over these chapters without Abbot's knowledge.

Much less hanging on every word.

As much as Pinetta hated to admit it, Abbot drew her effortlessly into Vesper's world, laid bare the delicate, pristine lives of proper families, undone by heartache and ruin.

As she read, Pinetta shook her head and dabbed at tears with a leftover Christmas napkin. Vesper was a truly tragic heroine, sublime in suffering, wounded, "crushed like a wild violet under a heavy boot." The effect was made worse by knowing the story's end. That after losing Philip, Vesper had acquiesced to a suitable marriage, only to bear a lifelong hunger in her heart for the man she loved. No wonder the pain of it finally broke her down. And now, at this very moment, she lay upstairs, dreaming, perhaps, of the man whose photo was on her nightstand.

Pinetta turned the page. Her eyes riveted to the first sentence.

Vesper Kimball, once the grand dame of Dennisonville society, became its oddity.

Tea at Kimball Pines

    Pinetta pushed the manuscript away and watched the steam seep from the simmering teakettle, glanced at the frost at the windows' edges. In the stillness, she could hear the grandfather clock in the hall ticking away the minutes of the first day of the New Year…365 days, which, for Vesper, would be exact duplicates of the days of the previous year and the year before. She would rattle around this magnificent house, full of fine aging furniture, art, relics from another era. Empty of people. *Except for me*, Pinetta thought. She left the table.

    Vesper Kimball, once the grand dame of Dennisonville society, became its oddity.

    The words echoed, hounding, haunting. At the foot of the stairs she listened. Vesper was not stirring. Pinetta walked to the living room window and gazed out at Second Avenue. At one time visitors had flocked to this house. Mr. Kimball's business associates had arrived for parties. Robert's friends had come to play. Vesper had welcomed the ladies of Dennisonville for receptions, teas, and holiday dinners. Who had she been back then? What had she offered? What talents and gifts had she boxed away along with her china and crystal? What opportunities had she closeted along with her formal gowns?

    It could've been me, Pinetta thought. *If I hadn't come to the Magnolia Arms….*

    In the pale morning light, a wisp of a notion took root and sprouted into resolve.

    The sun rose on 1979. A superb winter day, the sky a deep blue, the air clear and brisk, the clouds billowing, cottony, and silver-white. Not a hint of early morning fog or lingering dew.

    Truitt's eyes popped open. "I kissed Pinetta," he said to the new day, and almost sprang out of bed. He dressed, smoothed his hair over his ears, and hurried into the kitchen.

    Joan Cooper and Agnes were at the table.

    Agnes stood and hugged him. "Happy New Year."

    "Happy New Year to you. Is Pinetta here?"

    "No. Left early for Vesper's." She walked to the stove. "Breakfast?"

    "Just coffee." He took a chair. "How are you, Mrs. Cooper?"

    "Please call me Joan. I feel wonderful. Haven't slept so well since Abbot left."

Chapter 20 ~ Resolutions

"Have you seen him yet?" Truitt asked.

Agnes set a cup of coffee at Truitt's place. "He's still asleep. But we have a photo." She slid the morning paper to him. "He's come up in the world. I've never even *met* Harriet."

Truitt studied the photo of Abbot, front and center among the Dennisonville elite.

"This is how Abbot grew up," Joan said. "But he never liked it. Whenever we had parties like this, he would put in an appearance and then head back upstairs to his room."

"Are you going to ask him to come home with you?" Truitt asked.

"I don't know," she said. "His father would like for him to start grad school, but I—"

"Mom?"

Abbot, in a gray sweatshirt and jeans, stood in the kitchen door.

Joan leaped up from the table and bumped Truitt in her rush to the door. Weeping, she clung to her son.

"You're all right," she said, her voice muffled by his shoulder. "You're all right."

"Of course, I'm all right. What are you doing here? How did you find me?"

She let him go and wiped her eyes. "Never mind. Just let me look at you."

Abbot's mind raced. *Here's my excuse. I have to take my mother home.* They sat with Truitt.

Abbot spotted the paper and picked it up. "Oh, brother. I was hoping they wouldn't use my picture."

"I don't remember the last time you sang at a party," Joan said.

"Not my idea," Abbot said. "Not doing it again."

"Not till the concert," Truitt said. "I'm sure Donovan plans to give you a solo."

"Of course," Joan said. "This summer. I'll have to come back. Could I reserve a room?"

"Actually…" Abbot said, "I don't think I'll be here. I've been thinking about going home for a long time." He took his mother's hand. "Mom showing up…well, it's like a sign."

Agnes stared at him. "But what about your book? All your research?"

Abbot reached for his mother's coffee and gulped it down. "I have enough."

"Oh, sweetheart," Joan said, putting her arm around his shoulder, "that would be wonderful. The drive home won't be half so long, and your father—"

"I don't have much to pack," Abbot said, standing. "We can swing by Vesper's house on the way out of town and pick up my manuscript. I'd like for you to meet her anyway."

Pinetta, alerted by a call from Agnes, returned the pages to Abbot's desk and approached Vesper's door to wake her. Vesper would want to be dressed properly when she met Abbot's mother...and said goodbye. Pinetta turned the knob and peeked in.

Vesper was awake. Slippered feet gliding across the Persian rug. The sash of her white satin dressing gown tied around her prim waist, left arm extended, she gripped the hand of her unseen partner as she side-stepped back and forth, back and forth.

In her right hand was the photo of Philip March.

She was so beautiful; Pinetta was transfixed.

Vesper twirled, caught sight of Pinetta. Halting, she held Philip to her heart, bowed her head. "We danced till dawn—our last New Year's Eve together.... not Mr. Kimball."

Pinetta whispered. "I know."

"So now you know what a foolish old woman you work for."

"Love makes fools of us all," Pinetta said. "There's no need to hide the photo from me. If anyone understands, I do."

Vesper raised her head and found a friend looking back. "Time for breakfast?"

"Ready when you are. And there's news. Abbot's mother is in town. He's going home."

Sudden grief clouded Vesper's face. "Abbot's *leaving*?"

Touched by her sorrow, Pinetta tried to soften the blow. "He's been away a long time. His mother..." She walked to the bed, straightened the covers. "You know what a mother's tears can do. He decided on the spur of the moment."

Vesper returned the photo to her nightstand. "I'll miss him."

Pinetta fluffed the pillows. "They'll be here soon. Abbot wants to introduce you."

When Vesper came into the kitchen half an hour later, Pinetta picked up the corsage from the table. "This is for you. To celebrate the New Year."

Chapter 20 ~ Resolutions

Vesper, in a red wool skirt and white chiffon blouse, stood still while Pinetta pinned on the corsage.

"I haven't had flowers in a long time," Vesper said. "Do I look all right?"

"Prettiest girl in town," Pinetta said.

"That's what Papa used to say. Now they say, 'Craziest lady in town.' Don't they?"

Pinetta pulled out a chair. "I've never heard a single person call you that. They think you're…mysterious."

Vesper scooted up to the table. "Mysterious?"

"All the best women are," Pinetta said. "Part of their charm."

Abbot drove his mother to Vesper's house. While the women chatted in the living room, he excused himself to go upstairs to his "office." He removed the page he had left in the typewriter and added it to the back of the other chapters. Then he opened the drawer to remove the photos he and Prudence had been squirreling away. Nothing there. He rifled through stray pieces of paper—birth certificates, newspaper clippings, theater programs—and found only one photo, stuck in the back. A stiff formal family photo of Vesper, her parents, younger sister, and three brothers.

Not the image he was looking for—Vesper and Philip March, together, in formal dress, perhaps for the final time. He had already imagined the photo on the cover, along with his title, *The Jilting of Vesper Belle*. And his name…as author.

Prudence had nixed his original title: *The Jilting of Vesper Kimball*.

"You can't use *jilting* if you're going to call her Vesper *Kimball*. She was jilted *before* she was married. You'd have to use her maiden name."

Then she suggested *The Prisoner of Second Avenue* as an alternative. Abbot laughed.

"What's the matter?" she had asked.

"That's a play by Neil Simon."

Miffed, Prudence stiffened her jaw. "You just keep working. I'll worry about the rest."

Abbot had settled on using Vesper's middle name instead.

The longer he was away from Prudence, the easier he found it to be decisive.

He returned the photo to the drawer and ran his hand across the desk. He would miss sitting here every day. Miss this house. And Vesper.

Tea at Kimball Pines

"Don't do it."

Startled, Abbot looked up. Pinetta was standing in the open door.

Leaning into the desk, he nudged the drawer closed with his leg. "What do you mean?"

"You know perfectly well what I mean. Don't betray the woman who's been so kind to you. Either admit to her what you really plan to do or write some other story."

Abbot scooped up the precious pile of paper and clutched it to his chest. "I don't know what you're talking about."

Stepping in, she closed the door. "Come on, Abbot. You know we read the pages you left on the table at home. The secret's out."

"Vesper's story deserves an audience," Abbot said, parroting Prudence.

"Not like this," Pinetta said.

"This is my chance to make a name for myself." He walked to the door. "I've put too much work into this to quit now. I have to finish. I'm going down to say goodbye."

Pinetta followed Abbot downstairs and watched from the hall as he knelt by Vesper's chair. He took her hand. "Thank you for having me in your home. I'll miss you."

She placed her delicate hand on his cheek. "It seems right you should go home today. First day of a New Year. With your mother. There's no heartache like missing a child."

Abbot squeezed his eyes shut. "Is there anything I can do for you before I go?"

Pinetta stepped into the room. "Yes, there is. You can ask her to dance." She walked to the grand piano in the corner and began to play, "I'll be loving you…Always."

Abbot offered Vesper his hand. She stood. He took her in his arms and danced with her.

His mother had never seen him look so handsome.

Pinetta watched from the porch as Abbot backed the car from the driveway. She almost called him back, but remained in place, waving, frosty air stinging her face. If only there had been a little more time, Vesper might have been spared.

She closed the front door and put on a cheerful face. There was nothing to do now but prepare Vesper for the inevitable. She found her standing at the window.

Chapter 20 ~ Resolutions

"Heartwarming, isn't it?" Pinetta asked. "I love reunions."

"I'm happy for his mother. But it was nice to have him here. Upstairs. Tapping away on his typewriter." She turned to Pinetta. "You can go home now. I need to be alone."

"Are you sure?" Pinetta asked. "We could have lunch and maybe—"

Vesper was halfway to the stairs. "No. Thank you. I'm going to my room."

Pinetta watched her go. She had known Vesper less than a week. They were barely acquainted, much less on friendly terms. She could not put her foot down, demand Vesper return to the kitchen for a sandwich and a game of gin rummy. She cleared the tea cups from the coffee table and started toward the kitchen, pausing at the foot of the stairs to look up. The dark days after Guy Henry left, the long hours...which turned into months...she barricaded herself in her own room came surging back. *If anyone understands the need for privacy, I do,* she thought.

Half-hoping Vesper might change her mind, Pinetta dawdled as she cleaned the kitchen. When all was in order, she put on her coat and locked the back door on her way out. Keys in her pocket, she walked to the car, removed the tarp, and placed it in the trunk. She was backing out the driveway, when out of the blue, she said, "No," and put her foot on the brake. She pulled forward, parked, marched through the kitchen and upstairs to Vesper's room. Knocking as she entered, she found Vesper sitting quietly in a chair by the window.

Without a word, Pinetta stepped to the closet and took out Vesper's coat. Then holding it by the shoulders, she stood in front of the chair. "You're coming with me."

Vesper squinted her eyes, as if meeting a stranger. "What?"

"I won't let you sit here grieving over Abbot."

"My dear. I haven't left this house since my appendix ruptured two summers ago."

"All the more reason you should come with me now." Pinetta held out the coat.

Vesper's thin fingers tightened around the arms of the chair. "You've been here a week, and you think *you* know what I need?"

"Yes."

"Well, you don't. Besides that, Robert might come today. He has the day off."

Pinetta sat on the edge of the bed. "Robert is *not* coming. And deep down you *know* it."

Vesper drew back. "How can you say that?"

"Because I've been where you are. Smack dab in the middle of reality, but still clinging to a life I knew would never be mine again."

"Robert is my son…my heir…he knows—"

"I'm sure he's a fine man," Pinetta said. "But you shouldn't spend *one more* day alone in this house waiting for him, when out there"—she pointed to the window—"there's a whole town full of people who'd love to be your friends."

"Friends? Don't you mean a whole town full of people who'd love to get a peek at the old lady who lives in the big house?"

"They're not like that. *I know.* I came to this town kicking and screaming. But it was the best thing that ever happened to me." Pinetta could hardly believe she was saying the words coming from her own mouth. "Come with me. Stay for an hour. If you don't like it, I'll bring you right back. I promise."

Agnes was washing dishes when she heard the back door open. She wrung out the dishcloth. "You're home early. Did Vesper—?"

She turned. Vesper Kimball, a jar of preserves in hand, was standing in the kitchen of the Magnolia Arms.

"I hope you like strawberry," Vesper said. "Fiona's mother made them."

Behind her Pinetta Fraleigh was grinning.

Chapter 21

Impossible Dreams

Enoch Cooper, wearing khakis and a navy-blue polo shirt, slipped his feet into Brooks Brothers' alligator loafers and buttoned his yellow golf sweater. Hoping he had achieved the "casual" look his wife Joan had specified, he adjusted his black-framed glasses and smoothed his close-cropped gray hair. For him "casual" was unattainable.

Joan Cooper ushered Abbot into the upstairs study where his father Enoch waited. Their chilly encounter, the first in seven months, appeared more like an executive acknowledging a client than father welcoming a son. Stepping from behind his desk, Enoch extended his hand; Abbot took it. Joan, stationed by the door, shot her husband a warning glance, reminding him to follow her instructions. Enoch leaned in and gave Abbot a perfunctory embrace, their shoulders touching for an instant. Pointed to a chair, Abbot sat down. His mother sat next to him. Enoch, forcing a smile, said, "So… you're back. Your mother tells me you ended up in North Carolina."

Abbot nodded and was allowed to recount a quick summary of his travels.

"You never touched your bank account," Enoch said.

"Got odd jobs along the way," Abbot said.

Joan coughed.

Enoch glanced at her. "And you ended up as a newspaper reporter?"

"While he worked on his *book*," Joan said, arching her eyebrows.

Enoch took note. "Yes. About this book…"

Prudence O'Neill opened her business on January 2nd. She made coffee for hypothetical clients and sat behind her perfectly arranged desk in her profoundly quiet office, hoping the contacts she had made would pan out. Until then, she had nothing to do.

Only a manila envelope full of pilfered photos and a phone number where Abbot could reach her. But she had waited every day for the past week, and the phone had rung only once. A wrong number. She was beginning to panic.

The terrible risk she had taken, leaving Abbot to finish the book on his own, assuming the fire she had lit under him would keep burning without her fanning the flames, was not paying off. *Once I leave,* she had told him, *I won't exactly be the most popular person around, so I can't call here. You call me. From Vesper's house. Reverse the charges.* But he had not followed her orders, and she was in the dark about his book…*her* book…the first title of O'Neill Publishing. His silence was maddening, especially since she had assumed everything was under control. She was so certain she had planned for every eventuality. Overcome all Abbot's objections. Quieted his fears. Bolstered his ego. Fueled his dreams. *The holidays,* she had reasoned. *After the holidays, he'll get back to work. Then he'll call.*

Day after day she arrived at her office at 8:00, unlocked the door, and manned the phone. Day after day the phone remained silent. She closed the office and went home to her tiny overpriced apartment, only to repeat the cycle the next day.

On the last day of her first week in business, the phone rang. She grabbed the receiver.

"Abbot?"

"No. This is Enoch Cooper, Abbot's father."

She leaned into the desk to steady her nerves. "Mr. Cooper? I…never expected—"

"I'll come right to the point, Mrs. O'Neill." His tone was brittle. Clipped. Like a newscaster or the head of a Senate investigative committee. "I'd like to offer you a contract."

"Excuse me?"

"I've decided to go into the publishing business, and I need an experienced person to head that up. I'd like to offer you the position of executive VP."

"I…I don't understand. Why would—?"

"Abbot says you're the best in business, or will be, once you get established."

Her jaw dropped; perspiration beaded on her forehead. "Abbot. When did you—?"

Chapter 21 ~ Impossible Dreams

"This morning at breakfast."

"He's home?"

Mr. Cooper ignored the interruption. "I've had a contract drawn up. Sending it by registered mail. Look it over. We'll talk again in a few days."

"I'm flattered by your offer, but I just opened—"

"We can discuss details later."

Prudence imagined Enoch Cooper posed in a high-backed burgundy leather chair, gripping the receiver in his right hand as the fingers of his left hand tapped the desk blotter.

"I'm not sure I want to work for someone else," she said. "It's taken me a long—"

"I've already spoken to Daniel Ogden. Says you'll be a good fit for my company."

"Daniel? When—?"

"Putting this contract in the mail today. Contact information included."

"I'm not sure what Abbot told—"

"Everything. Your office is on a side street. Not a good location. You're hiring a local printer in a ghetto area, and you have no advertising budget."

"I'd hardly say—"

He chuckled, smug and condescending. "You're obviously not a businesswoman, or you'd realize I'm making you an offer you can't refuse. I'll be expecting your call."

Mr. Cooper hung up the phone and looked at his wife. "Satisfied?"

Joan nodded once. "Yes."

"Once she agrees," Enoch said, "…and she will…I'll send someone to get the photos from her. Abbot can finish his book, and I'll publish and market it. Will that make you happy?"

"Yes. But what about her? Won't she realize you're only—?"

He waved his hand. "Leave her to me. You drive a hard bargain, Joan Cooper. I didn't know you had it in you."

"I won't lose my son again. If publishing his book will keep him home, it's worth any price you have to pay."

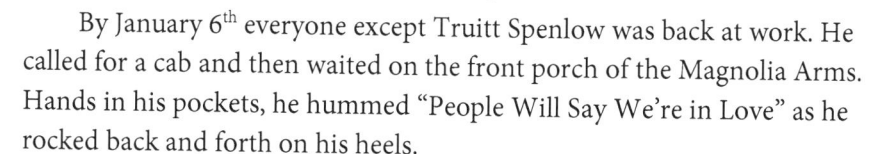

By January 6th everyone except Truitt Spenlow was back at work. He called for a cab and then waited on the front porch of the Magnolia Arms. Hands in his pockets, he hummed "People Will Say We're in Love" as he rocked back and forth on his heels.

He was on top of the world.

Tea at Kimball Pines

The terrible risk he had taken, arranging a date with Pinetta, and then daring to kiss her…twice…had paid off. He had never dared to dream she would fall into his arms and profess her love in return. He had even made allowances that making his intentions known might damage their friendship. But they remained on good terms. She had not rebuffed him, nor was she avoiding him. And now that Vesper had visited, Pinetta was basking in the sweet glow of success. Her lovely face was softer now, no longer lined with worry or the pain of failed dreams.

Choir rehearsals would begin tonight. For almost a month he had been furtively coaching the singers. The timid ones, like Gretchen and Verbena, were beaming with confidence. The gifted ones, like Lute, were gleaming with the promise of success. 'The whole town,' according to Agnes, was already anticipating the choir's debut. *It'll be like a classic '40's film,* she predicted. *Ordinary people having their one moment in the sun.* Truitt had not admitted to anyone he was glad Abbot Cooper had gone home. With him out of the picture, Lute was a shoo-in for the solo in "The Impossible Dream."

When Asa Ludlow pulled his cab next to the curb. Truitt, still humming, sauntered down the steps and climbed into the back seat.

"Mollie's Restaurant," Truitt said. "And take the scenic route. I'm in no hurry."

"Yes, sir," Asa said, peering at him in the rearview mirror. "You're that musician fella, ain't you? From Agnes' old school? The guy who made such a stir at the choir tryouts."

Truitt reached over the seat to offer a handshake. "Yes. I'm a musician. How much of a 'stir' I made I couldn't say."

"My missus told me the single ladies in town…of a certain age…are thinking you just might be the one for them. You interested in dating anybody?"

Truitt weighed his words. Agnes had coached him about being too chatty with either of the Ludlows. "Haven't dated much since college. Not sure I'd know how to go about it."

Which is true, he thought. *Nestor had to coach me.*

"I heard that Cooper fella left town."

"That's true."

Asa turned left on Broad Street. Ordinarily, he would have pointed out the Baptist church and talked about the recent Christmas cantata, but he was too busy tweaking his notes for the next tourist.

"Word is his father was near death and wanted to make amends with his son before he…uh…you know, went to his eternal reward?"

Chapter 21 ~ *Impossible Dreams*

Truitt laughed. "No. It's simpler than that. Abbot's mother came. I think she just wanted to see if he was all right. Going home with her was his idea."

"He still plan to publish that book on Mrs. Kimball?" Asa asked, hoping his tone was convincingly casual.

"I honestly don't know."

"And the Fraleigh woman is working for Mrs. Kimball?"

"Uh-huh." Bound by an oath of silence, Truitt kept Vesper's visit to himself. Asa would have run off the road if he had known.

"You meeting someone at Mollie's this morning, are you?" Asa asked.

"No. Just wanted to get out of the house. It's too quiet since Agnes and Nestor have gone back to teaching. Pinetta's at Vesper's and Ham's remodeling the kitchen at Fiona's house."

"Nice couple. Ham and Fiona. Don't know what took them so long."

Truitt shrugged. "Some things take time."

Stymied, Asa parked in front of Mollie's Restaurant. "Here you go."

Truitt climbed out. "Would you like to join me?"

"I'd like to, but have to keep at it. I retired two years ago, but couldn't make ends meet. Lucky they took me back."

Truitt pulled a $20 from his pocket and handed it to Asa. "Keep the change."

"No, sir. That's four times as much as—"

"I insist," Truitt said, waving. "Enjoyed the conversation."

Asa went on his way, satisfied he had made a friend, but not sure how.

Muriel welcomed Truitt at the door. "Dr. Spenlow. Your table's waiting."

Truitt took off his coat. "How did you know I was coming?"

"Agnes said I should expect you, since this is your first day in the house alone."

At home in the cheery atmosphere, Truitt settled into a chair and studied the menu. After ordering, he gazed around at the hodge-podge of retirees, uniformed workers, and tourists, listened to the gentle murmurs of quiet conversation. Across the room a burly flannel-shirted man, elbows on the table, was chowing down scrambled eggs. A businessman scanned the morning paper. Truitt let his mind wander back to the countless mornings he had eaten breakfast alone and gulped down a second cup of coffee in his windowless office in the "D" Building of Brighton Park Community College. How different his life—

"Dr. Spenlow?"

He turned to find a pleasant curly-haired lady smiling at him. "Yes?"

She was holding a paper napkin with both hands, as if she planned to read from it. "My name is Vivian Grant. I'm sorry to disturb you, but I have a question."

Glad of company, Truitt pointed to a chair. "Would you like to sit down?"

"No. I'm here with my husband. That's him over there by the window." She ducked her head. "He told me not to bother you."

"You're not bothering me. How can I help?"

"It's about the choir." She folded the napkin in half.

"Yes?"

"I hate to sound like a gossipy old hen…but I heard since you started giving voice lessons, everyone is feeling much better about the rehearsal tonight."

"You have friends in the choir?"

"Yes, but that's not"—she glanced at her husband—"what I wanted to ask. My husband, Walter, came to tryouts, but left before they called his number. On account of…"

"Donovan?" Truitt asked.

She nodded. "Walter used to sing all the time, but since he had a heart attack last year, he's…not the same. His confidence is gone. I can hardly get him out of the house."

"I'm sorry to hear that. I know how he feels. I had an accident a few weeks—"

"Anyway"—she folded the napkin again—"I heard Abbot Cooper left. I thought maybe Walter could take his place."

Truitt tried not to wince. "That wouldn't be up to me. I'm just a choir member like everyone else, but I'll talk to Donovan. Would Walter be willing to try out?"

"We'll cross that bridge when we come to it." She laid the napkin on the table.

Truitt unfolded it and read Walter's name and phone number. He tucked it in his pocket.

That evening, brimming with confidence, the community chorale paraded into the chorus room of Dennisonville High School and took their places on the risers. Possessed of a secret everyone shared, except Donovan—or so they thought—each one was ready to impress. They straightened their shoulders, checked their breathing, made sure their feet were hip width apart,

Chapter 21 ~ Impossible Dreams

weight equally balanced, chins parallel to the floor. Some trilled their lips. Others ran their tongues back along the roofs of their mouths to make sure their velums were raised. Serafina Rummage practice octaves. Hal Mayberry intoned chromatic scales. Pinetta played chords.

Donovan breezed in, draped his leather coat over an empty chair on the front row, and took his place behind the conductor's stand. No one was surprised when he did not take time for pleasantries. A hush fell over the cautious group.

"All right," Donovan said. "Stand and we'll start with warm-ups." He aimed his baton at Pinetta. She sounded a C chord. "On 'ah.'" He sang up to G and back to middle C.

They followed his example, moving up the scale after each run.

Truitt willed them to succeed, hoping Gretchen would keep tempo, Dinah would free herself to hit the high notes she could easily reach, and Corby would not tighten his jaw. Truitt's arm seemed to have a will of its own. He could not stop it from conducting from the wrist, keeping time, urging his students onward and upward. When at last Serafina and Mary Grace landed a high G, Donovan cut off the note with a wave of his baton and blinked his eyes.

"Not bad," he said. "But let's see what you can do with your parts."

Verbena could not resist glancing over her shoulder at Truitt. He gave her a quick wink and nodded at Donovan, urging her to give full attention to the conductor.

Their enthusiasm was short-lived. Forty-five minutes later, while they were soldiering through "Get Happy," Donovan hammered on the conductor's stand.

"Rubato. Ru-*ba*-to. The exact Italian translation is 'stolen time.' The challenge of..."

Tom Gibbons, on the back row, leaned in and whispered to Truitt. "What's roo-bah-toe?"

Truitt whispered. "It's singing a little before or behind the beat, but still staying on tempo. Think...Frank Sinatra."

Tom sat back. "Why doesn't he just say that?"

Donovan stopped mid-sentence, tilting his head left. "Is there a problem back there?"

Tom, who had come straight from Gibbons' Hardware in his tan uniform shirt with 'Tom Gibbons/Owner' embroidered above the left pocket, was in no mood to be scolded.

"No," Tom said. "No problem. I was just asking Truitt here what"—he rounded his lips with mock seriousness—"roo-*bah*-toe means."

On hearing the name 'Truitt,' the whole choir, eager for enlightenment, turned to listen.

"It's singing a little before or behind the beat," Tom said, as if he were explaining the merits of copper pipe to a customer, "but still staying on tempo. Think Frank Sinatra."

"O-o-oh," Serafina Rummage said. "That makes perfect sense."

"It does," Mary Grace said, taking advantage of the pause to catch Lute's eye.

"Truitt always knows how to explain things in simple ways," Gretchen said to Verbena.

Agnes, seated near the piano, rolled her eyes at Pinetta.

Wyatt Blackwell shook his head. Rehearsal was playing out exactly as he had expected.

Half an hour later, Donovan called them to a halt and reminded them to practice. Pinetta took her music and followed Agnes to the truck. Truitt stayed behind to talk to Donovan.

"I thought they did well tonight," Truitt said.

Donovan buttoned his leather coat. "All right for a first rehearsal. I've got my work cut out for me, but it's always that way when you start with a new group. Can't expect more."

"Might not hurt to end rehearsals on a positive note."

"Not the *first* rehearsal," Donovan said. "Don't want them getting too comfortable."

"Mind if I ask who's going to sing Abbot's solo, now that he's gone?"

"You. Of course."

"Why would you give it to me?" Truitt asked. "I'm not the only tenor."

Draping his muffler around his neck, Donovan tossed one end jauntily over his shoulder.

"You're the only one who could pull it off."

"No, I'm not. Lute could sing it…easily."

Lute had once sung it during a lesson and brought Pinetta and Agnes to tears.

Donovan grimaced. "The fat produce man? Think how he'd look in a tux."

"Pavarotti doesn't look bad in a tux," Truitt said.

Donovan headed to the door. "My colleagues at the university are expecting to hear a classically trained soloist. I won't feature some local yokel. The solo is yours."

"I don't *want* the solo. A community choir is supposed to give *everyone* the oppor—"

Chapter 21 ~ Impossible Dreams

The door to the chorus room slammed shut as Donovan breezed out.

Truitt kicked the conductor's stand. It sailed into the first row of chairs, sending them crashing into each other and knocking over a half-finished cup of coffee left behind.

Pinetta opened the door. "Agnes is warming up the car. Are you...what happened? Are you all right?"

"No, I'm not all right. Can you get some paper towels from the bathroom?"

When Pinetta left the room, Truitt righted the conductor's stand and began rearranging the chairs into rows. She returned with a yellow bucket on wheels and a mop.

"Checked the janitor's closet," she said. "Thought this would be simpler."

He swished the mop across the floor. "Donovan wouldn't know how to conduct a choir if directions were painted in letters on the back wall. *How he's kept a job all these years, I'll—*"

Pinetta blinked. "I've...never heard you talk like—"

He dunked the mop in the bucket and then slapped it on the floor. "I might have a little more patience with him if he didn't remind me so much of Finn Bigelow."

She stepped back to avoid a spray of soapy water. "Who?"

"Finn Bigelow. My first chair cellist. I had a friend...a good man...who came to college late in life. When he tried out for the orchestra, Finn humiliated him. I've always—"

"That wasn't your fault," Pinetta said.

Truitt gave the floor a final swipe. "I found a way around it. Let Bentley sit in on rehearsals. He was the janitor, so he had a key to the auditorium."

"Did Finn ever find out?"

"No," Truitt said, returning the mop in the bucket. "What are we going to do? I *know* what my singers are capable of. Lute *deserves* that solo."

"I agree."

He pushed the bucket to the door. "I didn't even get a chance to ask about Walter Grant."

Pinetta walked beside him. "Who?"

"Walter Grant. He's one of the people who came to tryouts, but left early. His wife approached this morning at breakfast. Asked if Walter could join us, now that Abbot is gone."

Pinetta laid her hand on Truitt's shoulder. "Maybe you could talk to Donovan tomorrow."

"Maybe." He waited while she opened the door. "You did a wonderful job tonight."

"I've been practicing at Vesper's house. She has a beautiful piano and loves to hear me play. I've caught her singing a couple of times. Wish we could get her in the choir."

Truitt pushed the bucket into the hall. "Think what the Ludlows would say."

Gray January days crept by. The second floor of the Magnolia Arms remained empty. Nestor offered Ham one of the rooms. He refused, insisting tenants would arrive "sooner or later." He could not find the words to tell Nestor he had rented Eileen Redmon's old apartment. He and Fiona were getting married.

Agnes was feeling better every day. The morning sickness was over. What she had been told was true—during the second trimester, an expectant mother is convinced "all's right with the world." She and Pinetta decided on "Winnie the Pooh" for the nursery. Ham painted the walls pale yellow. Pinetta made curtains.

Though Nestor still worried about money, he was grateful he and Agnes had teaching jobs. Their second semester classes met on the same days, so they enjoyed being together as they rode to school. Their love, tested by the intrusion of Nestor's past, had deepened. The ghosts, haunting him, had been silenced.

If they had a daughter, she would be named for his mother.

Truitt, spurred on by Nestor and Agnes, continued his pursuit of Pinetta. Advised to be subtle, he dreamed up dozens of small kindnesses to show her. A rose on the table. A box of her favorite tea. An offer to pick up her dry cleaning or return a book to the library.

Pinetta acknowledged him, but kept her distance, thoughts of Barton still gnawing at her.

She focused on her new job, soon becoming more than an employee to Vesper. Brought up in similar circumstances, they shared the same patterns and habits and eased into a mutual friendship. Pinetta knew instinctively what Vesper needed and provided it without being asked. But in one matter Pinetta resisted Vesper's will.

She refused to let Vesper remain alone.

Pinetta found a willing accomplice in Agnes, who was at her best when coming up with a plan. They hatched a scheme. One morning while Vesper ate breakfast, Pinetta put the plot in motion.

Chapter 21 ~ Impossible Dreams

"We've finished the nursery," she said, feigning interest in the morning paper. "Agnes wants you to come see it. What day would you like to go?"

Vesper looked up from her cornflakes. Something about the set of Pinetta's jaw made it impossible to object. "Thursday?"

"Perfect."

Agnes welcomed them and showed Vesper the nursery. Returning to the kitchen, they found the table set for lunch, Ham and Truitt waiting. Vesper was too polite to refuse. After lunch, Pinetta, as planned, "persuaded" Truitt to sing. They moved into the parlor. Vesper sat across the room, listening, right foot tapping.

Week after week Pinetta worked her way through a list of "safe" visitors—gentle souls who would neither gawk at Vesper nor badger her with questions. Verbena Vernell came first. She sat next to Pinetta as Truitt sang. When Gretchen Tate came the following week, she invited Vesper to stand at the piano. Vesper hummed along. When both ladies came the following week, Vesper sang along with them. Every visit lasted a little longer than the one before; every lunch ended with singing. The first Thursday in February, Muriel Porter left her assistant managing the lunch crowd and joined them.

Muriel catered their lunch. With good reason.

Vesper finished a third almond cookie and licked her lips. "Oh, my, I have no words to describe these."

"Wait till you taste them warm from the oven. Agnes has ordered them for the Valentine party. You'll be there, won't you?"

Vesper blushed. "Me? Oh, no. I haven't been to a party in—"

Pinetta refilled Vesper's cup. "We've reserved the restaurant for the 13th. We want you to come up with a guest list."

"And the menu," Muriel said.

Agnes touched Vesper's hand. "Say you'll come. It won't be the same without you."

Alerted by Gretchen and Verbena, the choir arrived for rehearsal half an hour early that night. Hal Mayberry, on the lookout for Donovan, stationed himself at the door, while Truitt addressed them.

"First, let me say how proud I am of the progress you've all made. You sound amazing."

"Because of you," Serafina said.

"Sure not because of Donovan," Corby added.

Tea at Kimball Pines

Truitt quieted the scattered applause. "We're going to have a chance to try out a few of our numbers. I'll let Pinetta explain."

She stood by the piano. "All of you know Vesper Kimball…by reputation. She's a respected member of our community and has given generously to civic causes."

"Like the library," Verbena said.

"All of us at the Magnolia Arms," Pinetta said, "feel recognition for Vesper is long overdue. We're honoring her at a Valentine party at Mollie's Restaurant. We want you to sing."

She explained the conditions. The party was a secret. No one was to announce Vesper Kimball would be there. They would sing three songs. And be ready for an encore.

"I don't know if any of you have ever found it difficult to be in a crowd," Pinetta said, "but I used to be that way and it's very—"

Hal waved from the door. "He's coming."

The Saturday before Vesper's party Agnes was perusing her "To Do" list when she felt her baby move. She closed her eyes, savoring the moment. Six months as Nestor's wife, and she still marveled at how her life had changed. Every morning she woke up next to him in the house she had dreamed of from the moment she found the photo Wilkie Brooker dropped in the parking lot of Brighton Park Community College. She and Nestor had been entrusted with the house's future—theirs would be the first child to live here since the Sutton boys thirty years ago.

The doorbell rang. Leaving the kitchen, she peeked into the parlor and spoke to Truitt, seated at the piano. "Lute's here. Ready for him?"

Truitt marked his score with a pencil. "He's early. Shouldn't be here till 10:00."

"Maybe it's Mary Grace, wanting to borrow something…again." They laughed.

But when Agnes opened the front door, she found Prudence O'Neill—not the last person she expected, but close.

"Hello, Agnes," Prudence said.

Agnes had never seen Prudence so disheveled. "What are you doing here?"

"I…I"—she coughed—"need to ask…could I come in?"

Agnes opened the door wider; Prudence stepped in and pushed it close.

Chapter 21 ~ Impossible Dreams

"If you're looking for Abbot, he's not here," Agnes said. "Went home New Year's Day."

Prudence unbuttoned her coat. "I know. Could I sit down? I've been awake most of the night, and I'm exhausted."

Agnes led her to the kitchen. Prudence scooted up a chair to the table.

"Coffee?" Agnes asked, rifling through the cabinet for a mug. The chipped one.

"Yes." Prudence looked toward the parlor. "Is that Truitt playing the piano?"

"Uh-huh." She kept her back to Prudence till she could calm her temper.

"I've never heard it."

"It's original." As Agnes poured the coffee, she considered what Ivy Leigh would do in this situation, took a deep breath, and faced Prudence. "He's debuting it on Founder's Day."

"Oh, yeah." Prudence chuckled. "I forgot. *Founder's Day.*"

Agnes set the mug in front of Prudence. "Did you come all this way to insult my town?"

No," Prudence said, clutching the mug. "That came out wrong. Sorry." She sipped slowly, trying to regain her footing. "I guess you're surprised to see me."

"I was surprised when you came two months ago," Agnes said, sitting across from her. "Surprised when you left without a word. So, yeah. I'm surprised you're back."

Rubbing her bloodshot eyes, Prudence stared at Agnes as if she had never seen her. Was this plucky young woman the same one who had cringed in her office a few short weeks ago?

"You're not going to make this easy, are you?"

"Make what easy?"

Prudence leaned her elbows on the table. "Please just let me get this over with."

A twinge of sympathy flickered; Prudence was undone. "Go ahead."

"First, I want to say how sorry I am for giving you a hard time...that day...in my office."

"You came all the way here for *that*? You could've—"

Prudence stuck to her prepared speech. "If I'd known you were pregnant, I would've—"

"Treated me better?"

"Yes. Anyway, since then I've...I've read your book and now—"

"You hadn't read it before you grilled me in your office?"

Prudence gulped. "Parts of it. But since I've opened my own office, I haven't been so busy and—"

"Ah. Now that you have only one manuscript and that one is mine...*now* you have time."

For lack of anything better to do, Prudence glanced at her watch. Five minutes in the house and nothing had gone according to plan. Might as well come to the point. She placed her hands in her lap and straightened her shoulders.

"I want to publish your book."

The doorbell rang. Truitt kept playing.

"You can't be serious," Agnes said. "Do you honestly think I'd let *you*—?"

Prudence held up her hand. "Let me finish."

"Not till you answer this. Are you still planning to publish Abbot's book about Vesper?"

"Yes.... and no. *I'm* not. Not exactly."

The doorbell rang again. The piano stopped.

"What's that supposed to mean?" Agnes asked.

Truitt appeared in the kitchen door. His eyes darted from Agnes to Prudence. This was not a conversation he wanted to join. "Oh. Prudence. You're...back. I'll get the door."

"Thanks," Agnes said, still zeroed in on her visitor. "Go on."

"You know Abbot is home," Prudence said.

"Yes. I always notice when there's one less person living in my house."

"His father's had a change of heart. Probably on account of—"

"His mother," Agnes said.

Ham opened the back door. When he spotted Prudence, he pulled the door closed and tiptoed down the steps to the driveway.

"That's my guess," Prudence said. "Anyway, a few weeks ago, Mr. Cooper called me. Said he was starting a publishing company. Offered me the job of VP."

"Mr. Cooper's gone into *publishing*?"

"Yes. He sent a lawyer with a contract. Promised me the moon. I won't go into all that, but I'll just say it looked good on paper. I signed it. I thought it would save me years of—"

"Why are you telling *me* all this?"

Across the hall Lute Monroe began to sing.

Chapter 21 ~ Impossible Dreams

"It was all a ruse," Prudence said. "They didn't want *me*. They only wanted—"

"The stuff you took from Vesper's house," Agnes said, smiling in spite of herself.

Prudence ducked her head. "Yes. There was nothing I could do but hand it over. I thought once I did—"

"You'd be on your way up the corporate ladder."

Prudence looked up. "Yes."

"Let me guess. You haven't heard a word from Mr. Cooper since."

"No. I don't know how I could've been so gullible."

"And now you think you can prove yourself to him by handing over a manuscript. And mine came immediately to mind."

"Of course. That's why I came here in November. To offer you a contract. Then I met Abbot here…well, I appreciate all you've done for me, and I thought I could repay you by—"

"Come on, Prudence. Do you honestly think I believe any of this? And even if I did, do you think I'd let *you* or your *company* publish my book after what you've done to Vesper? Do you know what Abbot's book will do to her? She'll be humiliated."

Lute's voice filled the awkward silence that descended, hovering between them.

Prudence's shoulders sagged. "I should've known better than to come here."

"Why did you?"

"I thought your book might be important enough to you that you'd—"

"Overlook everything else?" Agnes asked.

Prudence turned her head. "Beautiful song. Who's singing?"

"Lute Monroe."

"Who?"

"Never mind. Was there anything else?"

Prudence shook her head. "Would you at least think about my offer?"

"I won't associate with a company that's going to ruin someone's life." Agnes leaned in. "And for your information, Vesper is no longer in hiding. She comes here to visit once a week."

"What?"

"Uh-huh. Your 'fragile recluse' is turning into a social butterfly." Agnes held up the "To Do" list. "We're throwing her a party on Valentine's Day."

Prudence turned pale. "Does Abbot know?"

"No. Abbot doesn't know. We haven't heard from him since he left."

"Neither have I," Prudence said, pushing back from the table.

Agnes stood. "Would you at least tell us when the book is going to be released, so we can prepare Vesper?"

Prudence shrugged. "If they tell *me*. Well…bye."

For an instant, she thought of asking if her room was still empty and begging Agnes to let her stay.

Chapter 22

Practice Makes Perfect

 Prior to conducting the Dennisonville Community Chorale, Donovan Strode had led four choirs in eight years. Claiming to be "always on the lookout for talent," he had gone from a university to a community college, then a church, and finally landed at Dennisonville High School. Everywhere he went, he was deemed a "catch," because he always came so well recommended. Chairmen of music departments lauded him. The elder at Knotts Avenue Presbyterian Church composed a less effusive statement, since his conscience forbade him from *outright* lying. Nevertheless, he crafted a basically honest reference for the same reasons the schools had.
 To make Donovan Strode someone else's problem.
 It was whispered the Dennisonville Chamber of Commerce had nearly "come to blows" over Donovan's appointment as conductor. The main factor swinging votes in his favor was his implied "connection" with the faculties at UNC Chapel Hill and Duke, relationships which Donovan had exaggerated. No one thought to consult the parents who heard nightly reports of his outbursts from the teenage children in his choir. Therefore, the hapless Community Chorale was committed to his oversight.
 If it had not been for Truitt's instructing and encouraging the singers behind the scenes, the mutiny might have occurred much sooner than it did.
 Rehearsal after rehearsal, Donovan thinned out the numbers. Discerning a slightly sharp note, he swept down on the altos, singling out the offender, and giving her an impromptu lesson on pitch. She never came back, claiming her mother was ill, needing care. The procedure repeated with the basses. Two of them were absent the following week; one because of a *grandmother's* illness and the other due to an unexpected audit of his company. After each

practice, Truitt, Agnes, and Pinetta would fume and rage, and then eventually calm down, vowing to stay the course for the good of the choir.

When by February the chorale had dwindled to sixteen members and there was talk of changing the name to "chamber ensemble," Bridey Ludlow came to school to see Donovan.

Dropping her tote bag on the floor of the teachers' lounge, she folded her ample arms on her ample waist. "The planning committee is *not* happy," she said. "If *one more person*"—she wagged her index finger—"leaves the choir, I'm going to the mayor. You'll be replaced."

Insulted, Donovan glared at her. "Do you know how many choirs I've conducted?"

"Yes, I do." She lifted her tote bag, plunked it on the table, and searched for the document she wanted. Then holding it at arm's length like a royal proclamation, she read: "Four in the last eight years, two before that when you were in graduate school and two before—"

"All right. All right," Donovan said. "You made your point."

Bridey slammed the paper on the table. "If I wasn't so new to this choir business, I would've investigated you further, before I argued for you at our first committee meeting."

"And what would *you* know about choral music?"

"Not much. But I do know the people of this town. They are good and gracious people, who treat their neighbors with kindness and respect, which is *more* than I can say for you."

Standing, Donovan drew himself up to his full 5'7" and pushed his reading glasses up on his perspiring nose. "When I need a lecture from you on how to prepare for a concert, I'll let—"

Bridey stood firm. "I mean it, Donovan. One more bad report and you're done."

Leaving his résumé behind, she shouldered her tote bag and swished from the room.

Donovan sank down in a huff and snatched up the paper. Running his finger down the list, he relived each triumph. Why on earth was this catalog of positions held in respected academic and religious institutions a mark *against* him? Did people not realize a man of his talent and experience could go *anywhere*? Were they *so* bucolic they did not recognize a first-rate musician in their very midst? Did they have *no* appreciation for the years he had invested honing his natural abilities? How else could he produce such consistently dazzling productions? This list offered proof of his versatility.

Chapter 22 ~ *Practice Makes Perfect*

Instead of quaking in his wingtips, Donovan renewed his devotion to his methods. What the choir needed was more discipline, not less. *In fact,* he thought, folding the page, *I'll take this to the next rehearsal. Share some success stories of productions. Maybe then they'll appreciate what they have.* He tucked the page in his pocket. *Maybe they'll stop whining.*

At the next rehearsal, however, the choir met his self-adulation with blank expressions. Cutting his tribute short, he cued Pinetta to begin. Forty-five minutes later, he let them "take five." Instead of remaining in the chorus room as usual, he sauntered out into the hall to rub elbows with them—improve public relations. Finding no one near the door, he walked down the hall. As he neared the corner where the hall turned right, he heard voices. Stepping nearer the wall, he edged closer, stopped a few feet from the corner, and leaned against the lockers, out of sight, listening.

Though they were speaking in hushed tones, he recognized a few voices. Leaning in as far as he dared, he could make out some of what was being said.

"The party will start at 6:00," Agnes said. "So you should all be there by 5:30."

Pleasant murmurs followed. Donovan made out the word *piano.*

"Yes, Muriel rented a piano. Actually, a Steinway. If this goes well, she said she's going to buy one and provide dinner music every night."

Agnes shushed their quiet expressions of delight.

"Wouldn't that be nice?" Donovan recognized Serafina's voice. "Maybe she'll hire permanent entertainment. I've always wanted to do a dinner show."

More excited muttering and happy chatter. More shushing from Agnes. Donovan ground his teeth.

"Remember, Agnes said. "This will be Vesper's first time in public in many years. Please don't crowd around or stare at her. We're there to sing, not to gawk."

"She's a little nervous," said a voice Donovan did not recognize.

"Anything else, Truitt?" Agnes asked. Silence. "All right. February 13th. 5:30. Mollie's Restaurant. Women, black formals. Men, black suits, red ties. Main Street Florist is providing corsages and boutonnieres."

Another subdued eruption of joy.

"About time we got to show Truitt what we can do," a male voice said. "After all he's done for us. Can't sing two bars together without Donovan butting in."

Grumbling.

Truitt? Donovan thought. *They think Truitt is responsible for—?*

"We need to get back," Pinetta said. "Or he'll be out here looking for us."

Feet shuffled.

Donovan ducked into the nearest classroom. His back to the wall, he waited while they filed by and then peeked into the hall. Finding it empty, he marched back to the choir room.

He stepped to the conductor's stand, tapped his baton, and announced "You'll Never Walk Alone." Then led them through the rest of rehearsal without comment.

His grim silence made them more nervous than his usual interruptions.

After a tense hour, Donovan laid his baton on the conductor's stand. Squaring his shoulders, he fixed his eyes on the back wall at a point slightly above their heads.

"I need to announce a change in our rehearsal schedule." He moved his glasses to the top of his head, so the faces would be a blur. "I've moved our rehearsal on the 12th to the 13th."

Sixteen pairs of eyes widened. Serafina gasped. Verbena's mouth fell open.

"Why?" Agnes asked.

"I'll be out of town on the 12th. Academic conference."

Pinetta shot up her hand. Donovan acknowledged her.

"I can't be here on the 13th. And if I'm not here to play the piano, then no one—"

"Agnes can fill in," Donovan said.

"I can't be here either," Agnes said.

Gretchen waved. "Me neither. Uh...convention coming to town. Need to be at the motel to...check them in."

Scattered voices offered their own made-up-on-the-spot excuses.

Red-faced, Donovan held up both hands like a factory owner quelling a union strike.

"I'm the conductor," he said, thumping his chest. "*I know* the work that is to be done and how *often* we need to rehearse...*and for how long*. If you can't be *where* I want you, *when* I want you, I can't use you. Be here on the 13th or don't come back."

He stormed from the room, leaving the choir open-mouthed behind him.

Chapter 22 ~ *Practice Makes Perfect*

Wyatt Blackwell rose. "Well, that settles that. I'll see everyone at the restaurant on the 13th."

Two days before the concert, a postcard from Disneyworld arrived at the Magnolia Arms. Pinetta, who had brought in the mail, assumed it was from her sister Eve, who had posed for a photo in front of Cinderella's castle every year since the Magic Kingdom opened. She turned it over to learn it was not addressed to her, but to "Nestor & Agnes Carlyle," and read:

Hello from sunny Florida. Wanted you to know you have a new stepmom (and stepmom-in-law. Ha-ha). Married last week. Now on honeymoon. You see where. Love, Dad

Pinetta shoved the postcard between the bills and catalogues and left the pile on the kitchen table. Then she climbed the stairs to the third-floor window, where she stared out at the bleak, gray winter day, brown grass, bare tree limbs. This moment—finding out Barton was married—she had imagined many times. The final death knell of her ridiculous hopes. He had called only twice since leaving. To say the job was going well. And then later, that he bought a house, a fixer-upper, and when he finished remodeling, Nestor and Agnes could visit and "bring the baby."

He had never asked to speak to her.

Why should he?

But she had never stopped hoping the romance with Eileen would derail, and he would come back.

Agnes found the card when she came home. She showed it to Nestor and Truitt.

But no one brought up the subject at dinner.

The next day Truitt called for a cab. Asa Ludlow drove him to Hartwig Jewelers at the corner of First and Main.

"Wait here," Truitt said. "This won't take long."

"Getting your watch fixed?" Asa asked.

"No. Making the last payment on something I've had on layaway."

On the night of the Valentine party, Ham drove his truck to Kimball Pines. Enlisted as chauffeur for the evening, he would escort Vesper, Fiona, and her mother, Gladys, to the party. Vesper suggested they take the Buick, because it had "a better heater."

Tea at Kimball Pines

Agnes and Pinetta arrived at the restaurant early to look over the preparations. Nestor and Truitt, with plans of their own to discuss, followed later.

Arriving in groups of two of three, the choir, reverent as pilgrims approaching a cathedral, arrived at Mollie's Restaurant and entered the candlelit room. Agnes and Pinetta pinned on the flowers and directed the singers to their tables, set with china and centerpieces of red and white carnations. In awe of the occasion, everyone spoke in hushed tones. When Truitt called them to assemble, Verbena straightened Corby's tie, Gretchen buttoned Tom's shirt cuff, Mary Grace squeezed Lute's hand. Taking their places, they warmed up and sang one verse of "The Way You Look Tonight" before Nestor signaled. Vesper had arrived.

They returned to their tables. Pinetta left the piano and joined Nestor at the door. Agnes reminded everyone to talk among themselves and not to stare at the guest of honor.

Escorted by Ham, Vesper paused at the door, her mind darting back to the day she had stood in this very spot with her father, who had brought her to spend her birthday money, when this building had been *Schafer's Five & Dime*.

Ham felt her tremble. "You all right, Miss Vesper?"

"Yes. Just remembering." When he opened the door, she entered, surveying the room. "Isn't this lovely?"

Fiona and her mother, both misty-eyed, followed.

Pinetta met them. "Let me take your coat, Vesper. Your table's over here."

The choir, as instructed, pretended to be occupied with placing napkins in their laps, sipping from water glasses, complimenting each other's attire, but every eye, one way or another, peeked a glance at the mysterious woman they had heard about since childhood. But she fit none of the peculiar descriptions. At 72—everyone in town knew her age—she was lovely, elegant, with a sweet face and wisp of a smile. In her long-sleeved ivory white dress, she glided across the room like a fairy godmother, come to grant wishes. Agnes pinned on her corsage. Nestor pulled out her chair.

Dinner was served.

Remembering not to eat too much (or they would not sing well, Truitt had said), they dined on roast beef, potatoes, carrots, hot rolls with butter; sipped coffee and tea; and, as Muriel had promised, savored almond cookies.

Chapter 22 ~ *Practice Makes Perfect*

Vesper, seated with Ham, Fiona, and her mother, ate heartily, glancing often around the room, warming to the pleasant chatter of the other guests. Gretchen caught her eye and waved. Vesper waved back and whispered to Fiona, "That burly young man next to Mrs. Tate. Is that Charlie Gibbons?"

"No, ma'am. That's his son, Tom."

"You don't mean it. The last time I saw him…he was just…didn't he turn out well?"

Agnes, at a table with Truitt and Pinetta, winked at Nestor, stationed by the door to turn away uninvited guests. He winked back. Her heart swelled with love…and pride. Nestor had volunteered to take the first shift watching for intruders, so Ham could enjoy dinner with Fiona.

"Look at Nestor," Agnes said. "Isn't he handsome?" No answer from either Pinetta or Truitt. "What's with you two? Nervous about performing?"

Truitt shook his head. "Not about that." He felt the small box in his coat pocket.

Pinetta nodded at Vesper's table. "Not nervous. Irritated. About that empty chair. I invited Vesper's son. I thought he might come. He's been wanting her to get out of the house."

"Doesn't look like Vesper minds," Agnes said. "She hasn't stopped talking since they sat down." When she saw Ham place his napkin on the table and walk to the door to take Nestor's place, Agnes pushed back from the table. "I'm going to the kitchen to get Nestor's dinner."

Left alone with Pinetta, Truitt reached into his pocket. They were surrounded by people. Maybe he should wait to propose till they were alone, but, frazzled, he wanted to free his mind before the performance, so he could concentrate on conducting.

Clutching the box, he squeaked out Pinetta's name. "I know we only met a few months ago, but—" Before he could say any more, Nestor sat down.

"Any problems?" Pinetta asked.

"No," Nestor said. "Several cars drove by and a tall guy, walking a poodle in a pink sweater, but no one else. I think we've pulled it off."

Agnes returned with Nestor's dinner.

Truitt let go of the box; it slipped into the corner of his pocket. "Let's get started."

He stood by Pinetta's chair, offering his arm. She hesitated, noticed Agnes' scowling at her, and then put her arm through his and approached the piano. The choir took their cue and rose from their places. They lined up on the risers. Men in the middle. Altos on one side, sopranos on the other. Their audience was small: the guest table, seating three women; Ham at the door; Nestor alone at his table; Muriel and a kitchen staff of four. But it was enough. They had come a long way since auditions, worked hard, stuck together. This was their moment.

They opened with "Till There Was You." Four bars into Serafina's solo, Ham, watching the sidewalk from the window, slipped out the door. Agnes noticed and squeezed Dinah Latimer's hand to steady herself.

Outside, Donovan Strode, his hot breath billowing into clouds in the frigid air, was lecturing Ham. "I demand to be let in. That's *my* choir. *I've* trained them."

Ham, temper rising, crossed his arms over his barrel chest. "No one can *own* a choir. They're all individual people, who chose to come tonight. Without you."

"*I run this choir.*" Donovan hammered his top coat button.

Ham was unmovable. "Private party. The guest of honor made up a list. You were not on it. She doesn't even know you."

The first number ended. Donovan jerked his head toward the sound of applause and tried a different approach. "All right. The end of the song. I can walk in now."

Ham blocked the door. "No one comes in. That includes you."

"You hillbilly. What do you think you know about concert etiquette?"

Smiling at the appreciative audience, Agnes turned to Nestor, and cut her eyes in the direction of the door. Nestor glanced over his shoulder, noticed Ham was missing, and slipped outside just as Donovan, in a childish fit of anger, raised his arm to take a swing at Ham.

Ham raised his left arm in front of his face. Nestor darted to the right. Donovan's arm came down, bouncing off Ham's elbow. Nestor ducked behind Donovan, grabbed his left arm, and pinned it behind his back. Donovan doubled over, yowling, one arm throbbing, the other aching. Nestor let go. Ham took Donovan by the lapels of his expensive black leather coat and straightened him up, holding him firm, lifting him till they were nose to nose and Donovan's toes barely scraped the sidewalk.

Agnes leaned to her right in an effort to peek out the window, but the terror on the sidewalk was out of view.

Turning back to the choir, Truitt nodded at Pinetta, who played the opening notes of "Let There Be Peace on Earth."

"Put me down, you big lout," Donovan wailed. "Or I'll call the police."

Chapter 22 ~ *Practice Makes Perfect*

Ham chuckled. "Go ahead. The police chief's mother is one of the sopranos, and he's already heard an earful about you, believe me." Still holding Donovan by the collar, Ham lowered him to the ground. "Now you listen to me. This is a private party for a good friend of mine. In fact, that choir"—he tilted his head in their direction—"is full of friends of mine. Take my advice and go home. Save it for the next rehearsal."

Donovan brushed off his coat. "Next rehearsal...there won't be a next rehearsal for this bunch. It's only February. I have plenty of time to start over." He fumbled for his car keys in his pocket. "I'll be in the mayor's office first thing in the morning. I'll hold new auditions, advertise to other towns. They'll come swarming here for the chance to work with me."

"You do that," Nestor said. "The mayor already knows all about you. His brother was one of the tenors who quit two weeks ago."

Donovan snorted and sulked away into the starlit night.

Agnes was relieved to see Nestor give a thumbs-up when he returned.

For all the choir knew, Nestor and Ham had stepped out for a breath of fresh air.

The final words of the song drifted up, wafting through the room like a spring breeze. *Let there be peace on earth, and let it begin with me.*

Truitt turned and acknowledged the applause. The choir beamed.

"And now," Truitt said, "I would like to introduce a special number by Lute Monroe."

Pinetta panicked. Why hadn't Truitt told her Lute was going to sing "Impossible Dream"? She hadn't brought the music. Mortified, she was opening her mouth to apologize when Truitt turned to the conductor's stand and pulled some pages from beneath his scores.

Agnes left her place and took the music from him. Walking to the piano, she motioned Pinetta to return to their table. Truitt announced Lute Monroe and then moved aside as Lute took center stage to sing "Song of Eventide."

When the day begins to fade, evening comes, and all is night, I think of you...I think of you. When the sun begins to shine, daylight comes, and all is bright, I think of you...

A sublime moment, captivating all who heard, melding them to the singer, the sentiment, the surroundings. Lute—the perfect messenger, lent his voice to anyone who had loved and lost, loved with no hope of love in return, loved and been loved.

Agnes glanced at Truitt, his eyes riveted to Pinetta, the reason for the song.

Nestor, alone at his table, gazed at Agnes. He loved her more than ever.

Ham swiped at a tear with his shirt cuff; he wished his mother could have met Fiona.

Pinetta tried to focus on the choir, but finally ducked her head. The only "love" on her mind was Barton.

Vesper closed her tired eyes, sank back, and let her mind drift to the warm spring evening when Philip March had placed a bouquet of daffodils in her arms and whispered he would kiss her later when her parents were not watching.

The final note, hanging in the air like a benediction, was met with silence. Lute looked down at the floor, took his hankie from his pocket, and wiped perspiration from his face.

Muriel Porter was first to come to her senses, break the spell, and start clapping. The kitchen staff joined in. Nestor stood. Fiona left her place to stand next to Ham. Agnes pushed back from the piano, applauded, and motioned Truitt forward.

Vesper Kimball rose to her feet, and holding her hands high, clapped and clapped—for Lute, the choir, her friends, the evening—and then called for an encore.

Pinetta, the last to stand, smiled in the polite Pembroke way, and returned to the piano.

No one, including Vesper, wanted to leave. She mingled among them like a queen on a state visit to her subjects. Pinetta remained at the piano, playing softly, admiring the end result of her weeks of coaxing Vesper from the shadows.

She glanced around the room at Ham and Fiona, hand in hand; Mary Grace and Lute, side by side; Gretchen and Verbena, giggling at Truitt, who had said something to make them laugh. The choir, congratulating each other, hugging, and saying goodnight.

Agnes slid next to her on the piano bench. "Look what you've done, Pinetta."

"You could've played the piano just as well."

"Not the concert," Agnes said. "Look at *them*."

Pinetta chuckled. "Quite an assortment of people."

"It is. And if you hadn't taken this 'assortment of people' into your heart, where would they be today?"

Vesper approached the piano. "I'm glad to catch you both together. Thank you for a wonderful evening."

Chapter 22 ~ Practice Makes Perfect

"You're welcome," Agnes said.

"I'll see you in the morning," Vesper said. "We'll have to call Robert and tell him. He'll be so pleased. I should've thought to invite him."

"Next time," Pinetta said.

"It's been such a nice evening," Vesper said. "I hate to see it end. At least I still have the book to look forward to. We'll celebrate that. In the spring."

They watched as Vesper joined Ham, Fiona, and her mother at the door.

"We have to tell her," Agnes said. "We can't let the book come out and blindside her."

Nestor walked over. "You two ready to go?"

"I am," Agnes said.

"Mind riding with Truitt, Pinetta?" Nestor asked. "I'd like to take my girl home."

"Not at all," Pinetta said. "Good night."

By then the choir was drifting away, and the staff was transforming the room from formal dinner to work-day breakfast.

Truitt, having shaken the last hand and accepted the final thank-you, walked to the conductor's stand to pick up his scores. Pinetta, standing at their table, took the last sip of water from her glass, before handing it over to the busboy.

She suspected a conspiracy—her being left alone with Truitt. But she would not allow her suspicions to spoil the evening. Music cradled in her arm, she waited for Truitt. He tapped his scores on the conductor's stand and started toward her.

"Your baton," she said.

"What?"

"You left your baton on the conductor's stand."

"Oh," he said, darting back. "Can't forget that." He picked up his baton. Joining her at the table, he laid down his music and took the baton case from his chair.

Determined to keep matters casual, Pinetta pointed to the case. "I never knew conductors carried their batons in a case."

"My mother gave this to me, when I graduated from college. I could've bought a better one by now, but…"

"She'd be pleased," Pinetta said. "Ready to go?"

He looked up. "Not yet."

Watching from across the room, Muriel motioned the busboy to hurry to the kitchen.

Pinetta looked around. "Well, everything's done. Except facing Donovan at—"

"Not everything." Truitt took the small blue velvet box from his pocket.

Pinetta shook her head. "Truitt…I—"

He took her hand and knelt on one knee. "I know what I am. A funny little bald man with a nose a little too big. Not the stuff your dreams are made of. But we've both been alone long enough. There's no sense in it." He opened the box. "I'm asking you to marry me."

"Truitt, you don't know me. You think you do, but—"

Wincing, he set the box on the table, shifted his other knee to the floor and steadied both hands on the chair. "I should've never done this."

"Don't get me wrong," Pinetta said. "I'm flattered. It's not every day a woman my—"

Truitt reached out his hand. "Not that. I shouldn't have gotten on my knees. My leg isn't healed enough yet. Can you help me up?"

Pinetta put her hand under his arm and pulled him up as he pushed against the chair.

He rubbed his injured leg. "I didn't quite think through that. I practiced what I'd say, but the kneeling…bad idea." He closed the box and held it out.

She hugged her music tighter. "Don't misunderstand. I think you're a wonderful—"

He placed the box in her hand and closed her fingers around it. "Don't say another word. Keep the ring. Put it in a drawer. When you're ready to give me an answer, give it back. I'll put it on your finger or return it to the store."

"All right. And I just want to say—"

"No. No more tonight." They walked to the door. "Let me apologize for springing the song on you, but"—he shrugged his shoulders—"that was part of the surprise."

"It was beautiful," Pinetta said.

"It was for you."

They drove home in silence under the moon and stars.

Satisfied with the successful evening.

Utterly disappointed with themselves.

Chapter 23

As Time Goes By

The following day Donovan Strode spent his lunch hour crafting a letter to Mayor Jake Tanzler. He could have saved himself the trouble and eaten his bologna sandwich instead. By 8:30 a.m. it was already too late to present his plan to "start over."

Because Bridey Ludlow, the mayor's first cousin on his father's side, was at City Hall when the door opened. The mayor always let her in. As exasperating as she sometimes was, she had her finger on the pulse of the town and was a keen political advisor.

She had, almost single-handedly, won him the last election.

Dropping her tote bag on the floor, she grabbed a handful of mints from the crystal dish at the edge of his desk and wriggled into one of the tufted brown leather chairs.

"Jaybird," she said, munching, "I don't like to call in favors, but I've made a colossal blunder and I need you to help me get out of it."

Eyes wide, he blinked at her. She *never* admitted she was wrong. He ran his hand through his thick, wavy, dyed-brown hair, gray at the temples. "Blunder?"

"Uh-huh. Now you've known me my whole life, and you know I don't often put on airs…get all puffed up about my know-how." She bent over, pulled a paper napkin from her tote bag, and wrapped up the mints for later. "But this time, I've stepped in it, Jaybird, and you gotta help me out. Our reputation depends on it."

He hated it when she called him *Jaybird*. Especially in his own office. "*Our* reputation? You mean…our family?"

"*Yes*. Our *family*. Of Dennisonvillians. We are a family in this town, don't you agree? What we love most about living here. We're more than neighbors. We're in this together."

"In what together?" He glanced at his watch. The police chief had asked for an appointment at 9:00. And he was never late.

Her shoulders heaved as she drew in a deep breath and sighed. "It's Donovan. It's always Donovan. It's *been* Donovan ever since I pitched him to the planning committee."

"The music teacher at the high school?"

"Yes, that's the one."

He groaned. "It's not about the choir tour to New York, is it? Because I told them—"

"No. That's the least of our problems. It's the *community* choir…for Founder's Day."

"Oh. What about it?"

"We have to get rid of him. He's destroying morale." She tried to lean forward to tap on his desk for emphasis, but the arms of the chair held her fast. Instead, she made a fist and pounded it into her palm. "The choir is the centerpiece…the linchpin of the whole day. They can't just *sing well.* They have to be…happy…a living, breathing testament to the quality of life in this town. We'll have visitors from all over the state. People coming home. I want my Norman Rockwell moment."

A twinge of civic pride fluttered in his heart. "America, the Beautiful" echoed faintly in his mind. His phone buzzed. He answered. "Yes, send him in." He hung up and turned to his cousin. "Chief Wilde is here."

"Mikey? I haven't seen him in ages."

Pushing back from his desk, Jake stood, hoping Bridey would take the hint to leave. "Must be important. He called me at home last night. So, I really need to—"

"Understood. I'll call you tonight after supper." Gripping the arms of the chair, she pushed up. No result. Jake was walking around his desk to help when Mike Wilde stormed in.

"Jake," he said, removing his hat. "We have to talk about the choir." He lowered his 6'3" frame into the chair next to Bridey and straightened his crewcut in front.

"So, you *know*," Bridey said, relaxing back into her chair.

"Yes, I know," the chief said. "My mother's in that choir. I was happy about it at first, because I think she needs to get out more. Seemed like a good opportunity. And—"

"But you're not happy *now*, are you?" Bridey asked, cutting her eyes at Jake.

"No, I'm not happy. She's been telling me about this Strode guy for months. How he lords it over them. She's been sneaking off to the Magnolia Arms for voice lessons—"

Chapter 23 ~ As Time Goes By

"With Truitt," Bridey said, glad the subject had been brought up. "Yeah."

Jake leaned against his desk. "Who's Truitt?"

"Truitt Spenlow," Bridey said. "He's the one I came to talk you about. He's a friend of Agnes Carlyle's. Every bit as educated as Donovan. Maybe more so. And *everyone* loves him."

"She's right," the chief said. "Mama loves Truitt. And she was so worried something might happen at the performance last night that she asked me—"

"Performance?" Jake asked.

"Vesper Kimball's Valentine party," Bridey said.

Now that the party was over, Mary Grace Dodson had seen nothing wrong with sharing the news with a friend or two or seven and had called Bridey the moment Lute dropped her off at home.

"What?" the mayor asked. "Vesper doesn't go to parties."

"She did last night," the chief said. "And the choir provided music, but no one was supposed to tell, so Vesper could finally come out of her house without anyone bothering her."

"You'd think I would've been invited," Bridey said, "since the choir was my idea."

Knowing better than to let Bridey get a foothold, Mike spoke over her. "Anyway...Mama was worried, so she asked me to drop by just to make sure things were all right."

"She did?" Bridey asked, pressing her hand against her cheek.

"Uh-huh. So, I put on Muffy's sweater, put her in the back seat—"

"Muffy?" Jake asked. "You put your poodle in the police car?"

"My *wife's* poodle," Mike said. "And no, I didn't take the police car. Took my own car. Parked around the corner, put on a wool cap, pulled my scarf up over my chin and kept my head down as I strolled by with the dog."

Bridey would have been on the edge of her chair if she could have wiggled loose.

"And?" Jake asked.

"Looked in the window," Mike said. "Choir was singing. Truitt was leading. And there was Vesper sitting at a table, pretty as you please. Ham Hampton was by the door."

"Guarding," Bridey said, repeating what Mary Grace had told her.

"That's the impression I got," Mike said. "So I walked around the block, put Muffy in the car, and decided to hide out around the corner a while. Who do you think came by?"

"Donovan," Bridey said, nodding at Jake.

Tea at Kimball Pines

"And quick as that"—Mike snapped his fingers—"Ham was out on the sidewalk. Couldn't hear what he was saying, but Donovan was furious. Just as he raised his hand, Nestor shot through the door."

Bridey unwrapped her mints and fanned herself with the napkin.

"The wimpy choir director was going to try to take down Ham?" Jake asked. "Did he have a death wish or something?"

"Didn't last long," Mike said. "Nestor pinned his arm behind his back. Boy, did he holler. I decided everything was under control and went home. Wish I could hire those guys."

Wondering what else was going on he knew nothing about, Jake returned to his chair, sat down, and put his fingertips together. Bridey grinned. Now they had his attention. The story spilled out—Bridey and Chief Wilde trying to one-up each other with accounts of Donovan's tantrums and insults.

"But you should know all this, Jaybird," Bridey said. "Your own brother quit the choir two weeks ago. Didn't you think anything of it?"

Jake rubbed his chin. "Brothers don't talk about things like—" The phone buzzed. He picked it up and listened, motioning for Mike's attention. "You're kidding. We were just…no, no. Tell him I'll see him…What time? Fine. It won't take long." He hung up. "Donovan Strode called and asked to see me today. Said it was an emergency. He'll be here at 4:00."

Bridey gasped. "In that case, you'd better take notes, so you'll be ready."

The mayor complied, writing a full page as Mike and Bridey kept talking.

When the conference was over, Jake stepped behind Bridey's chair to anchor it while Mike took her hands and helped her up.

"Thank you, Jaybird," Bridey said. "You, too, Mikey."

The mayor walked them out and asked his secretary to hold his calls. He returned to his desk to phone his brother, who confirmed what he had already heard.

"Call Tom…and Hal," his brother said. "They'll tell you the same thing."

When Donovan arrived at 4:00, the mayor, yellow legal pad on his desk, listened politely as Donovan aired his grievances.

"I've written it all down here," Donovan said, taking the letter from his coat pocket. "I knew you couldn't address the city council without knowing my reasons—"

Jake took the letter and laid it on his desk. "So, what you're saying is you—as a professional musician—have found it impossible to work with this *amateur* group of singers?"

Chapter 23 ~ As Time Goes By

Jarred by the mayor's stern tone, Donovan tempered his response. "Not when we started, no, but as we've gone on...they haven't been as responsible as I—"

The mayor drummed his fingers on his desk. "Responsible. You don't call people who work all day long and then practice with *you* two hours a night, twice a week, 'responsible'?"

Donovan gulped. "What I meant was—"

"These people are volunteers. They're not being paid to be in the choir. And some of them—I hear—want to do well so badly they've been taking voice lessons on their own time."

Donovan felt suddenly hot. "I'm glad you brought that up. It's in the letter, but—"

"Practicing on their own," Jake said. "And Dr. Spenlow doesn't charge them. A man who's lived here only a few weeks seems to care more about this town than you do."

"The *town* is not the point. I was made conductor of this choir, and I have the right—"

The mayor glanced at his notes. "And Mrs. Fraleigh and Agnes Carlyle have been playing the piano for lessons *and* for rehearsals...out of the goodness of their hearts...and for the good of this town, and you have the nerve to come in here and ask me to tell the city council you want to 'start over,' throw these good people on the trash heap, and advertise to *other* towns for singers? Not on my watch."

Donovan snorted. "Who told you all this?"

"I've been on the phone all day. I started with my brother. Then Tom Gibbons. Hal Mayberry. Wyatt Blackwell. Then the ladies. They all tell the same story. So, here's what I'm going to do." Standing, he picked up the letter and put it in his coat pocket. "I'm going to hand deliver your letter to the council president. Once he reads it, he'll understand why I exercised my mayoral privilege and fired you on the spot."

"Fire me? People are coming from all over the state, several universities, to watch *me* conduct this choir. When word gets out I'm not involved, your crowd is going to be cut in half."

Jake stepped beside his desk and gestured to the door. "Thank you for coming by."

Donovan clambered up. "Mr. Mayor. I don't think you fully understand what you're—"

Jake walked to the door and opened it. "I understand perfectly. This unfortunate incident has reminded me why I entered public service. To look out for the people who elected me. I only wish they hadn't waited so long before asking for my help. A mistake I intend to rectify on my way home. Good afternoon, Dr. Strode. Your services are no longer required."

Twenty minutes later, Mayor Jake Tanzler arrived at the Magnolia Arms. Agnes, a half-eaten sandwich in her hand, answered the door.

"Are you Mrs. Carlyle?" he asked.

She gulped and wiped mayonnaise from the corner of her mouth. "Yes. I'm sorry. I'm just so hungry by the time I get home." She looked again. "Are…aren't you the mayor?"

"I am."

She opened the door. "I'm sorry. I've never seen you up close. In fact, we've never actually met. But I feel like I know you. Ivy Leigh is a big fan."

He stepped in. "How is she? Do you know?"

"Getting married. Here. In the spring. I'm sure you'd be welcome. But what can I do for you? Do you need to see Nestor?"

"No. Actually, I came to see Dr. Spenlow. I want to offer him a job."

The following week the choir met for rehearsal at the Magnolia Arms under the direction of their new conductor, Dr. Truitt Spenlow.

Nestor welcomed them, pointing the way to the dining room, where Vesper Kimball was ladling apple cider into white mugs and Fiona was overseeing a dessert table, laid end to end with dozens of cookies the mayor had ordered from Foster's Bakery.

The choir moved into the parlor. The sopranos took the sofa. Altos sat in the overstuffed chairs, some poised on the arms. Tenors and basses ferried in chairs from the dining room and kitchen, completing the semi-circle around the piano.

Pinetta and Agnes, entering last, were welcomed with applause.

Agnes giggled. "What's that for?"

"Everything," Serafina said. "Letting us take voice lessons here. Meet here tonight."

Pinetta slid onto the piano bench as Truitt entered. The choir greeted him with a standing ovation. He waved his hand to silence them and motioned them to be seated.

"First," he said, "I want to congratulate you on your performance. You've worked hard, and it's paying off. Now…how many of you have a friend who left the choir?"

Hands shot up all over the room.

"Two," Gretchen said.

Chapter 23 ~ As Time Goes By

"Tomorrow," Truitt said, "I want you to call them and invite them to our next rehearsal. This Thursday, 7:00, at the Presbyterian church. Reverend Ford has given us permission to practice in the auditorium."

"They have a lovely piano," Verbena said. "Better than the one in the chorus room."

"I agree," Truitt said. "One more question. How many of you know someone who was at the auditions and either left without trying out or didn't make the choir?"

Again, everyone raised a hand.

"Your second call should be to these folks," Truitt said. "Tell them another audition will be held Saturday morning, 10:00 a.m. at the church. They'll have a lot of catching up to do. But if they want to try out again, they're welcome."

"I wish we could get Abbot Cooper back," Gretchen said. "Has he gone for good?"

"Yes," Pinetta said, her firm response leaving no doubt the discussion was closed.

Truitt reviewed the changes he had made in the program. Lute would take the solo part in "The Impossible Dream." Tom, Wyatt, Corby, and the mayor's brother, Dan, would form a barbershop quartet. Together with Mary Grace, they would sing "Lida Rose" from *The Music Man*. Serafina and Dinah would sing "Friendship" from *DuBarry Was a Lady*.

"We'll prepare two encores," Truitt said. "And—"

"What about your song?" Serafina asked.

Truitt pretended to be occupied with his list. "I'm not sure it fits our program."

"It would fit *any* program," Gretchen said. "It's classic. We all want to sing it again."

"I agree," Wyatt said. "The whole town should hear it."

"We'll see," Truitt said.

That night they sang as never before. Huddled in the cozy room, rather than perched under an acoustic-tiled ceiling in a cavernous space, their voices blended as one. The sound was so beautiful, Verbena wept. Gretchen coughed, hoping to ease the lump in her throat. Agnes laid her hand on her stomach. Her baby, roused by the music, would not be still. Pinetta played brilliantly, glancing often at Truitt, following his direction, but also struck by how he had changed since he arrived, a tired man, broken in body and spirit. Tonight, he was vibrant, infused with passion and self-confidence.

Distracted, she lost her place in the music, fumbled. Truitt, still keeping time, glanced over his shoulder at her. *She never makes a mistake,* he thought.

Vesper helped Fiona clean the kitchen and then stepped across the hall to hover in the doorway of the parlor, her eyes drifting from face to face. As the music saturated the room and seeped into her heart, she ached with regret over the years she had shut herself away. Her closed doors and drawn curtains had kept out *these* people, who would have welcomed her into their hearts, filled her days with unforgettable moments such as this. Well, no more shivering from nameless fears. She had taken her first steps back into the waiting world and found it welcoming.

When the song ended, Vesper tiptoed in and tapped Pinetta on the shoulder.

"Fiona's taking me home now," she whispered. "I'll see you in the morning."

As Vesper left the room, Lute Monroe called out: "Good night, Miss Vesper."

The whole chorus joined in. "Good night"—"Night, Vesper"—"Sweet dreams."

Beautiful as a song.

Music in her head, Pinetta woke up humming. She turned on the lamp, stood up, and turned around to straighten the quilt. She never left her room without making her bed. Running her hand over the old familiar Coffin Star pattern, she noticed another of the faded purple blocks had come loose at the corner, the clumped batting sticking out. She poked it back in.

"Have to remember to fix that today," she said, fingering the tear. "Sometimes I think keeping this old thing stitched together is more trouble than—"

She frowned at the frayed edge. Why *did* she keep piecing these squares together? She gazed at her pale pink walls, pristine, rosy, in the glow of the lamp. This old quilt, red and purple, did not belong in this room…had not matched her room by the kitchen…or her room at Millie's, for that matter.

In fact—she put one hand on her hip—she had never liked this quilt at all. But it was a rite of passage for a Pembroke girl to receive one of Great-Aunt Connie's prize-winning quilts for a wedding present, and it was expected the gift would be on permanent display in case Great-Aunt Connie ever dropped by.

Because if it wasn't on display, every other Pembroke woman, no matter what age, would hear about it.

But Great-Aunt Connie had been dead for years.

"And wouldn't know where to find me, if she were alive," Pinetta said. "And besides that, I'm not married anymore."

Chapter 23 ~ As Time Goes By

Instead of straightening the quilt, she folded it and shoved it under the bed, giving it a final kick to push it farther under.

She and Vesper would go shopping today and buy a new bedspread.

She dressed and walked down the hall, surprised to see the kitchen light was on. Who else could be up at this hour? She quickened her pace, but hearing her name, stopped.

"Did Pinetta *ever* say anything about your song?" Agnes asked.

Pinetta tiptoed to the wall and edged nearer to the door, leaning closer to listen.

"Not a word," Truitt said. "Everyone else still talks about it. But to her…it's like nothing ever happened."

"She just needs more time," Agnes said. "Pass the sugar. It hasn't been that long since Barton got married. She's still not over it." A spoon clinked on the side of a bowl.

"I thought when she found out he was married, she might…I don't know…finally let go of him and look at me in a different way."

A chair scraped on the floor.

"It's not *Barton* she misses," Agnes said. "He never gave her the time of day."

Pinetta frowned. *Never gave me the time of day? The night I left for Papa's funeral he—"*

"Then what is it?" Truitt asked.

"She never stopped believing he'd come around. That one day he'd look up and really *see* her. Notice the things she did for him *every single day*."

"She said that?" Truitt asked.

I did not, Pinetta whispered, wondering how Agnes knew.

"No," Agnes said. "But I felt exactly the same way about my old boyfriend. Took me forever to come to my senses. Poor Nestor. I drove him crazy."

Keeping near the wall, Pinetta backed away from the door and then stepped to the middle of the hall. Clearing her throat vigorously, she breezed into the kitchen.

"'Morning," she said, brushing past them on her way to the stove. She busied herself with cups and teabags, keeping her back turned. "You two are up early."

Truitt stared at Agnes. She shook her head.

"It's this baby," Agnes said, too cheerily. "He enjoyed rehearsal so much he wouldn't let me get to sleep. Finally, I—"

"He?" Pinetta asked, pleased with her nonchalance.

"I did say, 'he,' didn't I?" Agnes giggled. "Just a feeling, I guess."

"We were…talking about…rehearsal last night," Truitt said feebly.

Turning around, Pinetta leaned against the sink and crossed her arms. "It did go well, didn't it? The room gave a whole new sound."

Truitt stirred his tea; Agnes studied her corn flakes.

Both unsure how to proceed.

Stalling, Agnes picked up the cereal box. "Corn flakes?"

"No. Stopped eating corn flakes when I was seven. I'll have breakfast with Vesper."

Pinetta took her tea to her room.

Agnes followed and stood in her open door. "What are you and Vesper doing today?"

Pinetta buttoned her coat. "Not sure."

"Listen, Pinetta. I'm not sure how much you—"

"How much I *what*?" Her voice chilled Agnes to the bone.

"How much I said to Truitt about—"

Pinetta turned red from her collar to her forehead. "About who I should love and who I shouldn't, who I should marry and who I shouldn't, what I should do now that—"

"I wasn't saying what you should *do*. I was only trying to—"

She tapped on her top button. "My feelings for Barton were real. I'm not some lovesick teenager who had a crush on the captain of the football team."

"I know that," Agnes said.

Pinetta sighed. "I don't have time for this right now. But in the future, I'd appreciate it if you wouldn't 'explain' me to Truitt or anyone else. It's not necessary."

"I'm sorry. It won't happen again," Agnes said, making a mental note to check the hall the next time she and Truitt were talking.

Pinetta whisked past her—"See you tonight"—and out the front door.

Agnes stepped in to turn off the lamp. Pinetta never left it on. Bed unmade. First time *ever*. Spotting a purple corner of the quilt shoved under the bed, Agnes knelt and pulled it out. Another sign. Pinetta was on edge. Unbalanced.

"About time," Agnes said. "Now we're getting somewhere."

Gripping the steering wheel, Pinetta stewed all the way to Kimball Pines. It was still early. Vesper would be asleep another hour at least. *I'll have time to calm down,* she thought.

But when she arrived, she found Vesper, standing at the stove, scrambling eggs. The table was set: complete with placemats, silverware, jam, honey, and the morning paper.

Chapter 23 ~ As Time Goes By

"Good morning," Pinetta said. "Did you have trouble sleeping?"

"Slept like a baby," Vesper said, spooning eggs onto a plate. "But I woke up with something on my mind and could *not* go back to sleep. Breakfast?"

Pinetta hung up her coat and sat at the table. "Love some."

Vesper, wearing a white eyelet-ruffled apron, served the eggs. "Scrambled okay?"

"Yes, thank you. Are you worried about something?" Pinetta asked, wondering if the answer would be 'when Abbot's book is coming out.'

For weeks she had waited for the right opportunity to bring up the subject, to explain about "poetic license," that Abbot might embellish the truth, tint the story with his own perspective, add details, alter facts. Reveal truths. Share confidences. But she could never bring herself to spoil Vesper's happiness. She was coming to life, like a wilted flower, plucked up from dry, sun-baked soil to be planted in the shade of a sheltering tree. So, Pinetta continued to gamble the book was not ready, and with any luck, still a pile of typewritten pages on Abbot's cluttered desk.

Opening the refrigerator, Vesper removed the egg carton. "Not worried. But something did upset me last night, and I can't stop thinking about it." She cracked two eggs into a bowl.

"What's wrong?"

She whisked the eggs furiously. "While Fiona and I were cleaning the kitchen last night, she told me she and Ham are getting married at *city hall*."

"That's right. The weekend of Fiona's spring break. They're short on money and decided to spend it on a honeymoon instead of a wedding."

The eggs sizzled as Vesper poured them into the skillet. "I won't hear of it. I've known Fiona since she was a child. She used to play in this very kitchen. I will not have her bumping into people paying parking tickets on the most important day of her life. No. That will never do. We'll have the wedding here."

Pinetta could not help laughing.

Vesper spooned the eggs onto a plate and walked to the table. "I don't blame you for laughing. I know it sounds like a hare-brained idea. The wedding's only two weeks away and—"

"No. It's not that. I think it's wonderful."

"You do? Then—?"

"Are you the same woman I had to *pry* out of this house a few weeks ago. Now you want to host the social event of the season and invite the whole town?"

Tea at Kimball Pines

Vesper grinned. "Not the *whole* town. Just half of them."

Over eggs and toast Pinetta caught a glimpse of the woman Vesper Kimball had once been, her eyes sparkling with purpose and hope.

When Pinetta came home that night, she found Agnes grading papers at the kitchen table.

"Fiona made soup," Agnes said, pointing to the stove. "Help yourself. I already ate."

Pinetta sat next to her. "In a minute. Could I talk to you?"

Agnes laid down her pen. "If it's about this morning, I just want to say—"

"No. It's not that. I need your help."

"That's what Truitt and I were talking about this morning. He's worried he's taking advantage of you, asking you to play for rehearsals *and* lessons, so he thought I—"

"No. Not the choir. Ham and Fiona's wedding."

"They're getting married at city hall. There's not much to do, unless you want to—"

Pinetta shook her head. "No. They're getting married at Vesper's house. We called Fiona today before she left for school. And then we went shopping...all day. My feet are killing me."

"What? How did this happen?"

"Last night, when they were doing dishes, Vesper asked Fiona about her wedding. When she said it was at city hall, Vesper put her foot down. She insists on having it at her house."

"*Vesper* wants to host it? Do you know what you've done?"

Pinetta held up her hand. "Not my idea. It's going to be a killing amount of work, but—"

"Not that. We can pull that off. I mean Vesper. Opening her home to the public? No one's going to believe it, and it's all because of *you*."

Pinetta shrugged. "I don't know if I'd say that."

Agnes snatched up her pen. "Let's come up a schedule. I can't wait to tell Ivy Leigh."

"I can't wait to tell Bridey Ludlow," Pinetta said.

At the next choir rehearsal, seven singers, including the mayor's brother, walked up the aisle of the Presbyterian church and slipped into their sections as if they had never been away.

Chapter 23 ~ As Time Goes By

Fifteen people showed up at the audition the following Saturday. Among them, Walter Grant, whom Truitt had invited himself. Everyone who tried out was added to the choir.

The following Saturday, the Dennisonville Community Chorale, 38 strong, flocked to the church and bustled in, chattering like children on the first day of summer vacation. From the stained glass windows lining the walls, saints and angels watched as tenors and basses shook hands and slapped each other on the back, and sopranos and altos slid over to make room on their rows in the choir loft. Truitt introduced the new members. Rehearsal began. Voices, confident, free, bolstered by each other, inspired by their conductor, soared up to the vaulted cedar-beamed ceiling and rained down on an audience of four.

Watching from the rear of the auditorium were Bridey Ludlow, Chief Wilde, and Mayor Tanzler, who had stopped by to see the new and improved choir. And Vivian Grant, who had insisted on providing refreshments.

The men set up the table. Bridey helped Vivian with the tablecloth.

"Walter looks happy," Bridey said.

"It's a miracle," Vivian said. "I feel like I have my husband back. Since he found out he made the choir, he's been a different person. Stopped thinking of himself as a 'heart patient.'"

Bridey called to her cousin Jake. "See there, Jaybird? I told you so."

"He looks great, Vivian," Jake said. "And just a few weeks ago, we were afraid we were going to lose him."

"*My* mama looks happy," Mike Wilde said, raising his hand to wave at her.

"Excuse me," a voice said.

A stranger had slipped into the vestibule. Red-haired, bearded, in a black suit, black tie, eyebrows knit, he resembled a pitiless Puritan, recently returned from pillorying a sinner. He reached into his coat pocket and pulled out a business card. Bridey snatched the card before the mayor could reach it.

"Ben Whitaker?" she read.

He took out a small notebook and flipped through the pages. "Do I have the right place for the…community choir?"

Chief Wilde took the card from Bridey. "What do you want?"

Even in civilian clothes, Mike was imposing. Whitaker stammered.

"I'm looking for someone named"—he consulted his notes—"Carlyle. I went to the house…on Belmont, but no one was—"

"And what do you want with them?" Jake asked.

"I work for Robert Kimball," Whitaker said.

"Vesper's boy?" Bridey asked. "We haven't seen him in—"

Whitaker sneered. "He's no 'boy.'"

Mike Wilde displayed his badge. "I'll ask again. What do you want with the Carlyles?"

Holding up his hands, Whitaker stepped back. "No need for that. I'm not looking for the Carlyles exactly. It's one of their tenants. Abbot Cooper."

"He left town ages ago," Bridey said.

Jake peered at her. "Why don't you help Vivian and let me and Chief Wilde deal with this?"

She pouted, but did as he said.

"Now what's this about?" Jake asked.

"Mr. Cooper has published a book about Mr. Kimball's mother." Whitaker read from his notes. "*The Jilting of Vesper Belle*. Presents her *and my employer in a very bad light. He's filing a law suit against Cooper. Defamation of character. Invasion of privacy. I need to—"

Mike spoke up. "We just told you. Cooper left town."

Whitaker peered around Mike to survey the choir. "But what about the Carlyles? Surely they have some idea where he—"

Mike shook his head. "Your business is with Mr. Cooper. Not them."

Whitaker tucked his notebook in his pocket. "So much for small town hospitality."

Agnes, watching from the front row of the choir, saw the mayor and chief stand shoulder to shoulder, blocking the intruder. She lost her place in the music, fumbled. Dinah pointed to the measure they were singing.

When the stranger left, Bridey barged into a huddle with the men. Agnes mustered up a fake coughing spell and left the choir loft. Pinetta watched her hurry up the aisle to the vestibule.

They both knew—what they had feared was happening.

Agnes approached Bridey. "What's wrong?"

Chief Wilde handed her the business card. "Someone looking for Abbot Cooper. Name's Whitaker. He works for Robert Kimball."

"Vesper's son," Bridey said.

"He's already been to your house," the mayor said.

Agnes studied the card. "What did he want?"

"Apparently," Bridey said, "Abbot finished his book, and Robert is not happy. He's going to sue."

"Sue?" Agnes asked. "It must be worse than we thought."

"You're white as a sheet," Bridey said. "You better sit down." She slipped her arm around Agnes and guided her to the back row of the church. "I'll get you some water."

Chapter 23 ~ As Time Goes By

Agnes squeezed her hand. "Get Chief Wilde for me."

Bridey motioned for Mike. He knelt in the aisle next to Agnes.

"What's wrong?" he asked. "Do you know this guy?"

"I don't know him, but I knew what Abbot was writing in that book. You don't think he'll go to Vesper's house, do you? Because we haven't told her yet. It will destroy her."

Without a word, Mike hopped up. "Come on, Jake. Let's go."

They arrived at Kimball Pines. The mayor bounded to the door and rang the bell. No answer. They parked at the opposite curb to wait. When there was no sign of Whitaker for an hour, Mike started the car and pulled away.

"Let's stop by the Magnolia Arms," Jake said. "We'll tell them everything's all right."

They waved at the mailman as they turned the corner.

He had been carting a heavy book since early that morning and was eager to lighten his load. He slipped a few envelopes into Vesper's mailbox and then pulled out the book, wrapped in brown paper, and propped it by the door.

Harriet Oxley-Friend brought Vesper home twenty minutes later.

"Need help getting in?" Harriet asked.

"No, thanks. I have my keys right here. Thank you for bringing me home."

"I would've picked you up, too, if you had asked."

Vesper smiled. "It was too much fun seeing the look on Asa Ludlow's face when I got in his cab."

"It'll be all over town by dinnertime," Harriet said.

"I hope I can tell Pinetta before she hears. If it weren't for her, I'd still be up there behind those closed curtains."

Vesper got out of the car and started toward the house. She spotted the package. *Could it be?* She hurried up the steps, unlocked the door, picked up the book, and walked inside. *Two surprises in one day. Wait till I tell Pinetta.*

The next morning when Pinetta arrived, she did not find Vesper in the kitchen. She slipped upstairs. Vesper's bedroom door was open. Pinetta peeked in. Vesper, in rumpled clothes, sat on the edge of her bed, her hands resting on her knees.

A book lay beside her on the bed.

"Vesper," Pinetta said, as she entered. "Are you all right?"

Tea at Kimball Pines

Vesper turned to her. "Why? Why would he say these awful things about me?" She picked up the book. "This picture. Of Philip and me. It was hidden in my room. He went through my things. This title. *The Jilting of Vesper Belle*? Jilting?"

Pinetta knelt on the floor by the bed. "I'm sorry, Vesper. When did this—?"

"It was here when I came home from the Garden Club meeting yesterday."

"Garden Club? If I'd known…I would've—"

Vesper's voice was hollow. "I wanted to surprise you."

"That's wonderful," Pinetta said. "Next time I'll drive you."

Vesper shook her head. "I'm not going back. Once people read this, I won't be able to show my face."

Pinetta stood. "Come downstairs. You'll feel better after we have breakfast and talk. After church, we'll have lunch at the Magnolia Arms. All right?"

"No. I'm too tired."

"Then I'll bring you some tea." Pinetta walked to the window. "And open the curtains. It's a beautiful day."

"No," Vesper said. "Leave them closed."

Chapter 24

Blessings in Disguise

Grasping the curtains, Pinetta bowed her head. "I'm sorry, Vesper. I've known for a long time what Abbot was doing. I should've told you, but—" She turned from the window.

Vesper had heard nothing. Head on the pillow, she had gone to sleep. Pinetta removed Vesper's shoes and covered her with the comforter. She took the book with her to the kitchen, laid it on the table, and called the Magnolia Arms.

"Agnes?" She tried to steady her voice, but failed. "Could you come over?"

"What's wrong?"

"The book is here. She was up all night reading it."

Pinetta sank down and slid the book toward her to examine it. No expense had been spared. Hardbound with a dust jacket. Abbot's photo on the back. His name as author on the front, under the haunting picture of Vesper and Philip.

Even if she had not known Vesper, Pinetta would have been intrigued and longed to open the cover, read the story, and know her better. So, she did. She glanced at the title page, skipped the "Acknowledgements," and turned to the dedication.

Dedicated to the managers, staff, and residents of the Magnolia Arms, without whom...

How could he? Associate the Magnolia Arms with *this*?

She turned to Chapter One.

Tea at Kimball Pines

On Second Avenue in Dennisonville, North Carolina, stands the Kimball Pines, a stately mansion where time stands still. Within its walls lives a lonely woman, as confined in her failed dreams as a canary perched in a gilded cage.

But unlike the caged bird, Vesper Kimball never sings.

The words stung as sharply as if she had penned them herself. *I should've done more...to try to reason with Abbot,* she thought.

In spite of herself, she kept reading, drawn in by Abbot's vivid prose, poignant, and from what she knew, accurate to the smallest detail. He had done his homework. And he was a gifted writer. The syntax was flawless, the descriptions elegant.

Agnes did not bother to knock. "Where is she? Is she all right?"

Leaving the book on the table, Pinetta rushed to Agnes and threw her arms around her. Agnes stood motionless as Pinetta hugged her for the first time since they had met.

"It's my fault," Pinetta said. "I should've told Vesper. Now we're right back where we started. Everything's been undone in one night."

Agnes guided her to the table. "In the first place, *none* of this is your fault." She sat across from her. "And in the second place, you don't know anything's been undone."

Pinetta closed the book and turned it around. "*Look* at the title. Vesper was expecting the story of her family. The legacy of the Kimballs. And instead she got *this. Jilting?*"

She let the book fall; it slammed onto the table.

Agnes picked it up. "Have you read it?"

"Yes." She rolled her eyes. "And it's beautiful. At least we can take comfort in that."

"I doubt Robert Kimball will 'take comfort' in that." Turning the book over, Agnes glanced at Abbot's photo on the back. "I wonder who brought it here?"

"I don't know. She fell asleep before we finished talking."

"So she doesn't know about the lawsuit yet."

"No. But she'll be so embarrassed," Pinetta said. "And she'll blame herself for upsetting Robert. We'll have to cancel the wedding. She won't want to go through with it. Not now."

"You don't know that."

"You didn't see the look on her face, Agnes. I know that look. I saw it on my own face in the mirror. Every day. After Guy Henry left...and I shut myself up in *my own* house."

Chapter 24 ~ *Blessings in Disguise*

"But you're not shut up in your house now, are you?"

Pinetta was not amused. "Obviously."

"How did *you* get better?"

"You know that. I went to Millie's, and she wouldn't leave me alone."

Agnes folded her arms on the table. "And then?"

Pinetta shrugged. "I came here and…moved into the Magnolia Arms."

"And?"

Irritated, Pinetta smacked her hand on the table. "We don't have time for this. I called you here to talk about Vesper. So, we can decide what to do about *her*."

"That's what we're doing." Agnes held up the book. "Hasn't it dawned on you?"

"What?"

"A book *like this* could've been written about you…*The Jilting of Pinetta*…uh…after all this time, I don't know your middle name."

"Jane," Pinetta said, jaw clenched.

"Jane. Of course."

"I know what you're thinking. 'Plain Jane.' Right? Perfect name for me?"

Agnes laughed. "Oh, Pinetta, stop it. The only person who thinks you're 'plain' is you."

"Then why did you say—?"

"Because 'Jane' is sturdy and no-nonsense, like you."

Pinetta frowned. "I'm not sure 'sturdy' is a word I like."

"It's what Millie saw in you. She knew, with a little prodding, she could drag you back into the land of the living. And here you are, and that makes you the perfect person—"

"Land of the living?"

"—to help Vesper. You've been where she is. And you know the way out."

When Vesper woke at noon, the curtains were pulled back and Pinetta was taking a blue dress from the closet. An open suitcase, fully packed, lay on the bed.

Sitting up, Vesper rubbed her eyes. "What are you doing?"

"Packing. You're going on a little vacation." Pinetta draped the dress across the foot of the bed. "A couple of weeks. Maybe longer."

"I'm not going anywhere." Vesper dragged her hand across the bed. "Where's the book?"

"Agnes took it home." Pinetta whisked back to the closet. "Want something to eat now or do you want to wait till after we get there?"

"We?" Vesper asked.

"Yes. We're going to lock up the house for a while. I managed to get a reservation at an exclusive bed and breakfast. You can have the room as long as you want."

"I'm not going anywhere. I was fine till I let a stranger through the door"—her voice rose, quivering with emotion—"and you see where *that* got me. Well, I've learned *my* lesson."

Pinetta closed the suitcase. "I'll put this in the car. Your coat's in the kitchen. Get dressed. We want to get there before dark."

Following Agnes' instructions—"Act as if nothing has happened and don't give her a chance to argue"—Pinetta hurried from the room and closed the door behind her. Leaning against the wall, she crossed her fingers and held her breath. When Vesper did not follow her into the hall, she slipped downstairs to the kitchen.

Half an hour later, Vesper appeared. "Maybe a drive would do me good. If the roads aren't bad. Have you checked the paper for the weather?"

"Yes."

Vesper gazed around the kitchen. "When will we be back?"

"When the time is right."

"Who'll take care of my house?"

"I've already made arrangements."

Pinetta helped Vesper with her coat, grabbed the car keys, and opened the back door.

When they pulled into the driveway of the Magnolia Arms, Vesper turned to Pinetta.

"You tricked me."

"Not really," Pinetta said. "You *are* on vacation and this *is* an exclusive bed-and-breakfast and you *can* stay as long as you want."

Nestor walked down the porch steps. He opened Vesper's door and offered his hand. Pinetta followed them with the suitcase.

The day passed quietly by. Vesper was never left alone to brood. After lunch, Truitt invited her to listen to a new arrangement and give her opinion. She dozed on the parlor sofa as he played the piano. She awoke. Pinetta served tea and insisted they review the wedding checklist, gently ignoring

Chapter 24 ~ Blessings in Disguise

Vesper's resistance. Nestor said he needed advice about tulips and asked Vesper to come to the greenhouse. When they returned to the kitchen, Agnes claimed to need help with the soup she was making. After supper, Vesper could stay awake no longer and asked which room was hers.

Agnes pointed toward her bedroom. "Nestor and I thought you'd be more comfortable in our room. The second-floor rooms are all empty. You'd be alone up there."

Vesper reached out to pat Agnes' expanding middle. "I won't have you walking up and down stairs when there's no need. You forget. I'm an expert at being alone."

"I didn't forget," Agnes said. "That's why we thought you should be down here."

"No. You'll be up early. Getting ready for work. I don't want you to have to tiptoe around because of me."

The issue settled, Nestor carried Vesper's suitcase to their old room.

Pinetta followed. She opened the suitcase and took out Vesper's nightgown. "We'll unpack tomorrow. Good night." She walked to the door.

"Pinetta," Vesper said. "Where's the book?"

"What book?" Pinetta asked and closed the door.

She returned to the kitchen where Nestor, Agnes, and Truitt sat at the table, gathered around the book like a jury deliberating over evidence in a trial.

"The hard part's over," Agnes said. "We got her out of that house."

They spent the rest of the evening discussing how to go on with daily life, while shielding Vesper from unwanted attention. Truitt offered to move his voice lessons to the church.

Nestor disagreed. "The choir kept the party a secret. They won't tell anyone she's here."

"And company would do her good," Agnes said. "Especially Gretchen and Verbena."

"Somehow," Pinetta said, "we're going to have to finish the wedding plans without her."

"I think the wedding will be a good way to keep her mind occupied," Nestor said. "When it comes right down to it, she won't want to disappoint Fiona."

Agnes brought up the subject of Robert Kimball. "Should we tell him Vesper's here?"

"He doesn't care," Pinetta said.

"But if he's looking for Abbot," Nestor said, "he'll want the story from her."

Temper rising, Pinetta rapped on the book as she spoke. "If Robert paid more attention to her, he would've *known* what was going on. What business is it of his *where* she is now?"

Truitt suppressed a smile. Pinetta was beautiful when she was angry.

Agnes jabbed Nestor's knee under the table.

"It's been a long day," Nestor said. "We can talk more about this tomorrow."

They all agreed and went to their rooms.

Agnes curled up next to Nestor. "Can you believe it? Vesper Kimball, sleeping upstairs in our house? Who would've dreamed?"

Truitt turned off his light and lay on his back, grinning at the ceiling. He was sorry for Vesper's trouble, but having her here meant Pinetta would be home all day tomorrow. And every day after that…for the foreseeable future. Maybe his luck was changing after all.

Dressed for bed, Pinetta propped up her pillows and reached for the book on her nightstand. Ignoring her conscience, shouting, 'Traitor,' she opened to where she had left off and kept reading the book, which had caused them no end of trouble.

Midnight. 1:00. 1:30. Pinetta could not stop reading until she reached the scene where Vesper was grieving over her son Edward, stricken with pneumonia. Heartsick, Pinetta closed the book, got out of bed, and put on her robe. She was walking to the kitchen for a glass of water, when she noticed a light on upstairs. She tiptoed to the second floor. Vesper's door was open. Her room empty. Climbing to the third floor, Pinetta peered down the hall. Vesper was standing motionless at the arched window, her frail form outlined by the faint glow of the clouded moon.

Pinetta edged closer. "Vesper. It's cold up here. Come back to your room."

No response.

Rooted in place, Pinetta called again. Since the day Barton's postcard had arrived, announcing his marriage, she had not set foot on this floor, made sacred by Barton's work, the site of her daily pilgrimage to serve his coffee.

Here…memories of him were thick and inescapable. But greater than her wish to flee was the need to help her friend. Drawing near, she took off her robe and draped it around Vesper's shoulders.

Chapter 24 ~ Blessings in Disguise

"Ham told me this used to be his room," Vesper said, eyes fixed on the street below. "And that he used to find you up here, standing at this window."

Chilled, Pinetta crossed her arms, hugging herself. "I used to sneak up here when he was gone. I think I may have been the reason he thought of taking out the walls and the door."

"And before that...this was Agnes' room."

"Uh-huh. I think she still misses it, but she won't admit it to Nestor."

Vesper pointed to the spiral stairs. "Ham told me about building the staircase. How Nestor's father showed up right when he needed help. Otherwise, he couldn't have finished."

In the dark, Vesper could not see Pinetta's face reddening. "Yes. I think that's the only reason Nestor let him stay. They had been...at odds for a long time."

Suspended between sunset and sunrise, stranded too far from either to remember the world had once been light and would be again, Pinetta fought off the feelings she kept at bay during daylight hours. Only half-listening, she leaned against the window ledge.

"...heard stories about him from Fiona's mother. She said when Nestor's mother died, his father...what was his name? I forgot."

"Barton."

"Yes, that's it. Barton. Was so heartbroken, he took off. Left his son. Was gone for years. Is that true?"

"Yes."

"Makes you wonder."

Standing, Pinetta inched toward the hallway. "Wonder what?"

"Do you envy someone that kind of love...or pity them?"

"I really couldn't say. No one's ever loved me like that." She motioned to the door. "It's cold up here. We should get you back into—"

Distant thunder rumbled.

Vesper tilted her head toward the stairs. "Have you been up there?"

"Yes," Pinetta said, inching toward the hall. "I'll show you in the morning."

Vesper placed her hand on the banister. "Will you walk up with me? I wanted to look, but couldn't find the light. Didn't want to fall and cause you more trouble than I already have."

Pinetta rubbed the space between her eyes. *I've got to get out of here. I'll tell her I don't know where the—*

Tea at Kimball Pines

But Vesper, already three steps up, was craning her neck to find the way. "I think I see a window from here. Is there room to stand?"

Pinetta sighed. "Wait. Let me look for the switch." She turned on the light and joined Vesper. "Go ahead. I'll walk behind you. It's steeper than it looks."

Rain, sheeting against the windows, pattered on the roof.

They reached the platform. Pinetta stood back as Vesper approached the window on the front of the house.

"The town looks pretty from up here. Doesn't seem threatening at all, does it?"

"No," Pinetta said. "Why—?" She was about to point out the folly of that idea, until she remembered she had once stood in the same place, thinking the same thought.

"I was so proud of myself," Vesper said. "Going to the Garden Club meeting." She glanced over her shoulder. "The lecture was on waxing camellias."

"My mother raised camellias. Well, our gardener did."

Vesper moved to the next window. "Prudence told me once the book was published, I might be invited to autograph books at different events. So, I thought I'd practice going out."

"I knew you could do it. You've come such a long way since—"

"The thing is…I actually enjoyed the meeting. They treated me like a celebrity. You wouldn't think I'd lived here all my life. I went to grammar school with some of those ladies."

The rain turned to sleet. Pinetta, shivering, rubbed her arms. "I'm sure they've missed you. You should remember that, instead of—"

Vesper stepped to the third window, overlooking the woods behind the house. "You wouldn't believe the silly ideas I had about how my life would be after the book came out." She laughed bitterly. "It's going to change, all right. I'll be more of a joke than I was before. Robert will be furious. He'll *never* come see me now."

Pinetta grasped Vesper's shoulders and turned her around. "You're not a joke. Don't ever think that. It's not your fault you trusted someone who took advantage of you."

"But why did he do it? I treated Abbot like a son. Let him look at my personal belongings, because I thought he was writing a *history* book. Not some sordid story about—"

"There's nothing sordid about your life. No one will think that."

Chapter 24 ~ *Blessings in Disguise*

Vesper pulled the robe closer around her. "How can you be sure?"

"Because I know what I think. It's a beautiful story about an honorable woman, who suffered losses, and went on living anyway."

"Like a 'caged bird'?"

"That's only part of the story. Not the end."

Bankrolled by Abbot's father, *The Jilting of Vesper Belle* disappeared from bookstore shelves as soon as shipments were stocked. Abbot gave interviews and crammed his schedule with as many book signings as possible. Before long, people were arriving in Dennisonville and slipping into Mollie's or Newman's to lay their copies on the table, order coffee, and quiz the servers about the "strange lady who lives in the big house." Eventually, reporters also arrived at the Magnolia Arms, "mentioned in the dedication." Whoever answered the door replied, yes, they knew Abbot Cooper. No, they had no idea where Vesper Kimball was.

Critical praise for "Abbot Cooper's debut work" was widespread. The people of Dennisonville, however, remained ambivalent, even after *The Dennisonville Chronicle* published an effusive review (written and paid for by the Cooper marketing armada). Though Vesper had never lived her life among them, she was one of their own and they did not take kindly to strangers' bandying her name about. Even Asa Ludlow, who had spent years propagating the Vesper Myth, was close-mouthed when strangers climbed in the back of his cab and asked to be driven to Kimball Pines.

"I'll take you there," he would say, "but she's not home. Out of town. Europe, I heard."

Nevertheless, tourists swarmed in, cameras in hand, standing across the street to stare at Kimball Pines, talking quietly among themselves about how beautiful it was, wondering about the lady inside, and then pointing to the window—positive they had seen the curtain move.

At last Bridey Ludlow had her wish. Dennisonville was "on the map," but no one, including Bridey, was happy about it. There was general agreement if Abbot Cooper "knew what was good for him, he'd better never show his face here again."

This public show of disdain, however, did not stop residents from reading the story behind closed doors and whispering about it wherever they met. Dennisonvillians, who had cut their teeth on Vesper Kimball stories, were finding her more fascinating than they imagined.

Tea at Kimball Pines

But none of the turmoil touched Vesper, safe inside the Magnolia Arms, her days filled with music, conversation, and enough daily chores to make her feel useful. The longer Vesper stayed, the more convinced Pinetta was that the "old days" were gone.

Nestor proved right about the choir. None of them mentioned Vesper's sitting in on their own lessons or attending the ladies' section rehearsals on Tuesdays. Once, during "If Ever I Would Leave You," Gretchen poked Verbena and nodded at Vesper. Doing needle point on the sofa, she was singing along in a clear, pure voice. One by one the ladies grew silent. Truitt stopped conducting; Pinetta kept playing. Vesper, mind elsewhere, finished the song, snipped off her thread, and raised her eyes. Everyone laughed, including her. Truitt added a chair to the circle and invited Vesper to join them.

Gretchen, sharing her music with Vesper, leaned in to whisper. "Walk me out after rehearsal. We need to talk."

The following morning after Nestor and Agnes went to school and Pinetta left to see Muriel about the wedding reception menu, Vesper hurried downstairs to see Truitt. She found him marking a score at the piano.

"Good morning," she said. "Is everyone gone?"

He stuck his pencil behind his ear. "Yes. Did you need something?"

"As a matter of fact, I do."

He scooted to the end of the bench. "Pinetta made muffins before she left. She said I—"

"No, no. I don't need food. I want to ask you a question."

"What is it?"

Folding her hands, she tried to be coy. "I was wondering about a song the choir sang at my party. Can't remember the title." She glanced at the ceiling. "Something about 'evening'?"

She knew the title perfectly well, but Gretchen had coached her to "sound innocent."

"'Song of Eventide'?" Truitt asked.

"That's it. You remember."

He nodded. "Yes. I wrote it."

"You did?" (A fact she also knew.) She rested one hand demurely on the piano. "I was just wondering if you were planning to sing it again...the choir, I mean...for Founder's Day."

Chapter 24 ~ *Blessings in Disguise*

He brushed a speck of dust from F# above middle C. "No, I don't think so."

"May I ask why?"

"That was a special occasion." He cleared his throat. "Some selections…don't fit into a particular program. I've made some changes. Lute has other solos. Don't want to wear him out."

"Couldn't someone else sing the solo?"

He tucked his chin to his chest. "The truth is I'm not ready to hear it again…for awhile."

"Weren't you pleased with how it went?"

"It was better than I imagined. That's…part of the problem."

"I don't understand," she said.

"I wrote that song…well, started it…a long time ago. About a woman I loved…and lost. I always wanted to finish it…hear it performed. I'd given up on that…till I came here…"

"Because?"

He shrugged. "I had time on my hands."

"And…inspiration?"

He met her gaze. "What do you mean?"

She had only guessed, but his bald head, glistening red, confirmed her suspicions. "I've been here more than two weeks, Truitt. I've seen how you look at Pinetta. Tell me I'm wrong."

"You're not wrong. The song was supposed to set the mood for my proposal. But it didn't work out that way. She kept the ring. Hasn't put it on yet."

Vesper shook her head. "I can't imagine being proposed to like that. When my husband asked me to marry him, it was more like a business proposition. *How* could she say no?"

"I can answer that in one word." He spit out the name as if it left a bad taste. "Barton."

"Barton? Nestor's father?"

The doorbell rang. Relieved to have an excuse to get away, Truitt hopped up. "That's Tom Gibbons. Comes for his lesson before work."

Vesper stepped aside to let him pass and then walked across the hall to the kitchen.

The parlor door closed. Truitt sounded a chord, and Tom Gibbons sang up the scale.

Tea at Kimball Pines

Sitting down, she tried to digest the story she had just heard. Pinetta. Good, steady, no-frills Pinetta had fallen for Barton, who had deserted his son, been gone for years, married—how many times?—and then showed up out of the blue.

What was Pinetta thinking? Vesper gathered cups from the table and walked to the sink. She turned on the faucet. Waiting for the water to get hot, she glanced out the window and spotted Annie May Goode on her way to school.

"Look at that pretty pink coat and beautiful long hair," Vesper said. "Isn't she—?"

Annie May caught her toe on a crack in the sidewalk. Down she went, banging her knees, skidding on her elbow, scraping her face. School books scattered; papers fluttered. Struggling up on all fours, she sobbed as she scrabbled for her homework.

Vesper hurried out the back door and rushed down the driveway. Bending over, she picked up the arithmetic book and then brushed the little girl's hair from her face.

"Poor dear," Vesper said. "That's a nasty scrape over your eye. Come inside and let me clean that up."

Wailing, Annie May clutched her books. "I'll be late for school."

"I'll call the office and tell them what happened." Vesper helped her up. "Then I'll walk with you to school. How does that sound?"

Annie May wiped her nose. "I'm not supposed to go anywhere with strangers."

Vesper put her arm around her and started back to the house. "I'm not a stranger. I've lived here all my life."

"I've never seen you before. Who are you?"

"Mrs. Kimball."

Annie May lifted her tear-stained face. "The sad lady who lives in the big house?"

"Yes, the lady who lives in the big house. But who told you I was 'sad'?"

"My mama." She sniffed. "She said you've had trouble and you tried to make the best of it, but after your husband died, you just couldn't take it anymore and quit going out."

Annie May recited the story like a lesson she had memorized.

Vesper fixed her eyes on her path ahead. "And how does your mama know that?"

Chapter 24 ~ Blessings in Disguise

"You went to school with my grandma. And my brother, John Roy, brings your groceries."

Vesper opened the back door. "You're John Roy's sister? Annie May?"

"Yes, ma'am."

"Well, in that case, we'll call your grandma. She'll tell you it's all right for you to come in the house. Will that make you feel better?"

Annie May walked up the steps. "You can't call her. Mama took her to the doctor."

"Then you'll just have to trust me. Your mama won't mind. I promise."

"All right." She laid her books on the table and settled in a chair. "John Roy was wrong about you. I'm gonna tell him."

Vesper took a dishcloth from the drawer, wet it, and wrung it out. "What do you mean?"

"He said you don't like kids, and I could never come with him to see your house."

Vesper sat next to Annie May and gently wiped the blood from her face. "Why do you want to see my house?"

Annie May winced. "Because it's the most beautiful house I ever saw. I've always wondered what it looked like inside. Everyone does. They say there's gold everywhere."

"They do?"

"Yes, ma'am. 'Closest thing we've got to a mansion in this town.' That's what Mama says."

Vesper returned to the sink to rinse the cloth. "Tell you what. You be a brave girl and let me put some medicine on your face and your knees. Then come back here after school, and I'll take you to my house. Would you like that?"

Annie May brightened. "You mean it?"

"Yes. And you can stay as long as you like. We'll have a tea party."

The secretary at Dennisonville Elementary School hung up the phone and tapped on the principal's office door.

She pushed up her glasses on her nose. "You won't believe who just called. Vesper Kimball. Annie May Goode fell and hurt herself. Mrs. Kimball's bringing her to school."

No one believed her, until Vesper, holding Annie May by the hand, strolled into the office for the first time in nearly 40 years.

Tea at Kimball Pines

Alerted to Vesper's arrival, the music teacher, school nurse, and janitor lingered in the office, trying to appear casual.

Principal Vaughan, straightening his tie, slipped out when he saw her arrive.

"Mrs. Kimball? It's nice to see you. Thank you for bringing Annie May. Is she all right?"

Vesper signed the visitor log the secretary slid across the counter. "Yes. Just had a bad fall. And please tell her teacher the story about her homework being ruined is *true*."

"We'll take care of it. Thank you."

Vesper pretended not to notice the half dozen pairs of eyes gaping at her. Instead, she bent down and whispered to Annie May. "Now, don't forget. Come back to the Magnolia Arms after school, and Mrs. Fraleigh will drive us to my house. I'll call your mother to ask if it's all right."

"Yes, ma'am." Annie May left for her class.

Vesper glanced around the office. "Hasn't changed much in all these years."

"It was painted last summer," the secretary said, almost chirping.

"Very nice," Vesper said, though she did not care for mint green. "Well, goodbye."

She was almost at the door when the secretary opened her desk drawer and pulled out *The Jilting of Vesper Belle*. "Mrs. Kimball." Vesper turned around. "Would you sign my book?"

Principal Vaughan shot her a withering look. "Mrs. Saunders, please."

She pretended not to hear. "Such an inspiring story. I had no idea."

Murmurs of agreement resounded through the office. The music teacher hurried back to retrieve her copy, half-read, by the mimeograph machine.

Vesper paused, like a frightened bird about to take flight. "Inspiring?"

Mrs. Saunders opened the cover. "Such a good example about dealing with loss. In spite of all you…well, you've done so much for our community…financially…I mean…"

Vesper returned to the counter and reached out for the book. "It's all right. I understand what you're trying to say."

Surrounded by admirers, Vesper's visit stretched to almost half an hour. She said goodbye and started home, breathing in the brisk air, blowing out through pursed lips to watch a little cloud appear, evaporate. She felt like skipping.

Chapter 24 ~ Blessings in Disguise

A car slowed and pulled to the curb. Gretchen Tate, on her way to her voice lesson, rolled down her window. "Vesper? What are you doing out here? It's freezing. Get in."

Thanking her, Vesper climbed into the car. On the way to the Magnolia Arms, she told the story of Annie May and the visit to the office.

"You should've seen it," Vesper said. "I signed one book after another. Before I knew it, the room was full of people. All of them wanting to meet *me*."

Gretchen patted Vesper's knee. "Of course they did."

"But why? They don't even know me. I'd never seen any of them till today."

"Don't you know? People in this town think of you as…part of who we are. You're our very own Emily Dickinson. We might not understand you, but you belong to us."

"No, I didn't know."

Gretchen turned onto Belmont Drive. "Without you we wouldn't have a nice library or park. Your scholarship fund has sent a dozen Dennisonville kids to college. Everyone knows it was you—not *Mr.* Kimball. None of those things happened till *after* he was gone."

"I did it for Edward. I always thought, if he had lived, he would've been the kind of man who would—"

Gretchen pulled up behind a pale blue Pontiac parked in front of the Magnolia Arms. "Whose car is that?"

"No idea," Vesper said.

They got out and stepped onto the sidewalk. Vesper read the magnetic sign on the door: *Ophelia Hunt. Realtor.* They started toward the house, but before they could investigate, a well-dressed woman walked by, got in her car, and drove away.

Standing in the open door, Truitt waved. "How did it go at the school?"

"Fine," Vesper said. "Better than—"

"Who was that?" Gretchen asked, pointing over her shoulder.

"My…uh…realtor," Truitt said. "I've been looking for…a house."

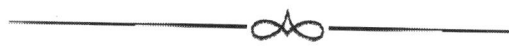

———∽∞∽———

Pinetta left her meeting with Muriel and drove to Kimball Pines. She collected the mail and toured the cold, vacant house. The longer Vesper was away, the more the rooms seemed like museum displays, collections of treasures, perfectly preserved.

Tea at Kimball Pines

But Vesper was not among them—at least for now.

Completing her second-floor inspection, she placed her hand on the banister and descended, imagining voices coming from the living room, pictured the sons she never had, the daughters she had hoped for, grandchildren playing on the floor.

Shuddering, she hurried past the empty chairs and sofa, unlit fireplace, and drawn curtains, down the hall to the kitchen. Glancing at the stove on her way out (she promised Vesper she always would), she climbed into the Buick and drove home.

Nearing the Magnolia Arms, Pinetta spotted a silver car in the driveway. She parked by the curb and then paused on the sidewalk to study the car. New. With a dealer's tag. BMW. Definitely not belonging to one of the choir members.

She stepped onto the porch and opened the door. She could hear Mary Grace singing "Ave Maria" in the parlor, conversation coming from the kitchen. As Pinetta walked down the hall, she sniffed Chanel No. 5. Heard Vesper talking. But who—?

Pinetta peeked in the kitchen.

Spying her, Vesper rushed over. "Pinetta, look who's here."

Pinetta's eldest sister, Miriam, stood and kissed her cheek. "Hello, Pinetta. Mrs. Kimball was just catching me up on all your news. Took me on a tour of the house. So…quaint."

Vesper, alarmed at Pinetta's blank expression, realized too late she should have met Pinetta at the door and warned her Miriam was there.

Pinetta fidgeted with her top button. "What are you doing here, Miriam?"

Miriam sat, crossed one nyloned leg over the other, and straightened her camel hair skirt. "I was in Washington, visiting friends at DAR headquarters."

"This is hardly on your way home," Pinetta said.

Picking up a spoon from the table, Miriam wiped it with a napkin. "After Eve visited, she told us about where you live. I wanted to see it. We had *no idea* you had a *new* job."

"Eve?" Vesper asked.

"Our youngest sister," Pinetta said. "She dropped by last November."

"Sit down, Pinetta," Miriam said. "You're standing there like a waitress taking an order."

Pinetta complied; Vesper bristled.

Chapter 24 ~ *Blessings in Disguise*

The final "Ave Maria" drifted across the hall. The parlor door opened. Mary Grace sashayed into the kitchen. "How was that, Vesper? Am I—?"

Vesper shook her head imperceptibly. Mary Grace halted, took in the scene, studied Pinetta's grim face. Truitt was right behind and, like Mary Grace, skidded to a stop.

Vesper gestured to Miriam. "You haven't met Pinetta's sister."

Awed by Miriam's coiffed, raven-black hair and expensive clothes, Mary Grace edged nearer to Vesper. Truitt stood behind Pinetta's chair and extended his hand.

"Truitt Spenlow."

"*Dr.* Truitt Spenlow," Vesper said. "And this is Mary Grace Dodson, our neighbor."

Mary Grace wanted no part of Miriam. "I have to be going now. Nice to meet you."

She scooted through the back door.

Miriam, hands in her lap, raised her eyebrows at Truitt. "Doctor? The local GP?"

"No," Vesper said. "Ph.D. Retired."

Miriam cocked her head. "Oh, so you were the one giving that...lesson."

Her wrinkled lip and condescending tone reminded Truitt too much of Dr. Elspeth Sherwood, the imperious school administrator he had left behind.

"Yes," he said. "You must be Pinetta's *older* sister."

"By ten months," Miriam said.

"Was Pinetta expecting you?" Truitt asked.

"I was on my way home from DAR headquarters in Washington. We hadn't heard from Pinetta since Christmas, and naturally, Mother wanted me to check on her. It was a short detour."

"It's my fault she hasn't had time to write," Truitt said. "She's our accompanist, and we're getting ready for a concert. Very busy schedule. She's working entirely too hard."

Her advantage slipping, Miriam sipped her tea. Cold. But she gave no clue. "So you're playing the piano now instead of cooking for a living. Do you make enough to support—?"

Vesper joined the fray. "No. Pinetta's music is community service. She *works* for me...my administrative assistant...managing my late husband's estate."

Miriam narrowed her eyes. "When did this happen?"

Tea at Kimball Pines

Vesper opened the cabinet and took out a soup pot. "I had heard about Pinetta and asked to see her as soon as she came back from your father's funeral. I knew Mrs. Hubbard had left, and she was free. Would you like to join us for lunch, Miriam?"

"No. Thank you." Not yet beaten, Miriam fired her final volley. "But I did want to meet Pinetta's fiancé while I was here. She said she wanted to bring him home for Christmas, but had to leave so suddenly for Papa's funeral. There wasn't time for him to 'change his plans.'"

Pinetta gripped the seat of her chair. "Actually, what I should've said was—"

Truitt placed his hand on Pinetta's shoulder. "That wasn't exactly true. I *could've* changed my plans, but I've been recovering from a car accident and I didn't want to hobble in on a cane the first time I met Pinetta's family."

Miriam pointed. "You? *You're* the fiancé?"

Vesper spoke up before she could think twice. "Yes. I gave Pinetta the morning off, so she could keep appointments with the caterer and the florist."

This at least was true.

"Then I must see your ring," Miriam said. "So I can describe it to Mother."

Pinetta squirmed. "I…I don't…have it…"

"The ring was too big," Truitt said. "It's at the jeweler's, being sized."

"Why didn't you let Mother know?" Miriam asked.

Pinetta spluttered. "It…all happened so quickly."

"They were going to elope," Vesper said. "But I found out about it and insisted they have the wedding at my house. It was going to be a small, private affair, but Pinetta has so many friends. Once word got out, the guest list just mushroomed."

After a respectable 45-minute visit, Pinetta accompanied her sister to the door.

Miriam put on her coat. "Everyone will be surprised about your news." She put on her leather gloves. "You couldn't have picked anyone *less* like Guy Henry. I never liked him, but at least he was taller than you…and had hair. But there's no accounting for taste."

"No, there's not," Pinetta said. "After all, you married Giles." She opened the door. Lute Monroe, arriving for his lesson, was lumbering toward the porch.

Miriam stepped through the door. "Where will you go on your honeymoon?"

Chapter 24 ~ *Blessings in Disguise*

"We haven't decided."

"You must let us know. If you'll be near Sumter, we could host a reception for you." She scrutinized the front of the house. "Nothing too formal."

Lute waited on the top step.

"Hello, Lute," Pinetta said. "This is my sister, Miriam."

He wiped his hand on his overalls and held it out. Miriam ignored it.

"I'm a little early," he said. "Truitt ready for me?"

"Yes. Come in." Pinetta stood back to let him enter.

Miriam shook her head. "I don't know *how* you live here."

"I don't know how I lived anywhere else."

Pinetta closed the door. Noticing Miriam's scent still hovering in the air, she grabbed Nestor's boot and used it to prop open the door and air out the house. She returned to the kitchen.

"Well," Vesper said, ladling soup into bowls, "I haven't had that much fun in years. That Truitt. I didn't know he had it in him, did you? When he said, '*older* sister,' I could barely keep a straight face."

"What about you?" Pinetta asked. 'Administrative assistant'? Where did *that* come from?"

Vesper set the bowls on the table. "I don't know. I've done a lot of things today I never thought I'd do." She told Pinetta about Annie May and the promised tea party at her house. "I always knew I'd know when was the right time to go back to my house. I guess that's today. Do we have anything to serve?"

"Nothing an 8-year-old would like."

"Then we'll go to the store. It's been a long time since I sat in my own kitchen. I'll get my coat." She walked to the door. "We should leave a note to say where we've gone."

Pinetta picked up the note pad on the table. She wrote *Agnes—*, tore off the sheet, crumpled it and started again. *Dear Truitt—*

I was married almost 30 years, and my husband never one time stood up to my sister when she made fun of me. In fact, he enjoyed it. I'll never forget what you did for me today. It was noble. Thank you. Tell Agnes I'm taking Vesper home. I'll explain when I get back. Pinetta

All the way to the store Vesper chattered about seeing her house. Pinetta listened, trying to sound enthused as she responded. But she couldn't help worrying. Had Vesper come far enough in the last few weeks to go back to living alone?

Tea at Kimball Pines

Pinetta drove Vesper and Annie May to Kimball Pines. After tea and cookies, Vesper took Annie May's hand and led her upstairs. Pinetta watched. *When was the last time,* she thought, *a child walked up those steps and ran down the hall?*

She returned to the kitchen to clear the table. Vesper was home. Upstairs in her old room. They would return to their routine. Pinetta would arrive each morning. They would have quiet meals. She would lock the house on her way out.

But maybe, Pinetta thought, *maybe Vesper's glimpse of the world was enough to keep her in it. And there's still the wedding to plan. We'll just take one day at a time.*

She glanced at the clock and went upstairs to tell Vesper it was time to go. She found them in Vesper's room. Annie May, sporting a long strand of pearls, white high heels, and a yellow, broad-brimmed hat, was putting clothes into a suitcase.

"What are you girls doing?" Pinetta asked.

Annie May looked up. "Miss Vesper let me try these on. She said next time I come over I can wear them."

Pinetta examined the suitcase. "Is she letting you take all these clothes to your house?"

Vesper laughed. "No. Those are for me. I'm packing a few more things to take home."

Chapter 25

Tears and a Journey

Arriving home after school, Agnes plunked her books on the kitchen table and headed straight across the hall to the parlor. Neither Corby Dudman, finishing his voice lesson, nor Truitt, paid attention when she passed by and plopped down on the sofa, her feet up on the arm, her arm over her eyes. Contented, she sighed. There was no place in the world like this sofa in this room in this house. Her baby jabbed an elbow—or a knee?—into her side. She pushed back. "You're glad to be home, too. Lucky kid. You get to grow up here."

Truitt sounded a final note and closed the lid on the piano.

"She awake?" Corby asked.

"Yes, but not for long," Agnes said. "Bye, Corby. See you at rehearsal."

"Think this baby will wait till after Founder's Day to make an appearance?" he asked.

"Hope so."

After Corby left, Truitt closed the French doors and pulled a chair next to Agnes.

"Could we talk? A lot happened while you were gone, and I'd like to tell you before Vesper and Pinetta come back." He took Pinetta's note from his shirt pocket and handed it over.

Agnes read. "Pinetta's sister was here? When?"

"This morning." He recounted the story.

She sat up. "Let me get this straight. You…and Vesper…told Miriam that Pinetta is 'managing' Vesper's estate and is engaged to *you*?"

He nodded. "I know. Unbelievable. Right? I don't know what got into us."

"That's amazing. Vesper. Locking horns with Pinetta's sister. And you. No wonder Pinetta thinks you're"—she scanned the note—"'noble.' Way to go, Truitt."

"But what now?" Truitt asked. "Her family will expect a wedding. She'll have to make up some reason why that doesn't happen."

"Nothing we can do about it today." Lying back, she closed her eyes.

He tucked the note back in his pocket. "There's one more thing...about Vesper."

"What is it?"

"You know a little girl named Annie May?"

"Yeah. She lives down the street."

"Well, Vesper saw her fall down on the sidewalk. She rushed out and brought her in. After she fixed her up, she *walked* her to school."

Her eyes popped open. "What?"

"Promised her a tea party at her house," Truitt said. "If she'd let Vesper help her."

"So that's where they are now? Kimball Pines?"

"Yeah. You think Vesper will come back or stay home?"

"I have no idea. Poor Pinetta. First her sister, and now this."

———————∞———————

Annie May's mother was watching from the window. When she saw Vesper's Buick pull into the driveway, she came out to meet them. Annie May thanked Vesper again and waved a final time before going in.

"See you tomorrow," she said.

Vesper waved back as they drove away. "Let's go to Mollie's. Dinner's on me."

Taking Muriel's suggestions, Vesper bought dinner for everyone and chose two desserts.

Night coming on, the friends drove home, each drifting in her own thoughts.

"They say you can't go home again," Vesper said. "Now I believe it."

"What do you mean?"

"The first few nights, after I left home, all I could think about was going back to my beautiful house. But when I got there today, it didn't feel the same. It was cold..."

"You told me to keep the heat turned down."

"I don't mean that. I mean...lifeless. Nothing there to warm you up and make you feel welcome." She turned to Pinetta. "Did you feel cold the first time you came in my house?"

Chapter 25 ~ *Tears and a Journey*

"Not cold. Just nervous."

She shook her head slowly. "You shouldn't feel that way in a home. I don't feel that way at the Magnolia Arms." She shifted the cake box in her lap. "I'm going to ask Agnes if I can stay...permanently. You don't think they'll mind, do you?"

"Mind? Of course not."

"I'll pay rent. I know they need the money. I've seen Nestor worrying over the bills."

She gazed out her window. "And Truitt will be glad you're home every day, instead of coming over to my house."

Pinetta turned to her. "Why would you say that?"

"Gretchen put me up to asking Truitt why the choir isn't singing 'Song of Eventide' for the concert." She cut her eyes at Pinetta. "He told me he didn't have the heart to hear it again."

Pinetta bit her lip. "I suppose he told you why."

"Yes, he did. And I told him I don't how you said 'no' to his proposal. Men like him don't come along every five minutes. If anyone knows that, I do. Haven't you read my book?"

When Vesper burst out laughing, Pinetta joined in. "I'm halfway through. I'll let you know what I find out."

Arriving home, Pinetta placed the carry-out bags on the kitchen table and walked across the hall to the parlor where Truitt and Agnes were still talking. She opened the door. "Where's the tablecloth, Agnes?"

Truitt whirled around. "You're back. How long have you...? We didn't hear you."

"We brought dinner," Pinetta said. "Vesper wants to eat in the dining room."

Glancing at Truitt, Agnes walked to the door. "The tablecloth's in my closet. I'll get it. And I'll tell Nestor dinner's ready." She squeezed Pinetta's hand as she passed by. "You okay?"

"Yes. I have a lot to tell you."

After Agnes left, Truitt ambled toward Pinetta. "I want to apologize for the mess I've gotten you into. But your sister made me so mad, I—"

She placed her fingertips against his lips. "I told you. Today was the first...and only...time someone stood up to my sister...for me." She leaned in and kissed his cheek. "I won't forget it."

Truitt blinked. "After supper, could we...talk? I have something I need to—"

Vesper, carrying the food to the dining room, appeared in the hallway. "Truitt, could you get my suitcase out of the car? I've run out of hands."

Agnes smoothed the cloth over the long table. Pinetta set five places together at one end. Nestor sat at the head of the table; Agnes on his left, Vesper on his right. Truitt, nervous as a teenager on a first date, sat across from Pinetta. When Nestor bowed his head to say grace, Pinetta reached across the table to take Truitt's hand. Noticing, Nestor prayed longer than usual.

Agnes put her napkin in her lap. "This is so nice. I'm starving. Thank you, Vesper."

"I hear you had a busy day, Vesper," Nestor said, spooning scalloped potatoes onto his plate.

Vesper laughed. "So has poor Pinetta. I've dragged her from pillar to post. To the store, then my house. We took Annie May home, and then went to the restaurant."

"I felt like a Hollywood agent," Pinetta said. "Everywhere we went people stared at Vesper like she was Katherine Hepburn. I thought the cashier at the store was going to faint."

"A star is born," Agnes said.

Vesper wagged her hand. "Listen to you. 'Star.'"

"She's right," Truitt said. "There's no reason you can't join the choir. Come to rehearsals at the church."

"We need another soprano," Pinetta said.

"You won't have to try out," Truitt said. "I've heard you sing, and you know half the music already from sitting in on practices."

Vesper looked from one to the other. "Well…I guess I could…come to practice. But—"

The phone rang.

"I'll get it," Pinetta said. "Probably Bridey. Wanting to know if what she's heard is true." Standing, she imitated her. 'Please tell me you did *not* take Vesper to the store today.'"

"Tell her we went to Mollie's, too," Vesper said.

Pinetta took the call in the kitchen. "Hello."

"Pinetta? Thank goodness you answered the phone. This is Gretchen."

"I was going to call you later and thank you for giving Vesper a ride today. She—"

"Did she tell you who was there when we got back?"

Pinetta was bewildered at Gretchen's impatience. "You mean my sister?"

"No. The *realtor*."

"Realtor? Why would a—?"

Chapter 25 ~ *Tears and a Journey*

"She was there to see *Truitt*. He's looking for a house. Did he say anything to you about it? He wouldn't leave before our concert, would he? We can't *do* it without him."

Short of breath, Pinetta leaned against the counter. "No, he hasn't said anything. But lately, we've all been occupied with—"

The doorbell rang.

"You have to find out what's going on, Pinetta. He may have gotten another job offer somewhere. He could go anywhere and earn a huge salary. A man of his caliber?"

"He wouldn't leave…just like that…without telling anyone."

Gretchen was inconsolable. "Talk to him, Pinetta. And then call me back *tonight*."

Pinetta walked down the hall. Nestor was talking to Mary Grace. She was in a panic.

"Don't worry," Nestor said. "I can leave right now."

"What's the matter?" Pinetta asked.

Mary Grace wailed. "Lute went to Raleigh today. He was waiting at a red light, and his truck was rear-ended. He had to have it towed. Now he's stuck there. And I can't go get him. I don't have a car. I thought Nestor could take me. I don't know who else to ask."

Nestor raised his eyebrows at Pinetta; she understood his plea for help. He did not mind picking up Lute, but did not want to be trapped in the car with Mary Grace.

Pinetta put her arm around her. "Try not to worry. Have you had supper?"

Mary Grace sniffled. "No…o… o."

"You can wait with us while Nestor goes to get Lute."

Pinetta went to kitchen for another plate. On her way back to the dining room, she saw Nestor and Truitt, coats on, at the front door.

"You're both going?" she asked.

"I thought Nestor could use the company," Truitt said.

He wants to talk to Nestor alone. Tell him he's leaving.

The women sat with Mary Grace while she ate and then headed to the parlor.

As Pinetta walked ahead with their guest, Vesper hung back, reaching out to grasp Agnes by the elbow. Agnes turned; Vesper held her finger to her lips and whispered.

"I don't want to be rude to that poor girl, but I *have* to talk to you. Tonight. Can you keep an eye on me and follow my signals?"

Agnes nodded, grateful to have any excuse to slip away. Loving your neighbor was one thing, but waiting for Mary Grace to stop talking long enough to take a breath was another.

Pinetta suggested a game of gin rummy, but Mary Grace refused, "too upset to concentrate." She chattered ceaselessly, peppering them with questions about Fiona's wedding, and letting them in on her secret. She was convinced Lute was going to propose. After an hour, Vesper decided she had been polite enough and stood up.

"I'd love to stay and talk more," she said, "but there's a lot to do tomorrow, and I really need to go to bed."

"Me, too," Agnes said, patting her stomach. "Sleeping for two now."

Pinetta seized the moment. "Vesper's right. We should all get some sleep. The men should be home soon. Can I walk home with you, Mary Grace?"

Mary Grace, who had two more stories to tell and a dozen more questions, nodded. "I was hoping we could sing some tonight, but I guess that can wait."

"I'll get your coat," Pinetta said, "and meet you in the kitchen."

They said good night in the hall. Pinetta closed the back door on their way out.

"Let's talk in my room," Vesper said. "I need some advice, and then I'll need to make a few calls. Oh, and I'll need a ride to Raleigh tomorrow."

"Don't you want to wait for Pinetta to come back?"

"No. This concerns her. And I don't want to tell her till I work out the details."

"Okay. But I need to make a call first. I'll meet you in your room."

Agnes picked up the phone in the kitchen and dialed. "Hi. I wanted to touch base with you before we turn in. We're still on for tomorrow? Right?"

In the time it took Pinetta to walk two doors down and back, her friends had gone to their rooms. She was relieved. She was all talked out and wanted to be alone. She left the hall light on and lay on her bed, door open, to wait for Truitt. *If he's leaving,* she thought, *it's my fault. He's never been anything but kind to me, and I've thrown it back in his face every chance I got.*

Exhausted, but determined to stay awake till Truitt came home, she grabbed Abbot's book from her nightstand and started reading. Her eyes closed. She slept.

Chapter 25 ~ *Tears and a Journey*

The phone woke her. Dazed, she glanced at the clock. 6:10? Couldn't be. She never slept that late. She was still dressed. Someone had covered her with a blanket. Closed her door. The phone kept ringing. She threw back the blanket. Dashed from her room. Truitt's door was open. Bed made. Had they even come home last night? The phone kept ringing. She stumbled to the kitchen. Grabbed the phone. Too late.

A note on the table. Agnes' handwriting. *Gone to train station. Back soon.*

Clutching the note, Pinetta sank down at the table. Truitt had left for the train station. Job interview. *That's what he was going to tell me last night,* she thought. *He couldn't wait any longer for me to make up my mind.*

Maybe he had left a note. She hopped up. Dashed to his room. Scanned his dresser. Nothing. Scurried across the hall to her room. A note there? No. Nothing. She had exhausted his patience. He had made up his mind to leave.

The full weight of what she had done flooded over her. Scenes flitting through her mind. Truitt. Singing with Gretchen when she lost her nerve at the audition. New Year's Eve. The kiss at midnight. Vesper's party. The proposal. And only yesterday... standing between her and Miriam. Hand on her shoulder. Sparing her from embarrassment. *The ring's too big. I'm having it sized.* She opened her top drawer, lifted out the blue velvet box, abandoned there since Valentine's Day. Heart breaking, eyes blurred with tears, she opened it, took out the ring, slipped it on her finger. A perfect fit.

She clasped her hands to her chest. Maybe there was still time. If she left now...She searched for the keys to the Buick. Gone. She ran upstairs to find Vesper. Her room was empty. Vesper had gone with them. *Why didn't they wake me up?* Without a thought of changing her wrinkled clothes, or even combing her hair, she raced downstairs and through the back door. Nestor's truck was in the driveway, the bed piled high with folding chairs, a blue tarp secured over the top, waiting to be ferried to Kimball Pines for Ham's wedding the next day.

Pinetta sized it up. She had never driven a truck, but desperate to get to the train station, went back to the house and snatched Nestor's keys from the pegboard by the door. She climbed into the driver's seat and cranked the engine. The chairs were stacked too high for her to see from the rearview mirror. Shifting into reverse, she looked in the side mirror. The driveway was impossibly long. The street impossibly far away. The windows were fogged. She could not find the defroster. She turned on the windshield wipers and put her foot on the gas.

Somehow she got to the street. Pushed on the accelerator. Hurtled forward, nudging the speedometer up, flying through yellow lights, slowing only to turn corners. Heard the chairs scrape together, tipping back and forth. But drove on. If they toppled onto the road, she would come back with Nestor to pick them up. Flying into the parking lot, she aimed for the terminal, jerked the truck over, scraping the tires against the curb. She yanked the keys from the ignition, tore past the "Taxis Only. No Parking" sign, and, barreling through the crowd in the terminal, raced onto the platform.

People everywhere. Which way to go? She looked both ways, leaned forward and back. Had to start somewhere. Turned to her right and pushed through the people waiting to board. By the time she reached the last car, the waiting passengers had surged into the train and the platform was almost empty. She started back, craning her neck to see into the windows. The train left the station. Worn out, she staggered back through the terminal and onto the sidewalk. A policeman, standing behind Nestor's truck, was reading the license plate and writing a ticket. She broke into a run.

"Wait. Wait," she called, waving. "I was only gone a minute. It was an emergency."

"Taxis only. No exceptions." He tore the ticket from the pad and presented it.

Pinetta climbed into the truck. Laid her head on the steering wheel. Too late. Truitt was gone. "The wedding's tomorrow. Why didn't he wait?" Behind her a taxi driver honked. She started the engine. Eased forward, past parked cars, suddenly aware of how unwieldy the truck really was. "Maybe he had no choice. They scheduled the interview. Said he had to come now or forget it." Sighing, she turned toward the exit. "Or he's signing a contract on a house somewhere. That's why the realtor came by." Ahead of her a car was reversing. She stopped to let it out.

In that moment, while she waited, she glanced in the side mirror. Six cars back a man was closing the trunk on a classic burgundy Buick. There was no mistaking him. It was Truitt. His bald head glistening in the rising sun.

Screaming, she threw the truck into park, pushed open the door, and broke into a run.

"Truitt. Truitt."

Grasping the door handle, he looked up and saw the woman he loved loping toward him.

Chapter 25 ~ Tears and a Journey

When Nestor saw Truitt step away from the car, he got out. "Where are you going?"

Truitt pointed. "It's Pinetta."

"How did *she* get here?" Nestor leaned in his open door to tell Agnes. "Pinetta's here."

Agnes left the car just in time to see Pinetta throw herself into Truitt's arms.

"Thank you. Thank you," Pinetta said, clinging to him.

"Thank you for what?" Truitt asked.

"For not leaving me."

"Of course, I'm not leaving. What gave you that idea?"

Releasing her hold, she gripped the lapels of his gray cardigan. Lifting her tear-soaked face, she snuffled, spilling out her heart onto the pavement. "Gretchen said…you're looking for a house. And last night, when you said you wanted to talk to me, I realized you were going to say goodbye."

"No," Truitt said.

But the floodgate, opened, could not be shut. "I waited for you to come home last night, but I fell asleep. And when I woke up, you were gone. I thought I'd lost you. And I realized…I love you." She held up her left hand to display the ring. "My answer's, 'Yes.' Yes. Just don't leave me."

Nestor peered over the roof of the car at Agnes in her own puddle of tears.

A man's voice yelled, growing louder as he came nearer. "Hey, lady, come back here and move this truck. I gotta get home."

When Nestor heard the word 'truck,' he stepped to the rear of the Buick. Peering toward the man, Nestor spotted his truck and gulped. He approached Pinetta.

"If you'll give me the keys to my truck, I'll move it. How did you—?"

She reached in her coat pocket and handed over the keys. "Don't ask."

Ivy Leigh Ransom opened the rear door and got out. "What in the world is going on?"

Agnes, too overcome to speak, could only point at Truitt and Pinetta.

"Ivy Leigh?" Pinetta asked, wiping her nose. "What are you doing here?"

"Torbert and I came for the wedding." She bent down and spoke to Mr. Hampton. "You might want to get out. I think we're going to be here a while."

"I didn't know you were coming," Pinetta said. "I would've ordered you a corsage."

309

"We weren't," Ivy Leigh said, "when the wedding was going to be at the courthouse. But when Agnes called and said the plans had been changed, we thought we'd surprise everyone. I can see now that wasn't a good idea."

Agnes could wait no longer to hug Pinetta.

"I'm sorry," Agnes said. "I should've told you last night what we were doing. But you *always* get up early. When I came to tell you, you were sleeping so soundly, I didn't have the heart to wake you. So, I covered you up and closed your door."

Nestor had backed up the truck to where they stood. Alarmed at the way the cargo had shifted, he motioned to Mr. Hampton, who helped him straighten the chairs and retie the straining ropes.

"Why don't we all go home?" Ivy Leigh said. "Torbert, why don't you ride with Nestor?"

"Yeah," he said, eyeing the sagging tarp. "We may be here awhile."

Ivy Leigh slid into the driver's seat. "I'll drive. I'm the only one who's not a mess."

Truitt escorted Pinetta to the car. She got in the back seat. He slid in next to her.

Agnes took the front seat. Ivy Leigh drove toward the Magnolia Arms.

"I'm glad you're back," Agnes said. "It's not easy being you."

Ivy Leigh glanced over her shoulder at Truitt and Pinetta and then winked at Agnes.

"I think you're doing just fine."

Pinetta lifted her head from Truitt's shoulder. "Wait a minute. Where's Vesper? Didn't she come with you?"

"Uh…no," Agnes said, eyes on the road. "Ham picked her up for breakfast. They're…"

"What?" Pinetta asked.

"They're…uh…Vesper needed to go to Raleigh today and knew we'd be busy with the wedding, so she asked Ham to take her."

"Raleigh? Why is she—?"

Sworn to secrecy, Agnes changed the subject. "Ivy Leigh, how do you feel about standing in as 'mother of the groom' tomorrow?"

Pinetta turned back to Truitt. "So, you're not moving to another town?"

"No. Why would you think that?"

"You told Gretchen you were looking for a house. I thought you'd finally had enough of me and wanted to get away."

He took her hand. "I wasn't trying to get away. I realized I can't keep having my students parade in and out of the house, especially after the baby's born."

Chapter 25 ~ Tears and a Journey

"I never thought of that. But you won't be teaching voice forever."

"I am now. I'm going to start a music school."

"Here? In town?"

"Of course, here. Where else? It would be foolish to disband the choir after Founder's Day. We've come too far. We're going to stay together, if everyone wants to. Tour. Maybe record. Once I get the school started, I'm going to hire musicians to teach instruments, too."

"A music school?"

"I've already joined the American Choral Directors Association. I never dreamed I'd be leading a choir instead of an orchestra. Or that I'd be married to the accompanist."

The wedding day dawned—when Vesper would lavish her unspent love on the young woman who had grown up in her house and served her faithfully. Deeming Pinetta's taste "impeccable," Vesper had instructed her to spare no expense to make the day perfect.

The formal living room had been cleared of its dark antique furniture. The heavy drapes drawn back, letting in the early spring sun. Rented white chairs, which had somehow survived Pinetta's fevered dash to the train station, were lined up in rows.

White lilies, white daisies, and yellow roses sprang up and spilled over the edges of white baskets and blue-and-white ginger jars. Intertwined with green ivy, white tulle, and white satin ribbon, blossoms garlanded the stone mantle and the banister. White candles glowed.

A white linen table cloth adorned the dining room table, an array of heavy hors d'oeuvres and delicate pastries spread from end to end. Topped with Vesper's Lenox ivory china bride-and-groom from long ago, a three-tiered cake waited on a round table.

A string trio, suggested by Harriet Oxley-Friend, provided music. Serafina Rummage sang "The Way You Look Tonight," and Fiona, in Agnes' wedding dress, descended the stairs. Ham, in a new navy-blue suit, sniffed loudly. Nestor, best man, slipped him a handkerchief.

Once Fiona was standing next to her groom, all eyes sneaked a peek at Vesper, radiant in rosy pink chiffon, wearing a corsage as "honorary grandmother." Pinetta, wedding coordinator, stood in the back, taking in the scene—the room full of friends, the house full of life. Not since the first choir audition had such an array of Dennisonville citizens been gathered under one roof. At home among Vesper's old friends—Garden Club ladies and the Dennisonville elite, who had known Vesper "before"—were her new friends—choir members, storeowners, schoolteachers, whose eloquent kindness had drawn her out of isolation.

Pinetta grinned as Bridey Ludlow jabbed Asa in the ribs for the fourth time. Wedged between his wife and Harriet Oxley-Friend, he could not keep his mind on the ceremony. He was too busy ogling the room he had so often described—erroneously—to curious passengers.

Pinetta gazed at the bride's side—Vesper with Fiona's family. And then at the groom's side—Ivy Leigh and Torbert, Nestor and Agnes, and Truitt. Her fiancé. When the minister said, "Let us pray," Pinetta bowed her head. Her heart was full.

Someone stepped beside her, a shoulder touching hers.

"Good work," Muriel whispered. "On everything."

Pictures were taken, food served, cake cut. Friends mingled. Engraved crystal cups in hand, ladies sipped punch and chatted. Men, balancing plates of stuffed shrimp and meatballs, slipped out the front door to sit on the porch or stand on the lawn.

Sensitive to Vesper's privacy, Pinetta hovered at the foot of the stairs to discourage curiosity seekers. But Vesper, Annie May and a friend in tow, dismissed her. "Go enjoy yourself, Pinetta. There's nothing here I'm afraid to lose. And no one here would hurt me."

Pinetta went in search of Ham. She found him, tie loosened, in the kitchen, talking to Muriel and eating from a paper plate. Seeing her, he swallowed and stood to embrace her.

"Thank you," he said. "Thank you for the wedding. Fiona deserved this. You've made her very happy. And me, too."

"You're welcome." She pulled back. "I didn't want to say anything till after the wedding, because I didn't want to steal your thunder, but I have news of my own." She held out her hand.

He swept her up, lifting her off the floor. "You did it. You said yes. I told you so."

"What?"

"The best kind of love is the kind that sneaks up on you."

The longer people lingered at the reception, the happier Pinetta was she had scheduled the wedding for 2:00. No one wanted to leave. Almost everyone was on hand when Fiona threw her bouquet. Mary Grace caught it; friends slapped Lute on the back. They gathered around as Ham and Fiona

Chapter 25 ~ Tears and a Journey

climbed into a borrowed car and drove away, tins cans, tied to the rear bumper, bouncing and clanking as they turned off Second Avenue. Friends were still in the street, waving, when a sleek black Cadillac, approaching from the opposite corner, honked at the crowd and parked by the curb.

Agnes grabbed Nestor's arm. "Who's that?"

Only the choir and a few others, who had been at the church the day Ben Whitaker came looking for Abbot Cooper, recognized the man who emerged from the backseat, opened the trunk, and pulled out a "For Sale" sign.

Bridey Ludlow wasted no time. She handed Asa her plate and pushed through the crowd to find Chief Wilde, who had escorted his mother and Vesper back into the house.

Without a word, Whitaker brushed past speechless onlookers, positioned the sign, and hammered it into the ground. At the same time, another man, some *thought* they recognized, opened the passenger door and sauntered around the front of the car, lecturing as he approached.

"*What* is going on here? What are you doing, trampling on this yard?"

It was Robert Kimball.

Mayor Tanzler stepped forward. "Hello, Robert. Haven't seen you in a while."

Chief Wilde appeared on the porch. The guests stood back to let him through.

"Where did all you people come from?" Robert asked. "Get off the grass. And move these cars."

Chief Wilde, jaw set, walked forward. "Your mother invited us." He had never liked Robert Kimball.

Agnes whispered to Nestor. "Should we get Vesper? Or just try to get rid of him?"

"It's her house," Nestor said. "She should know what's going on."

On his way to the house, Nestor spoke to Mr. Hampton and Hal Mayberry. "Go help the mayor. I'll be right back."

Afraid of a scene, mothers called to their children and walked quietly toward the porch.

Pinetta took Truitt's hand. "Come on. I've been waiting for a chance to put Robert Kimball in his place." They skirted around the group and stood next to Chief Wilde.

Vesper emerged from the house. The son she had once longed to see was not a welcome sight. She held out her hand to Lute Monroe at the foot of the steps. Chivalrous, he reached up.

She descended the steps. "Come with me, Mr. Monroe."

Robert raised his voice. "My *mother,* as you *all* know, is in a fragile mental state. Do you honestly expect me to believe *she*"—he swung his arms wide—"gave permission for *this*?"

"It's a wedding reception," Pinetta said, "and it was your mother's idea. This is *her* home and *her* yard. Not yours."

"Who are *you*?" Robert asked.

Slipping around Chief Wilde, Vesper spoke up. "Manager of my estate."

The mayor stood aside to let her through.

Robert roared with laughter. "Manager of your estate? Since when?"

"Since December," Pinetta said. "If you came around more often, you'd know that."

Chief Wilde whispered to Vesper and pointed to the sign.

Her face reddened. "What's that?"

"A 'For Sale' sign," Robert said. "You're coming to live with me and Pauline."

"She most certainly is not," Pinetta said.

Robert's eyes flamed. He jabbed his finger at her. "Stay out of this, little woman. It's none of your business."

Truitt moved between them. "I'll thank you to keep a civil tongue in your head when you're speaking to my fiancée."

Bridey Ludlow gasped. "What?" She rushed to Pinetta and snatched up her left hand. "You're *engaged*? When did this happen, Piney?"

"Not now," Pinetta said, eyes fixed to Robert. "You have no right to tell your mother what to do."

"I have every right," he said. "Her judgment is obviously impaired. Letting Cooper in here to invade our privacy. Publish that ridiculous book. Since it came out, I haven't had a single client come through the door who hasn't asked about it. And I'm sick of it. I'm going to put an end to it one way or another."

"There's nothing in the book about you," Vesper said. "Except a few pictures."

Petulant, Robert planted his hand on his hip. "*And* how I 'never visit.' I can't count the people who have lectured me about being a 'better son.' Well, I've had enough. You're coming with me. This house is too big anyway. Pauline has found a nice retirement community."

Chief Wilde held up his massive hand. "Wait just a minute. Your mother is in no way 'impaired' and doesn't have to go anywhere with you, if she doesn't want to."

Chapter 25 ~ Tears and a Journey

This met with such raucous agreement from the other men that Ben Whitaker began backing away, slipped around to the other side of the car, and slunk down in the back seat.

Robert's nostrils flared. "She's still *my* mother. I'm her sole heir. This house will come to me after she dies, so I have *every* right to—"

"Not exactly, dear," Vesper said. "I've made other arrangements. Just yesterday, in fact. I was going to write to you after the wedding."

"What *other* arrangements?" Robert demanded.

"Actually, I don't live here anymore. I moved to the Magnolia Arms. Because you're right, dear. The house *is* too big. But I'd never *sell* it. So, I went to my lawyer yesterday and—"

"You saw your lawyer without *me*?" Robert asked.

"Yes, without you. Even if I'd asked you to take me, you would've found some excuse to put it off, so I asked Ham."

Robert sneered. "Ham? Who's Ham?"

"The groom. You just missed him. Anyway, I've put the house in a trust."

"Good decision," the mayor said.

"Shut up, Jake," Robert said. "Nobody asked you."

The mayor held his tongue. For Vesper's sake, he would not create a scene.

"That's 'Mayor Tanzler' to you," Chief Wilde said. He turned to Vesper. "Say the word, Miss Vesper, and I'll show your son to his car."

"Thank you, Mike," she said, "but we might as well settle this now." She faced Robert. "The final document is being drafted. I'll go back in a week to sign it."

"Oh, well, I'll meet you there. When is the appointment?"

"I won't need you."

"I'll have to look it over. As the trustee, I—"

Vesper did her best not to appear smug. "I didn't make you the trustee."

"Of course you did. I'm your only son. Your sole heir. The house will come to me."

"No. It won't."

"Then who?"

Vesper leaned forward, pointing around the mayor at Pinetta. "Her."

"Me?" Pinetta asked.

"You can't do that," Robert said.

"Yes, I can," Vesper said. "And I did." She touched his arm. "I love you, Robert. You're my son. But you don't love this house or anything in it. It's only a bother to you. Like I am."

Chief Wilde dabbed at his eyes and shook his head. If he could have come up with a reason to arrest Robert Kimball and shuffle him off to jail, he would have.

Pinetta approached Vesper. "Are you sure about this?"

"Positive. This way I can keep the house and still live anywhere I want. You've already proven you can take care of it. You don't need *me* supervising."

Agnes could stand it no longer. She bypassed the crowd and stood next to Vesper. "You can live with us as long as you want to."

Outnumbered, Robert Kimball stormed back to his car and yelled from the curb. "Don't think this is over. I'm seeing *my* attorney tomorrow. I'll be back. You'd better start packing."

Agnes had had enough. "She already *packed* and moved into our house. And don't forget to take your stupid sign."

The assembly clapped and cheered.

Inspired, Lute Monroe jerked up the sign and pitched it into the street, just missing the shiny bumper of Robert Kimball's car as he retreated.

Robert learned his mother was right. She could entrust the house to anyone she chose. One week later, Pinetta signed the document making her the trustee of Kimball Pines. She and Vesper lunched in Raleigh and drove home to the Magnolia Arms.

In spite of advice from well-meaning friends, Truitt and Pinetta insisted on a quiet wedding. Pinetta was in no frame of mind to start making checklists again, until it was time to prepare for Torbert and Ivy Leigh's wedding in April.

On March 28th Pinetta Fraleigh, wearing a pale green tea-length dress and carrying a bouquet of yellow daisies, left her room and met Nestor at the foot of the stairs. Her arm in his, they ascended to the third floor. In front of the arched window, draped with ivy garland, stood Reverend Ford, Vesper, Agnes as matron of honor, and Truitt. When the minister asked 'who giveth this woman to be married,' Nestor answered, "My wife and I" and gave Truitt Pinetta's hand. Moving aside, Nestor took a small pitch-pipe from his pocket and sounded a note. Vesper began to sing.

Chapter 25 ~ Tears and a Journey

When the day begins to fade, evening comes, and all is night, I think of you...

Truitt thought his heart would explode.

After the ceremony, the five friends got into Vesper's car to "go out for dinner." They had all agreed this was an appropriate way to celebrate. But when they arrived at Mollie's, they found the restaurant decorated and the choir in attendance.

Gretchen was the first to congratulate the happy couple. "We couldn't let you get married without some kind of fanfare."

After dinner, Nestor gave a speech about Truitt, which was interrupted with applause so often, he thought he would never finish. Agnes tried to talk about Pinetta, but choked up so many times, she finally gave up, concluding her speech with:

"All I can say is, the first day I met Pinetta Fraleigh...uh...Spenlow...if you had told me one day she would ask to me be her matron of honor, well...I still can't believe it."

Nestor took the microphone again. "Thank you for coming. Let's give Truitt and Pinetta a final round of applause before—"

Truitt stood. "Could I say a few words?"

"Sure. They're all yours."

Truitt faced the crowd. "Thank you for coming. There's no group I'd rather share this moment with than you." He glanced at Pinetta. She nodded. "I was going to announce this at our rehearsal next week, but since you're all here, I might as well tell you now."

Word about 'Truitt and the realtor' had spread. So, when Truitt began, "After Founder's Day—" half the crowd gasped, certain he would finish with, "Pinetta and I are leaving."

Truitt held up his hands to quiet them. "After Founder's Day...I'd like us to stay together. Permanently. As the Dennisonville Community Chorale. If you agree."

They jumped to their feet. Gretchen hugged Verbena. Serafina hugged Mary Grace. Wyatt shook Hal Mayberry's hand. Tom clapped Corby on the back. Dinah Latimer picked up her napkin and wiped her eyes. Lute blew his nose.

Agnes tugged on Truitt's sleeve. "I think that's a 'yes.'"

"Wait," Truitt said. "There's more. Sit down, please."

"As you know, Vesper now lives at the Magnolia Arms and has made...my wife...the manager of her property. The three of us have been working on a plan for a while now. After we get back from our honeymoon, Pinetta and I will be moving in there."

"How nice," Verbena said.

"Not many newlyweds have a 'first home' like that," Tom said.

"We're moving in," Truitt said, "to be closer to our work."

"Our voice lessons will be there?" Serafina asked.

"Not right away," Truitt said. "But by the fall we plan to open the Spenlow School of Music."

Again, the audience leapt to their feet.

In all of Charlottesville, Virginia, there was no honeymooning couple who talked more endlessly about their bright future than Mr. and Mrs. Spenlow. The more they discussed the choir, the school, the house bustling with students, the more ideas came to them.

Small, intimate concerts and recitals in the living room. Group instruction in the larger rooms upstairs. Upgrading and enlarging the kitchen to provide meals for students who would attend the eventual summer music camps. And, of course, choir rehearsals and voice lessons.

"Have you decided which room should be ours?" Truitt asked. "I suppose you'd like to move into Vesper's room, but…"

Pinetta shook her head. "It would make the perfect room for group lessons and section rehearsals. Too large for just two people." Head down, she stirred her asparagus soup.

"You know more about the house than I do. What would you suggest? Robert's—"

"No."

"I hope you're not thinking of Edward's room, because I—"

She laid her hand on his. "I want to stay at the Magnolia Arms. We could move into Abbot Cooper's old room. Then I'd still be able to help Vesper. And Agnes…when the baby comes. That would be all right, wouldn't it? We've been happy there."

Truitt smiled. "I was trying to think of a way to bring that up. I don't want to leave either."

When Truitt and Pinetta came home, they found Vesper standing in the driveway, hands on her hips, admiring the building project underway—expanding the old garage.

Chapter 25 ~ Tears and a Journey

She hurried to the car and hugged them both. "Well," she said, over the hammering, "what do you think of it?"

"Nice," Pinetta said, "but will it be big enough for all three of your cars?"

"It's just for the Buick," she said. "I don't want you bothering with that old tarp any more. I sold the other cars while you were gone. Money for the school. How was your trip?"

"Wonderful. But it's nice to be home."

They entered through the back door and, suitcases in hand, headed to the hall.

"We moved a few things from your old rooms," Vesper said. "But Agnes said we should let you move your personal things when you got home."

Pinetta followed Truitt up the stairs. When they opened the door to their new room, they found it had been redecorated. New curtains. New furniture. Two chairs by the window.

Truitt set down his bag. "Well, looks like we're home, Mrs. Spenlow."

The next day Pinetta drove Vesper to the Garden Club meeting at the Delahunty House.

"Are you sure you won't stay?" Vesper asked. "Everyone wants to see you."

"Not today. I want to finish cleaning out my old room. There's a lot to move upstairs."

"All right, but at least give them a little wave. They're all staring out the windows."

Pinetta waved, but drove away before anyone could dash to the car.

When she came home, she heard Serafina vocalizing in the parlor. She paused at the door. Serafina waved and gave her a thumbs-up.

Pinetta entered the old familiar kitchen. In the stillness—her first unhurried moment in weeks—she savored the scene. In the sink—breakfast dishes Nestor and Agnes had left before rushing off to school. Not "unwashed dishes," but reminders of a couple with open arms and open hearts, who took people *in*. Had taken *her* in. On the table—a yellow legal pad scribbled over with names, phone numbers, the week's rehearsal schedule, goals for the music school. Her husband's handwriting. Evidence of a good-hearted, talented man, using his considerable gifts to teach "average" singers, help them realize their dreams.

She sat in "her" chair; memories, like noisy ghosts, clamoring.

Here—prim, trussed up in a starched blouse, she had withdrawn every day to rehearse her failed life, nurse grudges, nibble on tasteless cookies, sip lemoned tea. She looked over at her first room, now a cozy study. How many mornings had she awakened there, Guy Henry as her first thought? Then…Barton. At that stove she had prepared meals he never noticed. Not long ago, apron tied tight around her waist, she had stirred cranberry sauce, adding sugar because Barton liked it "sweet." Then dumped the whole batch on top of Bridey's pie. Shoved the garbage can under the sink.

Cranberry sauce. A good place to start cleaning.

Hopping up from the table, she grabbed the garbage can. Shoulders back, she marched to her first-floor room, swung open the closet door, removed the ten jars of cranberry sauce and dropped them in the trash. *Why had she kept them?*

Jars pinging and clanking against each other, she dragged the trash can to the bed, knelt down and reached underneath for Great-Aunt Connie's Coffin Star quilt. Rolling it up tight, she shoved it in the bag and tied the top closed.

Bending down, she pulled the plastic bag out of the trash can, tied it closed, and, cradling it like a sacred offering, carried it out to be rid of it once and for all.

A young, dark-haired woman, parked by the curb, watched Pinetta set down the bag, remove the black trash can lid, and heave the bag inside.

Hopeful, the young woman got out of her car.

Pinetta replaced the lid and brushed off her hands. "That takes care of that."

"That looked like it was heavy," the stranger said, coming closer. "I was going to ask if you needed help, but I couldn't get out of my car in time."

Pinetta turned. The newcomer held a book, Abbot Cooper's face peering out from the back cover. By now Pinetta—and most of Dennisonville—had grown accustomed to Abbot's bright-eyed readers showing up, unannounced. No one minded as much as they used to.

"Spring cleaning," Pinetta said, pointing to the book. "Are you looking for Vesper?"

Relief washed over the woman's face. "Yes. I went to her house, but no one was there." She opened the book and ran her finger down a page. "Then I remembered the author mentioned the"—she read—"Magnolia Arms in the Acknowledgements. Is this the right address?"

Chapter 25 ~ *Tears and a Journey*

"Yes, but Abbot doesn't live here anymore. If you want to meet him, you'll have to—"

"Oh, I don't need *him*. Only Mrs. Kimball. My mother sent me to find her. A friend of hers read the book and told her about it. Our lives have been upside down ever since."

"Vesper's not here right now, but if you have time, you can wait for her. She loves meeting new people."

The young woman gripped Pinetta's arm. "You *know* Vesper?"

"I work for her." She extended her hand. "I'm Pinetta Fraleigh…uh, Spenlow." She laughed. "Sorry. I just got married. Not used to my new name yet."

"*You* work for Vesper?" A smile transformed her troubled face. "Wait till I tell my mother I met the woman who *works* for Vesper."

Pinetta was amused at her celebrity status. "Come inside. You can call your mother, if it will make you feel better. What's your name?"

"Jenny McKendrick." She turned the book around to display the photo on the cover. "Philip March is my grandfather."

"Philip? Vesper's Philip? *He* read the book?"

Jenny nodded. "We could hardly pry it out of his hand to get him to eat and sleep."

Pinetta was stupefied. "Philip. *Vesper's* Philip is alive? I mean, he sent you?"

"No. I mean, yes, he's alive. More alive than I've ever seen him. But he didn't send me. My mother did. We didn't want to tell him we found Vesper, in case…"

Pinetta covered her face with her hands. "I have to sit down. Come inside. Call your mother and tell her you're here. Then we'll start from the beginning."

When they came through the door, Pinetta pointed to the phone. Jenny dialed.

"Mama. Are you sitting down? I'm at the Magnolia Arms. With Mrs. Spenlow." She smiled at Pinetta. "She *works* for Vesper. Yes, I'm serious. No. She's not here right now. She's at the Garden Club. I know. Well, apparently, things have changed since the book was finished. Mrs. Spenlow is going to pick her up soon. I'm going to meet her. *Today.* Don't cry, Mama. You'll get me started. What? Okay. I'll ask her." Jenny placed her hand over the receiver. "Mama wants to know if you think Vesper would be willing to visit Granddaddy."

Tea at Kimball Pines

Pinetta threw back her head and laughed. "Oh, yes…she'd be willing."

Pinetta and Jenny talked for an hour.

Then, leaving Jenny in Truitt's care, Pinetta drove to the Garden Club to pick up Vesper, practicing her speech along the way.

"*You'll never believe who showed up…No…*" She shook her head. "*I have good news. We have a visitor…No…There's someone at the house. A young lady came by to ask about…*"

Pinetta parked under an oak tree to wait. The story would have to be told here. She could not drive while telling Vesper that Philip March was alive and well. That he had never stopped missing her. That it had not been his decision to marry someone else. His mother, never the same after his father's suicide, had wheedled him into marrying the girl of her choosing and then lived with Philip and his family her entire life. That Philip's wife, who had given him three daughters, had died two years ago. He lived with his youngest daughter, Jenny's mother.

And he wanted to see Vesper. 'If she could find it in her heart to forgive him.'

Vesper appeared and climbed in the front seat. "Have you been waiting long?"

"No," Pinetta said, "but someone else has."

Harriet Oxley-Friend, last to leave the Garden Club meeting, locked the door of the Delahunty House behind her. She spotted Vesper's car still by the curb. Glancing at her watch, Harriet approached the car. Pinetta rolled down her window.

"Is everything all right?" Harriet asked. "It's been an hour since the meeting was over."

"Everything is perfect," Vesper said. "Just perfect."

Toting their book bags, Nestor and Agnes came through the back door at 5:00. At the stove, Pinetta tried to manage an offhand tone. "We're eating in the dining room again tonight."

"As long as it's soon," Nestor said, dropping his bag by the door.

Agnes sat down and slipped off her shoes. "Fine with me. I just want to sit down. My feet are killing me. And don't expect me to talk much. I've lectured all day."

Chapter 25 ~ Tears and a Journey

"No worries," Pinetta said. "Even *you* are going to be speechless. Someone's joining us."

"New tenant?" Nestor asked.

"No," Pinetta said. "But she's spending the night."

As Pinetta expected, when Agnes discovered who Jenny was, she screamed and threw her arms around her. Supper went cold while everyone talked. By the time they finally went to bed, they felt like they had known each other all their lives.

Agnes showed Jenny to Prudence O'Neill's room. She said good night, came downstairs, and got in bed with Nestor.

"Just think," she told him. "Vesper's in our old room. Truitt and Pinetta are in Abbot's room, and Jenny is in Prudence's room. Doesn't that appeal to your sense of poetic justice?"

"Yes," Nestor said. "But you realize Vesper won't be in that room for long, don't you?"

The next morning everyone rose early to have breakfast with Jenny. Friends for less than 24 hours, they all dreaded parting. Jenny promised to come back for Founder's Day.

"Stay for the week," Agnes said. "And bring your mom."

"She'd like that." Jenny kissed Vesper on the cheek. "See you in a few days."

Truitt cancelled his lessons for the rest of the week. He and Pinetta repacked the suitcases they had taken on their honeymoon, and two days later boarded a train with Vesper.

Pinetta spotted Jenny the moment they pulled into the station. Beside her, an older version of "Jenny," her mother, with the same kind eyes, and beside her a tall, gray-haired man. Pinetta would have recognized him in a crowd of 10,000. Philip March.

Patting Vesper's arm, Pinetta pointed out the window. "There he is."

Vesper placed her hand over her lips. "He hasn't changed a bit." She stepped off the train and into the arms of Philip March, the lost years melting away.

They were young again. And in love.

Nestor was right. Vesper did not come home. She would not be separated from Philip again. She instructed Pinetta what to do with her belongings; what to pack and ship to her, what to sell, and what to give to Robert.

Tea at Kimball Pines

"Anything except the grandfather clock," Vesper said. "Hire a company to pack it and move it here. A wedding present for Philip. He doesn't know I still have it."

The antique furniture, removed for the wedding, was never returned to Kimball Pines. It was sold at auction and the proceeds invested in the Spenlow School of Music. The formal living room was transformed into a recital hall named for Vesper March.

Throughout the spring, choir rehearsals continued. Wyatt Blackwell, appointed chairman of the board, asked Truitt why the choir had to wait till after Founder's Day to give concerts.

"If we toured to nearby towns," Wyatt said, "we'd have a following long before Founder's Day. *And* you can advertise the school."

Truitt took his advice. The choir gave three out-of-town concerts before spring was over. At each appearance, the members handed out brochures: one on the music school and the other on the Magnolia Arms. Inquiries and reservations for both were forthcoming.

By the time second semester was over, Agnes did not think she could go on teaching one day longer. She went home and started "taking care of herself," as Nestor had insisted. One afternoon, the phone woke her from her daily nap.

She answered. "Hello?"

"May I speak to Agnes Carlyle?"

"This is she."

"Mrs. Carlyle, you may not remember me. This is Daniel Ogden."

She nearly dropped the phone. "Yes, I remember you."

"I'm calling about your book, *Briarwood Manor*."

"What about it?"

"I'd like to talk to you about publishing it."

Agnes sat up. "Are you serious?"

"Your little town has made quite a splash lately with the success of Abbot Cooper's book. And that means *your* book…about your house…is now marketable."

The moment Agnes had dreamed of since her college days had arrived, and she could think of nothing to say, except, "*My* book?"

"I'd like to make an appointment to talk it over. I know your first meeting with Mrs. O'Neill did not go well, but I hope you won't hold that against us. She's no longer here."

324

Chapter 25 ~ Tears and a Journey

Agnes could not help laughing. "Yes, I know. She was here for a while, but we lost track of her. Do you know where she is? We have some mail we need to forward."

This was not actually true, but Agnes, riddled with curiosity, seized the moment.

"She tried to open her own business, but it didn't work out. Then worked for another publisher. Left there. She called me, begging for help. I felt sorry for her. So, I called my sister-in-law."

"Your sister-in-law? You called Elspeth Sherwood…at Brighton Park?"

"Yes. She needs an English teacher next fall. Prudence applied."

"Prudence is going to teach at Brighton Park? My old school?"

"In a way, you gave me the idea. Now, about your book? Would you consider letting me publish it?"

"I'll have to talk to my husband first. I'll let you know."

Agnes hung up the phone. "Imagine that. Prudence at Brighton Park. Well, if anyone can help her, it's Margaret." She picked up the phone and dialed her friend. "You'll never believe…"

When the choir took their places for the Founder's Day concert, Agnes was not with them. She was in the hospital with her son, Denver Ransom Carlyle. Rambunctious to the end, he arrived ten days early at a healthy 8½ pounds.

He was named for Jonas Grinstead's father. And Ivy Leigh.

As promised, Barton and Eileen arrived to see the baby. Pinetta welcomed them warmly and served a sumptuous dinner. Then she and Truitt drove to Kimball Pines to spend the night.

They climbed the stairs to Vesper's room.

"Marriage agrees with Barton," Pinetta said. "He's put on weight."

"And his hairline is receding," Truitt added. "Didn't you think so?"

After Founder's Day, the Spenlows devoted their attention to the official opening of the music school. Truitt conducted board meetings and interviewed applicants for teaching positions. Pinetta stayed busy in her office at the Magnolia Arms—her old room off the kitchen.

"There's no need for me to do paperwork at the school," Pinetta told Agnes. "If I have an office here, I can help with Denver while you're editing your book."

Tea at Kimball Pines

Early in September, Vesper March received a large manila envelope in her mailbox. *Abbot Cooper* was penned in the upper left-hand corner. Pinetta had forwarded it from Kimball Pines the same day she sent a card in an ivory white envelope.

"That Pinetta," Vesper said, on her way back to the house. "So thoughtful. As busy as she is, she always finds time to write." She called to Philip as she walked into the kitchen. "We have mail. From Pinetta."

She opened the large envelope and spilled out the contents on the table. The photos Abbot and Prudence had taken from her. She looked for a note. Found none. "Poor boy. He thinks he ruined my life and is trying to atone. If he only knew…"

She opened the other envelope. A formal invitation.

Dr. and Mrs. Truitt Spenlow
Request the honor of your presence
At the grand opening of
The Spenlow School of Music
17 Second Avenue
Dennisonville, North Carolina
October 4, 1979
2:00-5:00 p.m.
Faculty Reception
Free concert by the Dennisonville Community Chorale
Please join us for an afternoon of music,
Light refreshments, coffee, &
Tea at Kimball Pines.

Made in the USA
Lexington, KY
13 November 2019